The Land Beside

J.H.E. Lim

PARTRIDGE

To order additional copies of this book, contact
Toll Free +65 3165 7531 (Singapore)
Toll Free +60 3 3099 4412 (Malaysia)
orders.singapore@partridgepublishing.com

www.partridgepublishing.com/singapore

CONTENTS

ACKNOWLEDGMENTS

In loving memory of
my parents, Peter Soon Howe and Grace Ee;
my eldest sister, Glory Hong Lian
I wish to thank the following:
Jesus, the author and finisher of my faith
My husband, John, and two sons, Hugh and Ralph
Their wives, Betty and Shu Lin, and their children, for their
encouragement
Relatives and friends, whose interaction over the years have
enriched my life and theirs
All those who have helped me in some way to work through
the intricacies of life

AUTHOR'S NOTE

The Land Beside is a contemporary fantasy set in the twenty-first century. This book, the third in The Land series, is written for young adults and mature readers.

Josie, the protagonist, is now a young adult, going on twenty-two years of age. She has mysterious and unusual encounters in the land beside a house.

In the past, it used to be in the land behind. In later years, the adventures took place in the land beyond. In this story, she notices that the land beside her own home is open to her for more adventures. There, she meets aggressive people, robots, and menacing shamans whose skills stun her. How she overcomes them is part of the story in this book. Later in the story, she is zoomed to outer space, to a planet she has not visited.

Running parallel to her adventures are accounts of her relationship with the good, bad, and ugly people she meets. Now an adult, she has taken over the fashion design business which her mother started. In the office, she interacts with many other characters. The reader sees how she uses various communicative skills in her interaction with them.

She encounters a cousin she has never met before. Her father arranges for him to work with her. Before long, she discovers he has deep-rooted problems, which cause conflict in their relationship.

The values of trust, gratitude, friendship, and love are woven into the storyline.

BOOK REVIEWS

Book 1: *The Land Behind*
Book 2: *The Land Beyond*

Since *The Land Beside* is my third book in The Land series, I feel it appropriate to include some book reviews given by readers of the two earlier books.

BOOK 1: THE LAND BEHIND

Book review by Tricia Ariffin, 2020

Before this book, I have not read books written by Singapore writers. What led me to get the book was when I attended a book launch held by the author herself. I admit that after reading it, I did enjoy what was written. I can almost imagine her sharing her life story with real references to how she grew up in Singapore.

What was especially intriguing was my trying to figure out which character the author identified herself with and if the love described in the book was from her own experience. So real were the accounts given in the book.

But it turned out that this was not so after my chat with her. The reality of the characters is a testimony to her gift in creating people who are so real in their emotions and attitudes in this contemporary fantasy.

I was particularly impressed by the description of Josie, the protagonist. She came alive in the book!

From local delicacies, such as *nyonya* kueh, and popular dishes, such as fish-head curry, to setting the context back to the time where there was teatime in a spacious bungalow, it was interesting for me to see how an affluent family back then (and possibly even now) live.

It was not a lifestyle I grew up with, but since I met some of my parents' friends who grew up with similar backgrounds and whom I had the chance to have tea and biscuits with, reading about Josie's upbringing made me feel like I too was there, appreciating that kind of lifestyle.

Altogether, an easy read, but, certainly, a book hard to put down. I found myself curious to find out more about Josie's adventures!

It took me a day and a half of nonstop reading to finish the book. There was so much intensity that was built up into her adventures that I found myself spilling into the next chapter, wanting to know the end.

BOOK 2: THE LAND BEYOND

Book review by Michael Radon, 2020
The Land Beyond by J. H. E. Lim
Source: US Review of Premium Books

"Do you really trust me to know that when I share my experiences with you about my visits to the land, I'm telling the truth?"

After meeting the Celestial Gardener in her last adventure, Josie Yuen is left with an earring that is the key to visit the lands beyond her own—strange places and people that exist in a parallel existence to her reality. While this escape offers her moments of curious exploration and often a vision of a future to come, her life in her own world is changing with her maturity and demands her attention. Her cousin Jeremy, whom she has shared admiration with in the past, is a potential love interest for Josie. However, his freewheeling lifestyle with his university friends conflicts with her introverted and traditionalist upbringing. How can Josie navigate her own challenging life while juggling the secret of the land beyond and the information it provides her?

With some light fantasy elements, this is a clear and considerate coming-of-age story of a young girl who is still very much a student and a daughter, but who is also becoming a woman of her own right. Linguistic tics and food provide splashes of vibrancy that really bring to life the culture of every environment in the book, whether it's Singapore, Kuala Lumpur, China, or Canada. Josie's eagerness to be helpful and her strong moral compass make her an instantly endearing character and a role model for younger readers. Offering a global perspective and characters with good moral fiber, this story is an entertaining, character-driven work that's enjoyable to all audiences. It may especially resonate with readers who are transitioning into their own adult lives.

BOOK 2: THE LAND BEYOND

Book review by Tony Espinoza
By the Pacific Book Review, 2020
Title: The Land Beyond
Author: J. H. E. Lim

When creating a narrative that will not only capture an audience's attention but bring about a true connection between the reader and the characters, it is important to find a way to establish the culture of a character. As Henry David Thoreau once said, "It is not part of a true culture to tame tigers, any more than it is to make sheep ferocious."

In J. H. E. Lim's book, *The Land Beyond*, the author takes readers back into a modern-day fantasy world, where our world blends with another just adjacent to our own. The second in The Land series, the story follows Josie, who previously had discovered a world on the land behind her home. Having gained access to it, she must traverse these other lands while also growing her relationships with her friends and family.

Dealing with getting those close to her to believe her tales, she must discover the growing nature of her relationships as she delves deeper and deeper into these parallel worlds.

This is an engaging and fascinating read. The author does a great job of blending culture and personal relationships with rich character development for both the protagonist and the other characters in the protagonist's life. One of the more important relationships highlighted in this tale, that of Josie and Jeremy, really draws the readers in and gets them invested in the narrative.

This is the perfect read for those who enjoy fantasy-driven narratives in modern-day setting that highlight personal relationships. As a fan of the genre, it was refreshing to see a story that featured a heavy fantasy element but focused more on the growth and personal development of its characters.

This is a memorable, evenly paced, and entertaining read. Emotional and character driven, *The Land Beyond* by J.H. E. Lim was a truly creative and fantastic read that brought the fantasy genre well into a modern setting.

BOOK 2: THE LAND BEYOND

Book review by Joshua Lim Jun Yi, 2020

This is an enjoyable book to read. Although I am a young adult, I am certain the book will appeal to both younger and more mature readers alike.

I like the use of slang, colloquial expressions, and references to locations because I can relate to them.

The storyline is engaging and a good sequel to the first book, *The Land Behind.* Readers get to see the characters progress in their outlook on lifestyles and priorities as they mature.

It is interesting to read the intimate emotions and relationships explored between the two main characters, Josie and Jeremy, as they get to know each other's likes and dislikes.

I highly recommend the book for both young adults as well as mature readers!

BOOK 2: THE LAND BEYOND

Book review by Tricia Ariffin, 2020

This book is a natural progression from the first book, *The Land Behind*. It is interesting to see how the relationships of various characters develop in the story and where Josie's adventures would further lead to.

The characters have matured in this book. I appreciated that an idealistic portrayal of a loving relationship was not given in this book.

The pace of this book is quite different from the first novel, where there is more mystery here to uncover for the reader. There is also more development of each character (with some new ones added) and what they prioritize based on their life stages.

My biggest takeaway from this book is this: when someone loves you enough to believe what you yourself believe (even when they cannot see it at that moment of time), in due time, when they can see it for themselves that it is real, it's truly a profound moment.

BOOK 2: THE LAND BEYOND

Book review by Dr. C. Y. Chen, 2020

I am a retired professor from the National University of Singapore and thoroughly enjoyed reading the story, which transported me back to my days as a teenager.

The story takes place in 21st C, Singapore. It aptly incorporates aspects of Asian culture and family values in a relatively Westernized modern city state.

The story unfolds with the multifaceted world of a teenage girl. Readers are given insights into how she has been shaped by the convergence of both Eastern and Western cultures.

I feel that stories like *The Land Beyond* help to build the inner strength of younger people, particularly girls. Through descriptions of daily activities and choices of decisions made in the storyline by the characters, younger readers are given guidance in relating to people and social situations, whose views and lifestyles may be vastly different from theirs.

THE LAND BESIDE POEM

There is a land beside my house
Where unusual people
Make their appearance.

Robots emerge
Alongside people with evil intentions.
Their knowledge is mind-boggling,
Their skill is incredible.
They come and go
Like shadows in the night.

Some disappear into the night.
At other times,
In the land beside my house,
I am zoomed to outer space.

Who are they, these people,
Who visit the land beside my house?

ONE

At twenty-one, Josie is no longer a teen unsure of herself. She has matured in her thinking and experience but finds she has a lot more to learn of people and life.

Her parents Ruth and Joshua Yuen, no longer control her choices. However, they guide her whenever she seeks their advice.

As for Jeremy, the love of her life, he still has top place in her affections. He is in his last year of a PhD course in technology and environmental studies in a top university in the United States.

Before he left for his studies abroad, he suggested that they shelve their marital plans until he completed his studies. Josie and her parents were agreeable with this.

In the meantime, she achieved degrees in humanities and business management. Her father encouraged her to take a course in the latter when he learned of her intention to join her mother's successful fashion business.

She recalled him saying, "Since you've decided to enter the fashion design business, an understanding of business management will give you a boost."

As a result of her father's encouragement, Josie also took courses with upmarket designers in France and Italy to strengthen her knowledge and skill in that area.

When she took over the running of the company, she was determined to expand on her mother's vision and achievement. It wasn't long before she began exploring more markets worldwide.

* * *

It was a fine, clear day at the Singapore Open for the Asian Golf Tournament.

When Josie arrived at the Sentosa Pavilion, she couldn't spot her father. Her eyes scanned the crowded hall. Spectators were glued to the glass window to view the competitors playing on the *Serapong* course. She looked up and down the line of people. Her father's tall, broad-shouldered physique wasn't among them.

Next, her eyes darted to the other end where the lunch buffet table was laden with a sumptuous array of dishes.

Suddenly, her eyes picked out a familiar figure. It wasn't her father, but she recognized the man from his physique. He stood out above those around him. His lithe build and white golf shirt brought back memories of the time he spent in her house when he visited her family in Singapore.

Her heart leaped in keen anticipation. She missed him a lot, especially the times when he stayed in her father's house and they had chatted way into the night with her.

As she weaved her way through the thick crowd toward him, memories crowded her mind: of the time they met, of the start of their relationship, of the time when they had major differences in their perception of what was an appropriate lifestyle, and of the time when they eventually worked out their differences.

Josie's upbringing was vastly different from his. Ever since he was six, Jeremy had been educated overseas. His lifestyle was very liberal, influenced by his friends in England.

In contrast, Josie tended to be more conservative because of her upbringing. Her mother had a strong influence on her in her teen years.

Initially, this difference had put a stain on their relationship. However, their love for each other led them to overcome obstacles which were hindering their relationship.

As she threaded her way to the front, she saw the man as he stood there, listening intently to the group of men and women around him. He was head and shoulders above the others.

His side features displayed a tall, straight nose and thick, dark, wavy hair, which had attracted him to her when she first met him in Sabah when she attended a wedding there with her parents.

But she was puzzled. Why was Jeremy in Singapore? Didn't he text her to say he was too busy to fly back during the university break? Didn't he say he had much more research to do for his final paper? She knew he was in his final year of study at a prestigious American university.

A glimmer of hope arose. Perhaps he did find time after all. Perhaps he flew back just to see her!

When she came alongside him, she slipped her slim hand into his large hand, which was hanging loosely by his side.

She grasped it firmly before saying, "How nice to see you here! Thought you've too much research to do to come back!"

He turned his head fully to face her. A puzzled look crossed his clean-cut face.

"Have we met?" he asked in a pleasant voice.

Stunned, she stared up at the face above her. He was the splitting image of Jeremy. Yet his tone was different, and what he just said implied he didn't know her.

Jeremy was a baritone. The man looking at her had a tenor voice. Stammering, she uttered, "Je-re-my?"

His bewildered expression matched hers as he said, "Er, have you got the right person?" he gave a lopsided grin, which chased away the gloomy look on his face.

"It's always a pleasure to meet such a lovely person!"

Josie's face was a flaming red. She burst out, "Um, er, sorry, I thought you were Jeremy."

The man released a wider grin, revealing a perfect set of white front teeth. "Hmm, Jeremy, eh? Um, a nice name, but it's not my name."

He added gallantly, "Wish I was him, though."

The group around him was clearly amused. The guys laughed openly. The girl next to him sniggered. "It's a novel way of getting to know a guy!"

He gave Josie a short bow. "Henk. Henk's my name."

His hand swept the group facing him. "And these are my golfing buddies."

He tilted his head a little to the left, quirked an eyebrow, and then asked, "You are?"

Both the smile and the posture were unmistakably Jeremy's!

But the man waiting for an introduction had called himself Henk. He repeated, "You are?"

Josie was highly embarrassed. But she regained her composure. Another flush swept over her face. She muttered, "Um, sorry, er, thought you were Jeremy!"

His group of friends tittered again. Some were laughing outright.

"Hey, Henk, you lucky guy! To get such lovely woman to lay claim on you!" The man on his right clapped him on the shoulder.

The woman on his left chirped, "I'm jealous!" She slipped her hand into his and pulled him possessively toward her.

He loosened his hand from her hold. At the same time, the young man stood, studying Josie's flushed face.

He lifted her limp hand, kissed it, and released it before saying, "Shall we introduce ourselves again?"

His arm tapped his broad chest. "I'm Henk. This is Stella. That's James."

He pointed to the two people standing next to him. "And behind them are Jack and Benson. We're all golfers. Are you a golfer too?"

Josie could see he was trying to make her less embarrassed. She swallowed hard. Recovering her composure, she said, "Um, I'm Josie, er, yes, I'm a golfer too."

Graciously, Henk replied, "What a nice name, Josie. I take you're looking for a friend?"

He added, "And you think I'm him!" His melodious tone reminded her of Bobby, her Indonesian cousin.

She grabbed at his words. "Yes, yes. Thought you were him!"

"Lucky fella!" He grabbed a glass of red wine from a passing waiter. "Have a drink. We could all do with a fresh glass."

He shoved a glass into her hand and after he lifted his, said, "To our new friendship."

To the others, he said, "Hey, let's drink to our new friend!" They lifted their glasses politely. As the glasses touched their lips, a roar arose from those in front of the television. The group's attention riveted back to the scoreboard on the television.

Josie quickly left them in search of her father. She found him at the other end chatting with the new chairman of the golf club.

"I was wondering where you were," Joshua Yuen said to his daughter.

Casually, she asked him, "Is Jeremy here with you?"

Joshua looked surprised. "Huh? Isn't he in the States? Thought he was too busy to come back."

She decided not to say anything more. As she stared out of the glass window at the players on the eighteenth hole, she couldn't help wondering who Henk was. His resemblance to Jeremy was uncanny.

He had the same golf shirt design. His pants were white too—Jeremy's favorite color. His height was about the same. His build was incredibly similar. The way in which he stood made him a possible double of Jeremy.

Josie looked around for him, but the thick crowd milling around the room made it impossible for her to detect him. When the event was over, she left with her father for home.

Over dinner, a thought occurred. "Dad, does Jeremy have any other relatives about his age group?"

Joshua thought awhile. "Well, there's Shi Fang."

Josie remembered her. She stayed with them for two months when she came out with Jeremy on his first visit to Singapore.

"Er, I was thinking of a male cousin."

"Um, there's Bruce, Zech's son from Indonesia. He looked a lot like Jeremy. We went to Penang some years ago with him and his family."

"Er, not him. I mean another cousin, about the same age group."

"Well, best ask your mother that question. As you know, Luke, Jeremy's dad, is your mum's adopted cousin."

Ruth stopped eating. "Why the question?"

Josie shook her head. "Um, no particular reason. Just wondered. Earlier on, I thought I saw a young man who looked a lot like Jeremy."

Ruth laughed. "You're missing him, are you?"

But Josie persisted with her question. "Mum, the resemblance was uncanny!"

"Well, your aunt Jem is a better person to ask. She knows about Luke's relatives more than I do."

That night, Josie finished her dinner without knowing anything more about the mysterious young man.

* * *

That night, Josie had a dream. She was on a golf course. The marshal had paired her with three other golfers. Sharing her buggy was a woman called Fen.

Josie gave a start when she saw Henk. He was the one she'd met at the golf championship earlier in the day. He was wearing a white outfit.

He took the initiative and introduced himself and the other person sharing his buggy. "I'm Henk. And that's Jim."

Throughout the game, he never once showed any recognition of her. When they reached the halfway house, they stopped for a drink. Josie learned that all three were pursuing studies at the National University of Singapore (NUS).

Fen was studying computer technology. Jim was completing his thesis for an engineering degree.

Henk told them he was currently pursuing environmental studies at NUS. Earlier, he completed research in business studies in St. Gallen in Switzerland and secured a business degree.

Before he could elaborate further on his area of study, the marshal called them to tee off as the other party behind was waiting. After the eighteen holes of play, each went his separate way.

Josie awoke the next morning, still remembering her dream. She mulled over it.

Although she met Henk on the Asian Tour in the weekend recently, in her dream, he didn't seem to recall meeting her.

The next evening, Fred called her. "Got time for a quick meal?"

"Sure," she said readily. Fred was the friend of her cousin Justin. Their friendship began when Justin introduced them. She used to fly kites with him from a young age until her teen years.

Every weekend, Justin and his two friends Fred and Chin spent their time in the wide field across his house, flying kites. Josie had the opportunity to do this, for whenever Josie's parents traveled, she stayed with Justin's parents.

From Justin, Fred, and Chin, she quickly learned how to fly kites. The boys didn't mind her tagging along. She was useful to Justin, for she often retrieved his fallen kites for him.

However, she learned how to fly a kite skillfully only when she went to Bali with Jeremy, Fred, Justin, Chin, and Ella. There, Josie met her Indonesian cousin, Bobby, who taught her how to maneuver the kite adroitly.

At an early age, she also learned from Justin how to paste glass on the kite string for the kite fight.

Over time, the boys and Justin studied in different tertiary institutions abroad. Fred, however, undertook computer and environmental studies. He chose to study at NUS. At that time, it was offering a scholarship to incoming students. Fred was among those who qualified for it.

After graduating, he found work with a company which was involved in the creation of new, environmentally friendly devices.

Josie's recollection of the past was interrupted when Fred's friendly voice floated over the phone. "Shinji okay for you?"

Josie hesitated. "Um, it's a bit pricey." She knew how much Fred was earning. "Let's go to *Tampopo*. I like the *shabu-shabu* with the *kurobuta* pork."

"As you wish. See you in a bit." He rang off.

Although Fred's father was wealthy, Josie knew Fred himself earned a reasonable salary. He didn't want to use his dad's money to pay for his dinners with her. His mother died soon after he was born, and his father never remarried.

She liked Fred a lot. She was comfortable with him. When she reached her teen years, he confided his keenness to start a relationship with her.

She was touched by his affection but admitted she couldn't reciprocate his feelings for her. By that time, her heart was given to Jeremy. Fred knew about it, and he respected her for that.

Many years had passed since he mentioned his affection for her. Josie often wondered why Fred didn't find a girl of his choice. He was never short of a girl. At parties, many girls gravitated toward him. His friendly nature and wealthy dad were magnet points of attraction. He didn't have a steady relationship with any of them, although he escorted many to parties and outings.

Ella, Josie's longtime friend since school days, once commented, "Wonder why Fred has remained a bachelor for so long."

Chin, to whom Ella was engaged, made an astute remark one night when the three of them were out for dinner. "Perhaps he's waiting for Josie to break off with Jeremy! I know he likes her a lot!"

Whereupon Ella shushed him up sharply. "Don't talk nonsense! You know Josie's just waiting for Jeremy to graduate before they get married!"

Whenever Fred invited her out for a meal, he simply added, "For old times' sake," to make her feel comfortable. Josie knew what he meant.

They often chatted into the night about the times when they flew kites and visited Bali for the international kite competition. They reminisced over the Christmas and Chinese New Year parties they had with Jeremy, Justin, Chin, Ella, and a host of other friends.

Then they fell silent when they remembered that many of their friends had gone abroad for further studies and they were the only two of the old crowd left behind in Singapore.

That night, when she arrived at the restaurant, the place was filled. She spotted Fred at the far end. As she passed by a table of six people, she happened to glance at them.

Her heart skipped a beat when she caught sight of Henk, Fen, and Jim, the persons she saw in her dream. There were three others with him, Stella and Jackson, the friends Henk introduced her to at the Asian Tour, and another man she didn't know.

They were all laughing and chatting, except Henk. His face had a brooding look. Josie didn't know the reason.

As she weaved past the table, he looked up. A spark of recognition lit his eyes when he caught sight of her. And then she was gone as she headed toward Fred.

In that split second, he seemed to recognize her. But she didn't stop to acknowledge him, for she recalled the last embarrassing moment at the Sentosa Golf Club. She hastened forward toward Fred.

When she reached the table, he rose to greet her. He was his usual affable self. "I've ordered your favorite." He mouthed the words over the din of the room.

"How about you? Sharing it with me?" she asked.

"I'll take a bit of what you order. I've also ordered some sashimi just in case you want to eat it."

"No, you go ahead," she told him. "I don't usually take that. I'll stay with the *shabu-shabu*." Josie noticed he was thinner. His lean frame made him look taller.

"Heard from Jeremy?" he asked as she took the seat opposite him.

"Nope. He seldom calls. Time difference. We depend a lot on text messages."

His eyes scrutinized her in a brotherly way. "You've lost weight."

Josie burst out laughing. "I was just thinking the same about you."

"Did anything interesting lately?"

"Uh-huh. A few days ago, I watched the Asian Tour golf tournament at Sentosa." He was silent, listening to her.

"And guess what? I met a man who's the splitting image of Jeremy."

Fred asked, "Your cousin, Bruce?"

She shook her head. "Nope. He looked a little like Bruce, but more like Jeremy. And he likes to wear white too!"

Fred was silent, absorbing what she said. After a while, he asked, "Do you know him?"

"That's the strange thing. I went up to him thinking he was Jeremy, grasped his hand, and greeted him affectionately. He was startled because he didn't know me."

"I'm sure he was. I'd be too if someone as attractive as you grabbed my hand!" Fred grinned. "What did he do when you greeted him in that way?"

"As I said, he looked quite startled. Um, asked if we knew each other. His group of friends made a little joke about it." She went on, "Naturally, I was embarrassed."

The food arrived. They began their meal. After a short while, Josie asked, "Do you think Jeremy has a brother or a cousin I don't know about?"

"What do you mean?"

She couldn't come up with a rational explanation, so she fell silent.

"Did you ask your parents?"

"Uh-huh. They said they didn't know, um, suggested I asked Aunt Jem."

"Hmm, sounds reasonable."

They finished their meal. On the way to the cashier's desk, they passed by the table where Henk sat earlier. The party had left the room by then.

TWO

Josie was standing on the land beside her house. She saw before her coconut trees and a stretch of sandy beach running a long way. Her unshod feet sloshed on the wet sand. The waves washed over her feet as she walked along.

The sea breeze caressed her thick, long tresses as it blew strands across her face. She tasted the salt on her lips, for she was standing close to the water's edge.

She saw only one other figure in the distance. As she walked on, the sun grew hotter. The humidity increased. Her skin was burning hot. She decided to head for a shack a short distance to the left, where she spotted a vendor selling coconuts. As she approached him, she saw that some of the tops were shucked. Paper straws were stuck into two coconuts.

Scratched on the crude wooden signboard was the price: two dollars. *Hmm, prices have risen*, she thought. *Used to be just a dollar.* She pulled out two coins from her pocket.

The man handed her the coconut. As she sucked in the juice, it felt warm. "Yuck! Should have known. It's noontime!"

Since she didn't want to discard it, she continued sucking in the juice slowly. A sobbing sound caught her ear. It came from inside the atap hut. She craned her neck to detect the person. In the shadows within, she caught sight of a child.

"What's wrong with that child?" she asked the vendor.

He shrugged. "Don't know. Every day, cry," he said this in broken English.

"Why? Isn't his mother here?"

"No mother, no father." The thin, bony man shrugged and said, "Er, just appeared one day."

"My wife has been feeding him, but we can't afford another mouth to feed," he whined.

"Well, why don't you send him to the police then?" Josie reasoned. "They'll be able to locate his parents."

"I did," said the man. "But he ran back to my hut after a time."

"Has he got a name?"

"Uh-huh," replied the man. "His name's Henk!"

At that point, Josie awoke from her dream.

She mulled over the name. *Henk's an unusual name*, she thought. She recalled the Henk she met at the tournament. But she couldn't reconcile the adult she met with the child in her dream.

They were in the middle of tea when Joshua called. Ruth spoke awhile with him and then rang off.

"Your dad's bringing someone home later. Says he'll be staying with us."

Josie was curious. "Um, Dad's business friend? Um, staying in the annex?" She knew her father often invited his business friends for short stays.

"Probably." Ruth finished the cake on her plate and sat, sipping her coffee. She then asked Elsa, the Filipina helper, to set the table for two more for dinner.

"Er, Mum, is it all right if I didn't join Dad and his friend? Er, have some work to complete."

Ruth looked at her daughter. "It might be nice if you can join us later to meet the guest."

Josie was reluctant. Her father's business guests were often years old. She knew he owned several companies in Singapore and overseas.

All of them were involved in technology in some way. When they stayed over, they usually discussed over cups of coffee way into the night.

"Er, maybe, but can't say for sure." She left the table soon after. When she completed her work, instead of joining her parents, she took a nap.

By the time she awoke, it was past midnight. Her parents had retired for the night. Feeling hungry, she went downstairs to cook some instant noodles.

Someone was sitting at the table, drinking coffee. The aroma drifted to her. The dining room lights were dim. She wondered why the person hadn't retired for the night. Was he her father's business friend? She knew the annex didn't have kitchen facilities.

As she approached him, he half-turned his head. She let out a big gasp. It was Jeremy!

"You're back!" She exclaimed in delight. "When did you get back?" She reached him in two short sprints.

She hugged him from behind. As she bent to kiss the side of his cheek, it felt rough, so unlike Jeremy's, which was usually smooth and clean-shaven.

The person released her hands which were clasping his neck. His voice was filled with amusement. "This is getting to be a habit."

He tilted his head backward. The ceiling light fully illuminated it. Josie gasped again, this time more from shock. It was Henk smiling at her.

"How? Er, why are you here?" she asked falteringly.

"Why am I here?" He laughed out loud. "Joshua invited me to stay."

Bewildered, Josie said, "You're my dad's business friend? How come? His biz friends are usually much older."

He pulled out a seat for her. "Let me finish my coffee before it gets cold. Then we can chat. But why are you down here at such a late hour?"

"Er, um," she stammered. "I slept through dinner. Felt hungry, so I came down to make some instant noodles."

"Well," he said gallantly, "don't let me stop you."

She moved into the kitchen to gather her thoughts. She recalled the dream she had earlier when they were on the golf course. He told her he was doing studies relating to the environment. She wondered how he came to be her father's business friend.

When her noodles were ready, she carried her bowl into the dining room but found the guest gone. She ate the noodles slowly, her mind in a turmoil.

Did her mother know the guest resembled Jeremy a lot? Was that why she asked her to join them over dinner?

She concluded her parents must have known. Henk's resemblance to Jeremy was too close for them not to notice it. When she finished her noodles, there were still no answers to her many questions.

She returned to her room and soon fell asleep.

By the time she came down for breakfast the next morning, her parents had left the house. Of Henk, there was no sign.

"Where's everyone?" she asked Elsa.

"Gone out," the helper replied.

"And Jeremy?" Josie asked her.

She corrected her. "Not Jeremy. Henk."

"Er, don't you see the resemblance to Jeremy?"

Elsa shook her head.

Josie insisted, "Don't you think Henk looks a lot like Jeremy?"

Elsa shook her head. "Darker. More hair on top. Hair shorter too."

"But how about his head, his eyes, his neck, his build?"

"Not the same," Elsa repeated as she collected the plates and disappeared into the kitchen.

Maybe Mum is right, she admitted to herself. *I must have Jeremy too much on my mind.*

As she drove to her office, she tried hard to recall Henk. All that time, she was searching her mind for something about him which was different from Jeremy. But none of his features or physique appeared to be different. To her, Henk could be his twin.

Before long, she arrived at her office building. When she walked into the meeting room, the team was already waiting for her briefing. The buzz trailed off as she took her seat at the head of the table.

The secretary walked to the side table and poured her a cup of *tehsi* (a mixture of local tea with sugar and evaporated milk).

"Let's discuss the possibility of opening a store overseas, um, perhaps in Shanghai," Josie opened with the suggestion.

Phil, her assistant, chipped in. "Not a good time. The virus has some provinces in China on lockdown. There may be others following. We don't know yet."

"Ah, yes," Josie said. "Thanks for the reminder."

She looked around the table of core managers. They were in their twenties and thirties. "Any suggestions?"

She trusted their capability. Although they weren't highly experienced in the fashion business, they were well-informed on market trends. They knew which were still available for them to open new stores.

Prior to her taking over the business as CEO of the company, her mother was running it. Ruth had built a reliable team—a core of managers and designers she could trust.

Among them was an even mix of men and women. One of the design team members, a woman, was married, with a one-year-old child. Ruth had allowed her to work from home. She came for face-to-face meetings once a week or whenever there was a need to discuss something urgent.

Sometimes, she did video conferencing with Ruth. Joshua's technology enabled such facilities in the company for the young married person.

"Well, why don't we try Australia instead?" Josie called their attention back to her.

But the group wasn't enthusiastic. "The main cities in Australia are just recovering," ventured Kye, who joined the team a year ago. "The economy there, on the whole, is down."

After a short pause, Phil concluded, "Not a good time for expansion though. Suggest we consolidate what we have." He had joined the team at the outset. Ruth liked his design skill and organizational ability.

Anh, another member of the team, was originally from Vietnam. She came over to Singapore in her teen years and joined the company a year before Josie took over.

She ventured a reason. "The festive season is over. Might be a good idea to wait a while."

After a short pause, when Josie asked, "Anyone else with another suggestion?" she was met with silence.

She concluded, "Let's strengthen our existing markets then. Um, perhaps create new fashions." Signs of relief were visible on all faces.

When Josie returned late that evening, her parents were still out. Of Henk, there was no sign.

After a light dinner, she went to her room. After completing her work, she went to bed. A full moon was casting its rays of light on the side of her bed, close to the window.

Bozo, the toy dog her father had bought from Jersey island when she was a young child, lay beside her. She patted its head and covered it with a tiny blanket.

Before long, she was fast asleep.

The sound of someone sobbing woke her. It came from the direction of the land beside her house. From experience, she knew that something was happening there. She got up and headed for the land. But there was no one there. She walked on a little way. The sound of sobbing continued. She was puzzled.

She turned her head in that direction and looked. To her astonishment, she saw that the land beside her house had stretched to quite a distance, both in length and in width!

Incredible! The thought flashed through her mind.

She knew the house on the land had been demolished and there was nothing constructed yet. Since she didn't explore it in the daytime, she didn't know it stretched so far out.

When she was younger, there was a land behind her house. Later, when she became a teenager, the land extended into a land way beyond.

Recently, the land behind was shortened. That night, as she stood on the land beside it, she realized that it had stretched incredibly farther and wider. Instinctively, she felt there was something mysterious about the land.

The heartbreaking sobs interrupted her thoughts. She walked quickly toward the sound. She found a child there, tucked in the corner of a wooden shed. His head was bowed between his knees. He was sobbing his heart out.

Josie went up to him and touched his head gently.

"What's wrong? Are you hurt?"

He stopped crying. Tearfully, he looked up. "Want Mummy, want Mummy!" His face was grimy, unwashed, and grief-stricken.

Josie went out of the shed. She looked up and down the stretch of bare land. There was no adult around.

Feeling quite helpless, she went back to where the child was. By this time, he was sitting upright. He wiped his tears with the back of his soiled hand and then sat, watching her with curious eyes.

"Where's your mummy?"

The question triggered another bout of crying from the child. "Do you know where you live?" she asked. "I can take you home."

To her surprise, the child pointed in the direction of her home. "That's my home," she explained. "I'm asking where your home is."

He continued pointing in the direction of her home. She went outside the hut to look, hoping to find an adult.

A figure from the distance came striding toward her. When he came closer to her, Josie saw that it was the vendor who sold her a coconut drink in an earlier dream.

This is most odd, she thought. Nevertheless, since she had no alternative solution, she approached him.

"Are you looking for that boy?" She pointed to the child. The man nodded. "Yes. Henk. He's always looking for his mother. He doesn't know she died in a plane crash."

"Huh? How did you know that?"

The man nodded. "Heard his parents' plane was shot down some years ago over eastern Ukraine. The police told us. Soon after, we saw the boy hanging around here."

"Wasn't the boy told? Doesn't he have relatives who can take him?"

"The authorities couldn't locate his close relatives, so he was adopted out," the man revealed. "But he doesn't like his foster parents. He ran away from them.

"We found him in a shack, crying. My wife has been feeding him all this while. But we're poor. We can't afford another mouth to feed."

Josie asked, "Why does the boy keep pointing to my home? I live back there."

The thin, bony man shrugged. "Who knows! Perhaps he thinks his relatives are living there."

"Well, what're you going to do with him now?"

"I'll take him with me and send him back to the adoption agency."

"What's his name?"

The man said softly, "Henk," as he entered the shed.

Josie was surprised when she found herself back on her land. In the moonlight, she saw someone sitting on the steps outside the annex. It was the silhouette of a man.

Since it was her father's property, she approached him. He was holding his head between his hands.

When he heard her footsteps, he looked up. The moonlight acted as a floodlight.

Josie saw a weary, tear-stained face looking up at her. It was Henk, the man she saw late last night.

She approached him.

"Henk?" she asked tentatively. "You okay?"

"Yes," he said wearily. "Just tired. I'm going to bed now." He got up and left her.

Slowly, Josie made her way back to the main house, quite bewildered.

THREE

Josie had two pressing needs the next morning. The first was to find out more about Henk. The second was to know who bought the land beside her house.

It was strange that her parents never mentioned the sale of the land. It was stranger to know there was no house built there for some time now.

In the past, the land beside hers had a house and people. It was in a recessed part of the road. She seldom passed by it. Occasionally, in the past, she caught sight of a car from that house flashing by her gate with someone driving it.

Her opportunity came at dinnertime. Only her mother joined her. Of her father and Henk, there was no sign.

When she finished her meal, she raised the subject to Ruth. "Who's occupying the land beside our house?"

Her mother shrugged her shoulders. "Don't really know. On the day we returned from our long trip overseas, we realized the house was pulled down. Only the *rambutan* and *mango* fruit trees were left."

"Don't you find it strange?" Josie asked. "The entire construction demolished?"

"Well, we were away about two months. Nowadays, with modern technology, houses can be demolished quickly."

"Mum, what about Henk?"

Ruth raised an eyebrow. "Henk?"

"Uh-huh. The chap who's staying in the annex. What do you know about him? I think he looks a lot like Jeremy, don't you?"

Ruth laughed. She cast a sympathetic look at her daughter. "Actually, I think Bruce looks more like Jeremy. Why? Have you met Henk since he came two days ago?"

She leaned forward and studied her daughter's face. "If you must know, I see quite a difference. He's much darker. His skin is quite tanned as if he spent much time in the sun. His hair is much thicker on the top as if he hasn't had a haircut for some time."

Josie fell silent at her observation.

"Perhaps the only likeness to Jeremy are his ears. His ear lobes, like Jeremy's, don't turn outward."

"Mum, his eyes are deep set like Jeremy's."

Ruth looked more amused. "That doesn't make him look like Jeremy. A lot of guys have similar eyes. Height-wise, he is about as tall as Jeremy. But he has such a lost look."

Josie was startled at her mother's observation. "Lost look? What do you mean?"

Ruth looked at her watch. "Explain to you another time. Have to go now." She got up and left the table, leaving her daughter quite confused.

Josie drove to the office soon after breakfast. When she was twenty-one, she took over the running of the fashion business, which her mother started years ago.

In the middle of her meeting with the core managers, there came a knock on the door. It opened. In walked Joshua with Henk, to Josie's astonishment.

"What brings you here, Dad?" she stammered.

"Thought I'll introduce you to Henk, your new part-time business manager." He went around introducing Henk to the design team.

Although Josie was the CEO of the company, her father was still involved as the advisor. He dropped by the office occasionally.

She was taken aback by his announcement. He hadn't mentioned anything earlier about Henk coming to join the team.

"Can Henk join your discussion, or should he wait outside?" her father asked.

She collected her thoughts and quickly suggested to the group present, "Let's have a break. Meet later this afternoon."

Joshua looked at his watch. "Hmm, just twelve. Why don't we have an early lunch? Okay with you?"

She was still confused by what her father said about Henk being the business manager.

When he repeated, "Shall we have an early lunch?" all she could do was utter, "Yes, yes. Where do you plan to go?"

"Tanglin Club. Churchill Room. Quieter there than in the Tavern." He then barked out to Henk, "You can have the room next to Josie's office." He turned abruptly and left Henk and Josie to trail after him.

Joshua was a longtime member of the club. The Churchill Room, as he said, was a quieter place. That day, there were only three tables occupied as it was still early. They were shown to a table of Joshua's choice.

All this while, Henk didn't speak much. He answered only when he was spoken to. He took the seat next to Joshua, with Josie on his other side.

After Joshua decided on the wine and the set lunch for them, he went straight to the point. "Henk has a business degree and experience in marketing and sales. That's the reason I am asking you to let him join you."

When he saw his daughter's unhappy face, he went on to explain, "On a part-time basis. It's only for a year or two until he completes his environmental studies in the university."

"It'll help him earn some money. You'll find him an asset with his experience."

Josie watched Henk's somber face. A worried frown was etched on his rugged countenance.

As they were finishing their dessert, Joshua let out another statement. "Henk's your cousin, you know."

She choked on her tea. Spluttering, she echoed, "My cousin?"

Joshua sighed. "It's a long story. Henk's parents died in a plane crash when he was two."

"He was in Amsterdam then. The government there didn't know who his relatives were. As a result, they sent him to an orphanage because they couldn't locate any of his living relatives at that time."

"When he was older, he was later transferred to an orphanage in Sweden, which was run by some missionaries. It was only when I was offering a scholarship to an outstanding student in the mission school where he was lodging that I came to hear of his case."

"His name was mentioned as a candidate. I started a series of investigations for I wanted to know the background of the student I was offering the scholarship to."

"When I learned of his possible relationship with Ruth's family, I ran a trace on his parentage. After a long while, I found that he's the real son of Yanna and Talia, who were the much older cousins of Luke and Zech."

"The relationship details are complicated, so I won't go into details. Luke and Zech were adopted by Yanna and Talia and then sent by them to Singapore for their education in their early years."

"Much, much later, Henk was born to Yanna and Talia. As I said, he's their real and only son. When Luke married Su Jen, as you know, they had a son, Jeremy. So Henk is Jeremy's cousin."

"Amazing! Incredible!" was all Josie could utter. She was dazed by so much information piled on her over lunch.

Joshua continued, "The missionaries running the orphanage had a problem with Henk in his early years."

"He often ran away from the home, looking for his parents. The authorities arranged for him to stay with foster parents. But that didn't work out."

"He ran away from them too. Said he didn't like the foster parents. When he grew older, they sent him to another orphanage. It happened to be the one in Sweden. By that time, he was in his late teens. The school he attended found he excelled in science subjects, economics, and mathematics."

"The principal recommended him for a scholarship for biz studies in a university in Switzerland for his results were so good."

"Ironically, I was the one funding the scholarship for outstanding students from that mission school. He joined St. Gallen, a university in Switzerland. There, he achieved an MSc degree in business administration."

"Academically, he went from strength to strength. Then he joined various businesses. But he never stayed long. He left whenever he thought he had information about his parents."

"I lost touch with his movement after some years. It was only when he applied to study in Singapore that I came to hear of him again."

Josie looked at Henk to see his reaction to what her father was telling her. But she could read nothing from his impassive face. From her father's account, she discerned he had a restless spirit.

"And now you want him to join our fashion design company?" Josie asked.

Joshua leaned forward, grasped his daughter's cold hand, and said earnestly, "You're his only known cousin. You can help him adjust. He's been a lost soul for too long."

"Will you help me?" Henk asked in such a humble tone that she found it difficult to reject him. "At least I know I've some relatives here."

However, inwardly, she was doubtful. Can finding his relatives help him settle down when deep down he was still looking for his mother?

When would he be reconciled to the fact that his parents were no longer alive?

When he repeated his need for help, she saw the pain in his eyes, but she detected a note of hope in his voice.

She answered him, "Henk, when you put it that way, how can I say no?"

She was of two minds: wanting to help, yet not sure of the outcome. Didn't her father say he often ran away from the orphanage when he was young? And that he never stayed long in a job?

Instinctively, she knew he was a risk factor. But he was her cousin, desperate to be with his relatives to fill the void with the loss of his mother. Her father had often told her in the past that families ought to help one another.

Although her managerial training told her not to take him in, her emotions sympathized with his suffering.

She took refuge in procrastination. "Can I think about it? Um, right now, I have a lot of work that needs to be done in our company."

"Dad, I understand Henk is doing environmental studies in NUS. If he joins us part-time, he'd be like the interns we take in," Josie said to her father.

"Are you aware that interns in our company earn a pittance? Are you suggesting that we give him a salary?" her eyebrows were puckered into a worried frown.

Just then, her eyes shifted to Henk. He gave her a winsome smile as he pressed her hand. Her heart did a flip. Jeremy used to smile like that whenever he wanted to win her over to his argument.

She wished Jeremy were there to hear her father's proposal and help her decide. In decisions, two were better than one, she learned. Three cords were stronger where unity was concerned.

Deep within, she knew her father was determined to give Henk a chance. She knew him well enough to know he wanted to help Henk work out his loneliness and confusion. At the same time, he also wanted to help him earn some money. She knew her father's nature, always stretching out a hand to help someone in need.

Her aunt Jem, a counsellor, and her husband, Don, a medical doctor, had also worked with many to overcome their past problems. They helped such people to move from uncertainty to stability.

She recalled Don's repeated call to her in her earlier years regarding Bella, a wayward young adult. "Give her a chance. Help her adjust."

His call and Jem's remark kept flooding her mind over lunchtime. "Those who have much should help those who have little."

Joshua's reassuring pat on her hand brought her back to reality. Both men were looking at her, with hope shining out of their eyes.

But all she could give them was a lame reply. "I'll think about it, Dad."

Henk returned to the office with her. Her father had decided earlier to let Henk take the smaller room next to her office. She called the receptionist to have the cleaner clean it.

"Henk, since your room is being cleaned, why don't you come to my office. You'll have to excuse me if I don't chat with you, as I've some work to complete today."

In her office, he picked up the reams of fashion designs from the wall shelves and leafed through them while Josie made various phone calls.

After a while, she saw him wander outside the office to speak to Tia, the secretary. Through her glass door, Josie saw her leading him to the library much farther down the corridor.

Just before five o'clock, Henk returned to her office. His first remark on entering her room was "You have a healthy business. Been browsing through the reports."

They left for home soon after. Midway, Henk said, "I'd like to buy you tea. Can we stop somewhere for it?"

"Well, we're passing by the Tanglin Club soon. There's tea served in the lounge."

The sides of his lips quirked in a small smile. "But I want to take you to a place where I can pay for your tea. I have money, you know. Been working in the past year."

She shrugged. "Small matter, Henk. It's my dad who'll be paying for our tea. He's the member."

The lounge wasn't packed. They took a seat in the corner table facing the glass window.

"I'm grateful you're allowing me to join you part-time," he said as he poured the Jasmine green tea into her cup and he took a coffee. Josie could see he was assuming she had already agreed to let him join her business.

Josie confessed, "Um, I really don't how it's going to work out. But I guess I must trust my dad's foresight. He has much experience, as you know."

"Afraid I don't know much about your business," Henk said apologetically. "But if your father allows me to stay on, I'll get to know the business, as well as you and your family, a bit more."

Her recent visit to the land beside and the memory of the child crying flashed through her mind. It prompted her to ask, "Are you still looking for your mother?"

She saw a startled look in his eyes. "Why do you ask? She died a long time ago." He added, "And my dad too."

When he said that, there was anguish in his eyes and his voice. Josie felt bad that she raised a sensitive point with him. But she was curious to know his feelings and whether he could, with time, come to terms with the loss of his parents.

Somehow, the memory of the child in her dream crying stayed with her. Was he the same Henk, now an adult sitting, facing her, and having afternoon tea with her, as the crying child? And had he reconciled with his loss?

"I'm sorry, didn't mean to pry into your past."

He said nothing but just picked up a scone and buttered it before spreading strawberry jam over it. He handed the other half to her.

"Cousin," the words came out awkwardly, "would you like this half?"

His word evoked memories of the time when Jeremy used to call her his beloved cousin.

Cousin, she thought to herself. She hadn't heard the term for a long time now. Not since Jeremy left for his studies overseas.

She raised her eyes and met his. "Cousin! I like the word. Now you have relatives you belong to."

He said nothing. He just looked at her with a strange expression in her eyes. There was a faraway look reflected in his eyes. Her mother had first brought that look to her attention when she told her that Henk had a lost look in his eyes.

Just as they were finishing their tea, a couple came by. "Hello, Josie, your dad's not here?"

It was Jim and Lin, friends of her parents. Josie stood up. So did Henk. "Um, no," she said in reply. "Er, by the way, this is my cousin Henk."

Lin smiled a greeting. "Er, don't think we met him before. We met most of your cousins." She turned to Henk. "From where?"

"Sweden," he answered politely.

"Sweden!" Jim exclaimed in surprise. "Thought your cousins were from Indonesia and Sabah, Josie. Didn't know you have one from Sweden."

She said nothing, for she didn't know how to explain Henk's lengthy background. Since she knew Jim was waiting for an answer, she felt obliged to supply a brief explanation. "Henk studied and worked there for some years."

Jim stretched out his hand. "Nice to meet you, Henk."

When they got home, Henk went straight to the annex. Although he told her he wanted to get to know her family more, she found in the weeks ahead that he preferred to keep to himself.

In her room, she texted Jeremy about Henk. His reply was, "Keep your distance. You don't know what kind of person he is."

The message left her wondering why he was giving her a warning. He never met Henk, so how could he know there would be problems in her work relationship with him?

FOUR

When Fred's call came the next day, it was a welcome relief. He hadn't called for some time. She wondered what caused his silence. He used to invite her for dinner every fortnight.

His voice sounded excited. "Join us for dinner?"

"Us? Tonight?"

"Yes, yes," he said breathlessly. "I want you to meet Kay."

"Kay?"

"Uh-huh." He named a place she hadn't visited with him before. She had to *Google* for the road map.

The Japanese restaurant was tucked at the end of the road. The parking space was tight. Josie breathed a sigh of relief when she finally found a space. She was sandwiched between two cars and had to squeeze to get out of her car.

Japanese-style paper lanterns hung over the dim, low entrance. The inside of the restaurant was even dimmer. She looked around for Fred and spotted him in a corner table. He didn't stand up to hail her as he usually did. He was sitting next to a short, rather-plump girl.

When Josie came to their table, Fred simply said, "So glad you can join us."

He indicated the opposite seat. He was missing his usual hug and kiss on her cheek.

Kay was unsmiling. Josie saw her examining her critically. She was used to women examining her. Her beauty seemed to put them at a disadvantage. Kay was no different. She neither nodded to acknowledge her nor stretched out her hand in greeting.

Josie took an instant dislike to her.

Fred, on the other hand, smiled warmly at her. "So glad you can join us tonight."

He turned to Kay, squeezed her hand that was on the table, and introduced them, "Josie's an old friend."

Ouch! Did he have to say that? Josie thought. He made her sound very old.

Fred reached out for Josie's hand, which was on table too. But before he could touch it, she withdrew it from the table.

They had started on the wrong footing, Josie realized. She didn't know Kay and was upset that Fred hadn't told her anything about her in the weeks before.

When the waiter came to take their order, Fred told her, "I ordered the usual."

But Josie, feeling quite piques by Kay's cold attitude, replied, "I'm tired of the old. Would like something new." She saw the surprise in Fred's eyes, when she said it.

She hailed the waiter. Then she leafed through the thick cardboard of faded old photos of various dishes. They were the same ones as those in the restaurant, which she and Fred used to frequent.

She took her time. After a while, she pointed to a small plate of fresh salmon and tuna. Fred looked puzzled. He knew she didn't like *sashimi.* He knew she liked the *shabu-shabu* with the *kurobuta pork.*

"Er, don't you want the *shabu-shabu*?"

She snapped, "I'd like a change."

She saw Kay snuggling close to Fred. "I'd like the usual," she cooed to him.

After he gave their orders to the waiter, Fred leaned back. Kay's hand was still linked into his.

"I'm sure you'll want to know how Kay and I met."

Josie didn't answer him. She sat, sipping the iced green tea.

"Our date was arranged by Cloe." Fred could see from Josie's expressive eyes that she didn't know who Cloe was.

Kay giggled as she disclosed, "Cloe's our computer matchmaker."

Josie choked. She knew some young ones resorted to it but never thought that Fred would use it.

"Cloe's incredible, Josie. She knows what I like and the type of girl I want." Fred sounded enthusiastic.

Unsmiling, Josie thought, *Doesn't Cloe know you liked me?* She realized she'd put the verb in the past tense.

Opposite her, Kay was bubbling, "It's like a dream come true. I did a series of input, and Cloe came up with a whole lot of photos of men who are possible dates for me.

"Cloe arranged those dates. Finally, after some trial and error, I ended up with Fred. He was the closet match."

She leaned closer to Fred. "And you think I'm the best match too, don't you?"

Josie protested in her mind. *Can't be true. Fred used to say I was his best choice. What went wrong? Didn't we have such good relationship all these years?*

She heaved a big sigh. *Time to move on. Mustn't regret.* She consoled herself with the thought, *I still have Jeremy.*

Outwardly, she said insincerely, "So glad for you both." When Fred saw her giving a quirk on her lips, his face exuded a smile of relief.

A tear fell. Josie couldn't help it. Quickly, she turned aside to open her silk purse. She pretended to look for something but instead pulled out a tissue.

The waiter came with their order. They ate in silence. From time to time, she could feel Fred's eyes on her.

She knew he knew she didn't like *sashimi*. And she knew he wondered why she ordered it. She took a while to finish it.

Fred asked if she wanted to order dessert. But all she wanted was to go home. She made a pretense of looking at her gold watch.

"Um, think I've to leave now. Expecting a call from Jeremy." She knew it wasn't true but felt she had to add it as an excuse for leaving them.

"Who's Jeremy?" Kay's high-pitched voice interrupted her thoughts.

"Oh, er," Fred stammered as he explained, "he's Josie's friend. Mm, they have relationship. They'll probably get married after his graduation."

Kay looked pleased. She snuggled closer to him. "Um, we don't know when we'll get married, right, Fred?"

He looked embarrassed. "Um, still plenty of time." Hastily, he picked up the bill and headed for the cashier's desk.

"Have you known Fred for long?" Kay asked. Josie only nodded, unwilling to share with her how long her friendship with Fred had been.

With nothing more to say, their conversation petered out. From the corner of her eyes, she saw Fred coming back to them.

She got up abruptly, picked up her silk purse, and left the table without another word.

When she got home, she called Jeremy. She needed to hear his voice. It was near midnight. His sleepy voice reminded her of the time difference.

"It's me," she began.

"Huh? What time is it?"

"I need to talk to you about Fred."

His voice was clearer. "Something happened to him?"

"Uh-huh. He's found a girl."

"Er, that's good, isn't it? He's been single for a long time." She heard him yawning.

"It's not that. He found her with Cloe's help."

"Huh? She's his friend too? He has two girlfriends?"

"No, no."

"Her friend?"

"No. She's a computer."

There was a pause.

"Are you still on the line?" she asked.

"Yes, yes. A computer? Sounds weird. Is he so desperate to get a girl that he has to ask a computer to find a girl for him?"

Josie nodded, although Jeremy couldn't see her. She stifled a sob, but he heard it.

"Let's talk on the video call. You sound like you're crying. Do you miss him that much?"

So as not to offend him, she quickly switched the focus to him. "I miss you. When are you coming back? Now that Fred has a girl, I've no one to take me out for dinner."

"Ah, so that's the reason you're upset. Well, I'll be returning soon as I finish my research and hand in my doctoral thesis." He added comfortingly, "Won't be long now."

Josie didn't want Jeremy to see her upset face. She knew it wasn't right that she should be so upset.

Shouldn't she be glad that Fred finally found a girl? What upset her was that it was a computer who found the girl for him. It sounded so cold-blooded.

Jeremy's voice came over the headpiece. "You there?"

His warm, loving voice comforted her. "Well, don't get so upset. Fred may change his mind."

"The computer can't be a 100 percent right. Fred's dealing with a human being. Everyone has moods."

"When he finds out this woman has bad moods, he may not want to continue his relationship with her."

A ray of hope flashed through her mind. Jeremy was right. The computer couldn't predict human moods. Or could it? Technology is so advanced these days.

"I miss you," she breathed into the phone.

"Still crying?" His tender voice touched her.

"No, not over Fred."

"Don't cry over a lost friendship. He still cares for you. After all, you're like a sister to him. He knew you longer than I did."

She heard him yawning again. "I'll ring off now. Need to catch up on my sleep. Good night, my beloved cousin. Have a restful night."

Jeremy was right. She was like a sister to Fred. She grew up with him. She flew kites with him, together with her cousins Justin and Chin, when she was nine. A sister shouldn't get upset when her brother finds a girl.

She should be happy for him, shouldn't she? She looked at the bedside clock. It was nearly two. Puffing up her pillow, she settled her head on it and was soon asleep.

* * *

The creaking and cranking of what sounded like a mass of machines woke her. From her window, she could see lights in the land beside her house.

Hurriedly, she changed and headed for the place. But there was no one around. She heard the groaning of machines again. Her ears detected the metallic sounds to the left.

When she looked through the large glass window, she couldn't believe what she saw!

Robots! A whole mass of them inside what looked like a warehouse. She saw machines marching around in the building.

She decided to go inside to investigate the unusual scene. As she entered, she saw little robots, medium-sized ones, larger ones, and even huge sizes, looking clumsy. Some larger ones kept bumping into the smaller machines.

They emitted a buzz, which grew overwhelmingly louder as she walked farther in. The machines were all busy. Some were churning out messages on their screens in languages she couldn't understand.

On one side, ten machines were flashing the same sort of text. On the right, another five were giving out texts of a different kind. It looked like an Arabic type.

A third lot on the left typed out Japanese characters. Yet another lot revealed Chinese scripts. She walked around them to see what the other machines were producing. Some had designs. When she peered at their screens, she was astonished to see clothes designs.

Just then a bell resounded through the hall. All the whirring stopped. Everything froze. There was total silence.

Is this their rest period? Josie wondered.

Josie looked up and down the large hall. Nothing moved. The mass of machines seemed to be asleep.

Can't be, she reasoned. *Machines don't take naps, not in the sense that humans take afternoon naps!*

The silence was unnerving after a while. She was the only one breathing. She was the only human awake there. Just as she thought of moving out of the building, there was whirr close by. This was followed by three other similar whirrs.

A small robot slid close to her. Then another, a little taller, came in front of her. And then an even taller one. The last one was the tallest, about her height. Soon a good number of smaller robots moved in line, arranging themselves next to the first one.

Looking at them, Josie couldn't help but conclude, "They look almost like a family. Child robots, a mother, and a father."

In the next instant, her reasoning took over. "But they can't be! The smaller ones can't be their children. They can't procreate like humans."

Then the little one spoke. In a high-pitched voice, just like a child's, it asked in a monotone, "What're you doing here? Are you a new robot?"

The robot next to it, a taller one, examined her. "You look strange. You're not dressed like us."

The tallest of the three, in a louder voice, said, "Are you one of the newer designs?"

The machine's arm reached out and plucked her jeans as if to check the material.

Josie backed away immediately. The robots closed in on her. Their machines began to purr, softly at first, then a little louder, as they examined her.

Soon they woke all the other machines in the hall. The sound was incredibly overpowering.

The second-tallest one demanded to know, "Where are you from? We can see you're different. Are you from a different batch? What's your serial number?"

"Er, I'm not a robot," Josie began tentatively. "I'm a human."

The whirring increased in volume as the machines began to search their memory boxes. The second-tallest one, which Josie designated as the mummy of the group, reached out a mechanical hand and pinched her arm.

"Ouch!" she exclaimed. "That hurts!"

The family of machines, for that was what they looked like, drew closer. Their arms stretched out to pinch her.

"Don't do that!" she hollered. "Stop that! It hurts."

Immediately, the smallest robot replied, "We don't hurt." Then it stretched out its thin steel arm. "Here, pinch it."

That made Josie angry. "Of course, you won't hurt. You're made of steel! I'm made of flesh. I've veins and muscles and blood vessels!"

"You have them?" the daddy in the group was curious. "Where? Let us see." It stretched out a thin steel hand and pinched her flesh.

"Stop that!" Josie screamed in pain. "That hurts."

"I don't see any blood coming out," said the mommy of the group.

"Oh, so you know about blood." Josie then decided to distract them with logic. "Well, I'm different from you lot. I'm human, and humans bleed when we're cut."

The middle robot cut in. "I don't see any blood. I know about humans," it boasted. "Don't you know we're created superior to your kind? We can do things you can't!"

Josie had heard of robots with high AI. She didn't know why, but her heart began to palpitate more quickly. She began to feel a little afraid. She was one human against so many intelligent robots.

She looked for a way to escape them. But there were so many of them. And she didn't know how fast they could run.

The little robot pinched her arm again. "Don't do that!" She rebuked it sharply. "I told you it hurts. Can't you be kind to me?"

"Kind? What is that?" the daddy robot asked. This made her realize that robots didn't have the emotions and feelings which humans have. They were made differently.

Instead of explaining its meaning, she tried to confuse them by adding more emotions to the list. "We have compassion and love. We cry when we're hurt. We also hate when someone does evil things to us."

"Stop, stop!" the daddy robot whirred loudly. "What're all those things you listed?" It looked down at a box placed in its front—the program box. A thin steel finger flipped it open.

Josie saw a whole series of lights flickering. She realized it contained whatever its creator had put into its program. Everyone was silent, watching the daddy robot do a search.

"You won't know what feelings are because you just don't have that in your input!" she jeered at them in her anger.

A monotone demanded, "What do you mean when you say we can't feel?"

"What I'm saying is true! You don't have emotions like humans have! You're built differently. You're cold machines."

"Huh? You mean you're a warm machine?" the mummy robot challenged her.

Josie thought to herself, *Hmm, its vocabulary does include cold and warm. It knows that warm is the opposite of cold. But I don't think it can feel cold and warmth.*

Knowing the meaning of a word is quite different from feeling the sensations of warmth and coldness, she thought.

To test this out, she pretended to hug her arms. The group of robots was watching her. "I'm feeling cold now, in fact very cold! Do you feel cold too?"

"What is cold?"

As Josie suspected, the robots didn't feel changes in temperature. "It's a feeling," she said. "I can't explain it. I can just feel it in my body."

"Well, since you're here, teach us then," the tallest robot demanded.

The others moved closer to her. All of them opened their boxes. She became more afraid, for she knew she didn't have the skill to add to their program.

"Look," she said desperately, "I can't help you. My creator is quite different from yours."

"Who's your creator?" demanded the tallest robot. "Why can't our creator give us the same emotions?"

"I don't know. All I know is humans have souls."

She watched the expressionless faces of the robots. She had deliberately moved into an area of discussion which she was sure they couldn't comprehend.

To confuse them further, she added, "And emotions."

"How many emotions?" the daddy demanded.

"Many."

"We want them and souls too!"

"You can't have souls," she argued. "Only people who have souls can go to heaven or hell. Those who've done right, according to our creator, will go to heaven."

Josie sensed their puzzlement, although their faces didn't register any emotion.

Suddenly, the little robot cried out, "I want a soul! I want to go to heaven too." The other little robots began demanding too.

"Look what you've done!" the daddy robot exclaimed. "You've started a rebellion!"

From the import of its words, Josie knew it was cross with her. But its voice was just a monotone, which didn't connote anger.

She knew human voices had inflections and pitches which reveal their states of emotions, but robots didn't have them. The little robots continued clamoring in their high monotones for a soul. They began to choke and splutter because they couldn't cry.

There was nothing in their system that was created to make them cry when they were upset. They had no tear ducts like human beings.

They could wail, however. Their volume would rise and fall. And the first child robot who spoke to her did just that. Like a high-pitched siren, it wailed, "I want a soul! I want a soul!"

Josie looked at the bigger machine, which she likened to a mother, for want of a better term. But she knew it didn't have the function to comfort the little machine like that of a human mother.

She watched to confirm her belief. It didn't stretch out its spindly arms to enfold the smaller machine to comfort it. It couldn't. It wasn't programmed to do so. It just stood by coldly, stiffly, with no expression of compassion.

It dawned on her how different they were from humans. They had no souls or emotions too. They couldn't cry when they were hurt. They couldn't get angry. They were just machines.

Suddenly, a middle-sized mass of steel demanded to know. "What about us? Don't we live on too?"

This triggered a thunderous echo throughout the hall from the other robots. "How about us! Why didn't our creator give us souls?"

Suddenly, what followed their outburst was silence, an ominous silence, as they waited for her answer. Not a breath stirred the air around her because machines have no breath. Just purring sounds.

Josie couldn't sense any anxiety rising in them, but the outcry of their words implied their anxiety.

When the machines were anxious, their purr grew louder in volume. She attempted an answer. "Your creator can't create souls. Mine is the only one who can. My creator breathes life into us and gives each human person a soul!

"Your life span depends upon a battery." To console the machines, and she didn't know why, she added, "But they're rechargeable!"

As she stood there, confronted by the large number of robots, it hit her that, however advanced and intelligent robots were, they were still not superior to human beings in many ways. There were some things which made them inferior to humans.

Her mind rolled back to Chloe, the machine who chose a woman for Fred. She took comfort in the knowledge that Fred would one day realize that Chloe couldn't choose for him a perfect woman to be his wife.

There's no such thing as a perfect partnership. Relationships must be worked out over time. Like hers and Jeremy's! Only time would tell if Kay was the right match for him. At the back of her mind, Josie felt certain that Kay wasn't! She knew Fred too well.

She edged her way closer to the exit and quickly escaped from their presence. Hurriedly, she made her way back to her land.

Dawn was beginning to creep over the sky above. Pink streaks of light flashed across the sky. The land beside her house was just a blur when she looked back.

FIVE

It wasn't long before Josie and Henk fell into a regular pattern. In the mornings, she went to her office, while he attended lectures at the university.

Ruth accepted Henk's appointment without much objection. Josie suspected that it was her mother who suggested to her father that Henk take up the part-time job to help her expand the business.

Joshua, knowing that Henk's hostel and tuition fees were high, had invited him to lodge with them. And Henk readily accepted his offer since it saved him money.

The part-time job suited him well, for it gave him some earnings. The course of study required him to travel abroad as the students had to study the environments of different countries. He needed the extra money for the trips.

In the weekends, he joined the family after dinner to hear the news. When Jeremy was in Singapore, he used to sit with them in the living room after dinner. But after he left for the States, there was a void, until Henk came.

He sat in the same sofa which Jeremy used to sit. Whereas the latter participated in discussions with Joshua over news items, Henk remained silent.

A month after Henk settled in, Josie had a dream. She was in the land beside her house. She was drawn to a voice sobbing and crying, "I want my mummy."

This time, she knew where to find the boy. She walked along the bare stretch and headed toward the shed at the end. When she pushed open the broken wooden door, she saw a boy huddled in a corner.

"Don't you know where your mummy is?" she asked.

He stopped crying. "She's with Daddy," he said in a heartbroken voice.

"Where are they now?" she persisted, wanting to know if the boy knew about his parents.

"Not here, not here. They've left me." He started crying again. She stooped beside him.

"They haven't, you know," she said gently. "They're just in a different place. You might meet them someday."

"I want them now, now." He stomped his foot.

"Well, you can't," she said kindly. "Why don't I take you back to where your foster parents are." She lifted his hand, but he snatched it back.

"Don't want them, don't want them," he cried out loudly. Continuous sobs racked his thin body.

"Well, do you want to stay with me then?"

He stopped crying. "With you? Who're you?"

"Your cousin." The boy stopped his crying, digesting her information.

In a tentative voice, he asked, "You'll look after me?"

Josie stretched out her hand and stroked his thick mop of hair. "My parents will."

"You have parents?" He was curious. Then he began to cry loudly. That was a wrong statement to make, Josie realized, for it triggered another loud sob from the boy.

"Look, you can't stay alone in this shed. Come home with me. You can stay with me if you like." The offer caused him to stop crying. She pulled him up and walked outside with him.

The next thing she knew, she was walking back alone to her house.

As she passed the annex, she saw Henk sitting on the step of the annex, with his head bent between his hand.

"Henk." She approached him boldly. "You're with us now, your relatives. I'm your cousin, remember?"

He lifted his head and looked at her with tearstained eyes. "My cousin?" he said this slowly as he digested the information. "My cousin," he repeated, as if to convince himself.

"Yes, yes, your cousin," Josie said firmly. "You've found us, your relatives, me and my parents."

He said nothing but just sighed heavily. In the shadows, he got up and went inside the annex.

Josie went back to the main building with a heavy heart. She'd discovered Henk's secret—his longing for his mother.

Her visit to the land beside had shown her his deep sense of loss. Although he was now a mature person, he didn't seem to have overcome his loss. There was a tear in his soul, which she couldn't repair.

Josie found an opportunity to speak to her mother a week later concerning Henk's emotional problem. She didn't mention her visit to the land beside for she knew her mother didn't believe in her visits to the mysterious land.

When Josie was a young child, she used to visit the land behind her house. But Ruth had dismissed her visits as only dreams and even nightmares. Knowing her mother's tendency, Josie took a different approach, making it appear that she knew it from Henk's sharing.

Ruth was sympathetic. "With such a deep-seated problem, only time can heal. On our part, let's show him love and kindness.

"Your father has done well in allowing him to stay with us. That way, we hope Henk will realize he still has relatives and people who love and care for him."

In the weeks ahead, Josie didn't see any change in Henk. He often remained quiet. Over dinner, he spoke only when Joshua asked him his opinion. Moreover, he didn't have any conversation starters.

Perhaps, he's missing his friends, Josie speculated inwardly. She recalled the group he was with when she first met him at the Asian Golf Tour, the boisterous friends he seemed so relaxed with. And she wondered why he didn't socialize with them anymore.

* * *

About the same time, the world economy took a downturn. Most people were glum, for the market conditions were depressed.

The fashion design market didn't have ready outlets abroad. That was the reason Josie was surprised when one day, Henk suggested a trip to Mongolia.

In reply, she told him, "Er, don't you realize the economy has taken a downturn. Um, don't think it's a good time to expand."

"I'm aware of it," Henk answered. "That's the reason I'm suggesting your team go to Mongolia to get fresh ideas for their designs. Instead of expanding, the team can spend the interim time creating new fashions.

"When the market conditions improve, we can then think of expanding. The team will have more creative ideas when they see the fashions of the men and women in Mongolia."

"Men!" Josie exclaimed in surprise. "You're thinking of moving into men's designs?"

"Why not? You have men in your team who are capable of producing outfits which men will want to buy."

"Well, let's have a tentative discussion first," she told him. "See what the team thinks."

The next day at the office, Henk made a proposal to the team. "This isn't a good time to expand. Instead, why don't you people in the design team think of creating new fashions?"

"What're you thinking of?" Phil, the chief designer, asked. He was voicing the question of the other members. Without hesitation, Henk came out with his proposal, as if he knew already what he wanted.

"The fashions we now have, have been revolving around what the company has been selling for some years. I'm thinking of moving us into other types of fashion designs."

Everyone looked at him expectantly. "Why not try designs of, say, a Mongolian type?"

There was a confounded silence. Josie was the only one who wasn't surprised at Henk's proposal. To give the team members time to think over the proposal, Josie declared, "Let's have a tea break."

When they remet an hour later, Phil inquired, "Why Mongolian? Most of their dresses are the kaftan types. Will they sell well in Singapore?

Kye, the other designer in the team, stated his opinion. "Most are full length. Loose. Can be elegant though. Depends on the type of material."

"Aren't they similar to the Hawaiian muumuus?" Lea asked. She had joined the company recently.

Anh contributed a point, "They might sell well in the December months in Singapore when the weather is cooler." Her former work experience with some fashion houses in Paris made her an asset to the company.

"They'll sell well in the winter months in Europe," Lea added.

"We can innovate. Use linen for the cooler months and in the winter season," Josie suggested. "And thinner cottons in the summer."

"I agree with Josie." Henk supported her point. "You guys can create a slightly different fashion. Um, you don't need to copy the Mongolian fashions exactly. As Josie said, you can innovate."

He went on, "What I suggest is for some of you designers to fly out to Mongolia with Josie and me. See the real thing. Talk to those there in the fashion business."

"Er, Henk, you realize we don't speak their language. We've never been to that country before," Josie pointed out immediately. He gave her a benign smile.

He revealed, "I know a company there. Um, worked with them some years ago. One of the chaps can be our interpreter. I'll get him to arrange for us to see some models and outfits."

Josie was disconcerted by his information. Clearly, he'd anticipated their agreement to visit Mongolia even before he spoke to them.

But her team of designers was accommodating. They were a little bored sitting in the office, designing clothes which were already in fashion. What they were looking for were fresh ideas.

Phil agreed. "Why not. I'm game if Josie's agreeable."

Josie said bluntly to Henk, "But you're not with the design team. And we don't have contacts right now with any fashioner designers in Mongolia."

Henk looked a little sheepish. "Well, I know a man who used to do some business in Sweden. I can contact him. He might know someone in the fashion business."

"And then what?" Josie asked pointedly. "While we're talking fashion, what will you be doing?"

"Um, er, I was thinking of contacting one of the lecturers in the environment and forestry department. I understand there's one in the National University of Mongolia."

"Perhaps, I can glean something from their research which will help me in my thesis."

The others applauded. "Good idea, Henk." But Josie was a little disturbed to learn that Henk had planned for himself to be included in their visit to Mongolia without first discussing it with her.

Phil said aloud, "I feel we should visit Ulaanbaatar if Henk can contact someone there in the fashion business."

On hearing this, Henk said eagerly, a little too eagerly, in Josie's estimation, "Yes, yes, I can ask my contact if you like."

"Um, I'll have to discuss this with my dad before I decide."

When Henk replied, "I've proposed the idea to your father," Josie stiffened at his words.

He added, "Joshua is agreeable if you accept the idea."

"What!" Josie flared up at his words. "You discussed it with my father even before you spoke to me!" She was clearly upset. She vocalized her distaste in a raised tone.

Sensing an argument rising, the others quietly vacated the room.

Henk tried to placate her. "Er, it isn't what you think, Josie. I happened to mention it to your dad only yesterday over breakfast."

"Oh, great!" Josie's hands rested on her hips as she said this. "Who's running the business. You or me?"

"You, of course!" Henk said quickly, sensing her anger.

"I should hope so!" Her voice took on a metallic tone. "I don't like you discussing my business with my father before you come to me."

"It isn't what you think, Josie." He tried to placate her again. "Just thought we're cousins and you wouldn't mind. I didn't intend to go behind your back."

"I should hope not! Don't ever do that again, Henk. I don't like it! Don't presume on my niceness just because we're cousins!" She snapped as she picked up the files and headed for the exit.

"Sorry," he apologized.

When she left the office, she was livid. Why didn't her father let her know what Henk proposed to him! She decided to speak to him later that evening.

As it happened, Joshua was later coming home. Henk didn't join them for dinner. Her chance came only when her father went to the living room at news time.

She went directly to the point. "Dad, why didn't you let me know you agreed with Henk about the Mongolian visit?"

Joshua saw her upset face. "I didn't agree with him. I simply said he should speak to you and the team."

"Well, Henk implied you agreed with his suggestion. That put me in a bad light with the team."

Joshua looked at his daughter's flushed face. "Aren't you overreacting a bit? I'm not sure what he told you, but take it from me, it wasn't an agreement with him."

"Oh." Josie's anger subsided at her father's gentle tone. "I guess it's his way of saying it which offended me."

"What upset me also was that Henk appeared to have planned his own visit there too. He's assuming I'm including him in our visit there."

"Henk knows you're in charge, Josie," her father said placatingly. "Look on him as an asset. He's farsighted in some ways, especially where business is concerned. He has the experience to back him."

"I'm sure if he goes, he'll be of help to you in some way. He knows some of the people there from what he told me. As far as I know, you haven't any contacts there if you're planning to go to Mongolia."

"He'll be an asset in your company if you give him a chance to adjust to your way," Joshua assured her. "I'd never agree to anything without your consent."

With her father's sympathetic eyes on her, Josie simmered down. Inwardly, she admitted, *Maybe I'm overreacting.*

She slid toward him. "Sorry, Dad, it's just that Henk burst out with the suggestion in front of the team without consulting me first.

"What's worse is that he brought your name in, as if you'd agreed with him."

Joshua squeezed his daughter's hand. "I guess you're still new at being the boss, eh? Take it easy. Look upon

Henk as an asset. He has much business experience and knowledge."

He added, "He may not have the social graces which we know. Sometimes, his words or attitude may even offend."

"Guess so, Dad." She sighed.

"You're missing Jeremy, I know. It won't be long now before he returns and joins my company."

"I know, I know, Dad."

He patted her arm comfortingly. "Well, what do you think?"

"About what?"

"The possibility of visiting Mongolia and looking at their fashion designs."

She wrinkled her nose. "Not sure. I understand most of their garments are long. More like the kaftan or the Hawaiian muumuu."

"Well, you can always shorten it to suit our tropical climate. You've good artistic talent. Get your design team to do some sketches."

"Include some of the Mongolian color combinations. When your mother and I visited the country, she was impressed with the holiday *deel*."

"The *what*?"

"The *deel*. In summer, the colors are bright blue or green, mostly block colors. Some have a sprinkling of linear designs."

"Some of the younger women choose a claret silk, which they wear with a silk sash of contrasting color. They looked quite attractive in the outfits when we saw them."

Josie's eyes widened. "You mean you've seen the women in such outfits?"

"Uh-huh. The male *deels* are wider, with somber colors. You could make them less colorful for the men in Singapore. Might sell well here."

Josie threw her arms around his neck. "You're a genius, Dad. I didn't know you know so much about fashion wear!"

He grinned widely. "Must have rubbed off from your mother."

That night, Josie went to bed feeling very relieved she had a father who was wise and so thoughtful of her.

* * *

Around two in the morning, she was awoken by a loud whirring sound close to her bed. When she opened her eyes, she jumped up with a start.

Standing next to it was a small-sized robot with the lights on its box flickering.

"What're you doing here?"

In a high-pitched flat tone, the little robot said, "I want what you said you have when you visited us that day."

"Huh? And what's that!"

"A soul!"

"*Wh-at*?"

The lights in the box flickered wildly. "Yes. Can you ask your creator to give me a soul and emotions?"

Helplessly, Josie looked at the robot. "Does your mummy and daddy know you've come out of the land beside?"

The robot replied, "I don't have a mummy and a daddy. I'm just me, one of a kind. I have a program different from the larger ones. Can I stay with you until I get a soul?"

Josie was aghast. "You can't just come and live with me. This makes you a runaway."

"What's a runaway?"

"Hmm, I see it isn't in your vocabulary range. Well, when you run away from your parents, er, I mean, from the other larger robots and come to me, this makes you a runaway from your family of robots!"

The small robot's face registered a blank. Josie wasn't sure if it understood what she was saying.

Finally, it said, "They're not my parents. They're robots like me, only a taller and a larger size. They, too, don't have a soul."

He added, "If I have a soul, I'll be superior to them."

Josie was at a loss. She just didn't know how to explain to a machine what a soul was. Just then, an idea came into her mind. "Perhaps my dad can explain it to you tomorrow morning."

"You mean you have a larger person you call Dad?"

Josie could see the little machine had no idea of family relationship.

"Can I stay with you now?"

"It's quite late," Josie explained politely.

"Late? What's late?"

What a dilemma, Josie thought to herself. This little machine doesn't have a vocabulary input on time either.

"I'm tired. I want to go to sleep," she announced. "I'll decide in the morning."

"What do you mean? Sleep? Morning?" asked the little one.

Josie scratched her head in despair. Just then, she caught sight of two switches on the robot's box.

Ah, the switch box. I can put it to sleep, she thought hopefully. She stretched out a hand to flip the switch.

"Don't do that!" The robot protested. "That'll put me out of action." Josie was glad she saw a way to stop the machine.

"Don't worry," she said, "you'll wake up when I wake up tomorrow morning."

Without hesitation, she flipped the switch. The lights went off. The whirring sound died down.

When Josie awoke the next morning, she forgot all about her conversation with the little machine. After breakfast, she suddenly recalled it, so she dashed up to her room.

She scanned the room but couldn't locate it.

Hmm, must have dreamt it. She was relieved it was only a dream. How else could she explain its presence?

SIX

The week they were due to leave for Mongolia, Fred called her. "Dinner?"

Josie was reluctant. "With Kay?"

"N-aw, she's not free. Just you and me."

Josie was still reluctant. "Why? Are you inviting me only because Kay can't make it?"

There was silence. "Um, just thought I owe you an explanation."

"About what?"

"About Kay?"

"You're free to choose who you want to date and have a relationship with." Then she added softly, "Even if she's your computer's choice!"

"What's that? What did you say?"

When she didn't repeat her words, he asked, "Well, how about it? I'll come and fetch you."

She agreed because she didn't want to appear churlish. After all, as Jeremy reminded her, Fred was like a brother to her.

She was on the phone when she saw Fred walking along the corridor of her office. Through the glass door, she saw him conversing briefly with Henk.

When he entered her office, she could see his smile was guarded. "You have a nice office," he commented.

"You didn't tell me Henk's working here." He didn't sound pleased.

"Er, Dad arranged it. Long story. Tell you over dinner."

He nodded. "Looks like it'll be a long dinner. I've much to share with you too about Kay." He went ahead of her.

On the way out, she met Henk. Nodding his head toward Fred, he asked her, "Is he Jeremy?"

Josie was surprised. Didn't she see him speaking to Fred when he entered her office? Didn't Fred tell him his name? "No," she said abruptly. "He's Fred. An old friend. You met him earlier."

"Er, briefly only. He didn't tell me his name," Henk said. Fred was waiting at the door. Josie beckoned to him. When he came up to them, Henk greeted him.

"I'm Henk, Josie's new cousin."

Fred was amused. "New? You mean newly discovered cousin."

"If you like." Henk shrugged his shoulder and turned away. Josie sensed her, too, wasn't friendly with Fred.

In the car, Fred said, "Same place?"

"Don't you want to try some place else?"

"Maybe. Do you?"

"Yes," she said emphatically.

He drove around a bit. She asked, "Where are you taking me?"

"Um, trying to find a place we both like."

Josie couldn't resist saying, "Have you tried asking Chloe?"

He was silent. She goaded him further. "You said Chloe knows everything about your likes and dislikes. Would it know what I like? Er, what we both like?"

He scratched his temple. "Hmm, hadn't thought of that concerning you."

"You mean the computer decides only on certain people? I thought it knew about all your friends, girlfriends, I mean."

After a while, she added, "Maybe, you didn't give it any input about me. After all, come to think of it, I'm not your girlfriend, um, just your good, old friend." She put on a stress on the word *not*.

After a while, he said, "You're angry and upset."

Josie burst out, "Of course, I am! Getting a computer to choose a life partner for you. That's stupid!"

"I don't think so. Chloe knows Kay likes the things I like, the food, the movies, the books . . ."

"Stop, stop!" Josie screamed at him. "Does it know about the times you and I enjoyed flying kites? About how you told me you cared for me?"

Fred drove his car to an empty car park lot. He took her hand and caressed it.

"Josie, Josie, if you broke off from Jeremy tomorrow, I'll be the first to ask you to marry me! You know how much I care for you."

"Tell me, are you willing to give Jeremy up for me?"

He drew her closer to him. "If not, will you help me find a girl who can be my lifetime partner?"

Josie said stiffly, "You have Chloe."

"Chloe doesn't know my true feelings, Josie. If it did, it would have recommended you. It knows only the facts I put in. It's only a computer."

"You didn't tell it anything about us?"

"That's personal and private information. Only you and I have privileged access to it." She saw him frowning in the shadows of the car.

"It only knows the interests I feed it. That's why it came up with Kay."

A sob from Josie caused him to pull her closer to him. He gave her a tender kiss on the forehead. His hand caressed her smooth face.

In a voice charged with emotion, he said, "Now let's find a restaurant before I cause you to be unfaithful to Jeremy."

That put a smile on her face. "Would Chloe know that?" They both laughed at the ridiculous thought. They drove away from the car park in a lighter mood.

After a while, they ended up in the same restaurant they used to frequent.

When the *shabu-shabu* came, Fred asked as she was cooking the pork slices, "Tell me about Henk. How did he come to be in your office?"

"Dad arranged it. He has some biz experience. Has two degrees and some work experience. He's now pursuing environmental studies."

"Is he an intern with your company?"

"No, he comes in on a part-time basis because of his work experience and qualifications. That way, it justifies his salary."

"Well, don't get too close to him." He reached out for Josie's hand and caressed it again. "I'd be jealous."

She withdrew her hand. "We're leaving for Mongolia next week." A look of disapproval crossed his face.

He asked curtly, "Alone with Henk?"

"No, with a team of three designers. Henk thinks we can get fresh ideas for our fashion design."

"Well, don't get too close to him. There are things you don't know about him."

A warning bell sounded. Jeremy had given her a similar warning earlier. She stared at him. "What sinister thing do you think he's capable of?"

"Don't know. Offhand, all I can think of is what you shared with me about him. Um, that he's still looking for his parents, especially his mother."

"You said he told you they died in a plane crash. Er, that it was shot over Ukraine. And if so, why?"

He saw shadows of doubt chasing across her smooth face, the face he came to love ever since she was in her *tween* years.

"You also mentioned he never stays long in a job. Why does he keep moving jobs?"

"Can't say for sure. Fred, there are many reasons why a person moves from job to job."

"Well, just be careful, that's all."

"Jeremy gave a similar warning. Do you have a sense of foreboding regarding Henk?"

He patted her hand. "Maybe, but right now, I can't say exactly what it is I'm uneasy about regarding Henk. Um, it's just a feeling."

She smiled. "Do you think Chloe will know?"

"I'm not even sure if Chole can predict a feeling."

"Well, you and Jeremy have shaken my peace. Um, don't want to dwell on uncertainties. I want a good night's sleep."

In the car, just before she got out, Fred gave her a hug and a kiss. Her eyes widened.

"A brotherly one," he said, grinning. "For old times."

* * *

That night, Josie found herself wandering in the land beside her house. As she walked on, she realized the building which had all the robots in an earlier visit wasn't there that night.

A grey veil like a fog was gradually creeping along the street. There was no one else around. As she walked on, she had a feeling of dread, of heavy oppression, which she couldn't explain.

After a short while, she stopped to watch the veil. It was like a canopy moving slowly toward her. It seemed as if there were hands holding each end of the veil as it floated down the street, covering some of the houses which lined the road she was walking on.

Strangely, she saw the veil bypassing a house and then another one. She couldn't understand the reason for this. As she stood beside the house, she happened to look at its doorpost. Smeared across it was a dark maroon liquid.

What is it which has caused the grey veil to bypass that house? she wondered.

Meanwhile, the veil was approaching her. As it passed over a house close by, Josie heard screams and wails of people's voices. Utterly confused, she tried to look inside a house next to her. But the windows were all tightly shut.

Suddenly, she felt hands whisking her inside an open door. She was astonished. Inside, the house was lit with many candles. She blinked her eyes and made out four figures, two adults and two children. The mother was huddled with the children.

The male adult put his hand across his lips to caution her not to utter anything. The other three were looking at her with fear overshadowing their faces.

From outside, many more wails and cries sounded. Just then, a loud swishing sound could be heard, as if something were brushing over the very house she was pulled into.

Then the sound passed. The two adults heaved a loud sigh of relief. "It has passed us. We're safe," the woman muttered.

Josie found her voice. "It? Who has passed over your house? Why?"

The man spoke. "You must be a visitor to our land. Just as well when I saw you, I pulled you inside and shut the door just in time before the veil passed over our house."

"Otherwise, you'd be like the others, killed by the spirit of death with its gray venom."

When Josie heard this, she shuddered and turned pale. "Killed, did you say killed? By a spirit of death?"

Thoroughly confused now, she demanded to know. "Why? Who would want to kill your people?"

The woman put a hand over her lips. "Ours is not to ask why. We only know we're saved tonight by the blood smeared over our doorpost."

Bewildered, Josie asked, "Blood? Whose blood?"

The little girl answered, "The lamb."

The woman pulled a small book from the table and shoved it into Josie's hand. "Here, take this. Read it to understand our customs."

Josie reached out to take the book, but as the woman handed it to her, it dropped to the ground. She bent to pick it up. But she saw that the floor was not the mud floor of the house she entered earlier.

When she looked around for the book, she couldn't locate it. It was then that she realized she was back in her room.

Hurriedly, she dashed to the window and saw the grey fog receding from the empty land beside her house.

The next morning, her parents and Henk were already seated when she joined them for breakfast. Joshua was commenting on the news he read from the newspaper.

"The virus seems to be spreading fast. There are some rumors some countries have come up with a vaccine. But they're still in the experimental stage."

When she heard the discussion, Josie recalled her adventure in the land beside. She shuddered to think that the spirit of death might be passing over her land and many other lands on the planet.

* * *

Meanwhile, the design team for Mongolia made last-minute preparations for their trip. They were scheduled to leave the next day.

Joining Josie were Henk, Phil, Lea, and Kye. All were members of the design team, except Henk, who was the business manager.

Joshua invited them over for dinner. As he ladled the fish maw, sea bass slices, Chinese melon, and sea cucumber into his soup bowl, he asked Henk, "What arrangements have you made?"

Ruefully, he confessed, "At this stage, I don't know much. I contacted Arban, a Mongolian who I met years ago when I was on a business course in Sweden."

"He told me he's drawing a list of possible meetings for the team."

"That's it?" Josie asked.

Henk nodded. "Uh-huh. That's all I know at this stage. I guess we'll have to wait until we meet him."

Ruth said, "In the meantime, let's eat what we bought for dinner. In Mongolia, I understand they eat a lot of mutton."

Her eyes swiveled to her daughter. When she asked her, "Can you tolerate mutton?" Josie didn't answer her. Instead, she asked, "Isn't there anything else to eat?"

Henk offered an answer, "There're plenty of canned food and grains. Some restaurants offer Mongolian barbecue. They're more expensive, of course."

Josie's eyes lit up. She loved Mongolian barbecue and had taken it in a restaurant in Singapore.

"You can pack your favorite biscuits, Josie," Joshua suggested. "How about the rest of the team?"

They were quiet that evening as they considered what they should bring for their trip.

When Joshua asked them a second time, Phil said, "We'll survive. Will pack biscuits too. Um, won't be spending too much time there, I take it."

"Instead of waiting for your friend, er, Arban, right, Henk?" Joshua said, "I suggest when you arrive that you create some designs from photos which I'll pass you after dinner. Ruth took some on her last visit there. Um, just in case, the man hasn't finalized any arrangements."

Joshua added thoughtfully, "Er, there's a possibility he might be waiting for you before he makes any conclusive arrangement."

Ruth told the team, "We visited the country some years ago and saw that the men and women wear long outfits, especially in winter. They are similar in design to the kaftans."

"However, during summer, such clothing can be too warm," she concluded.

When Lea, a trim figure, asked, "What's Mongolia like?" everyone looked at Henk.

"You were there not too long ago. Why don't you tell them?" Joshua invited him. Henk cleared his throat, a habit Josie noticed he had whenever he began to speak.

"Um, it's landlocked between Russia and China. Far from the sea. Deep within eastern Asia."

"It has a continental type of climate," he explained.

"As Joshua said, winters are long and cold. So better pack a long coat and warm clothing as were heading into winter this trip."

Phil suddenly burst out, "Um, didn't that historical figure Genghis Khan rule over it a long time ago?"

Ruth said, "You're right, Phil. And his ancestors too. I believe the Mongol Empire collapsed and split up somewhere in the late seventeenth century. After that, Northern Mongolia was colonized by the Manchus of China."

"That was during the Qing dynasty," Joshua contributed to the conversation. "But that dynasty collapsed in the earlier part of the twentieth century. Mongolia's religious leader was then made as head of state."

He scratched his head as he tried to recall. "I forgot his name. It's such a long one."

Joshua went on, "When you're there, you'll probably find Mongolian names quite long. But I know you chaps will probably shorten them for your convenience."

"Will they mind if we shortened their names, Dad?" Josie wanted to know.

"Hmm, don't really know. I haven't tried it out. But if you meet the younger ones who have been to university, I expect they'll be quite tolerant about it."

"What're the people like?" Josie asked.

Joshua took a long look at his daughter. He saw her eager face, surrounded by the others in her team, all wanting to know. "I think I'll leave that to you, young adults, to find that out.

"You'll be there about a week, depending on what you can get out of this trip."

Ruth nodded in agreement. "As far as I remember, the Mongolians are generally nomadic in nature. They're quite independent people. Also, frank and outspoken."

"Socialize with them. Find out what they like. Enlarge your circle of friends," she encouraged them.

Both parents knew the young adults adapted easily. They were confident the team would get along with the young they met there.

SEVEN

Later that night, after the others left, Josie went to bed.

In the early morning hours, she was awoken by the strong fragrance of flowers. She opened her eyes and saw baskets of flowers surrounding her bed.

She recalled the time when she was fifteen years old. She had a similar experience. Hurriedly, she changed.

However, when she entered the land behind, she found that the length was shorter than the last time she had an adventure on it. She recalled it used to stretch to another land way beyond.

She walked on. The scent of fresh blooms filled the night air. Following the scent, she turned to the left, where the land beside her house was located.

It was a land which used to have a house, but the owner had sold it. The owner had torn down the house, but he hadn't constructed a new one.

From the side of her eyes, she caught a glimpse of acres of land stretching to the left.

Hmm, didn't know the land beside my house is so long and so wide.

She was astonished to see masses and masses of blooms all over the land. It was more like a field of flowers! They were exuding a strong scent as she headed in that direction.

There was no pathway carved out for her to walk along. In the far distance was a waterfall. She recalled seeing one in an earlier adventure. The scene was vaguely familiar.

Her heart began to palpitate in anticipation that the Celestial Gardener might be there. She longed to meet him again. It had been a long while since she met him.

She remembered he had such an overpowering presence. Meanwhile, she had to cross the mass of multicolored blooms. Tiptoeing along the edge, she brushed against the foliage of plants and flowers.

Sharp thorns pricked her bare skin. But in her keenness to meet the unusual man, she ignored the pain. From past experiences, she knew the pain didn't last long.

The perfume of flowers followed her all along the way. Trees of different foliage appeared before long, filling the air with the fragrance of fresh fruits. She looked upward and saw great bunches of fruits, varieties of them, hanging down from low branches.

If only I can pluck them and bring them home. They smell so good. They must taste good, she thought.

After what seemed a long time, she arrived at a waterfall. Flowing down from a high wall was a torrent of milky water.

She approached it. She could barely make out another garden beyond it, for the water was translucent. A memory chord stirred. She'd been there before. She knew that to get across to the other garden, she had to cross the waterfall.

As she stood there contemplating on what she should do to get across, she noticed something different. The water was milky white. Occasionally, it changed into clear transparent liquid.

Will my clothes be drenched with milk when I cross the waterfall? she wondered. Soon, she realized, there was a timing when the water changed from transparent into a milky substance.

"I'll time it. I'll cross it when the water is transparent." She calculated. It seemed an age.

The water tumbling down continued to be milky white. When she noticed the change, she dashed across the waterfall. But she didn't reckon for the medium-sized rocks at the bottom.

She tripped over one and fell right into the middle of the rushing waterfall. It caused her to tumble down. The torrent there was heavier than the previous time.

She was suddenly made aware of a strong smell of milk as it washed over her body. She looked at the water. It had changed from clear transparent into milky white within an instant. She sat on the rocks, with the milk pouring profusely over her head, her body, and her clothes.

Oh no! She was dismayed. *How can that be?*

Before she took the plunge, she had calculated the timing when the water would change. It wasn't even a minute yet. It wasn't due to change until two minutes later. Yet it did. Could it be that her timing wasn't correct?

Realizing it was pointless to try and work out the problem, she picked herself up, smelling like a baby who just drank a bottle of milk. Only this time, it wasn't mother's milk!

It had a different taste when she licked her lips. It was extremely fresh, like it'd been pressed straight out of a cow. And it tasted delicious! She stood there, drinking her fill, until the milk changed into transparent water.

It washed her from the head to the toe. Most amazing of all, it refreshed her. The water, too, tasted different from the tap water in her house.

Immediately after that, she crossed over to the other garden. The plants were different in texture from those she left behind. The petals looked like silk. She couldn't be sure if they were real, so she touched them.

It had a silky feeling. She examined one closely. It looked real. She tried to pluck one out from the stem. It wouldn't budge. In her keenness to get one, she pulled and pulled.

A voice said, with some annoyance, "What we have planted, don't destroy!"

She looked up and saw him. A tall figure enfolded in a bright, luminous light. The man she had longed to meet! He was standing some distance away.

She blurted out, "I'm sorry, Sir. It's just that I wanted to bring it home to show my parents."

The deep, rolling voice said, "What's planted here stays here!"

Josie hung her head in shame. "I'm sorry, Sir. It wasn't my intention to destroy!"

"What was it you wanted to ask me?" the voice asked.

"Huh?" Josie was puzzled. She hadn't requested an audience with the Celestial Gardener, although she had hoped earlier to meet him again.

There was a pause. "Er, I thought it was you who wanted to speak to me, Sir."

The deep, rolling voice said, "I do. You're going to Mongolia tomorrow."

"Huh? How did you know?"

He didn't satisfy her with an answer. Instead, he cautioned her, "Beware of the shamans."

"Huh?" Josie had no idea who they were.

He wasn't forthcoming with an explanation. Instead, he advised her, "Wear your armor at all times."

"Huh? Armor?"

She was beginning to sound stupid by uttering so many "huh" questions.

"You have it. The book tells you about the full armor. Wear it. Protect yourself at all times." After giving that cryptic instruction, the figure disappeared.

The little figure, who used to appear in the past to explain things to her, wasn't there to explain what he meant. Since there was nothing else to do, Josie walked back to her land.

Bit by bit, the scenery was withdrawn as she moved away from it. First, the waterfall. Then the vast garden. Before long, it was swallowed up in the darkness of the night.

Soon, she realized she was standing on the boundary of her own land. As she walked back toward the main building, she could see a light from a window in the annex. She knew it was from the room Henk was occupying.

The hour was late. She wondered why he hadn't slept yet. From the window outside, she could see into the bedroom. His bedside lamp was on. She could see him seated on the bed, reading a book.

She recalled what the Celestial Gardener told her to do, "Read the book. Put on the armor at all times."

And who were these mysterious persons he warned her about, the shamans?

She decided to return to her room. Her mind was filled with many thoughts as she walked back.

Dawn began to filter across the skies above. Light-pink streaks of light chased across the azure-blue sky. She saw the colors from the window in her room.

Before long, she fell asleep.

* * *

The team left Singapore for Ulaanbaatar in Joshua's private jet. Before they boarded with their masks on, security and temperature checks were done on each member.

Throughout the island, such checks had become the new normal. The journey took over nine hours. When they arrived, the private jet was directed to another landing site. The single runway, with its one direction only, was reserved for bigger international airlines.

Josie slept most of the journey, while the others read. After the jet touched down, Henk led them to a much smaller building. She fell in with his instructions to them.

From a young child, she was used to her parents guiding her wherever she travelled. Out of habit, she accepted Henk's guidance.

A Mongolian man by the name of Arban met them. He was tall and broad shouldered. He wore a sepia kaftan made of sheepskin. On his head was a black cone-shaped hat with a red top.

He spoke good English. "I managed to get two family rooms. Each has two beds and a private bathroom."

"The girls can share a room. However, their room is quite a distance away from the men's family room."

He added apologetically, "There are no cafes nearby."

Josie was glad her father had advised them to bring their packets of tea, coffee, and biscuits.

A minivan stood ready to transport them. After they loaded into it, before long, they were passing a row of container type structures. These turned out to be the family rooms.

Arban unlocked a room with a large, heavy iron key. There was only one key for each family room, he told them. He left them and then drove the men to where their room was located.

When Josie and Lea entered, they saw that the space was tight. Two narrow beds close to each other lay a short distance from the entrance.

There was no cupboard where they could hang their clothes. However, there was ample space beneath the high beds for them to store their suitcases.

Opposite the beds was a long window with tempered glass. At the base of the window was a long table. On it were two mugs, two teaspoons, an electric kettle, and a box of tissues.

Lea commented, "Hmm, very compact."

She opened the bathroom door, which was just where the tempered glass window ended. The space was large enough for only one person. It revealed a shower and a high shelf, on which were two large bath towels.

"No hand or face towels, I see," Lea observed. "Just as well we brought ours."

It didn't feel cold inside, although there was no heater visible. Lea threw her suitcase on the bed in the far corner. She left Josie to take the bed closer to the entrance.

Picking up the kettle, she went into the bathroom to fill it. She then pushed in the electric plug to boil the water.

"Did you bring any coffee?" she asked Josie.

"Don't drink coffee. Brought some packets of *tehsi*."

"Hmm, just as well I brought the *kopisi* packets!"

Josie told her, "I'm taking a hot shower."

From her suitcase, she pulled out a cardigan and pants. After that, she disappeared into the narrow bathroom. She emerged a short while later, feeling quite refreshed.

On the table was a mug with *tehsi* mixed in it. Lea had found the packets in Josie's opened suitcase, which she took out and arranged neatly in a row along the long table.

On it, she also placed the biscuit boxes, *tehsi* packets, as well as her own *kopisi* packets and barbecue, cheese, and corn chips.

Lea was sitting on her bed, nibbling from an opened barbecue chip packet. Josie took out a biscuit from another box laid on the table. She sat on the edge of the bed, nibbled it, and sipped the drink.

She asked Lea, "Why don't you have a shower? It'll refresh you."

There was no response. Josie turned her head and saw her fast asleep. Her drink lay unfinished on the table.

Hmm, guess I'm not the only one who sleeps easily, Josie thought. *Hope she doesn't snore.*

At dinnertime, Henk knocked on the thick metal door. On opening it, Josie saw him and the others. She woke Lea. The group then drove to a restaurant some distance away.

Arban had arranged for them to dine there. On the long table were bowls of noodles, pasta, and bread laid out in the center. At the end of the table were four mixed vegetables in large bowls.

In addition, there were three plates of mutton and beef slices. The wooden chairs and tables were arranged at the side.

Henk instructed them, "Why don't you help yourself to the pasta, veggies, and meats? The hotpot will come in a minute."

It wasn't long before a waiter entered, carrying a huge Mongolian hotpot. Everyone was hungry. They eagerly threw chunks of meats and vegetables into the large boiling hotpot.

While waiting for the meats to cook, they sipped hot green tea from their mugs. The fragrant aroma filled the air around them. It smelled strongly of mutton and oil.

When Josie noticed some other food pieces in the pot, she asked Arban, "What's in there too?"

He gave a wide, toothy smile. "In Mongolia, we cook the entire animal. Eyes, intestines, the head too."

Immediately, Lea released hers back into the pot, the ones which she had spooned out into her bowl.

The men weren't choosy. They ladled into their bowls whatever was in the pot.

The soup had a higher sodium level than what Josie was used to. And it was spicy. She decided to pour it onto the noodles, knowing the bland noodles would absorb the high amount of salt and oil.

There was no small talk around the table, for the acoustics in the room was bad. It made any attempt at conversation difficult. But the other groups sitting around were impervious. They chatted loudly above the din, with each one speaking at the same time as another.

On the way back to their family rooms, Lea asked Henk, "What's your room like?"

"No different from yours. Tight."

"Are the three of you sharing a room?" she asked inquisitively.

"Yes," he replied.

"Are there enough beds for the three of you?" she questioned. "I thought each room has only two beds."

Phil intervened. "We manage. We're not fussy. Used to roughing it out. We push the beds together. There's enough room for all three."

Josie knew the space must be tight, for the beds were narrow. The two men were slim, but Henk was quite large. She passed no comment.

Instead, she asked, "What're our plans for tomorrow?"

"Arban has arranged for us to meet a designer," Henk said. "He'll show us some of the clothing his team has. Since it's quite a distance from here, we'll start early."

"We'll have to use yaks or camels to get there."

Everyone fell silent at his information. No one had ridden on the animals before. Josie didn't even know what a yak looked like.

Kye, a Singaporean in the team, confessed, "I've never ridden on either one. How different is it from riding a horse?"

Henk grinned. This was the first time his face relaxed since they left for Mongolia. "Quite different. If you're sitting on a camel, you bump down and up a bit. But you soon get used to the swaying motion.

"The yaks are bulky. They resemble the American bison in some way."

The next morning, after breakfast, they saw a few camels and some yaks lined up outside. When she saw the yaks, Josie was nervous. As Henk told them earlier, the yak looked a bison with its bulky, hairy body and horn.

She didn't know Henk was watching her until she heard his voice. "Er, if you don't want the yak, use the camel." She studied the camel. Its height put her off.

Henk explained, "You sit between the two humps. The animal will sit on the ground for you to climb aboard. Er, there's a trainer who will guide it."

"Um, isn't there a jeep? What about the minivan we took from the airport?" she asked anxiously.

She didn't want to admit to the others, but she'd ridden on a pony only once before. It was an excitable young animal, supposed to be tame, but obviously wasn't. It had thrown her off. And she never asked for a ride on one after that.

She was relieved when Lea, too, voiced her doubts. "Yah, I agree with Josie. I'd like to go in a minivan. Feel secure. I've never ridden on a horse before."

Arban was standing close by. He shook his head in disbelief when he heard the two women. "Every Mongolian girl rides these animals."

"Well, in Singapore, every girl takes a bus, MRT, or car! Animals like these don't exist in my country," Josie retorted.

Henk explained, "The minivan is for city use. Not good for terrain like this, especially to where we're going."

"If you people want to meet the designer and his assistant, you'll have to learn to ride one of these." His large hand swept the animal which was standing quietly by. All of them were flicking their long horse-like tails at the flies buzzing around their bodies.

It was a stalemate the team could see. The women were nervous and anxious. Although the men were willing to try out the ride, none of them had ever ridden on them before.

Without warning, Henk jumped astride a yak and rode off. "What's he doing?" Josie yelped. "Riding off like that!"

Phil laughed aloud. "Showing off, I think, to you girls. Wants to impress you with his prowess!"

"Well, he's impressing the wrong person!" Josie growled in annoyance.

Lea contradicted her. "Well, I'm impressed! I could never ride so fast, let alone climb a camel or a yak!"

Arban corrected her, "You don't need to climb a camel. Its trainer makes it sit on the ground and you then sit between the humps."

The morning sun was shining strongly down on the group as they stood there, huddled together. But it didn't dispel the cold. A mild breeze blew. It brought a cold shiver on them.

"Henk doesn't seem to be returning. Can you take us to where the outfits are?" Josie questioned Arban.

"He'll return," he said confidently.

"How would you know? He told you?" Josie asked.

"I know him." Arban quirked his lips in a smile.

His remark caused Josie to wonder about her cousin. She herself knew so little about him, yet this Mongolian seemed to know more about him than she did.

When she said, "'You do? How long have you known him?" Arban looked at her quizzically and then said, "Oh, long enough."

"What's that supposed to mean?"

"We worked together for about a year in the past."

"Well, I don't want to stand out here in the cold." Josie stamped her boots to start the circulation in her cold feet. She hugged her arms around her thick, long cashmere coat.

Arban observed her and then commented, "You don't have enough fat to generate heat within you!"

She thought it rude of him to pass such a remark, especially since she wasn't a man. But she said nothing in reply.

Suddenly, he lifted his large arms and pointed to the distance. "He's coming back!" Everyone looked.

Instead of the yak, a jeep appeared in the far distance, heading toward them, whipping up a trail of sand dust behind it.

Sure enough, it was Henk. He zoomed up to Josie, got out dramatically, and swept an arm toward the jeep.

"Your chariot, madam!" Everyone laughed in relief.

Henk looked at the men. "You guys can ride the animals."

Lea quickly put up her hand. "I'll ride with Josie in the jeep." Without further ado, she climbed into the back seat.

Henk grinned at Josie. "I guess she's left the front seat for you. I'm driving. Hope you don't mind."

The jeep had thick opaque shades on both sides. Henk leaned across her to pull down the one on her side. He left the one on his side rolled up.

Josie was relieved. His thoughtfulness touched her. Henk then drove off and left the others to ride behind them.

Naturally, Henk arrived at the destination before the men. A small gray building stood before them. At the side, there was some construction going on for a taller, larger building. A scaffolding draped the exterior.

When Henk strode inside, Josie and Lea followed him. A narrow corridor led them to another door at the end.

Henk knocked on the door twice before pushing it open.

EIGHT

Lea and Josie gasped when they saw a bevy of fifteen outrageously beautiful tall young women facing the opened door, with enchanting smiles.

Josie immediately looked around for Phil and Kye, knowing that the latter, especially, had an eye for beautiful women. But the two hadn't entered the room.

She turned to look at Henk, but he didn't seem in the least impressed. Perhaps he had seen them before?

She remembered seeing some Mongolians who were waitresses in an Arab restaurant in London, England, who were tall and elegant. She and her parents were visiting the country at that time. The waiters there were tall and striking in looks. At the restaurant, she and her parents learned that they were recruited from Mongolia.

However, the ones Josie now saw in front of her were even more striking and refined in looks and dressing than those in the restaurant in London.

She moved farther into the room. Three models came to greet Henk. There was no shaking of hands or hugging. Their faces merely exuded pleasure at their meeting him again.

With nods and smiles, the three women said in a chorus, "Henk, *sain bain uu* (are you well)?"

In return, he smiled broadly. "*Sain*, well."

He next turned to Josie and Lea and introduced them to the Mongolian girls. "These are my friends. They're designers too."

The three nodded and smiled. One said to them in English, "Are you well?"

Henk then left them and went to the other end of the room to greet an older man. After that, he led the man to Josie and Lea and introduced them.

"Max, these are my friends Josie and Lea." The two nodded and smiled at him. Max was a tall, broad man, so typical of the other Mongolian men they were to meet later in their visit.

Just then, behind them, the door opened to admit Phil and Kye. Introductions were made again. As Josie expected, both men were beguiled by extraordinary beauty of the models.

Henk told his group, "Max is the design manager. He speaks English. So do the girls. Some of them have attended the National University of Mongolia."

Josie was impressed. "After graduation, do they choose fashion designing as their career?"

Max told her, "It depends. Most are part-timers only. A few are professional models." He went ahead of them, speaking as he walked. "Let me show you the clothes in the various sections.

He turned to Henk. "What kind of fashions are you thinking of?"

Henk, in turn, indicated that he should be speaking to Josie regarding fashions.

She clarified to Max, "Um, we're here to create new fashions. We'd like to look at the fashionwear of men and women first before we create our own designs. Um, we're here to get some fresh ideas."

Josie herself had no idea what the team was going to design. She was hoping they'd come up with some new ideas once they viewed the outfits of the Mongolian men and the women.

They continued walking until they reached another curtained section. Max drew aside the curtains. Rows of brightly colored garments faced them. The team drew in a deep breath at the sight of them.

The outfits closest to them were thick padded tunics in a sepia brown and in different shades of gray, from deep to light gray.

Josie lifted the top layer to look at the undergarment. What she and the others saw was a sheepskin.

Max explained, "That's stitched on in winter to generate warmth to the wearer. The sheepskin lining the padded tunic is designed to keep the wearer warm."

"Do both men and women wear such tunics?" Phil asked as he pushed himself forward to feel the material.

Max nodded. "The man's tunic has a wider cut. In winter, the colors are subdued, darker. Similar colors to those worn by the Western men and women in winter."

"I take it that in spring and summer, the colors are lighter and brighter," Josie concluded.

"Similar to the Western counterparts in some ways," Max concurred.

"In summer," Josie contributed her knowledge, "in the West, women's blouses are in solid, block colors, plain red, orange, and even bright green."

"In springtime, the material is lighter with floral designs to represent spring flowers. Is that the same here?"

"In Mongolia," Max said, "the women wear light, bright blue or green colors. The material may sometimes even be silk types. Some have linear designs on the front. They're plain, not necessarily floral."

He then asked, "How about in Singapore?"

Josie said, "The women wear clothes which match the Western counterparts. We import them from the West. Some of our clothes, however, are imported from Japan and South Korea."

"This means when their clothes are made for summer, we will import summer dresses."

Kye's eyes ran down a row of dresses farther along the hanger. "Do you have a name for this fashion?"

"We generally call it the *deel*," Max explained. "That's the *dan deel* fashion commonly chosen by women."

Josie recalled her father saying that Ruth was impressed with the *deel*.

Max ran his hand down the loose tunic, which reached down to the calf. "As you can see, it runs halfway between the knees and the ankles. Your people call it the midi length."

"The thicker padded material with the underlayer of sheepskin is our winter *deel*," he continued to explain.

Josie fingered the long sleeves and the high collar. She asked her team, "Don't you think this resembles the *cheongsam*? It has three buttons that slant downward from the collar to the right side."

She stepped aside for the others to examine the outfit.

Lea ventured an opinion. "Quite similar, but with no slit at the sides of the hemline. I expect in summer, the material will be much lighter."

"In our country, we use cotton, linen, polyester, and sometimes silk," Josie explained to Max.

She fingered the buttons. "These are strips of cloth tied into intricate knots and stitched on to the material."

Max nodded in agreement. "There are some with more decorative stones chosen by the wealthy."

"Ah, yes," Josie said. She explained to Max, "In our country, we use pearl buttons and even genuine jade or ruby stones for upmarket buyers."

Max revealed, "In Mongolia, each ethnic group's *deel* is identified by the way the *deel* is cut. The color choice tells a Mongolian which ethnic group the wearer belongs to."

"Hmm, very interesting indeed," Josie observed. In turn, she informed him, "In our country, each ethnic group has its individual fashion and design."

She expanded on the information. "The *sari* is a thin decorative long material worn over a short inner tunic by Indian women. It's distinctly different from the *baju kurung* worn by women of Malay origin."

"I must visit your country and bring my design team to see some of your clothing. Your range of clothes sounds most interesting. We can exchange ideas and create new fashions," Max exclaimed in delight.

"Tell me, in your country, are the much older married women full-bodied like the ones in our country?" His question took Josie and the team by surprise.

Quickly, Josie asked, "Why? Are the fashions for them different from the young unmarried ones?"

He nodded vigorously. "They are indeed, but the difference is more pronounced in the hat designs."

As if anticipating Josie's request to see them, he said, "I'll take you to see them another time. They're not kept in this building."

"Er, Max, unfortunately, the hat isn't popular with women in our country, except, perhaps, for those who take up golf," Josie explained apologetically. "In Singapore, only Western, Japanese, and some South Korean women wear hats for special occasions like a wedding or event."

She looked at her watch. "Um, time we break for lunch. It's nearly two. Wonder where Henk is." She looked around for him. Nobody could locate him.

"Let's look outside," Phil suggested.

They exited the building. Outside, they caught sight of Henk chatting with a Mongolian model. He was leaning against the side of the jeep with his arms folded.

The model was standing close to him, dressed in a bright turquoise gown. She presented an alluring figure, with the breeze blowing her long dark hair and brilliant gown against the backdrop of the mountains.

The yaks were lined in a row, waiting. There were no camels around. "Ready for lunch?" Henk asked when Josie came alongside him. She took her seat beside his, while Lea climbed to the back.

After a lunch of diced yak meat, rice, and fried vegetables at a small, nondescript restaurant quite a distance from the family rooms, Josie returned to her room. Lea didn't accompany her back.

She was alone in the room when a knock sounded on the door. She opened it and saw Henk.

"Lea's going on a tour with Phil and Kye. I'm taking you to visit an orphanage."

Josie's eyes widened. "Hmm, didn't know there's one here."

"Not just one, a few," Henk informed her. "Some of their parents died from accidents. Some are from poor families. When the mothers go out to work, there's no one to look after the children, so they're put in the orphanage." He studied her for a moment.

"But why are we visiting an orphanage?"

"Your father asked me to take you to look at them. Wants your opinion on them." He cleared his throat. "Um, they need funds for their education program."

Josie fell silent. She knew her father had been supporting several orphanages in other countries. Henk had benefitted from the education fund which was donated to one of them.

He looked at her dressing speculatively. "Want to change into something else?"

"Um, don't think so. I'm quite comfortable in this." Her hand swept the length of her thick woolen blouse and trousers as she said it. He turned and left her abruptly, leaving her to dash after him. Outside was the jeep.

When she was seated, he asked her, "Would you rather not visit it?"

"Er, you've made arrangements with someone haven't you?" she asked. He cleared his throat and coughed a few times before he said, "Yes."

"Well, let's go then." Before long, they arrived at a small building. She was expecting a larger building, considering that Henk had said it housed some orphans.

She was more surprised when a small-sized man of average height came forward to greet them. She came to expect Mongolian men to be tall, large, and heavily built based on the ones she saw earlier.

Henk seemed to know him. "This is Altan. His parents are Turks. He's a volunteer in this orphanage."

Josie had earlier learned their way of greeting. She nodded and smiled widely at him without offering her hand.

He returned the greeting in the same way. When he said, "*Sain bain uu* (are you well)?" Josie replied, "*Sain.*" He looked pleased when he heard her greeting. He bestowed her a friendly smile and spoke quite good English.

As he led the way into the small dark hall, a tall, thin, grim-looking, surly man emerged from a side room.

He was unsmiling. Henk greeted him in the usual way. Then he turned to Josie and said, "This is Boh."

When she greeted him, he gave her an unfriendly glare. His small eyes drew into slits. The deep lines on his narrow forehead doubled until there was no space for more lines.

He continued casting venomous looks at her. When she saw fires flaring out from his eyes, she instinctively recoiled from him. She fell backward into Henk, who was close behind her. His hand steadied her.

"You all right?" he whispered into her right ear. She straightened and moved away from him. She was very puzzled and alarmed. Who was this man who shot out fires from his eyes? Outwardly, she said nothing.

Henk didn't seem to see anything untoward about the man, for he just continued chatting with him.

A room further in revealed a collection of young boys. They weren't the chubby ones she saw earlier in the restaurant when they had lunch. These were thin. Their cheeks were dry and ruddy. Dressed in long dark-brown garments, with a sash tied around the waist, they hung around, looking miserable.

Their outfits reminded her of the boys in her country who attended gym sessions. They wore similar-styled outfits, but theirs were much shorter.

In contrast, however, the facial expressions of the schoolboys in her country were relaxed, and they smiled often. The boys in this orphanage, now facing her, had no smiles and exuded only looks of curiosity.

She remembered Henk in the earlier days when he came to stay with her family. His face was usually tense and moody.

He didn't smile often. He, too, was raised in an orphanage in his early years.

Altan's voice drew her attention back to him. "These children are from homes where fathers are alcoholics. Many of them have single mums."

"There's a small percentage of women who are alcoholics. They're struggling with their addiction. Um, have no time for the kids. Most are from poor homes. Some mothers are unable to look after them because of poverty or alcoholism."

Josie began to understand as Altan unfolded their sorrowful background. Many of the boys looked lost and bewildered. She discerned there was no joy in their soul.

Perhaps they haven't experienced true parental love, Josie thought to herself.

Boh was standing at a distance, at the other end of the long room. He beckoned to Altan. When he spoke to him, Josie was surprised she could hear from that distance what he was saying to him, "What does this woman want? Why is she here? Does she want to adopt a child?"

Altan replied, "She's here to donate money."

From that distance, Josie saw surprise on Boh's face. She thought to herself, *He probably thinks I'm too young to donate*, and he was right, for it was her father who would, on her recommendation, be donating.

A little boy came boldly up to her. He tugged at her hand to catch her attention. "Why are you here? Do you want to take me home with you?" He was speaking in Mongolian.

To her surprise, she could understand what he was saying. She opened her mouth to reply in Mongolian, but only some gibberish words came out.

He gave her a blank look, indicating he didn't understand her language. She bent to speak to him in English. "No, I just came to visit you."

Henk came alongside her to interpret it for him. As he did that, Josie wondered, *How did I understand the boy earlier?*

She said nothing of this to Henk but tried to comfort the little boy, who began sniffing and crying. She patted his head and hugged him.

Boh strode across to her. In an accusing tone, he said, "Look what you've done to this child! Do you think your money can buy our children?"

But Altan immediately hushed him up. "She's not here to take the child. She's here to financially support our education program."

"She'll be like the other groups, wanting to change our children's way of thinking," snarled Boh.

Josie was taken aback by his aggression. *Oh, so that's what he's thinking. No wonder he's so angry!*

Turning to Henk, she said loudly, intending that Boh should hear her words, "No point staying. Let's go."

With that, she strode outside. A flustered Altan chased after her. "Please, please, excuse Boh. He doesn't understand that you're here to help us fund the education of these children."

"Like the other shamans, he's an animist by belief. He's afraid you'll change the children's way of thinking."

Shaman, where had she heard the word? She searched her memory but couldn't come up with anything apart from what Altan had said to her that Boh was a shaman, who was an animist.

She ignored Boh. In turn, he shunted her and walked alongside Henk and Altan. When she got into the jeep, she didn't even say goodbye to Altan.

She was mad with Boh's accusation. Henk tried to calm her down as he drove. "You mustn't be upset with Boh. He's just afraid that the groups offering to fund the orphanages will influence the children to accept their faith."

"Well, Boh's accusation is unjustified!" Her breath came out in short gasps. "He shouldn't make sweeping judgments of all groups. If his belief is so strong and secure, what has he to fear?"

"Does he make money out of the orphanage too?"

"No, no, nothing like that," he hastened to explain.

"Well, seems to me that Boh's so immersed with his beliefs that he fears any group who donates money!" Josie said heatedly.

He patted her hand. "Don't let him upset you. Your father has helped many orphanages before. Remember, I'm one of the beneficiaries. Without his help, I couldn't get a higher education."

"Think of the far-reaching good results," he urged her. "You should pray over this with your parents. If you feel you should help this orphanage, then go for it. If not, there are other orphanages who'll accept the donation."

Josie was silent over Henk's suggestion. He leaned toward her and said earnestly, "The good usually outweighs the bad when your heart is sincere."

Josie simmered down. When they reached the family room, she saw that Lea wasn't back. She went in and took a hot shower. Just as she got into bed for a rest, a knock sounded.

She opened the door and saw Henk there.

"Er, can I use your room? Um, need a shower," he said sheepishly.

"Huh?" she didn't know how to respond to his request. It was unexpected. She couldn't connect with the reason he wanted to use the shower until he explained.

Sounding apologetic, he said, "Phil locked the room. He took the only key with him. I'll have to wait in the cold till he returns." He looked so weary with his stooped posture and disheveled hair that she didn't have the heart to turn him away.

"Er, there's only my towel and Lea's. You can use either one. And after your shower, you can, um." She stopped abruptly, not knowing what to say next.

He stood waiting expectantly in the open door. Then she added lamely, "Er, you can make yourself a cup of coffee, Lea's, if you like, for I brought only tea." She felt sure Lea wouldn't mind.

"And er, um, er," he stammered, as if not knowing how to vocalize his thoughts. A flush spread over his face and neck as his words came tumbling out. "Er, and after that can I rest in the other bed?"

He muttered, "Didn't sleep well last night," with his eyes cast downward, not wanting to meet hers. She was again uncertain how to respond to him. But his tired face caused her to accede to his request.

"Sure, why not!" A cold wind blew into the room. She shivered and said quickly, "You'd better come in. It's getting chilly outside."

After he went into the bathroom, she got into bed. She pulled the thick coverlet up to her neck, punched her pillow, turned to the side, and closed her eyes.

She heard Henk running the hot shower tap. After a short while, she heard the click of the bathroom door.

Then she heard the electric kettle whirring and, a short while later, the click as the auto switched off.

She heard Henk pouring out the hot water and stirring the coffee. Then all was quiet.

She'd fallen fast asleep.

NINE

A loud rapping on the door woke her. Lea's treble tone floated through. "Josie, open up. It's me!"

She got up but found the door unlocked. Of Henk, there was no sign. He must have left the room without her knowing.

A rush of cold air swept into the room when Lea pushed past her. Outside, it was already dark.

"Brr, it's quite chilly," Lea intoned. She switched on the room light.

"Are the others back yet?" Josie asked.

"Uh-huh. We saw Henk just as the tour van dropped us off."

"Where?"

"He was walking toward the meeting point. He seems to know his way around," she commented. "I'm taking a shower. Meet the guys in fifteen minutes for dinner."

"Er, where?"

"Henk said he'll come and call us. He seems to know you don't like the cold."

"Who does! Like the cold, I mean!" Josie retorted. "Do you?"

"Nope, not me!" With that, she pulled off her thick sweater, threw it on her bed, and went into the bathroom.

Josie looked at Lea's bed for signs that Henk had rested on it. All she saw was a nicely made-up bed, with the coverlet neatly pulled up to the pillow.

When Lea emerged, she told Josie, "Make me a cup of coffee, will you?" Josie started the kettle and tore open a coffee packet.

Lea's sharp eyes saw an opened packet in the bin below. "Have you been drinking my coffee? Thought you didn't like coffee."

Josie blushed, as if she had done something wrong. "Er, Henk came by after we got back. He used your packet, not knowing it was yours. Sorry, I don't have a coffee packet to return to you. You can have my *tehsi* if you like."

"Naw," Lea said generously, "it's all right if it's Henk. It's all right, too, if you want my coffee. I brought many packets. He's been so helpful to us since we arrived. I like him."

With that, she stirred her mug vigorously. "You should have come with us on the tour. The scenery is quite varied, with stretches of sand. Some are orangey red, some reddish yellow."

"Was the tour interesting?"

"Uh-huh. If you've studied geography, you'll appreciate it even more. Our tour took us past upland steppes, deserts, and semideserts. We even saw high mountain ranges with snowy caps. I remember seeing a lake on the way back."

"Oh, yes, we were told that a few hundred of the mountains are sacred to the natives, the Mongolians." She sounded excited as she narrated.

"You know what? When we stopped for a drink, the tour guide introduced us to the person who ran the small place. His father was there. The chap told us his dad's a shaman."

The word caught Josie's attention. There's that word again.

"Did you know they have magical powers?" Lea revealed.

"Did his eyes flash out fires?" Josie asked. "I met someone at the orphanage whose eyes did that. He was quite a surly chap!"

"Well, the one we met didn't have eyes like that," Lea answered. "Shamans have magical powers, you know."

The word stirred in Josie's mind. Where had she heard it before? Something niggled at the back of mind.

"Did the one at the orphanage exude fires from his eyes? How frightening!" Lea asked.

Josie decided to confide in her. "Yes, that one did. Quite upsetting to see the fires in his eyes. I sensed something wasn't right. You said they have magical powers?"

"Uh-huh," Lea replied. "Best avoid that chap. If he does black magic, that is worse! In Malaysia and Indonesia, I know some of them do black magic. Um, even cast evil spells!"

"Fortunately for us, the one we met was genial. Nice and chatty." She suddenly stopped talking and looked hard at Josie.

"What's wrong, Lea? Why are you looking at me like that?" Josie asked in alarm.

"You said you saw fires coming from that man's eyes?"

"I did. First time I ever saw it in a person. The last time that I saw fires they were from the eyes of a stone image in one of my adventures to the land beyond."

"Hmm, how interesting. Yah, I heard about your adventures. Are they just dream experiences?"

Since Josie felt she'd shared too much already, she quickly said, "My mother thinks they're just dreams."

"Well, if you say the man in the orphanage had fires coming out of his eyes, that could mean you have eyes which can see into the spiritual realm.

"I was told those who practice black magic can not only cast evil spells, but they also have fires flaring from their eyes." Lea gave a shudder when she said this.

After a pause, she suddenly blurted out, "Hey, Josie, you might be gifted with special spiritual eyesight, you know."

"Huh, whatever do you mean?" Josie was intrigued by what she said.

"In my church, some members are given this gift. They can see ghosts, as well as people like this man you mentioned, who have fires in their eyes. Some can also smell spirits when they are present in a room."

Lea looked at her excitedly. "Wouldn't it be nice if you have such a special gift." She clutched her hand and said, "If I ever go to a graveyard at night, I'll take you with me. Then you can see if there are ghosts there!"

Josie pulled her hand away. "Don't frighten me. I wouldn't want to see a ghost. So scary! And I'd never visit a graveyard at night, for sure!"

Lea looked at her admiringly. "You're special, you know. Having such a gift is precious. Not many have such a gift of discernment. It's related to the senses, the eyes, the nose, and even the ears."

"What do you mean by the ears?"

"Just that you can hear people talking, even when they're fifty or more meters away from you."

"Really?" Josie thought back to the time when she heard Altan speaking to Boh. They were quite a distance away from her in the orphanage.

Lea was unstoppable. Like a fountain, she spurted out more. "You know that chap I told you about whose dad was a shaman?"

"What of him?"

"His son told us his dad was an intermediary of some kind between the human and the spirit realms."

Josie plugged her fingers into her ears. "Stop, stop, I don't want to hear anymore of such talk! You're giving me goose bumps just hearing you!" She rubbed her arms vigorously.

"Poor Josie. Did you have a bad experience with that man at the orphanage?"

"Yes, yes, I did." Josie was quite agitated by this time. "He had venomous eyes. Was angry when Henk said that he brought me there for a visit and to talk of possible funding."

"Accused me of wanting to use the funds to change the children's minds to my way of thinking."

"What!" Lea exclaimed in disgust. "Whatever made him think that?"

"That's just it. I didn't mention anything about religion. He just got all huffy and puffy."

"You know shamans are steeped in their animistic beliefs," Lea explained. "Well, on the tour, I learned that shamanism and Buddhism were suppressed in the twentieth century by the socialist government. Did you know many of the monasteries and texts were destroyed at that time?"

"Yes, yes," Josie answered, more agitated by now. "That's recorded in history books. But I'm not concerned about their religious beliefs. Frankly, I don't care to know about them."

"My dad is looking at the possibility of donating some money to help the orphanage. Henk said he wanted me to look over the place to see if they needed any funding. That's the only reason I went."

Lea said sympathetically, "They're the losers if they're going to be so uptight about an offer of funding. I'm sure there are other orphanages who will appreciate your dad's offer of funding."

The word *shaman* kept tugging at her mind. Where had she heard it mentioned? Or had she read it somewhere? But she knew it wasn't from history books. She sensed inwardly it was from someone quite recently. But who?

Her memory search was interrupted when a knock sounded, and the door opened to show Henk. "Ready?"

He was waiting in the jeep by the time the two women came out. He drove off after Josie and Lea boarded.

He didn't mention anything about using Lea's bed, and Josie felt it wiser not to say anything too.

The night air was nippy. The jeep didn't offer any protection. There were two jeeps this time. Henk drove one, while Phil drove the other.

Soon, they arrived at a brightly lit restaurant. Judging from the exterior with its modern decorations, Josie and the others could see it was an upmarket restaurant.

"You'll like it here," Henk told them. "There's top-quality Mongolian barbecue served inside." From the time he stepped into the restaurant, it was clear he knew his way around.

When they entered the warm restaurant, Henk showed them the coat room just a little way inside. Two slim young women, taller than Josie, welcomed them. After taking their coats, they gave each a disc with a number.

Another staff led them into a private room. They took their seats on the stained, varnished dark wood high-backed seats. Drinks were served without them asking for them.

"You have to go to the buffet table outside to make your barbecue selections," Henk announced.

The range of meats and vegetables on the buffet table was large. Lea exclaimed delightedly, "I can't believe it. There are so many varieties to choose from!"

Henk passed a plate to Josie. Lea looked at the wide range on the table and listed them enthusiastically. "Beef, pork, chicken, mutton, fish, prawns. What shall we take?"

Josie laughed when she saw Lea's face. "Take the lot if you like. We can share them."

Before long, Lea and the others began filling their plates with the meats and seafood. Phil came next to Josie. "Can I pick out some crabs and shrimps for you?"

Henk immediately told him, "I can help Josie, Phil." He lifted a pincer and picked up some noodles. "Some ramen? Vermicelli?"

But Josie responded, "Thanks, Henk, I can manage." She moved away to the vegetable section at the end of the table. When her plate was filled to the brim, Henk immediately took it from her.

"I'll take it to the cook," he offered. "You pick out the sauces to jazz up your meats." He moved toward the cook. He must have felt her eyes on him, for he turned and beckoned her.

"Come and see the food being cooked." Josie went with him to watch the cook empty her plate onto a huge round griddle. Smoke filled the large vent above as the meats sizzled on the hot griddle.

"Egg?" the cook asked. "One?"

She lifted her finger to indicate two. The fragrant aroma from the grilled meats soon filled the air around.

Henk was standing beside her without any plate in his hand. She asked, "Not choosing your food?"

"I'm having dinner later with two friends."

"Friends?" she asked. But he didn't offer an answer.

When the cook handed her the plate, Henk took it from her. "I'll put this on the table for you. Why don't you choose the sauces?" And with that, he left her.

When she returned to the long table, Lea was choosing the sauces. She oozed out appreciation when she saw the range of sauces.

"Why don't you take some? I'll take another lot. That way, we can have a variety to dip into." Josie liked the idea.

"And I'll take a few more." Kye came alongside them. His plate was also filled to the brim.

"Kye, why don't you give your plate to the cook?" Josie suggested. "I'll take the sauces back to the dining room."

The cooked meats were waiting on the table for her. The vegetables, Josie saw, were lightly fried. The sweet potatoes were buttered and oven roasted. Placed in the center were bowls of rice. Cans of beer and green tea served in dainty cups were on the side table.

Before long, they all settled down to a sumptuous meal. The first few minutes were spent munching the meats. A short while later, Lea voiced their appreciation.

"Mm, this is delicious."

When they were nearly done, Phil was the first to ask.

"Henk, how did you know this restaurant?"

Kye shared his observation. "The staff seem to know you."

Henk nodded. "Been here a few times with my business clients."

"You mean you worked here before?" Lea was wide-eyed. She turned to Josie. "Did you know this?"

She didn't for Henk hardly shared with her about his past business ventures. She used her fork to pierce the last piece on her plate and popped it into her mouth to avoid giving an answer.

It was Henk who revealed, "I don't discuss my past business with Josie. Most of the time, I share it with Joshua, her father."

Phil declared, "Ah, Joshua is indeed a wise man. He's well respected in the technology field."

"When you finish dinner, I'll take you to a cafe where there's gourmet coffee," Henk offered.

"Sounds good." Phil applauded. "I was despairing of having good coffee in this place."

Lea suddenly said in a loud voice, "Josie doesn't take coffee!" All eyes were on her.

"Don't mind me," she answered generously. "I'll go where you all go. I can hardly take in anymore."

It was a small cafe a short distance away. When they arrived, the hour was late. There was no one inside when they walked in. They placed their orders at the cashier's desk, paid for them, and waited for the coffee.

Henk disappeared from the cafe. As they were sipping their fragrant coffee, he appeared with a mug, which he handed to Josie. "For you, chai tea. That's the best I can get." He added almost apologetically, "Er, no *tehsi* here."

Josie was touched. "It's kind of you, Henk. I wasn't expecting it. Chai tea is good enough." She made a pretense of sipping the tea. It wasn't to her liking, but she knew Henk was watching her.

"Don't finish the cup if you can't, Josie," he said, as if he knew she didn't like it.

"Um, as I said, I'm quite full." She set the cup down.

Lea immediately stretched out her hand for it. "I can drink the rest of the chai tea if it's OK with you."

When they got into the jeep, Josie murmured to Henk as she brushed against him, "Sorry, I couldn't finish the chai tea. As I said earlier, I'm quite full." She gave him a smile of appreciation. He squeezed her hand to show he understood.

"Anything for you, cousin," he said softly. This time, he said the term less awkwardly. Then he started the engine.

When they entered their family room, Lea passed a comment. "Henk likes you a lot. I can see. He watches over you."

Josie shrugged indifferently. "He's my cousin. Most probably grateful my father helped him get a scholarship in his earlier years and a part-time job in my company.

"He told me he was able to save some money when my dad allowed him to stay in the annex free of charge."

That night snuggled under the coverlet, she wondered who Henk was meeting so late that night. Before long, she fell asleep.

* * *

Josie was standing outside the family room in her thick, long coat. It was a chilly night. The temperature had dropped to below zero.

Angry voices outside had awoken her. She got up to investigate, for one of the voices sounded like Henk's.

But when she went outside, there was no one around. Strangely, no other buildings were around. Ahead was a road of baked sand. Her eyes could see it running a little way up, and then it stopped.

Her ears caught the sound further on of three people having a heated argument. It came from the land beside the one she was standing on. Snatches of conversation among the three floated across to her.

Although she was some distance away, she could clearly hear some of the words. "Parents, informer."

Those words intrigued her. The last word was an unusual choice. It wasn't a word in her everyday vocabulary.

She crossed over to the land. As she drew closer, she saw them. One of them was Henk. She recognized him from his height and broad shoulders and from his habit of clearing his throat before he began a sentence.

"You're sure my parents were informers?" his voice was tense, urgent.

"Quite sure," retorted the shorter man.

"Who were they working for?" Henk demanded.

"Maybe the Russians, maybe another party. Could even be the Chinese." The man dropped his voice.

Josie edged closer so that she could hear better. Henk's vocal output was uneven.

He was breathing heavily when he asked, "What were they involved in?"

"Oil purchase. It was a deal gone bad. Your dad took the money but didn't give them the right information about the deal. They claimed the one he gave them was false. Now the other party wants the money back."

"How much money?" Henk cleared his throat again.

"Millions." Josie heard him give a low whistle.

However, he immediately butted in, "That's odd. You sure the deal was only in millions, not billions?"

"That's what I was told."

"But oil purchases nowadays run into billions of dollars," Henk argued. "Did they fix the plane so it would appear to crash over Ukraine?"

"Maybe. Who can tell? Unless there's an investigation. Even then, no investigation team will know your parents were informers. They'll only report that two passengers were killed."

It was an incredible piece of information which Josie was hearing that night. She found it hard to believe. Was she having a dream?

The shorter man's voice floated across the still air. "Be careful. They're looking for you. They know your parents have a son."

Henk's voice came across angrily. "Why should they want me? What can I tell them? Nothing!"

The taller man said, "They want the money back. The deal didn't go through because the info was inaccurate."

Henk's tense voice rose in volume. "That's ridiculous. As far as I know, my parents gave them information. They paid for it. Whether the deal went through or not isn't my parents' problem."

"Tell it to them. That's all we know. Be careful, that's all we can say to you." The men took off, leaving Josie quite bewildered over what she overheard.

From Henk's agitated tone and frequent coughing, she knew he was very disturbed by what the men had shared.

Josie turned to return to her family room, but, to her utter dismay, she couldn't find it.

She reasoned that since she turned left to get there, she must now turn right to get back. But, on her right, there was just a small piece of land with a dead end. No containers with family rooms were visible.

She blinked hard and looked again. To her surprise, the land facing her changed into a longer stretch. She suddenly heard footsteps running toward her.

She turned her head and saw Henk closing the gap. She didn't know why, but she began running away from him. She sprinted away, her heart palpitating in anxiety.

She was very relieved when she suddenly saw the family room appearing before her. She hastily ran to it, wrenched open the door, and slipped inside. Just in time!

She stood panting against the door. To her relief, she saw Lea fast asleep, with a pillow covering her head. Josie locked the door and took off her thick, long coat.

After she changed into her silk pajamas, she crept into her bed. What she heard disturbed her peace of mind. It took her a long time to fall asleep, for her mind was busy replaying the earlier conversation and the warning given to Henk.

He had an unknown enemy out there. How was he to know who they were?

She couldn't believe Henk's parents were informers. For whom? Over what? Oil?

And what about the money? Millions of dollars? Not billions? Henk was skeptical over the amount stated by the man.

Was Henk supposed to know about its whereabouts? If he found it, he'd be rich overnight, but he'd be in danger. Didn't the man tell him some men were looking for the son to retrieve the money?

It was a mystery she couldn't unravel.

From his answer, Henk appeared to be in the dark.

TEN

She awoke when she felt a hand shaking her. On opening her eyes, she saw Lea standing over her.

"Hey, time for breakfast. Henk's outside."

Josie sat up. "Uh, don't think I'm ready for breakfast. I've a heavy head. Want to sleep in."

"Okay. You sure you are all right? You look pale."

"Er, just tired." Josie snuggled under the coverlet and pretended to go back to sleep.

"OK, I'll let Henk know. Want me to bring back a bun for you?" Lea asked. But Josie feigned sleep and didn't answer her. She heard the door opening and then shutting.

She tried to go back to sleep but couldn't. She was still highly disturbed by what she overheard last night.

Many minutes later, a strong rap on the door sounded. Henk's voice came across. It sounded urgent. "Josie, it's me. We need to talk!"

Somehow, she was expecting that he might want to talk to her about last night's cryptic conversation.

He saw her in the dark and recognized her. He even chased after her. Why? To talk to her most probably. And why had she run away from him? She had no answer to the last question.

"We need to talk," he repeated urgently as she opened the door. When he entered, he studied her face for a reaction to his request. But all he saw were puffy eyes.

"What about?" she pretended ignorance by yawning and rubbing her eyes. "I need to shower and change."

He sighed at her reluctance to talk. Sensing it strongly from her words, he had no alternative but to say, "Go ahead. I'll make you a cup of *tehsi* and a coffee for me."

He produced a large bun. "Er, brought back one for you."

Josie disappeared into the bathroom. When she came out feeling quite refreshed, she saw Henk seated on the edge of her bed, sipping coffee and nibbling corn chips.

"What was it you wanted to talk to me about?"

"Last night."

She swallowed the hot *tehsi* and then nibbled on the bun. In a calm voice, she asked, "What about last night?"

He went directly to the point. "How much did you hear?"

"What do you mean?"

"Come off it," he barked out. "You were standing in the shadows. I saw you. You saw me speaking to the men."

"Huh? I did?"

He was so positive he saw her that it made her think it must be real. If he saw her, then it couldn't have been a dream.

"Can you clarify please?"

He gave her a long hard stare. "What's there to clarify?" he snapped. "I was talking to the Mongolian men. You saw us."

"Remember, I told you last night at dinner that I was meeting two men?"

"One had news about my parents." His eyes searched hers for some reaction. Josie did her best to keep her face blank under the pretext of her drink.

To solve the mystery of the site of the land beside she asked, "By the way, where did you meet them? In the city? In a cafe?"

Henk continued staring hard at her. Then he said slowly, "In the stretch of land outside the family rooms."

"But, Henk, there's no stretch of land there. Neither is there a stretch of land outside my family room. There are just lots of small container-like family rooms around."

Inwardly, she was confused. There was no doubt now after what he said that he was in the land beside. He wasn't even close to the family rooms.

Since she wanted him to confirm if her dream was a reality, she got up and went outside. She needed it, to prove to herself too that it wasn't a dream, and that the conversation did take place.

The cold air hit her face. A slight breeze caused her to shiver. Seeing her only in the T-shirt and jeans, Henk hurried back to take her long coat, which he draped over her.

She strode farther to where she thought she saw a piece of land beside the plot yesterday. There was nothing but more container-like rooms.

She stood in the cold. The sun shone strongly down. Behind her was Henk. She asked, "Did you meet the men somewhere near here?"

He stopped, scratched his head, cleared his throat, and looked around. "Er, no, not anywhere here. The scenery here is different. Unlike last night."

Josie knew he was right because she had stood on the same piece of land. Since she didn't want to keep pushing the point, she declared, "I'm hungry now. Can you take me for breakfast?"

He set aside his insistence on an answer from her and waited outside for her. She went back to her room and changed into warmer clothing. Then she put on her thick, long coat before they drove some distance to the cafe where the others were just finishing their coffee.

"Hey, good to see you up," Phil greeted her with a warm smile. "Join us for breakfast?"

Josie greeted him with a wide smile. She had come to like him ever since she knew him. She found him emotionally stable. He always thought through areas of discussion which were perplexing and often came up with rational suggestions.

Phil was almost as tall as Henk. He was slim and lithe but tended to slouch. Although he was only in his thirties, his hair was thinning a lot. When he stood, he often leaned sideways with his right hand in his pocket.

Josie found him supportive and loyal. In her view, Phil was an asset to the company.

In her team, there was Kye, the designer, who was creative and artistic. He was sensitive to different hues of colors for the designs. He was attracted to beautiful women and always dating models, tall, slim ones.

And he loved music. When he was in the design room, he put in earplugs so that he could hear music from YouTube. He could work for hours and often forgot about lunch or tea, unless someone called him to join them in the lounge.

Like Kye, Lea was highly creative. She could turn an ordinary design into a work of art. She saw designs popping out from different fabrics. Josie had no doubt that Lea would successfully innovate the Mongolian *deel* outfits and produce new styles.

Lea's heart-shaped face with its widow's peak, high-cheeked facial bones, and light-brown eyes could have made her a beauty of some sort. Unfortunately, her skin was pockmarked because of bad acne attacks in her teen years which had left scars.

Josie encouraged her to see a skin specialist, but Lea had resisted. "No point wasting money. I tried some creams, but they didn't help me."

In the months she worked with her, Josie discovered that Lea had strong likes and dislikes. Once she made up her mind to like someone, she loyally defended the person when others opposed her in her decisions.

Josie was glad Lea liked and respected her a lot. On this trip, she noticed Lea's affections leaning toward Henk!

When Josie took stock of the team who was working with her, she was grateful they joined the company.

Of Henk, she had mixed feelings. He challenged her mentally and emotionally and caused her to be alert all the time he was with her. He often appeared to be uncaring about her feelings, for he shot out remarks which bordered on insults.

She recalled him saying forthrightly, "Why do you have such dull designs? Who would want to buy them?"

His choice of words stung her and often riled the team members. Sometimes, he said things to them with a sneer. This caused her to be mad at him, for he seemed so insensitive to their feelings.

In a meeting once, he belted out at Kye, "Do you think you deserve to be in the team?"

In defense, Kye retorted, "You're not the one who appointed me. Ruth did."

With Lea, he showed his disapproval openly. "Your designs aren't fit to be put in the fashion shows."

"Well, Josie approves," Lea would snap back.

There was such a tension whenever Henk came into the meetings that Josie felt it necessary to raise the matter to her father.

One night after dinner, she mentioned the problem to him. He helped her realize that Henk came from a different background.

"Raised on hard soil," her father reminded her. "He was raised without loving parents. In the orphanage, the caregivers were often cold toward the children. They were also blunt in their speech to the children.

"Their callous attitude may have rubbed off the kids. Many take the appointment for the money only."

Then Joshua would add softly, "Kids need love and kindness. Most orphan kids lack that."

"But times are changing. More missions nowadays are appointing caregivers who are kinder in their care of orphans."

Josie recalled the tender care her parents gave her. In her young age, her father would read stories of men and women who were strong and courageous, those who rendered help to needy families and orphaned children.

Although he travelled a lot, he never neglected to read to her whenever he returned from his visits abroad. Her every need was met by both parents.

Whenever Henk needled her, Josie recalled her dad's observation of his hard life in the orphanage. This caused her to exercise self-control in her answers to Henk's criticisms.

However, Josie later learned that Henk wasn't always hard and nasty in his interaction with her. There was the other side of him that she came to see months later, the tender, caring side. She felt sure this arose out of his gratitude to her father for his kindness to him.

As the days of knowing him lengthened, Josie often caught a faraway look in Henk's eyes when he wasn't talking to anyone. It was as if his mind was on someone he missed.

When she came to know him even better, she changed her opinion that he looked a lot like Jeremy. His face, although handsome, had a tough, rugged look, which was lacking in Jeremy.

The first time she met him at the golf tournament, he had seemed so charming. But, in later meetings with him, his charm seemed to be overshadowed by his troubled thoughts.

As the frequency of their meetings increased because of their work, she noticed that he seldom smiled. But when he did, his broad smile revealed a row of even white teeth. His irresistible smile reminded her so much of Jeremy.

She often found herself catching her breath whenever Henk smiled at her like that. It was in such moments that she saw his resemblance to Jeremy.

During his stay with her, she noticed he developed an affection for her. "Like a sister," he said to her when her eyes questioned his hugs to her. "Never had one. You're my first real cousin."

"And how about Joshua?" she remembered asking him. He would grin and say, "Um, like a father to me. I never knew my own dad. He died when I was only two. Most of the time, it was my mother who looked after me. And she died too."

A shadow crossed his face, and tears collected in his dark eyes whenever he mentioned her.

From that day on, Josie avoided raising anything about his mother or his childhood.

* * *

That morning in Mongolia, after Josie finished a quick breakfast, Henk announced to the group, "We're visiting a millinery, the place where hats are designed and produced."

Josie argued, "Henk, don't forget we design dresses only."

"Might be good to see them," he insisted. "Broaden your perception of fashions. You never know, you might branch into such designs one day.

"I've already arranged it with Altan," he told the group.

Josie pursed her lips in disapproval. Phil, however, supported Henk. "That's a good idea, worthwhile to take a look since we're already here. Besides, Singapore is becoming quite cosmopolitan in its population."

There were two jeeps waiting to transport them. They arrived at a large building. Altan was there with his cheerful smile. By now, everyone knew how to greet him in his language. That pleased him, they could see.

He wasted no time in ushering them into the first hall. There were dummies dressed in the Mongolian national costumes, complete with traditional headwear.

When the team saw the vast array of headdresses, there was a hushed silence. They were overwhelmed by the intricacy of the designs.

"The ones here have been produced over the years." His hand waved toward the lot close to them.

"As you can see, there are a variety of sizes. These are designed for different purposes. Farther away, there are newer fashions."

Josie commented, "Reminds me of the English. I know they love to wear hats. For every major event, English women have hats designed for the occasion."

"You attended some of them?" Altan asked.

"Oh, yes," she replied enthusiastically. "Some are really outstanding! Those were designed individually for women from the upper class."

"Do you have any yourself?" Lea asked curiously.

"Plenty. When I was in England, Mum would ask me where I was going to store them when I returned to Singapore."

Kye immediately asked, "Where did you store them?"

She laughed. "I didn't. In Singapore, it isn't the *in* thing to wear hats. I gave them away to my English friends."

"You didn't!" Lea said, sounding quite shocked. "Some must have cost you quite a bit!"

"Well," Josie confessed, "I sold those which were very pricey. My friends can afford to pay for them."

Phil said, "And did you use the money to buy more hats?" Josie didn't say anything in reply.

Altan then suggested, "Let's move to the other hall. You can see hats designed for different seasons, for the young and the old."

"The ones in the next hall are for everyday use. The young adults, too, wear hats. Um, ah, in another hall, you will see designs for various ceremonies."

They moved to the next hall. The fashions and colors dazzled them. "Look at the trimmings!" Kye called out as his fingers ran across an ornate one. "This design is quite remarkable!"

Altan explained, "The colors chosen depend on whether the hat is designed for a man or a woman."

"Men gravitate towards sober colors. In winter, their hats range from dark brown to gray and even black."

"Women have a wider range. The young adults, for instance, choose more colorful hats, even for winter wear." Henk suddenly appeared next to Josie.

"Don't the hats also denote the rank of the wearer, Altan?" he asked.

"They do, indeed! Different tribes choose their own colors and designs."

Kye released a deep breath. "Wow! I'm impressed."

"There's big business in hat fashions," Henk said to his cousin. "Think about it. Now that the team's here, they can pick up some idea on the various fashions."

Phil was encouraging. "That's good advice, Henk. We'll certainly think through your suggestion."

He turned to the rest of them. "Well, team, let's start sketching."

Josie cautioned them before they started, "We must bear in mind, though, hat making is a different art and skill. The configuration is quite different!

"Lea, why don't you fill your pad with ideas you gain from the designs here? Um, innovate and come up with designs which might be suitable for women back home."

Lea laughed. "I've no idea what's suitable for the women back home, for frankly, I haven't seen women wearing hats when they go shopping or lunch out. All I know are golf hats which they wear on the course. But I'll try, anyway!"

"Kye, why don't you fill in each design with colors which harmonize. You're good at that. Work with Lea," Josie instructed him. "After you draw them, fill in the drawings with colors. Choose colors young adults might like."

She cautioned Henk, "I don't think men in our country wear hats. Much too hot and humid. Even in weddings and funerals, I don't see our men wearing hats."

She hastened to add, "Except perhaps golf caps. Um, on the golf course, some women tend to have caps which are quite fashionable. But many are imported from Japan and South Korea."

Henk suggested, with some foresight, "We can keep them in view for our future expansion into Western countries. I know the men there wear them, hats, I mean."

They sketched even as they moved around the hall. There was no table. Every member had portable hand-sized pads to fill. The silence was broken only by the scratching of the styli on the drawing tablets. From his backpack, Kye fished out a box of color styli.

As soon as Lea and Phil completed their pads, he took them and filled in the colors. It was teamwork that morning. Josie herself, a professional artist in her own right, came out with new and innovative designs.

After their sketches were completed, they moved back to the first hall, which was filled with traditional dresses.

Josie nipped into the hall which had dresses for young adults. Her hand flew across the drawing pad. Before long, she filled them with more innovative designs.

Henk moved around the halls to check on the team. When he entered the one where Josie was completing her design, he said sincerely, "I'm very impressed with my cousin."

"Lea tells me you're a professional artist. Where did you complete your studies?"

"I did some postgrad courses over the years with the SCAD art school on location in France," she said briefly while continuing with her sketching.

When he said nothing, she stopped sketching to look at him. In his eyes, she saw admiration for her.

At lunchtime, Henk came in to stop the work. He told them, "We're leaving now for lunch. First, we'll go by the rooms and have the women change their clothes, before we leave for the lunch venue."

"Why?" Josie asked. "Can't we go like this?" her hand brushed down the length of her outfit.

Henk grinned and said mysteriously, "Er, not where we're going."

"Where are you taking us?" she and others were brimming with curiosity. Henk didn't say anything. He seemed to be enjoying the mystery he was creating.

The others crowded around him with questions in their eyes. But all he said was "Let's go. We don't want to be late for lunch." They got into the jeeps and headed back to the family rooms.

Inside, Lea asked Josie, "Do you think we should change into something dressy?"

"Don't really know. Henk didn't say where exactly we're going to," she replied. "To be on the safe side, let's change into something fashionable but not too dressy."

She chose a dark-blue cashmere dress with an elegant long cashmere coat and a white collar. Lea wore a deep-maroon turtleneck cashmere top and black woolen pants.

When they emerged, the three men whistled encouragingly. Henk led them to a small tour coach.

Josie's eyes widened. "A coach? Where are you taking us?"

He grinned again, making him look much younger. He was a little younger than Jeremy, Josie knew, but his troubled mind had an aging effect on his looks.

"You'll know when we get there."

He whipped out a smartphone and spoke softly into it. "We're arriving in ten minutes."

Josie wondered who it was that he was speaking to.

ELEVEN

Before long, they approached a tall building. When the group looked at the word *Holiday Inn* etched on the front of the building, they gasped.

Josie caught sight of a couple waving to them. When she recognized them, she shrieked, "It's Mum and Dad!" The moment the vehicle stopped she tore open the door but found it locked.

Behind her, Henk said calmly, "The driver will get it opened soon." When the door slid open, Josie tumbled out just as her mother came up to her. She hugged and kissed her.

Soon Joshua, too, was hugging and kissing his daughter. He held her at arm's length and said, "You look quite burnt and rosy!"

The others came out at a more sedate pace. They greeted Ruth and Joshua with warm smiles.

"But what are you doing here?" Josie asked Ruth.

"Well, your father is here for two days to look at some orphanages. I decided to accompany him, more to see how you're doing."

"Let's go inside before we freeze." Joshua led the way inside, with a loving arm around his daughter.

Ruth walked on the other side. They presented a picture of a loving family to the others.

Joshua led them straight into the dining room. A long table was reserved for them. As they pulled out their chairs, Joshua told them, "The lunch menu is already selected, and the food will be served soon."

He sat at the head of the table, while Josie sat on his right. Ruth sat next to Josie. While the others were about to take their seats, Joshua's voice floated across the long table. "Henk, come and sit next to me."

He was about to take his seat at the other end of the table when he heard Joshua calling out to him. He promptly went to Joshua and took the seat next to him.

"How's the team doing?"

"Not bad, Sir," he said respectfully. "They did a lot of sketching of various fashions earlier."

Josie eagerly added, "Yes, we even drew designs of hats and boots."

He looked genially at his daughter's flushed face. "You planning to go into the hat fashion? Well, Ruth, what do you think?"

Ruth laughed and patted her daughter's hand. "She has free rein to produce any fashion which is good for business."

Henk said, "It'll go well with Western women and men, if we expand." And then added as an afterthought, "Even Japanese and Chinese women and female golfers in Singapore wear them."

When the food arrived, everyone tucked in hungrily. It didn't take long for them to finish their meal.

"Coffee, anyone?" Joshua offered. "I think this place has gourmet coffee." He hailed a passing waiter for a menu. While everyone was placing their order, Joshua asked his daughter, "Jasmine green tea or chamomile?"

Josie chose the latter. When lunch was over, Joshua told Henk, "Take the others back to their rooms. Josie's staying here with us for the two days we're here."

Henk nodded. "And. Henk," Joshua added, "I've got a room for you here too."

A flash of appreciation lit his eyes. "That's very kind of you, Sir, but I think I'll return with the others."

Ruth whispered something to Joshua. He emitted a big smile. "Good idea, Ruth."

He addressed the group. "Would any of you like to stay over at my expense?"

There was a stunned silence. Then Phil timidly asked, "You mean you'll pay for all our rooms?"

Joshua gave a genial smile. "Why not? Won't break my bank."

Lea let out an exuberant yell. "Yippee! Thank you, thank you, Mr. Yuen. I'd love to stay in this hotel."

She turned to the group. "Hey, guys, I think this offer calls for thanks from all of you!"

They responded immediately. Josie ran to give her father a hug. "Thank you, thank you, Dad!"

"Well, I guess it's left to you, Henk, to organize the rooms. Tell Reception to check the group in."

"Certainly will, Sir," Henk replied with a happy grin.

When the team left them, Josie accompanied her parents to their suite. With his arm around her shoulder, Joshua said, "We've a surprise for you in our room."

Josie loved surprises. Every birthday, her parents bought something unexpected for her. That day, she was puzzled. It wasn't her birthday yet.

"What surprise, Mum?" Ruth smiled mysteriously at her daughter.

"You'll like it. Your dad saw it in your room. He thought you might want it to be your companion for the time you are here."

"Is it Bozo?" she asked. Bozo was the toy dog she had placed on her bed ever since her father bought it for her from Jersey island during their visit there.

"Nope. Something better." He inserted the card key and entered, followed by Ruth and Josie.

A loud clicking and whirring sound caught their ears. Then a high-pitched monotone droned out, "Josie, Josie, you're here! Can you help me get a soul?"

To her horror, the little robot came clicking toward her. She took one look at it and ran behind her father, screaming hysterically, "I don't want it! Take it away! I don't want it!" Her panic threw her parents into a state of bewilderment.

Screaming out, "Switch it off, Dad," she burst into tears. Joshua immediately complied. He flicked the switch of the machine, and it whirred to a stop.

With arms around his daughter, he led her to the couch in the adjoining sitting room.

"There, there." He spoke to her as if she were a little girl. "What's so wrong about a robot?"

She buried her face into his chest. "I don't like it. Take it away. I just don't want it."

Ruth held her hand and kept patting it. "Are you afraid of it, Josie? What happened to cause such fear in you?"

She stopped crying when she suddenly realized that she needed to come up with a rational explanation. How was she to explain to her parents that the little robot came from the land beside their house and had been pestering her?

As far as her parents were concerned, the land beside was empty, waiting for the contractor to build a house on it. She took refuge in her mother's words.

She blurted out, "I'm afraid of what it can do if it's programmed wrongly."

Joshua frowned when he heard it. "What do you mean by programmed wrongly?"

She didn't know how to explain it, so she said nothing. Occasional sobs choked her. "I just don't like it!"

Joshua stroked his daughter's long tresses in his effort to calm her. "What was it saying before I switched it off? I found it in your room last night.

"I thought you might like it if I brought it over here. It can help you in your designing."

When she heard her father's words, she grew a little calmer. She repeated, "I just don't like robots!"

Her father said comfortingly, "There's nothing to fear. Robots can be programmed to do what we want them to do. What if I get my programmer to do an input into this little machine into something you like?"

"Good idea," Ruth agreed. "Your dad found it in your room, Josie. He thought you bought it as a toy, although nowadays robotic function is more sophisticated than just a mere toy to play games with it."

When Josie saw both their puzzled looks, she felt guilty about her reaction. They had brought the robot out to please her, and here she was throwing what might appear to be a childish tantrum.

Suddenly, she recalled Fred and Chloe. "Don't like it. It might turn out to be like Chloe."

"Huh? Who's Chloe?" Ruth's eyes reflected her confusion.

Joshua laughed aloud. "Oh, so you think this robot might predict who you are to marry." She nodded miserably for want of a better answer.

Joshua explained to Ruth, "Chloe is a robot which Fred . . . you remember Fred? Um, the machine he used came up with a name of a girl who could be his steady."

"And?"

"Chloe told him the girl's name was Kay, I think. Right, Josie?" he asked her. She nodded, relieved that her father had taken over the explanation.

"Well, isn't that good?" Ruth still looked confused. "I mean, isn't it time Fred found someone nice?"

She paused awhile and then added, "Is this Kay not the right choice? Is that what you're afraid of Josie?"

Her daughter said nothing. Joshua consoled her.

"Josie, Josie, the computer can only come up with whatever data you put in. Fred must have given some data for Chloe to come up with a name like Kay."

"This person, Kay, must have the same interests as Fred. That's how the computer came up with the match."

When his daughter remained silent, to ease her anxiety, he suggested, "Why don't you work with my programmer when you return to Singapore? Get him to do whatever input you like."

He saw relief on her face. "Suggest you wash your face now. Then go to the shops with your mother to get yourself a nightdress and some other attractive clothes."

Ruth hugged her daughter. "Would you like to go shopping with me?"

Josie apologized, "Sorry, Mum and Dad, for getting so worked up over a little robot."

After she left them, Joshua spoke to his wife. "I sense there's something deeper about the robot which Josie isn't telling us. When I get home, I'll ask my programmer to take it apart and find out what its creator has put in."

Since Ruth was tired, she was contented to let her husband handle that part of the problem.

After refreshing herself with a face wash, Josie entered the sitting room. She saw Henk deep in conversation with Joshua. The earnestness on his face showed he was sharing something serious.

Joshua looked up as she picked up her handbag close to where they were sitting. "Ah, ready to go out?"

When Ruth came out of the bedroom, Henk stood up. He walked with them to the door and saw them out.

As they approached the lift, Ruth said to her daughter, "Henk's adjusting well. How do you find him? From what your dad tells me, he had a hard childhood. Wonder why his parents' plane crashed."

When they emerged from the hotel entrance, a cold blast of wind chilled them.

Meanwhile, inside the hotel room, Henk was telling Joshua, "I've some strange information to share with you concerning my parents. I met a man, a Mongolian, who contacted me yesterday."

"That's good news, isn't it?" Joshua commented.

"Good and bad."

"What do you mean?"

"Good in the sense that he knew a little about my parents and the possible reason for the plane crash."

"Bad in that my parents were supposed to have been involved in an oil deal that went horribly wrong."

"Huh?" Joshua's eyebrows creased heavily.

"Uncle Josh, the man said my parents were paid to pass information to a party regarding an oil deal with another party. Apparently, my parents never passed them the right information."

He leaned closer to Joshua. "The chap said they took the money and ran off."

"How much are you talking about?"

"A few million."

Joshua shook his head. "Can't be right. Oil deals go into billions nowadays, not millions."

"That's what I thought. It seems the other party never got the deal clinched. They wanted the money back. I was told my parents took it and disappeared."

"Somehow, the other party found out where they were and rigged the plane, which they were in."

"Too far-fetched to believe." Joshua sipped his coffee and sat back in his chair thoughtfully.

He then asked, "What does this informer expect from you?"

"He told me the other party wants to know where the money has gone to. Um, said the persons he was working for knew I am the son."

Joshua looked searchingly at the young man. "And you really know nothing. Um, no inclination at all?"

"You'll have to believe me, Uncle Josh, when I say I've no idea whatever about the money. I didn't even know my parents were involved in such a scheme!"

Joshua sat up. "It sounds quite complicated. If what the man says is true, then you'll be watched."

"They'll be watching me in vain then," Henk said. "I know nothing of any money." There was a long pause as both men thought over what they discussed.

As Henk sat there, he recalled seeing Josie in the land beside theirs that night. But was that person Josie? It was very dark. The height, long hair, and side profile of the person resembled Josie's. And the long coat she was wearing looked like the one she had.

But, if she was Josie, why had she sprinted away from him? That was the mystery he wanted to solve when he went to her room the next morning. But he was puzzled why she evaded giving him a direct answer.

He looked at Joshua and wondered if he should share with him the information about Josie. He felt his uncle's sincerity from the moment he met him. His extreme kindness impressed him. But he knew, too, that Joshua doted on his daughter.

He wondered what Joshua's reaction would be if he told him about Josie's presence. As if sensing Henk had something else to share, Joshua asked, "Is there something else you wish to tell me?"

Hesitatingly, Henk shared, "I think Josie was present that night. She might have overheard our conversation."

He saw Joshua giving a start. The older man asked sharply, "Did you involve my daughter in this? Don't you know these people can be dangerous?"

Hastily, he replied, "No, no, Uncle Josh, nothing of that kind. I didn't invite her to come with me. It's just that when I was speaking with the man, I saw a figure who looked much like Josie in the shadows some distance away.

"But, come to think of it, the person was about sixty meters or more away, so how could she hear our conversation?"

"How did you know it was a woman?"

"The person had long hair, which was blowing in the breeze, and a long coat, which I thought looked like Josie's."

"Not possible. From that distance in the dark, you can't be sure it was Josie," he said this emphatically.

"Besides, if you say it was about sixty meters or more and you were both talking in hushed voices, even if it was Josie, she probably," he trailed off, as he thought of something.

Henk immediately said, "You're probably right, Uncle Josh. I tried asking her the next morning, but she didn't seem to know what I was talking about."

Joshua had stopped completing his sentence because he remembered his daughter's special gift. She could hear a conversation which was even sixty meters away.

He recalled an incident on the golf course when she hit her ball a long distance away. When he teed off after her, his ball went to the right where the trees were.

A man from the other course was looking for his ball, which had gone across to the same clump of trees where Joshua's ball went.

When Joshua found his ball, the man claimed it was his. There was an argument about its ownership until Joshua showed him the red star marking which Josie had put on all his balls.

"For your protection, in case you lose them," she told him. "Jeremy puts a yellow star on his golf balls. I'll put a red on yours."

Joshua recalled what Josie said when they eventually met up on the green. "Did the man claim your ball was his?"

"How did you know what he was saying?" he asked her.

"I heard your conversation, Dad. The man sounded angry." That was the first time Joshua learned his daughter could hear words spoken over a long distance.

He never revealed to her his knowledge of her gift.

However, what some may think is a gift, Josie simply dismissed as something natural she was born with.

But that day, Joshua didn't tell Henk about his daughter's ability to hear a conversation so far away.

Inwardly though, he was troubled. If what Henk said was accurate, then what was Josie doing on the land late that night?

To know more, he asked Henk, "Were you on the land beside the family rooms?"

Henk scratched his temple. "You know, Uncle Josh, there's something strange about that place."

"What do you mean?"

"Well, when I asked Josie if she was present that night and had overheard my conversation with the man, she asked me to show her where the meeting took place."

"When we went outside the family room, there was no land beside the rows of family rooms."

"Well then, your meeting must have taken place at some other place." Joshua offered a logical solution.

"Did you arrange to meet the two men earlier at another venue?"

"Uh-huh. I arranged to meet them outside the cafe where the team had their after-dinner coffee."

"I remember leaving the cafe with the group. When I returned to the place later, the men didn't show up. The next thing I knew, I was on a piece of land away from the family rooms."

"You'll have to sort out this mystery, Henk. I wasn't present. But let me warn you, I don't want Josie mixed up in whatever it is your parents have done. Keep her out of it, do you hear?" his voice was serious and stern.

"I've no intention of involving her, Uncle Josh. I know how precious she is to you both."

The doorbell rang. Joshua went to the door. In walked his wife and daughter, laughing. They were carrying some parcels with them.

"Ah, I see you've been doing a lot of shopping," he jested.

He then turned to Henk. "Your room's a floor down."

"Thanks, Uncle Josh." Henk picked up the card key, nodded to Ruth and Josie, and vacated their room.

TWELVE

That night, Josie slept in the adjoining room her father had arranged for her. She was tired and fell asleep quickly.

The sound of children singing woke her up. When she opened her eyes, she was surprised to see a group of about twenty girls in their teen years surrounding her.

Most were crippled. Some were limping, some had crutches, and others were in their wheelchairs. They were facing her and singing familiar melodies which she heard before.

Where am I? She looked around. They were on a piece of land beside a building. The girls looked as if they were giving a performance to her. She was the only spectator.

When the girls finished their song, a burly man and a thin middle-aged woman ushered them across the land into the building beside it.

When the woman passed Josie, she invited her to follow the procession into the building. Before Josie entered, she looked back and saw the piece of land beside where the building stood.

The surrounding land looked familiar. It reminded her of the land she was standing on when Henk spoke to the man two nights earlier.

However, before she had time to recall, the woman hastened her to go in with them.

"The girls want to meet you. They're excited. They hardly have visitors from abroad." Josie was led to an inner hall.

A chair was pulled up for her in front of the girls. None of them squatted. Some were standing in their crippled state; some were in the wheelchairs.

"These girls are special," explained the burly man, who came up to Josie and handed her a program sheet.

"We're training them to sing. They have extraordinary voices. You're invited to assess them."

He pulled a lame girl forward to meet her. "This is Ariana. She has a remarkable vocal range. We're training her for the international teen vocal competition, which is coming up soon."

"You're the judge for now. You must choose the best girl for the upcoming competition."

Ariana stood shyly next to Josie. Her face was aglow with excitement at having been chosen to meet Josie.

Up close, Josie saw that her skin was very dry and peeling. Her cheeks were a ruddy red. She was thin and shabbily dressed.

"Why don't you tell Josie your name?" the middle-aged woman encouraged.

The girl whispered, "Ariana."

Josie complimented her. "What a beautiful name."

"Sing for her," the burly man urged.

There was no piano to accompany her. She sang a cappella. Her voice burst out into the most beautiful range of notes. She was like a nightingale performing for the solo visitor.

When she finished, she attempted a bow but lost her balance, for her lame leg bent over. The woman quickly picked her up. Josie saw tears flowing down her face.

She clapped for her. "That was lovely, Ariana. Really superb."

"You really think so?" the girl smiled through her tears, as she struggled to be stable.

"Yes, yes, I do," Josie replied sincerely.

"Where did you learn our language?" the man looked quite puzzled.

"Huh? Was I speaking in Mongolian?"

The next thing Josie knew, she was sitting on the floor of her bedroom. She had tumbled out of her bed!

As she picked herself up, she remembered she was in the adjoining room in the hotel where she was spending the night with her parents. She was wearing her new nightgown, the one she bought earlier with her mother.

Just then Ruth came into her room, smiling. "Had a good sleep? There's coffee on the table in our room. Why don't you get changed? We're going down for breakfast soon."

Hurriedly, Josie changed into her sweater. It was on a hanger beside the shower door. It was the one she had on in her dream last night.

She stared at it a long time. Was it a dream she had? And the teenage singer, Ariana, was she real? Her voice was still ringing in her ears when she completed her dressing.

She plaited her hair and looped a thick strand across the back of her head. When she emerged, only Ruth was sitting, sipping coffee. Its fragrance wafted across to Josie.

"Your father's taking us to an orphanage this morning after breakfast. The girls there are special. They're gifted with lovely voices."

Josie gave a start when she heard this. "What do you mean, Mum, special?"

Ruth smiled broadly. "Special in many ways. Their voices are great. They're being prepared to enter an international competition for the handicap."

"Handicap?" she echoed her mother. "And Dad's been asked to sponsor their trip?"

"Clever girl," said her mother. "You can anticipate what I'm going to tell you."

"Well, if you're not going have coffee, let's go down to meet the others."

"Are the others joining us too?"

"Nope. Henk's taking them to another fashion house." She paused and looked at her daughter. "Would you rather join them instead?"

Josie was unsure. The thought of going to an orphanage to hear the girls sing didn't excite her. Yet she felt compelled to go just to verify if her dream was true and if there was a girl called Ariana.

The others were about to finish their breakfast. They greeted Josie enthusiastically. But her mind was busy with her thoughts.

Henk came up as she poured out the tea. "Had a good night's sleep?"

"Why?" she asked defensively.

"Oh, just the usual question I ask everyone." He gave her a penetrating look.

I'm overreacting, she said to herself. *Henk wouldn't know about my dream.*

"We're visiting another fashion house. Your dad said the three of you are visiting an orphanage."

Josie nodded and helped herself to the blueberry yogurt cup laid out on the table. Lea came up to her.

"Is that all you're having for breakfast? There's a whole array of pasta and noodles at the other end. Want some?"

"Uh-huh. I'll help myself to them after I eat these." She indicated the items on the tray she was carrying.

When she was nibbling on the buns, Henk came up, carrying a cup for her. "Tea," he said. "Plain chamomile."

"Thanks, Henk," she replied gratefully. Throughout her meal, she was silent, thinking about her dream. In contrast, the others were chatting among themselves.

Joshua was sitting two seats away from her. "If you want to go with the others, we can always meet up for lunch."

Hastily, Josie answered, "I'll go with you and Mum. Want to hear the teens sing. They have lovely voices."

"You heard them singing?" Henk asked in a surprised voice. Josie saw her parents and the others looking at her. She smiled. "Maybe in a dream."

She had become quite adept at skirting answers to questions by referring to them as her dreams.

When they arrived at the orphanage, Josie recognized it as the same building she saw in her dream. A large piece of land with baked orangey red soil lay beside the small plot where the building stood. Behind were hills spread out in the distance.

"It's the only building here," she commented to her parents.

"Uh-huh. There's good potential," Joshua observed. "I think the three committee members running it are looking for funds for its expansion."

"Didn't they say they're hoping to build a special gym of some kind to help the handicap?" Ruth verbalized.

Joshua nodded. He repeated, "There's good potential. All they need are sponsors."

"Dad, they don't mind if some churches offer them the funding?" Josie recalled the reluctance of Boh when she visited the first orphanage.

Ruth looked surprised. "Mind? Why should they?"

"I was told by Altan that people like Boh are afraid the organizations who provide funds will try and change the children's minds. He's a staunch animist."

"Well, this particular one isn't owned by people like Boh," Joshua explained. "In fact, there are a few others who are only too happy to get mission organizations to help fund them."

He added, "And provide people to help them in the actual running! I understand a great many of the parents are poor and some are alcoholics."

Someone emerged from inside. He was a tall, big man, broad shouldered, with burnt cheeks and a broad forehead. On his head was a triangle hat with a white circle at its peak, which, Josie learned, indicated the native group he belonged to.

He announced, "I'm Erden. My name means treasure." True to his native custom, he didn't stretch out a hand to them. Josie and her parents nodded their greetings.

When Josie said, "*Sain bain uu* (Are you well)?" to him, he looked surprised but pleased.

He replied quickly, "*Sain.*"

"Where did you learn the greeting?" Joshua asked.

She grinned, feeling quite pleased with herself. "From Altan."

Erden led them inside. Facing them was a group of girls, all handicapped in some way. Josie remembered them as the ones she saw in her dream. She looked around for Ariana but couldn't spot the girl in the group.

When she blurted out to Erden, "Where's Ariana?" he looked surprised. "You know her?"

Josie offered no answer. Her father asked, "You've been here before with Henk?"

She shook her head. She didn't give any explanation. It was Erden who replied, "Josie can't have met the girl. I never met her before today." When he clapped his hands, the group arranged themselves in a neat row.

Her parents were offered seats in front. Erden drew up another chair for Josie.

There was no piano. When Erden lifted his hands, the group sang a beautiful, lilting melody in a cappella style. Their voices harmonized well, trilling at the high notes. The volume peaked to a crescendo. Then the sound gradually sank into a whisper.

It was a wonderful rendition of "O for the Wings of a Dove" by Felix Mendelssohn. The visitors clapped their appreciation.

"This is excellent," Ruth enthused. "Such a high standard! Who taught them?"

Erden puffed up his chest a little. "I did."

"That's excellent, indeed." Ruth repeated, "Where did you get your training?"

"I was trained in London before I decided to return to my country and train some my people. When I tested the voices of this group of girls, I saw great potential."

Joshua clapped and said, "You did well, indeed. Their standard is high."

Just then, a girl emerged from the shadows, followed by a large woman. Josie recognized her. It was Ariana. In turn, she recognized Josie. She limped toward her.

"Josie, Josie." She clasped her hands in delight.

Ruth was astonished. So was Erden. "You know my daughter? Where did you both meet?"

There was silence. How could Josie tell them about her visit to the land the night before?

Erden questioned his daughter in his language. He translated her answer to the group. "Ariana said she met Josie with another group of girls yesterday."

"Huh?" Joshua was perplexed, Josie could see. She laughed and said, "Maybe in a dream, Dad."

He was quite used to her dismissal of visions with her explanation of "in a dream." And he knew his daughter didn't want to tell the others about her dream.

To change the subject, he asked Erden, "Is there another group we can hear? If they're as good as this one, I might sponsor them too."

Erden's eyes were shining with delight. "You mean you're willing to sponsor another group?" Without waiting for Joshua's response, he said sadly, "Alas, this orphanage has only one such group!"

"Well, let's visit another orphanage then," Joshua told his family.

When he saw Ariana clutching his daughter's hand, he suggested, "Josie, would you like to stay here awhile with the girls while your mother and I visit another home? We'll come back for you."

"Yes, that would be great, Dad," she replied eagerly.

Erden showed them out, while Anu, the older woman, ushered Josie and the girls into a smaller room. There were plates of biscuits and some glasses of lemonade on the table.

The girls hurriedly grabbed the biscuits and munched on them. "You're back," Ariana breathed her pleasure as she sidled beside Josie.

"Yes, indeed," Josie replied. "I'm so pleased to see you again."

"You understand our language?" Anu was surprised.

"What do you mean?"

"Ariana spoke in Mongolian, and you answered her in English.

"I did?" Josie was beginning to realize that she could understand their language, but only at times. Outwardly, she had no explanation to give.

"Does Ariana understand English?"

"A little. We have English lessons once a week."

Ariana said, "You have such beautiful skin and hair." She stroked Josie's cheek but immediately received a sharp rebuke from Anu.

"Mind your manners! You shouldn't touch the visitor physically." Tears collected in the fifteen-year-old's eyes.

"It's all right, Anu. She's curious. Probably wants to feel my skin."

"It's bad manners!" Anu said disapprovingly.

The other girls took courage and blurted out to Josie, "Can we touch your cheek too?"

Anu clapped her hands. "Enough!" she barked out. Keep your distance from the visitor!"

Ariana muttered softly, "I wish I was as lovely as you, Josie." Tears fell. "I'm so ugly."

Josie patted her arm, but she was mindful of Anu's remark that there should be no touching. "You're beautiful in your own way. God has given you a lovely voice. That's beauty in some way."

"No," said the young teen. "I'm not. No one will want to marry me! My leg is ugly!" She indicated her lame leg.

Josie was surprised at her words. At fifteen, the girl was thinking of marriage already. *Did Mongolian girls marry at such a young age?* she wondered. However, she didn't ask Anu, feeling it best to refrain from such a question.

The girls surrounded her. One demanded, "Tell us a story."

"That's a good idea," Josie said, wondering what story she should tell. She looked around her. All of them were lame in one way or another. Some were in wheelchairs.

And they were all in their teens only.

Anu smiled. "Yes, it's good if you can tell them a story. They're so depressed most of the time."

"Why don't we ask the girls to sit, Anu?"

She got up and began carrying upright wooden seats from the wall. Then she arranged them in a circle with Anu's help and sat in the center.

There was a hush. The girls' eyes were focused on their visitor. Josie began, "Like all good stories, mine will begin this way: Once upon a time." A loud applause from the girls rose.

"Once upon a time, there was a young teenager. She had rich parents. But she wasn't happy."

"Why, Josie?" Ariana asked.

"Hush, Ariana, mind your manners. Don't interrupt Josie," Anu snapped.

"Well, let me go on with the story, Ariana," Josie said. "You can ask me questions after I finish telling you the story. Um, to continue."

"The teenager's name was Lai. She was lonely as she lived in a village which was far away from the other villages. She had no close friends."

"Did she have an impediment, Josie?" another girl asked.

"Huh? Impediment?"

"Yes, like a lame leg."

"Oh, well, she didn't. But it depends on what you regard as a setback. Some people don't regard their impediment as setbacks."

"Why not?" the girls chorused.

"Well, if you let me tell you the whole story, you'll realize what I mean."

The girls fell silent.

"Um, to continue."

"There was a rich man in the next province. When it was time to marry, he looked for a rich bride. But all the ones he saw were from poor families in the villages close to his."

"His mother urged him, 'You must get a girl from a rich family. There's one in another province. I'll make the arrangement of you.'"

"Now this man was a filial son. He allowed his mother to arrange a marriage for him. She chose Lai because she came from a rich family."

"After his mother arranged the wedding, he showed the girl's photograph to his friends. Some passed nice remarks. Some had derogatory remarks. But all of them agreed on one point."

"'Her nose is too large for her face.'"

"The man, whose name was Jack, told his mother about it. But she swept aside their criticisms."

"'She'll make you a make a good wife. Besides, her family is wealthy, and she's the only child. In addition, she's obedient and will please you in many ways.'"

"Her words persuaded him to marry Lai. The wedding day came. The two got married. His mother was right. Lai was obedient. She pleased him in many ways. Even his friends complimented him."

"But they kept nagging him about the one feature which they deemed was her defect - her large nose."

"Meanwhile, his friends married beautiful models. But they all came from poor families. The models had married his friends for their wealth."

"They spent his friends' money on upgrading their looks. And they bought expensive jewelry and cars."

"Not long after that, Jack's friends told him that their wives were draining their money. Lai, on the other hand, invested Jack's savings wisely. Before long, he became richer than all his friends. But he wasn't happy."

"Whenever he looked at his wife, he saw her large nose. He agreed with his friends that her nose was too large for her small face. It looked out of place."

"They influenced Jack to take her to their wives' plastic surgeon to reshape her nose."

"'Why?' Lai protested when she heard his proposal. 'I'm comfortable with my nose. I can breathe well. It doesn't disturb me.'"

"'But it disturbs me,' Jack said to her, 'whenever I look at you. All my friends' wives have tall, slim noses. Why can't you please me?'"

"Lai wasn't happy. She didn't want to submit to a surgeon's knife. She cried many days. This made her nose very red. It upset Jack more."

"He pleaded to her, 'Do a nose reshape. I'll get the most renowned surgeon to do it for you. Money's no problem for us.'"

"Her decision came when she learned that Jack was eyeing a beautiful model who had a lovely nose like that of a Greek goddess!"

"She learned too that the model came from a poor family and was looking for a man to support her needs. Lai's fears overcame her reluctance. She finally agreed."

"Jack was overjoyed. He looked at hundreds of nose shapes from the photographs of the ones the plastic surgeon had."

"However, the shapes were all the same as the other women from his province."

"When he showed them to Lai, she protested, 'But they're all the same shape. If I have Dr. Tze do the job, my nose will be the same as hundreds of other women he has worked on.'"

"But Jack was adamant. The day was set. Dr. Tze did the usual job. He reshaped her nose in much the same way as all the other women in the province."

"When Lai was finally fit to meet the public, Jack held a party to celebrate her new nose. Lai was happy for her husband. But when she saw the hundred other women with the same nose shape, she wasn't."

"She knew she wasn't unique anymore. She looked ordinary, just like the other women in the society. At the party, all the men spent the evening admiring the women's noses!"

"Because Jack was the richest man in that province, his wife's nose was the most complimented. And Jack was the happiest man that night when he went to bed."

Josie continued her story, "The next day, when Lai's mother visited them, she saw her new nose. She was distressed."

"'Why did you agree to have it reshaped? Don't you know your nose is your fortune?' her mother asked in distress."

"'Whatever do you mean?' Lai asked her in alarm."

"'Our village has a belief that every woman has a feature which brings in wealth into the family. And with yours, it was your large nose.'"

"Lai looked at her worriedly. 'Oh no, you mean from now on our fortunes will dwindle away?'"

"Her mother wailed, 'I don't want to think about it. Your nose has been cut! This means your fortune will be cut too!'"

"There was great distress in the household that day. When Jack learned about the prediction, he turned pale. He apologized to his wife for his folly. 'I don't think having a perfect nose is so nice after all!'"

And with that, Josie ended the story. She looked at the girls. They were all tearful. One said, "Poor Lai."

Another said, "What a foolish man she married!"

Ariana declared, "I don't think being perfect is so nice after all. From now on, I won't complain about my lame l leg! I have a great voice." She turned to the girls. "We all have great voices. What's a lame leg after all!"

Claps from the entrance sounded. "Hear! Hear!" Everyone looked in that direction. Joshua and Ruth stood there, clapping for them.

Ruth declared, "Josie is right, and so are all of you! We may have imperfections, but we have other features which are great. We can always work around our problems with God's help!"

It didn't take Joshua long to agree to sponsor the choir group which had Ariana in it since he couldn't find another group whose voices were as good.

It was arranged that they would visit Mongolia, where the international competition would be held, closer to the time.

When the team completed their designs, they decided to return to Singapore.

Just before they left, Josie commented to Henk, "I thought my dad said Mongolians have long names. The ones I met all had short names."

Henk grinned. "That's because I shortened them for your benefit!"

THIRTEEN

The day after Josie returned, Fred called her. "Dinner tonight?"

She wasn't delighted. "Is Kay coming too?"

There was a pause. When Fred's voice said, "I've broken off with her," Josie said nothing. Inwardly, she was glad for her friend.

They met in the same Japanese restaurant. Fred hugged her warmly. "You look lovely. But your skin's so dry."

Josie smiled. "You notice it? The sun there was hot. The air was so dry. My skin will return to normal now that I'm back to the humidity here."

When the *shabu-shabu* came, she ate it with relish. Fred sat silently opposite her, just watching. She didn't ask him about Kay, but he knew she was waiting for an explanation.

"Mm, about Kay," he began hesitantly after a long while. Josie continued drinking her soya soup. "We just didn't gel."

In a burst of confidence, he blurted out, "Kay was too accommodating. I didn't like the way she kept agreeing with everything I said. It was like speaking to a robot!"

"It wasn't conversation in the way real conversations go. I like a woman who argues, gives her views. Not aggressively though, but oh, you know what I mean!"

He threw his hands up in despair.

Josie went on eating while listening all the time. She used her chopsticks to pick up more vegetables from the pot. When the *kurobuta* pork slices were cooked, she picked up two and placed them in Fred's bowl, knowing that he liked them.

She posed a question to him. "Are you going to ask Chloe to look for another girl for you?"

Fred was munching the pork slices. He stopped and looked at her and then said emphatically, "No way!"

He revealed, "I've come to realize relationships cannot be predicted by robots! Um, that is, unless a man wants a robot-like woman who agrees with him in everything!"

"I like relating to real humans, not robots. I prefer a lively conversation when I'm with a human companion. I like arguments, um, not aggressive ones though, but challenges and exchanges of ideas."

He paused and looked at the woman who'd been his friend for years. Then he blurted out, "Someone like you, Josie! I like the way you contribute to our conversation every time we meet."

"Er, you may be maddening at times, but that's what I like about a woman like you. We may even quarrel, but that just spices up our conversation."

He added, "And we always make up in the end!"

She was a little alarmed at the enthusiastic way Fred was describing his relationship with her.

"But, Fred, I'm only an old friend, not your special girlfriend!"

He laughed. "I know, I know. A favorite old friend! I'm so glad we've kept our friendship all these years!"

Josie's worried brow cleared. She spooned some of the *shabu-shabu* soup into his empty bowl.

"I'm glad we're good old friends, Fred." Somehow, the word *old* didn't sound so bad after all.

"Will you help me find my life partner, Josie? You know so much of my likes and dislikes. I trust your choice."

She shook her head sadly. "No, Fred, I'm not a computer. You'll have to find a woman who meets your needs yourself. Only you know what's best. My choice may not be your choice."

She grasped his outstretched hand across the table. "But we'll still be good old friends. That'd be nice."

Fred looked at her with tender eyes. "I respect your suggestion, Josie. Now what would you like to order for your dessert?"

Cheekily, she said, "You know. We've been such old friends that I don't need to tell you, right?"

He retorted, "I'm not Chloe!" And they both burst out laughing at his answer. The light banter helped to dispel the tension between them.

* * *

The designer team settled into a routine. From the masses of drawings and sketches they brought back from Mongolia, they set about innovating and creating new designs.

A month passed. They were still working on the fashions. What they liked, they kept. What they didn't like, they shelved. A few, they discarded.

Henk flitted in and out of the office. He wasn't in some days. "Attending lectures," he told Josie.

One late evening, he entered Josie's office just as she was packing up. "Have dinner with me?"

"Are the others joining us?"

"No, just you and me." His tone was serious. So was his face.

"Is it important? I'm a little tired. Prefer an early night."

"Very important," he said curtly.

She wondered what it was that he considered so important. "Where?"

"There's a newly opened restaurant serving Mongolian barbecue. I'll drive you there."

Before long, they reached their destination. When they were shown to their table, Henk placed the order without asking for her choice. He seemed tense and nervous and kept clearing his throat a lot more.

They watched the beef and chicken slices sizzling on the grill. Instead of sitting opposite her, Henk took the seat next to her. He was quiet, sipping his beer.

After a short while, he reached out for her hand. Grasping it tightly, he asked, "Will you be my wife?"

"What!" Startled, she pulled her hand back.

"Will you be my wife?" he seemed to be pleading her.

Annoyed, she snapped, "What kind of a joke is this? I'm tired, Henk. Let's eat up. I want to go home after this."

His face crumbled. "I'm not joking. I'm asking you to be my wife."

She scowled at him. "It's not funny! You know I'm engaged to Jeremy. Besides, you're my cousin."

"So is he."

Josie was thoroughly disconcerted. When he invited her for dinner, his terse voice indicated that he had something serious to say to her. Now she knew.

"Josie, I need you to be my wife," Henk said earnestly.

"Let's pay the bill. I'm going home!" Her sharp tone indicated her anger.

"Hear me out," he said pleadingly.

"Well, you'd better give me a good reason for your proposal. I've no intention of breaking off with Jeremy. He's coming back by next year. We've discussed our marriage plans!" She moved farther away from him to the edge of the seat, after she declared it firmly.

"I know, I know," he replied agitatedly. "I just need to borrow you for a while."

"Now you're offending me!" Josie scowled. "What sort of woman do you think I am, huh?"

Henk saw not only anger but also bewilderment in his cousin's eyes. "Sorry, I didn't mean it that way. It's just that I need a woman to be my wife for a short while so that I can enter China as a businessman who has a wife."

"China? This is getting wilder! Why China? Which part?"

"Shanghai." He looked at her flushed face and saw her narrowing her eyes, as she tried to work out what he was trying to say to her.

"Do you remember the last time we were in Mongolia? You overheard the man telling me about my parents?"

His words caused Josie to exercise caution. She didn't want to admit that she saw his meeting with the stranger from a distance. "What about him?"

"He contacted me this morning. Told me he knows a man in Shanghai who has more information about the oil deal that went wrong. Um, this man is in the fashion business," he informed her.

"So why can't you go in as a single businessman?" she challenged him.

"Can't. This man knows my parents have a son who's single. If you go in as my wife, he won't suspect it's me. I'll say I'm the son's married friend."

"And what more, we can genuinely say we're in the fashion biz. Your biz is legit."

Since Josie was an intelligent woman, she could foresee the outcome. "What sort of a fool do you think this man is that he'll fall for such an explanation from you?"

"All I want is to find out more about my parents," he said pleadingly, "whether they were genuinely involved in a swindle or if they were framed. I'll pretend I'm looking for information for their son."

"Look, I promised your dad I wouldn't jeopardize you in any way."

"Oh, so you've been talking to my dad without speaking to me first! I think that's very sneaky of you!"

"Josie, Josie, it isn't like that at all." Henk sounded sincere and apologetic.

Josie leaned back. "I don't know, Henk. I really don't know. It seems so far-fetched." Her anger turned to sympathy for him when she saw his crestfallen face.

"We can go in on the pretext of wanting to connect with him concerning his fashion business. You can even talk to this chap about the possibility of doing a joint show to make it appear genuine. It'll be above board."

Josie usually made decisions without much delay. But with Henk's proposal, she was hesitant. "Let me talk to my dad about this."

"No, no, you can't!" Henk interjected quickly. "I don't want him botching up the opportunity for me by rejecting my proposal about marriage with you."

"It's only for a fortnight." His eyes begged her for help. "Nothing can go wrong. All I want is information to clear my parents of any wrongdoing they're accused of."

"Will you help me?" he beseeched her. He could see her calculating in her mind.

Then she burst out, "How about passports? Mine will be in my single name."

"That's not an issue. Many young married women today have maiden surnames written in their passports."

Josie knew he was right. Her friends didn't have passports with their married name. In meetings, they were all addressed as miss, not missus, unless they specified otherwise.

A few had joint names. A woman whose surname was Tan may have a Tan-Koh in her passport to indicate her married status. But that wasn't so popular with the younger married women, who preferred to keep their single surnames.

She saw tears collecting in his dark-brown eyes, the eyes which looked so much like Jeremy's. "Is that so important to you? Clearing your parents' reputation?"

"You'd do the same if they were your parents." Josie knew he was right. She'd never let anyone besmirch her parents' names.

After a long pause, she yielded. "OK, but I'll do it only once. Jeremy must never know about our arrangement. I suggest you refrain from calling me your wife in our meeting with this man."

Relief flooded his tired eyes. He said gratefully, "Thank you, cousin."

However, what they forgot was that people may make plans, but some don't go the way they intend them to go.

In Josie's case, circumstances prevented the venue from being held in Shanghai. The virus spread diverted many away from that city.

Henk informed her of this. "We're moving our meeting to Mongolia instead. I was just told this last night by Wu, the man from Shanghai."

When the design team heard that Josie and Henk were flying to Mongolia to meet the man from Shanghai, they were curious.

"Why are you two going there?" Lea asked. "Isn't the fashion designer from Shanghai?"

"The virus is spreading," Henk said. It was a good enough reason.

Josie left Henk to inform Joshua and Ruth. Naturally, not knowing the real reason, they were supportive.

The next day, they flew into Mongolia. At Josie's insistence, Henk booked adjoining rooms in the Holiday Inn. Josie was relieved when he signed them in under their individual names.

Unfortunately, the manager recognized them. He was affable, but not chatty. To Josie's relief, he didn't ask the reason for their choice of adjoining rooms.

The meeting was arranged over lunch. When they went down to the restaurant, Henk introduced himself to Wu who was a tall, handsome Shanghainese. His suit was expensive. The material was of mixed cashmere and silk, Josie could see.

He didn't stretch out his hand. Instead, he gave her a formal bow. His reason? "Virus!"

Henk clucked sympathetically. "Bad?"

"Getting worse daily. More deaths."

He invited them to sit in the seats opposite him. Before he sat, he asked Henk, "Your wife?" his head indicated Josie. "You told me you're married."

In a brilliant move, which surprised Josie greatly, Henk said, "No, my wife's twin. My wife can't accompany me here. She's a silent partner in Josie's fashion business.

"By coincidence, Josie came to Mongolia to meet some other fashion designers."

"Twin, eh?" Wu mused over the word. "Is your wife joining you later?"

"She's back in Singapore. Um, has another business, which isn't in fashion. Um, didn't feel she wanted to travel. Too many security and health restrictions."

Wu nodded emphatically. "Quite right, quite right. I too wouldn't travel if it weren't for my business." He seemed satisfied with Henk's answer.

Josie herself was immensely relieved that Henk hadn't introduced her as his wife. Earlier, she was worried over how she would explain it to her parents and Jeremy.

Wu said, "Let's have lunch. I've ordered the set." He waved to a passing waiter for attention.

After clearing his throat, Henk said awkwardly, "Er, by the way, my wife, er she, my wife's twin sister, runs a successful fashion business."

"Yes, you said that earlier," Wu reminded him. "I too have a thriving business in Shanghai. Used to have a few outlets in Hong Kong, but my wife and I have closed them. All that turmoil in Hong Kong isn't good for business."

He addressed Josie, "Where are your stores?"

"In Southeast Asia, France, and England."

Lunch was almost over. Josie sensed Henk was anxious to maneuver Wu into giving the information he was supposed to have regarding his parents.

The opportunity came when coffee was served. Henk went directly to the point. "You have information about my friend's parents?"

Wu nodded emphatically. "It contradicts what you told me over the phone."

"In what way?" Henk's voice was curt.

Wu cleared his throat. "Mr. Henk, your parents were more deeply involved than what you told me. They weren't just couriers."

"Not my parents," Henk quickly corrected Wu. "My friend's parents. I'm married. He's not."

"Oh, yes, yes. I was told he is single. But your names are similar—Henk."

Josie felt him tensing at Wu's observation. She quickly intervened, "Mr. Wu, Henk's a common name in our part of the world. Quite a few men in Indonesia have that name."

She added, "And in Holland too, men have that name." Wu gave no response to her clarification. Henk, who was sitting next to her, gave her hand a squeeze of thanks.

Looking intently at her, Wu asked Henk, "Does Josie look very much like your wife? You said she's her twin?"

"Oh yes," Henk said glibly. "Could pass off as her double."

"Ah, they must be identical twins then," Wu said. "Your wife must be very beautiful, judging from her twin's looks." Josie saw admiration shining out of Wu's eyes.

"Mm, yes, yes, my wife's very lovely. She could be a model herself."

Hastily, Josie interrupted him, "Er, we're here to talk about our friend's parents."

"Ah, yes," Wu replied. "They were deeply involved in espionage. Have been for many years. The wife was more cunning. I hear she drew her husband into it. He was a successful businessman."

"What kind of business?" Henk prodded him into sharing.

"Oh, import-export. The kind which enables him to travel widely. That was how the wife used the business to make contacts overseas as a cover-up for her espionage work."

Henk was silent, mulling over the information.

"What about the oil deal that went sour?" Josie asked.

Wu's eyes shifted to her. He appeared to study her intently. "You know about that, Mrs. Henk, um, Josie?"

"Our friend said he didn't believe it involved only millions of dollars. We know oil deals today are big business. Very big," she emphasized.

Then she continued, "We're wondering how it could involve only millions."

"You're very astute, Mrs. Henk, um, Josie. You're right." Wu's eyes probed hers. "I didn't believe it too. Felt in my guts that the man was framed."

She felt uncomfortable at the repeated mistake of Wu. Twice, he addressed her as Mrs. Henk.

Was it intentional? Did he suspect that they were putting on a show? Did he know Henk was the real son?

Inwardly, Josie was dismayed. *Oh no, this is getting more complicated than I thought.*

When Henk recovered his poise, he questioned Wu. "Framed? Why do you say that?"

Wu shared his suspicion. "Your friend's parents were small-timers. They never went into big deals as far as my informers know."

Henk cleared his throat and coughed a lot more, indicating his nervous state. "Do you know anything more?"

"That's all I know for the moment. I'm due to fly off in an hour's time. I'll keep in touch if you like."

"Um, by the way," Wu added as he got up, "I prefer to speak directly to your friend. No offence."

Henk nodded. "We'll see. The reason my friend didn't want to come and meet you was that he was told he was being watched. His life might be in danger."

He added, "He was told the other party desperately wants the money back. That's why he asked me to meet you."

"Yes, yes, there's danger," Wu admitted. "He needs to be very careful." With that, Wu signed the bill the waiter brought. He nodded to them and left.

Back in their rooms, Henk commented, "This is getting more complicated. I don't want to involve you anymore."

Josie was annoyed. "You don't think, do you, Henk? Wu has met me. Do you think he can forget me so easily? Anyway, that was a brilliant answer you gave him."

"Meaning?"

"When you introduced me as your wife's twin!"

Henk laughed. "Introducing you as her twin came out instinctively. It wasn't premeditated. I just felt I shouldn't implicate you by claiming you're my wife. Um, just want to protect you."

FOURTEEN

Later that day, they flew back to Singapore. When Henk reported to Joshua what transpired in the meeting, the older man was astute in his estimation.

"He could be fishing for details. From what you said, I've a strong feeling he suspects you're the son. By the way, did he ask the reason why Josie was present?"

Henk simply said, "He did. I told him she is in the fashion business and came out with me to meet some designers."

What he concealed, though, was that he introduced Josie as his wife's twin. Although it might be a future problem, he felt he could deal with it should it arise later.

* * *

The night they returned, in her sleep, Josie heard loud voices arguing. The night air carried the sounds through her window.

This woke her. Something was happening outside. The sound of voices arguing fiercely came from the land beside.

She went outside to investigate. Much farther on, she saw two figures. She crept closer.

"I'm telling you the man I spoke to was not the son's friend. It was the son himself!" The voice sounded much like Wu's.

A guttural voice shouted belligerently at him. "Then why did you tell him so much?"

"I didn't," Wu protested. "I simply told him his parents were more deeply involved than what he liked to think."

He added, "Um, there was a woman with him. He claims she's his wife's twin. You need to check her out."

The stockier figure with a strong foreign accent asked, "Why was she present?"

"He told me she is in the fashion business and came out with him to meet some people in Mongolia who are in the same line."

"What about the money? Did he say anything about it?"

"He's cunning. Like his mother. He revealed nothing. Just kept prodding me for more information. If you like, I can arrange another meeting with him."

"No, wait, this isn't a good time for travel. Also, he'll be more cautious when he's suspicious."

"Then what do you want me to do?"

"Wait and see. I'll send my men to observe him."

The two men parted. One walked towards Josie. She shrank back under cover of the darkness. Passing close by her, he smelt heavily of bad body odor.

He didn't see her as he strode back to the land which led back to her house. She trailed him. Then she saw him no more. He seemed to have vanished into the night.

As she walked back to her house, she knew it wasn't a dream. By some strange coincidence, the meeting took place in the land beside her house, and she could overhear their plot. But she couldn't explain how it came about.

It was a mystery for several years now how she could hear a conversation some distance away and, at a time, before the real event occurred.

But she didn't bother speculating. What worried her more was whether she should tell what she heard to Henk or her father.

She fell into a troubled sleep.

The next day, when she reached her office, there was no one around. The team was busy with their designing.

At midmorning, Henk strolled into her room. "Lunch?"

"Where? I'm avoiding crowded places."

"How about here in your office? There's a small lounge at the end of the corridor. Bought two Subways."

"Oh, so you knew I'd been staying back in the office." The lounge was empty. The others had gone out for lunch. Henk placed the two long sandwiches on plates. He mixed a coffee for himself and a *tehsi* for her.

When he finished his sandwich and asked, "What do you make of it?" she knew what he was referring to.

"I feel you're not safe. I don't trust Wu."

"Me too," Henk shared.

Josie was surprised at his agreement. "Did you sense this strongly, or is it just a hunch?"

"Wu didn't tell me anything apart from saying that my parents were more involved in it than what I know. I think he's fishing. And I feel he suspects I'm the real Henk."

"Then that puts you in real danger." She leaned forward. "Do you really not know anything about your parents?"

Henk avoided her eyes and didn't respond to her question.

"Didn't you have any inkling your dad was in the import-export business?" Josie persisted in her probing.

She was startled when he said, "Your dad knows."

"Huh? How?"

"Don't forget your father has several contacts overseas. He made inquiries about my background before he agreed to offer the scholarship to me."

"He found out I was somehow related to him. If he knew that, then he must also know my dad ran an import-export business."

Josie digested the information. "Don't tell me my father knew your parents were in espionage?"

He shrugged. "Hard to say. He didn't disclose anything to me." Then he shared, "I had a dream last night. It was so real that I wasn't sure if it was a dream or whether it happened outside my room."

Josie gave a start. She was all ears. She recalled her own night encounter vividly. He watched her eager face, all aglow with expectation.

When he thought back, he was glad Joshua turned out to be not only the man who offered him the scholarship but also his relative. He was grateful that he had also persuaded his daughter to offer him a part-time job in her company.

Over time, as he worked with Josie, he found her argumentative at times but knew it wasn't her fault. It was just that he didn't understand her ways.

In the past, he came across many who were hostile, unfriendly, and downright rude to him. In the orphanage, the workers weren't accommodating with the children.

As a result, he built up a tough front. He learned not to expect kindness from anyone he dealt with. Like the other orphans, he was denied answers to his countless questions.

When he was younger, there were two different sets of foster parents who adopted him at different times. But their harsh attitude and severe discipline on him caused him to run back to the orphanage.

He envied those who had kind foster parents. He longed for the day when someone like them would adopt him. But he waited and waited, until he reached his later teen years. Still, no loving and kind people came to adopt him. By that time, he gave up hope.

Then one day, when he least expected it, Joshua appeared. He came to interview him for a scholarship.

The missions committee had recommended him. His scholastic ability had qualified him for the award.

He recalled Joshua's first question. It had nothing to do with his scholastic ability. He was taken aback when Joshua asked him, "Do you know God?"

What sort of question was that in an interview for a scholarship? But Joshua had repeated the question.

Afraid that he wouldn't get selected, he'd muttered, "Yes," more to please Joshua.

"How well do you know God?" was his next question.

That's a hard one, Henk remembered thinking. *What answer should I give?*

He recalled blurting out, "I know he sent you to interview me."

When he saw the frown on Joshua's face clearing, he knew that somehow he'd given an answer which he accepted.

His next question was just as hard. "Will you be willing to go to church each week and study the Bible?"

I didn't even know what a Bible was. The mission school never gave the children one, he recalled.

The thought *Who would give me one?* ran through his mind as he sat that day facing Joshua, who was waiting for his answer.

Finally, he answered aloud, "Yes," more to please him. And he recalled Joshua fishing out a small white leather-bound Bible, which he handed to him.

"Don't let the words of this book depart from you. Read it daily. It'll bring life to your soul and prosper you."

Henk remembered nodding vigorously, more to impress his interviewer. From then on, life wasn't the same.

The day Henk left the orphanage, he didn't have a foster parent. Instead, he had a future, one with two academic degrees, which were made possible with Joshua's generous funding for him at two prestigious business colleges, and another with a family he could call his own.

In addition, he had a home he could go to after his lectures at the university and after work in his cousin's office. He was like any normal adult person with a family to go home to!

Josie's question called his attention back to the present. "What was the dream about?"

"Huh?" He was jolted by her words. She repeated her question.

He narrated, "Deep in the night, I heard voices arguing. One sounded like Wu's. He said some things to another person, things I couldn't hear clearly."

Josie was excited. "Did the other person have a foreign accent?"

"Huh?" Henk knitted his eyebrow and scratched the side of his head in puzzlement. "You heard it too? In your dream? That makes two of us."

She avoided giving him a confirmation. Instead, she asked, "What did you hear, Henk?" for she was anxious to know what he heard.

"I heard the other voice saying he'd have me watched. I also heard Wu telling the man he knew I was the son."

Josie's forehead creased. What he told her tallied with what she heard. "What're you going to do now?"

He shrugged, another habit he came to display whenever he was worried and didn't know what answer to give. Just then, voices along the corridor sounded. The others were returning from their lunch.

When they entered the small office lounge, Lea was vocal. "Hey, you two didn't you go out for lunch?"

She caught sight of the Subway paper wrappers. "Oh, you bought something in. Afraid of the virus spread?"

Henk just took the mugs, washed them in the basin, and then popped them on the rack. Josie merely said, "Let's get back to work."

She didn't know that the thought of someone watching them made a deep impact on her mind. It wasn't until she started looking around for possible watchers that she realized it.

Whenever she went out with Henk, she gave a start whenever she saw a man staring at her. One day, she mentioned it to him.

But he only laughed. "Josie, if you weren't with me, if you were with another guy, I'd also want to watch you."

"What do you mean?"

"Aren't you aware how lovely you look? Not just your face, but in your dressing as well. Like a model. And that skin of yours is the envy of many women." His words caused her to rethink.

She mumbled, "Hmm, didn't think of that. Just thought of Wu's warning, that's all."

"Relax. Don't let it bother you." He comforted her with a smile. "Anyway, the one they'd be watching would be me, not you."

But Josie couldn't dispel the uncomfortable feeling that she was being watched. She mentioned it to Henk a month later.

"Is someone watching you when you're alone or whenever you're with me?" he asked her.

She frowned, trying hard to recall. "Can't remember."

"Well, bring a notebook with you. Be like Sherlock Holmes."

"Who?"

"You know that chap in the fiction books. That supposed detective who can solve crimes."

"Note the time, the venue, and." He stopped. "I've an idea. You can draw. Well, draw the face of the person who you say is stalking you."

"What a good idea, Henk! Will do that."

Within a month, Josie came up with different sketches of men she felt were watching her. She showed them to Henk. He studied them seriously.

After looking through the two pads of sketches, he gave a comment regarding three of them. "These look like the same man. Where was he when you sketched him?"

She consulted her notebook. "Near the cafe around the block of my office building. All about the same time, five thirty."

"Oh, then there's nothing sinister about the man." He dismissed her suspicion. "Probably works in the same office block as you or in the next block."

"He could be stopping at the cafe for a cup of coffee. Um, probably about the same time as you, after office."

She gave a huge sigh of relief. "You think so?"

When he saw her anxious face, his long arms stretched out and hugged her. "So sorry I gave you something to worry about. Wish I hadn't asked your help. Now you'll suspect every guy who eyes you."

"Can you erase the thought from your mind?" he urged her.

She sighed. "Will try to."

FIFTEEN

At the dinner, Joshua told his family, "Henk's not joining us. He's the moderator for a discussion at the university. He'll be back late."

He took the book next to him and handed it to Josie. "I told him I'll give him this later tonight. If you're not asleep by then, can you go by the annex and give it to him?"

"I know he usually reads it before he sleeps. Says that's the only time he can expand his knowledge on what's in the book."

Josie looked at the book. It was larger than the small book Joshua had given her years ago when she was younger.

"Hmm, didn't know Henk reads this."

"Oh, yes, he's been reading it since I gave one to him at the interview for the scholarship. But that was years ago."

"He told me the small one I gave him is quite worn out, so I promised to get him a new one. The chap's quite thrifty, I realize. Didn't want to buy a new one."

Ruth joined in the conversation. Smiling, she said, "Perhaps he's waiting for you to buy one for him."

Joshua smiled. "This is the kind of book I wouldn't mind buying for anyone."

"What if Henk returns late, Dad?"

"Oh, he usually returns about eleven. He texts me to let me know whenever he's back."

"He's beginning to look on you as his father." Ruth smiled affectionately at her husband. "I'm glad he's more relaxed. When he first came, I noticed he was very tensed. Seemed guarded even, before he answers anyone."

"Er, Ruth, don't forget he had a hard life in his earlier years. The people in the orphanage weren't kind. The kids there were told that they should be seen and not heard."

"You know about his life there, Dad?"

"I met the ones running it. Stern, unfriendly folks. I'm glad the orphanages in Singapore have nicer helpers."

He added, "Um, especially the ones run by our church."

Ruth laughed aloud. "You're just biased."

She turned to Josie. "How's your relationship with Henk? Look on him more like a brother? More importantly, is he looking on you as his sister?"

Josie shook her head. "Hard to say, Mum. He's moody. Sometimes, so considerate and kind to me. At other times, surly and abrupt."

"But I must say, he's not like Justin who was downright mean to me in my early years. Henk's different."

Ruth sighed. "We all change over the years. Even Justin. He was more disciplined after he served in the army."

"Regarding Henk, Josie, help him adjust. Show him some *familial* and *agape* love. Kindness and love never fail to heal broken emotions," Ruth appealed.

"Not easy, Mum." Josie sighed. "He doesn't reveal much of his past sufferings. Keeps his emotions bottled up inside."

After dinner, she went up to her room. She continued to review and innovate on the various drawings her team had submitted. When her head began nodding, she decided to turn in.

As she got into bed, she suddenly remembered the book for Henk. She texted him, *U back yet?*

She was surprised to read his text. *An hour ago. Waiting for you.* She texted back, *Coming with the book now.* Hurriedly, she wrapped a short coat over her nightgown and left for the annex.

When she reached it, she saw that the door was ajar. After knocking on it, she went in. Henk was sitting on the couch in his pajamas, reading.

She recognized it as her father's old pajamas. She couldn't help exclaiming, "Hey, that's my dad's!"

He smiled. "Yes, he gave me four of his good used ones. No point buying new ones when I can fit into them. We're about the same height and weight."

"He also gave me six of his shirts and pants. They're in good condition. He told me he wore some of them only once because he has so many others."

Josie recalled her father saying Henk was thrifty. She was glad her father's clothes fitted Henk.

He looked quite pleased as his hand ran down the length of the pajamas. "This one fits nicely. Looks quite new too."

"You certainly look good in them," she commented, not knowing what else to say.

"I do? Look good in this?" he smiled at the thought.

A flush crept across her face. She mumbled, "Er, sorry, guess it's not the right thing to say." She tried to repair her mistake by adding, "I'm sure you look good in the shirts too."

Then she hastily thrusted the book to him. "Um, this is from my dad."

He took it and immediately flipped it open to a chapter. Then he patted the seat next to him. "Come, let's read it together. It's an important chapter."

Curious, Josie asked him, "Why is it so important?"

His face grew serious. "It's about your armor, our armor. It's both defensive and offensive."

"Are we going to war?"

"We're in a daily war, don't you know?"

Unclear as to his meaning, she sought for clarification. He looked up at her as she stood there.

"If you stand over me, you can't read what's in the book." He patted the seat again.

Then he pointed to the chapter and handed her the new book. She sat and read the entire chapter.

Understanding dawned on her as she read. When she handed the book back to him, he stated, "Now you know."

"Read it daily," he urged her. His dark eyes were somber. "Put on your armor daily to protect yourself."

Josie felt a little ashamed. She hadn't been diligent in her reading. When she was younger, she used to read the book every night before she went to sleep. Now that she was older, she dipped into it only when she needed to be comforted by the words.

Her own little book had several tags to help her locate the appropriate verses. She looked at the table but saw no tags on it.

"Don't you have a tag, which you can put in the new book on the chapter I just read? Um, for your reference."

"Don't need it. Although this is a new book, the chapter sequence is the same as in the other book."

He watched her contemplatively. "Do you have a book? I can loan you my smaller one. But you'll have to return it to me once you get your own."

He took the smaller, worn-out book by the table, the one next to his bed. Tapping on it, he said, "This is like an old friend."

"You know, this is the one Joshua gave me when I first met him at the orphanage for the interview."

"I remember his instruction. 'Don't let the words of this book depart from you. Read it daily. They'll bring life to your soul and cause you to prosper.'"

He paused awhile, recollecting the past. "Joshua is right. Whenever I'm anxious, I'll recall a verse to help me. I'm sure he must have given you a book and told you the same thing."

A depressed look flooded his face when he uttered, "You're more precious to him than I am." He bent his head over the small leather-bound book which her father had given him and put his lips to it.

A heavy sigh escaped him. He put the book by his side and clutched his head in his large hands. Loud sobs racked his body.

Josie looked on helplessly, not knowing how to comfort an adult person in despair. As he continued to sob, she urged him, "Don't dwell on the past anymore, Henk. You're here with us now. We're your family. We love you."

He repeated her words, "You're my family now." He kept muttering the words, as if to reassure himself of the fact. "Yes, yes, you're my family from now on."

Tenderly, she repeated her assurance. "You're my cousin, Henk. No one can take that fact away from you."

Another sob issued from him. She pulled out a tissue from the box and wiped his flowing tears. She sensed his deep longing to be loved and his loss of his parents, especially his mother.

And she felt utterly incapable of filling this void. She wanted to help him overcome his loss. But how? Her inexperience didn't yield the appropriate words for her to utter to him. So she simply remained silent.

Her presence seemed to comfort him as he released his grief. When his sobs lessened, he wiped his face with another tissue she handed him. They both sat in silence for a short while.

Then she said gently, "It's quite late, Henk. I'm going back to my room."

She left his room with a determination to help him, but how she'd do it, she didn't quite know. When she shut the door behind her, her own eyes were full of tears.

* * *

It was deep in the night. Josie was fast asleep. The clashing sound of metal woke her. The sound came from the direction of the window.

She got out of bed. The flashing of metal in the dim light outside caught her eye.

What is it? she wondered. *Looks like a fight.*

Two dark figures appeared to be jumping about, avoiding each other, as their long weapons flashed about. As usual, her curiosity impelled her to investigate.

She instinctively turned left toward the land beside. She knew that whatever activity took place now occurred in that land.

Above, a dim, watery moon emerged but withdrew almost instantly behind thick black clouds when the metals clashed, as if afraid of the clashing. Only the harsh sound of metal scraping against metal could be heard in the silent night air.

The sound moved farther away from her. Her keen ears followed it, and she moved a little closer. As she stood watching, she saw the slimmer man prancing about wildly, as if in a trance. His body shivered vigorously. He jumped up and down, slashing the air around him, in a bid to destroy whoever or whatever was in his path.

Metal continued scraping against metal as the two swords clashed often. At times, a loud piercing sound issued as metal hit harder against metal.

The other man, the taller one, seemed to be trying his best to evade the slashing of what appeared to be a sword. He was jumping to the left and then to the right. At times, he ran to the back and then sprang to the front to slash out at his opponent.

When the moon came out from behind the black clouds, she caught a glimpse of the person facing her. Shocked, she released a long, loud gasp.

It was the Mongolian shaman, the one with fiery eyes, whom she met in the orphanage! Her gasp must have been loud, for it penetrated the two fighters' ears. They stopped their prancing and looked around.

Quickly, she withdrew into the shadows of the wall.

Just then, the other man turned. Josie gasped louder when she recognized him as Henk! Both men looked around, as if trying to locate the person who had released the vocal vibration into the night air.

Suddenly, she saw Henk's eyes lighting up when he recognized her. At the same time, Boh recognized her.

With eyes shooting out fires and a sword flashing in his hand, Boh advanced menacingly toward her. He was twirling it like a baton.

Fear caused her to be frozen on the spot.

Henk's shout galvanized her into action. "Run, Josie, run!" But when she tried to run, she realized she couldn't. She was rooted to the spot. Fear and apprehension had paralyzed her.

She saw Boh approaching her fast. Henk's voice shouted out urgently, "Put on your armor! Your armor!"

Alas, she had forgotten to put it on. It lay within the book by her bedside. The clashing of metal sounding so close to her caused her to cringe.

Henk shouted more urgently, "Run, Josie! Where's your shield? Your sword?"

She thought in panic, *Yes, yes, my sword!*

Out of the blue, she recalled what Henk told her earlier when she was with him in the annex. "Your armor is both defensive and offensive."

What's the offensive armor I can use? She racked her brain. Desperately, she tried to recall. But her mind was blank. Boh was almost upon her.

Henk shouted, "The word, the word, your two-edged sword!"

What word? She searched her mind desperately. What word was he sword? Her offensive weapon?

Henk, by that time, had reached her. She was crouching on the ground, petrified. Just as her hand was about to cover her head to protect herself, she saw Henk spewing out some words from his mouth.

The words turned into a blazing shaft of fire aimed straight at Boh. An amazing thing happened. She saw the shaft piercing Boh.

Then he evaporated right before her eyes!

It all happened so fast. The next thing she knew, Henk was bending over her and lifting her up. Gently, he remonstrated her, "You forgot your sword. Didn't I tell you to put on your armor daily?"

She was sobbing in fear. "I know, I know. Mustn't forget. Thank you, Henk. I thought Boh was going to kill me. His eyes were shooting fires at me."

Henk reproached her gently, "You forgot you have a shield too, which can quench his fiery arrows."

She couldn't answer him. But she was overcome with relief to know he was there to help her.

"Josie, the armor is complete. There's a piece given to protect every part of your body."

Josie clung to him. "I forgot that!"

Tenderly, he said, "That's what cousins are for Josie. To rescue each other in time of need."

Josie looked at Henk with apprehensive eyes. "He evaporated, Henk. Where's he gone to?"

"Ah, the words I spewed out must have sent him right back to where he came from." Josie didn't understand what he was saying. What words did Henk utter that were so powerful and could have caused Boh to evaporate right in front of her eyes?

She limped back with him. At the boundary of their land, he released her hand.

The next thing she knew, it was bright morning. The sun's rays shone strongly on her face. As she turned away from the glare, she vividly recalled the night fight.

The horror, the terror, and the fear had caused her to be petrified and overwhelmed. Then she recalled Henk's timely rescue.

It must have been a nightmare, she concluded. *A horrible nightmare!*

But was it?

As she was about to get out of her bed, she saw the small white book on the side table. It lay open, as if someone had turned it for her. It was opened to the very chapter which Henk had asked her to read.

What was clearly revealed there were the various pieces of armor given to protect every part of her body.

She recalled him urging her to put on the special armor daily.

But she hadn't, to her own peril!

SIXTEEN

A few weeks later, Josie had a surprise call from Kim Chi, her old school friend. It had been some years now since they communicated. Influenced by her single mother, she was known for her tendency to mix only with children from very wealthy families.

After Kim Chi went abroad for her studies, Josie lost touch with her. Her loud grating voice brought back unpleasant memories of her schooldays association with her.

"Hey, Josie, it's me Kim Chi. Let's have dinner tonight. I'm back. Got married last year."

"Ask Fred and Jeremy to join me and my husband. I'll book the Gourmet Emperor." Josie knew it was a very pricey, newly opened Chinese restaurant.

It had been some years since she heard from Kim Chi. Her voice over the years hadn't changed. It still sounded like gravel scraping on granite.

"Are you there? Did you hear me?"

"I heard you, Kim Chi. What a surprise indeed. Jeremy isn't in Singapore. Studying abroad. But Fred is. Will ask him."

"Is he married by now?" Her inquisitive nature was still there.

"Er, I think you should ask him this yourself."

"All right, but why so secretive? Arrange with him to meet me, will you? Seven thirty tonight."

Josie called Fred, who didn't express surprise. When she told him that Kim Chi had asked if he was married, he laughed.

"What's so funny?"

Still laughing, he explained, "She connected with Qian, her husband, a man from Shanghai, through the computer. Didn't you know?"

"Oh no! And she's happy? Hmm, didn't know you knew about her marriage."

Fred appeared tickled at the thought. "I hear she's very happy. I'm sure her computer input must have been for an obedient husband and one who's a billionaire."

"Well, both her demands were met in this chap. I hear he comes from an extremely wealthy family."

"You've met him? You seem to know a bit about him."

"From the grapevine." Josie could hear laughter in his voice.

"Well, we'll meet him tonight," she replied. "Er, will see how he is."

The Gourmet Emperor was one of the new top restaurants in Singapore, designed for clients in the percentage of the wealthy in the business world.

Its exterior was opulent. Only Rolls-Royce and such make of chauffeur-driven class of cars rolled up to its entrance.

Extremely well-dressed women, some sporting Ruth's unique cheongsam designs, emerged from these cars in stiletto high heels, studded with genuine diamonds.

When Josie arrived in a taxi, the bellhops were taken aback. They were used to wealthy clienteles in a Rolls-Royce rolling up. Those arriving in a taxi, they dismissed as persons of low prestige.

As a result, they stood by without opening the door of the taxi for her. Josie was annoyed. She was dressed in her office outfit, which was made of silk. Her buttons were genuine diamonds, but the bellhops didn't know this. They had dismissed her as a guest who wasn't wealthy and of no consequence.

At about the same time, Fred arrived in his Rolls-Royce. When he got out and spotted Josie, he immediately went up to her and gave her a hug.

"You didn't go home to change into an evening dress?" he asked.

"Um, didn't think it necessary." She took his arm. Together, they entered, leaving the bellhops with mouths wide open when they realized their assumption of her was wrong.

Kim Chi was splendidly dressed. She sported the latest upmarket Shanghai design. Diamonds decorated her thick, small ears.

A heavy chunk of top-grade diamond necklace lay sprinkled down the front of her dress. The jewelry dominated so much of her that guests around were dazzled by them rather than by the person.

But just as well, Josie thought. For without her jewelry, Kim Chi's own figure wasn't much to draw gasps. She'd grown rounder. Her weight made her appear shorter than the time when she was at school.

When Josie entered with Fred, Kim Chi was effusive in her greetings. Her wrists jingled with the diamond bracelets as she shook their hands vigorously. The ceiling lights caught the sparkle of the diamonds.

Josie wasn't sure if the action was intended to attract attention to her diamonds.

Kim Chi embraced Fred and planted kisses on both his cheeks, while her husband watched them passively.

She pulled him forward. "Come, come, meet my oldest friends, Josie and Fred."

Qian was a thin man of average height, just a bit taller than his wife. Clearly, he was not used to all that hugging and kissing. He himself didn't make any attempt to hug Fred or Josie. He merely stood aloof and looked at them with a pale, serious face.

He spoke very little English. When he attempted to speak, his answers were in monosyllables. On the other hand, his replies in Mandarin were fluent.

Josie and Fred, too, were fluent in Mandarin, having learned it at a young age from primary school until they graduated, but Qian didn't know this.

His outstretched hand didn't grasp the other person's hand firmly. He stretched out a limp hand, perfunctorily touched Josie's and Fred's hands, and immediately withdrew his.

Kim Chi had booked a private room. A waiter dressed in a tuxedo hung in the background, carrying an ornate teapot. From time to time, he poured tea into the tiny intricately carved Chinese teacups. It was enough to yield just a sip before it required refilling!

The preordered dishes appeared the moment they sat. Kim Chi dominated the conversation throughout the meal. Her frequent use of the pronouns *I* and *me* excluded her husband.

She never once said "we." Josie realized there was little change in her over the years. Her old habits were still there.

"Why aren't you married?" Kim Chi shot this out bluntly to Fred. "I expected you to marry Josie."

A flush filled his face and Josie's, but he didn't satisfy her with a reason. Instead, he smiled graciously and turned the conversation back to her.

"Why don't you share with us how you both met?"

She giggled delightedly. Grasping Qian's hand, which was placed at the side next to her, she lifted it and kissed it several times. "The computer matched us."

Fred couldn't help looking at Josie when she said this.

"You should try it, Fred," she said enthusiastically. "It's not good to remain single so long."

"How did the computer come out with a right match for you?" Josie asked. "Did you do much input?"

"Nope. I simply did one, and the computer came up with Qian's profile. It was the perfect match for us. We met for lunch, and he proposed."

"Just like that, huh?" Josie stated.

"Uh-huh. He told me his dad, old Qian, encouraged him to find a rich wife."

"My input was for an obedient man who can get along with his wife in every way. The second was for a wealthy man."

"Did your data focus on PRC men only?" Josie asked.

"Nothing of that sort. I said any man. It went online. The data was accessed by men internationally."

Josie gave an inward shudder at the thought of so many men reading the data.

"Did you submit a photo of yourself?" Josie was curious.

"Of course. But it was one of myself when I was ten years younger and slimmer," she said candidly. She was quite open about this.

Josie and Fred looked at Qian when she said this, but his face was impassive. It made them wonder if he understood what his wife was sharing with her friends.

Kim Chi grasped his hand lovingly. "Qian contacted me via e-mail. Said he'd like us to meet up."

"Er, what did you send as input about yourself?" Josie was very curious about this.

Kim Chi thought for a while. "Um, I said I was very wealthy, came from a family among the top 10 of the wealthy in Singapore.

"His input said he was looking for a wealthy woman. Looks were secondary to him according to his data." Kim Chi giggled a little when she said this.

Fred exchanged looks with Josie again. They knew Kim Chi's input wasn't true. She had a mother who was single and not even among the averagely rich.

In kindness, they kept silent. *Does Qian know?* Josie wondered inwardly. He couldn't have. Otherwise, he wouldn't have asked her to marry him within a month of their meeting.

He seemed to dote on her. Josie watched him as he continually spooned rice, steamed vegetables, and soup into her bowl, while he himself ate sparingly. Her every wish was his command, it appeared.

She wondered what would happen when Qian and his father sought to use her family wealth to expand their family business.

When the dessert was served, Kim Chi asked Josie, "When are you getting married to Jeremy?"

"Perhaps next year," Josie replied sweetly.

"How about you, Fred?" Kim Chi said. "You should try computer matchmaking."

Fred replied, "I prefer to choose my own woman. Computers aren't always accurate. They predict women, or men, who agree with you in everything. Doesn't spice up a conversation."

He looked at Qian pointedly when he said this, but the man seemed impervious to this. Josie surmised he may not understand the nuance of Fred's deliberate look.

Josie lifted her glass of red wine. "To each of us. Kim Chi, I wish you and Qian the best in your marriage," she added sincerely.

He gave her a blank look, but Kim Chi was appreciative. She lifted her glass and smiled at them and then nudged him to do likewise. He took his cue from her and lifted his glass.

As they were leaving, Fred offered Josie a lift home. He then turned to Qian and asked in Mandarin, "You OK for transport?"

Kim was vocal. "Qian drove us here in his Rolls." She said this with great emphasis on the make of his car.

"Why don't you get the car?" she told him. "I'll wait outside for you." He obediently left her.

In the car, on the way to Josie's house, Fred passed a remark about Kim Chi. "How can she be happy with Qian as her husband. He's too docile!"

"Oh, Fred, that's not a nice thing to say. If he's happy submitting to her, then I'm sure their marriage will work out well. I know there are some men like him."

She added, "My friend told me that if a mother trains a son to obey her implicitly, then when he marries, he'll transfer that obedience to his wife."

Fred predicted darkly, "Wait until Qian finds out her billions are only in the thousands. What do you think he'll do?"

Josie replied, "I shudder to think of the consequences. But their future isn't ours to worry about, right?"

She added, "Right now, let's think about yours."

Fred sighed. "I've stopped looking for a woman, Josie. I'm contented with just having the occasional dinner with you."

"And with Jeremy when he returns," Josie added this deliberately to remind him of her commitment to Jeremy.

When Josie went to her room that night, she received a call from Jeremy.

"How's my beloved cousin doing?" he asked warmly.

"Missing you a lot," she replied. "Wish you were back in Singapore." When she saw his face on her video call, she commented, "You look thinner and darker. Have you been golfing?"

"Uh-huh, for exercise and some fresh air. Some of the golf courses in the States are great, others average."

"How about you? Been busy designing? Who have you been going out with? Socially, I mean."

"Kim Chi invited me to meet her new husband. Said they were computer matched." On the screen, she saw him frowning. "Is that wise of her?"

"Can't say as they're just married. He's the silent type. Could be due to a language problem. He may not know we're fluent in Mandarin. But he accommodates her wishes readily. Um, in her usual style, she dominated our conversation."

"Our? Did she invite Fred?" he asked sharply.

"Yes," she said shortly.

"And she invited Kay too?" he waited for her answer. There was a slight silence before Josie said, "Um, Fred broke off with her. Found her too agreeable. Prefers a woman who argues a little. Said it spices up their conversation."

"A person like you?"

She didn't answer him. She knew Jeremy didn't like her to get too close to Fred.

To move the attention back to him, she asked, "Jerry, when are you coming back? I miss you a lot."

"Um, missing you too," he replied. "I'm working hard to finish the thesis. Know what? Remember the visit we made to the land beyond before I left for the States?

"Remember the call by the Celestial Gardener to restore the environment?"

"Yes, yes," she replied eagerly.

"I've gone into research into how to restore overused and neglected lands through technology. Learned that many farmlands today are abandoned because of lack of farmhands. I'm onto a project on restoring neglected lands with the use of technology, without the need for heavy use of labor."

He added, "And I'm thinking of ways to make Singapore less dependent on imported labor through the use of technology."

He continued, "Land is precious in Singapore. There are many uses for them, besides accommodating tenants only. In the States, there're a host of great ideas using technology to address environmental problems."

"That's great, Jeremy. Perhaps you can use technology to restore infertile land in our part of the world."

"That's been on my mind for some time," he shared. "Well, time to log out. Have a restful night. Love you, my beloved cousin." He threw her a kiss on the screen.

SEVENTEEN

The evening Joshua returned from overseas, it rained a lot. There was a thunderstorm. The thunder rolled around in the garden outside. In fearsome smashes, it hit the trees around and uprooted some.

Josie and her parents were at the dinner table when they heard it rolling and crashing around.

"Sounds like heavy rain approaching," Ruth said.

"Um, I can even smell it coming," Josie said matter-of-factly as she spooned a ladle of *petai* cooked in tamarind gravy and minced meat onto her plate.

Joshua looked at his daughter contemplatively. Over the years, he came to recognize that she had an ability to sense many things.

He remembered that she had often told him to stop their golf game because she smelled the oncoming rain. Josie had issued the warning, even though the sky was clear and bright. And she was always accurate in her prediction.

When Henk came in from the storm several minutes later to join them, Josie heard a loud clicking and whirring accompanying him. It competed with the loud roll of the thunder. Her face turned pale when she saw the little robot sliding on its wheels by Henk's side.

"Your reprogrammed toy!" Henk announced. She sat tense. Although she heard his words, she wasn't sure if the robot had a new memory. She was still expecting to hear the high-pitched monotone of the robot whining out her name. But it didn't.

Joshua confirmed Henk's information. "I got Henk and my programmer, Kin, to do a reprogram of the robot."

Josie was silent. She was still nervous, although her father had said its data input was changed.

"What would you like to call it? You can work with Henk after dinner and do any input you like."

Inwardly, her mind was in a whirl. The three looked at her when she didn't offer any suggestion.

"Josie, did you hear what your father said?" Ruth broke her silence.

She swallowed hard. "I don't want it," she burst out. "Don't like robots," she declared vehemently.

"Huh?" Henk was puzzled. "But it's every young person's dream to have a pet robot."

"Um, just don't want it," she stubbornly repeated.

"It can help you in your fashion design." Henk tried to be helpful.

She gave a visible shudder. "Just don't want it. It looks odd, rolling around. Can't stand robots."

Ruth said persuasively, "But many young adults find it cute."

Her daughter retorted, "I don't find it cute. This one's quite ugly. Fat and tubby."

Joshua agreed. "Josie's right. In terms of looks, it isn't elegant. Even its voice doesn't sound human. Just a high-pitched monotone. But despite its flaws, it has its uses. New slimmer shapes are being designed to serve us in many ways."

"Where humans can't operate, robots can. They're invaluable. Our company has AIs of different levels of sophistication."

"You know when Kin, my programmer, took out the data box to reprogram it, he noted something odd."

"Whatever do he mean?" Ruth asked.

"The circuits don't seem to be anything like the ones we use here. The sensors, encoders, are totally different."

"And what more, Kin wasn't able to erase one input. Seems to be stuck in the groove. He was able to erase the others, but this one just kept repeating, 'I want a soul. I want a soul.'"

Josie gave a start when she heard the words. The demand was the one she heard the little robot nagging her that night in the land beside when she visited the factory building. Other robots, too, had joined it in its insistence on having a soul. That had annoyed her immensely.

"Perhaps it comes from another land, Dad. You should take it apart and destroy its micro controller. Then put in a new one."

"Hmm, it's strange that you should say that. Kin said about the same thing. I mean, that this robot didn't seem to originate from our country. He also revealed that it isn't from any country he knows, like the States, China, or even India."

Josie fiddled with her spoon nervously. Then she urged him, "Destroy it, Dad."

Henk cast her a speculative look before he intervened, "No, don't do that. Let me take it apart. I will take it to the university and ask some colleagues to have a look at it.

"If it comes from another land, it might be interesting to know which land. There must be a serial number which will enable us to trace the country of manufacture."

"Yes, yes," Josie agreed eagerly. "Take it away. I've no use for robots. Phil and Kye do their designing on the computer. We don't need a robot."

They left the little robot near the entrance. After dinner, they went to their rooms.

Josie had a restless night in her father's house. She was just about to fall asleep when a whirring and a clicking sound woke her.

She jumped up in alarm when she saw the robot by her bed. "How did you get in?" she asked sharply.

"Your door wasn't locked." Josie recalled that she hardly locked her door at night.

"Well, what do you want?" her tone showed her anger. She knew what the little robot wanted before it whined, "I want a soul. Can you give me a soul? You have a soul."

She was exasperated. "Stop pestering me for a soul. I can't give it to you. I'm not your creator. Besides, you're not a human."

"Your creator is a person, a human, just like me. He isn't the same as my creator. You're just a machine."

The little robot was silent. "Well, in that case, since you're so unfriendly, I'll return to my land."

"Yes, yes, go back to your land." She shooed it away with her hand. "You're of no use to me. I don't want you in my house!" She barked at it. She knew machines had no feelings, so she had no qualms in insulting it.

"All right," it said in its monotone without exhibiting any feelings of being hurt. With a loud whirr, it left her room.

From her window, Josie watched it rolling on its wheel toward the land beside. She surmised it was probably going to join the other robots, which she saw assembled there some time ago.

She was very relieved and felt less nervous when she returned to bed. She hoped it had left her for good.

The next morning, when Henk looked for the robot, he couldn't find it. "Did you take it?" he asked Josie.

"Why should I take it?" she retorted. "I told you I don't like robots!"

"Well, it's, er, sort of disappeared." Henk scratched his head, looking quite perplexed, as his eyes scanned the room for it.

When Joshua came down, he, too, was puzzled over its disappearance. "Where could it have gone to?"

"I wouldn't worry about it, Dad. It may have gone back to the land where it came from." When she said that, both Joshua and Henk cast her an odd look.

* * *

A week later, Jem and Don returned from their extended overseas trip. They invited Josie and her parents over for dinner.

"Uncle Don, Aunt Jem." Josie ran to hug them when she entered their house. "You've been away a long time!"

"Yes, indeed." Jem hugged her. "Been a long time since I last saw you all. I remember you left for France to study in a design college just before we left Singapore on our trip."

She held her at arm's length. "Let me look at you!" She and Don examined her critically, but affectionately. Their niece had a special place in their hearts.

Don remembered her as an infant. He used to cradle her in his arms at night whenever Joshua traveled overseas for his business. He often came over to help Ruth with the infant.

Usually, by nightfall, Ruth was too exhausted to look after her baby. She didn't employ a nursemaid to help her, for her friends had influenced her against it.

They told her the nursemaids from across the Causeway were untrained professionally. They were more of a hindrance than an asset, always insisting on a high pay.

Moreover, they insisted on buying new pots and pans. Although the old ones were still in good condition, these women complained that they weren't. After working for six weeks, they usually left and took all the old utensils, which were still in good condition, with them.

As an infant, Josie slept most of the day. But at night, she cried a lot. Don had volunteered to go over to their house to do night duty. Not that he minded. He loved babies, especially his relatives'.

That night, as they chatted with her parents over dinner, Josie saw that both had grown much older. Although Jem's short hair was fashionably cut, gray streaks were visible. Don's thick hair had thinned a little. He, too, had more gray streaks visible.

Elsa, their Filipina helper, had aged too. She wasn't as spritely as she used to be. Ah Ho, the *ma cheh* maid from China, was no longer with them. Whenever Jem and Don were away on a long trip, she'd stay with Josie's family, more because of her meals.

That night, Don ordered their favorite dishes - sea bass cooked in Thai style with hot sauce, chicken *rendang*, soup filled with fish maw, and sea cucumber. There was pineapple rice too.

Jem commented as she took her seat, "You've grown lovelier now that you are nearly twenty-two, Josie. Is Jeremy still studying in the States?"

"Uh-huh. He's returning next year. We plan to get married when he returns."

"That's wonderful news, Josie." Don cast her a very warm, affectionate smile.

Ruth asked him, "And Justin? How is he?"

"Doing medical studies in the States," Don shared.

"Taking after the old man, eh?" Joshua jested.

"We were surprised at his choice," Don told them. "After he gained a degree in science, we expected him to return. But he told us the aptitude tests all showed his inclination toward medicine."

"That's indeed nice for you, Don. Congratulations." Joshua clapped him on the shoulders.

"Your work must have influenced him in that direction," he said to Don.

There was much laughter and rejoicing at the family reunion that night. Just as they were starting on the dessert of sago and pomelo and the green bean soup, Ruth informed them of Henk's presence.

"He's a long-lost relative. When Joshua learned of this, he did some research on Henk's background."

"What do you mean research on his background?" Jem was intrigued by what Ruth said.

"Henk was an orphan when I first met him," Joshua explained. "When I offered the orphanage a scholarship to support their best student for a course of study in a business college, they recommended him."

"He did so well that he was offered a place to do a higher degree in another business school. I agreed to sponsor him for the business studies. I saw good potential in him."

Don concluded, "The results must have been excellent for you to you agree to sponsor him, Josh. I know you help only the top student."

"Hmm, from an orphanage, eh?" Jem commented. "What happened to his parents?"

Ruth leaned forward. "They died in an air crash. But what Josh learned is the surprising part about Henk."

"After he decided to offer the scholarship, he made a search to find out who Henk's parents were. And guess what?"

Jem and Don leaned forward to hear what she was going to share.

"Josh found out that Henk's father, Yanna, was Luke's much older cousin. Since he and his wife, Talia, didn't have any children after they were married for a year, they adopted Luke and Zech, who were their much younger cousins."

"Yanna and Talia were rich. They sent Luke and Zech to Singapore to be educated here, for there were some good schools even then in our country."

"After Yanna and his wife had Henk some years later, they left for Holland to pursue business there. Luke and Zech were left with distant relatives in Singapore to continue their studies."

Don let out a whistle. "What a small world! Fancy finding out about a relative who's in Holland!"

"That's great news, Josh!" Jem exclaimed. This means that if Yanna was Luke's cousin, then he was my cousin on our father's side."

Don kept repeating, "Amazing. Small world indeed!"

Jem asked, "Is Henk in Singapore?"

"Yes," Ruth answered immediately. "He's staying with us. Studying at NUS. Joshua also arranged for him to do part-time work in Josie's company as the business manager there."

Don remarked again, "Incredible! When do we get to meet him?" He rubbed his hands in anticipation.

"Tomorrow, if you like."

It was arranged then that they came over for dinner the next night. Joshua and Ruth didn't mention anything to Henk as they wanted to surprise him. They told Josie about their decision.

"It would be nice to see his reaction," Ruth said. Josie was excited, for she loved surprises.

At breakfast the next morning, when Joshua casually said to Henk, "Come back in time for dinner, will you?" he raised his eyebrow in inquiry.

"Want you to meet two special people," Joshua said but didn't elaborate.

When they left the table, Henk asked Josie, "Who're they, these special guests of your father's?"

"Oh, you'll know when you meet them." Josie went along with the mysterious game. She could see he was quite mystified.

At seven thirty that night, Jem and Don called to inform Joshua that they would be late.

He told his family, "Let's not wait for them. Let's begin dinner."

Half an hour later, the doorbell rang. Josie ran to open the door for them. Henk heard her effusive greeting and their equally enthusiastic replies.

Joshua, Ruth, and Henk stood up to greet them as they entered. "Henk," Joshua announced, "these are Jem and Don, your other relatives."

Henk's jaw dropped. He was dumbfounded. Clearly, he wasn't expecting to meet another relative. When he said nothing, Josie tugged at his arm. "Henk, another aunt and uncle! Isn't it super?"

In a daze, he muttered, "Yes, yes." He was trying hard to assimilate what Josie told him.

Don immediately gave Henk a bear hug. So did Jem. "Wonderful to meet you, Henk. Welcome to our family circle," Jem burst out in greeting.

Tears flooded his eyes. He was so overcome by their enthusiasm that he was speechless. To give him time to recover from his shock, Joshua announced, "Hey, let's eat before the food gets cold."

Everyone pulled in their chairs. Henk didn't eat anything. He just sat there, looking at Jem and Don, studying them. The others began chatting among themselves.

Don asked, "How did Henk's parents die? Josh, you mentioned a plane crash?"

"Yes," Ruth answered him instead. "Josh did diligent search on Yanna and Talia's background. Took him some years before he found out that they were Henk's real parents."

She went on, "Henk was only two years of age when his parents died. Initially, no one in Holland knew who his relatives were. The authorities put him in an orphanage run by the state after the air crash when they couldn't find his relatives."

"A year later, he and some other boys from that orphanage were transferred to another orphanage for older boys."

Joshua continued with the information, "When Henk entered his teen years, he was transferred to yet another orphanage. This one was run by a mission group."

Jem said, "Hmm, didn't know mission groups ran the orphanages."

Oh yes, they do." Ruth told her. "They heard about Joshua's scholarship offer. Yearly, as we told you, he sponsors bright students from orphanages overseas run by missionaries."

She added, "They invited Joshua to consider their brightest student. Henk's name came up. The principal of the school where Henk was sent to study gave a glowing report of the boy."

Joshua affirmed. "Every year, it's been my habit to sponsor a bright student from an orphanage. Henk's name came to my attention."

A sudden hush descended on the dinner table when everyone thought of it at the same time, although no one uttered the thought outwardly.

It was Josie who vocalized their collective thoughts. "Mum, don't you think it's too much of a coincidence that Henk's name should be brought to Dad's notice for the scholarship award?"

She went on, "And don't you think also that it's too much of a coincidence that Henk is our relative?" Ruth and the others nodded their heads in agreement.

"Josie, we fully agree with what you just said," Ruth declared. "There's someone up there in heaven who's guiding Henk, for sure, so that he can be reunited with his relatives."

There was another hush as everyone digested her words. Henk was overwhelmed by her revelation. He burst out crying loudly.

Ruth immediately rushed up to him. "Henk, Henk, don't cry. We're all so grateful you can be reconciled with our family."

He sobbed out, "Aunt Ruth, I'm crying from gratitude. I was hoping for years that I can find my other relatives. But my hope seemed to diminish with time."

He continued sobbing. In between tears, he said, "I almost gave up in despair when out of the blue, Uncle Josh appeared to help me."

Jem intervened, "Let him cry, Ruth. He's releasing all his despair and frustration over the years."

The women, too, were tearful that night when they realized how God had helped Henk find his relatives after all his years of frustration and despair!

EIGHTEEN

Many weeks after Henk discovered he had another set of relatives besides Josie and her parents, he went about with a lighter heart. The frown hanging over his brow cleared.

When he visited the office, the team and Josie could see that he was no longer tense. He had a lighter spring in his gait.

Everyone was happy for him, for they knew about his unfortunate childhood experiences. They were all touched by the news of Henk's reconciliation with more relatives.

One evening, Josie returned from the office, feeling quite exhausted. She staggered in. Just as she reached the dinner table, she stumbled, startling her parents and Henk. He immediately got up, rushed to her, and helped her to a seat.

Shaking a little, she rested her head on her hand. Her face was white as she sat there, looking quite miserable.

"Shall I call Uncle Don?" he asked her parents.

Ruth replied, "Yes, yes, please do." She held a glass of water to her daughter's lips. "Take a sip. Could be all that rushing about."

The moment Josie sipped the water, she vomited violently. Her parents and Henk stood looking at her helplessly. Henk snatched a napkin and wiped her face and mouth.

Before long, the doorbell rang to announce Don's arrival. "Where's Josie?"

Henk pointed to her. Don felt her pulse and popped a thermometer into her mouth. When he read the temperature count, his face was troubled. "Thirty-eight degrees."

"Henk, help me get her up to her room." Josie was light enough, so he carried her up to her room. He placed her on the bed, while her parents stood anxiously, waiting for Don's advice.

He looked at his niece and then said, "I'll give her something to bring the temperature down. This may be a bad case of flu or." He stopped and looked at the parents. They knew what was on his mind.

Joshua vocalized everyone's fears. "If it's the other virus, how soon will we know?"

"I'll have to do a test to ascertain," Don informed them. "The medical team taking the samples will come to my clinic only on Monday morning. If they don't come by, we might have to take her to the center to test."

"In the meantime, if her temperature rises, let her suck some ice cubes. Old-fashioned way, but it helps. Place some ice in a towel on her forehead."

"That's all we can do for the moment."

Joshua added, "And pray."

Don nodded in agreement. "I'll let Jem know. We'll all pray." He left them with a heavy heart.

Ruth changed Josie into a light nightdress. "We'll take turns tonight watching Josie."

Since Joshua knew his wife couldn't do without a night's sleep, he offered, "Ruth, I'll take the night shift."

Just then, Henk's voice sounded. They'd forgotten about him in their anxiety. "I can take turns with you and stay with Josie in the later part of the night, Uncle Josh."

When he saw Joshua looking at him speculatively, he assured him, "I can do with very little sleep. Whenever I study for my exams, I need sleep for only an hour or two, and then I'll be refreshed."

"You sure?" Joshua asked doubtfully.

"If I can't, I won't say I can, rest assured. It's the little I can do to return your kindness to me. Just tell me what to do with Josie."

Joshua was relieved to hear Henk's offer. He himself was very tired, having just return from a long overseas flight. He was looking forward to a good night's sleep. But then this happened to his own daughter.

Henk suggested, "Why don't I take the first shift?"

He looked at Joshua. "Uncle Josh, you look very tired yourself. As I said earlier, I can do with very little sleep. I'll put on an hourly alarm on my watch to check on Josie's temperature."

Joshua was grateful for his offer. He left the room after instructing Henk on what to do. "Keep the window open. Have the fan on. Sponge her if her temperature rises. Use the ice cubes in the small fridge on the landing."

"Will do that, Uncle Josh." Henk cooperated.

Ruth came in a while later to check. She was relieved when she saw Henk sitting close by Josie. Placed on the table next to him was the thermometer.

After they both left him, Henk settled on the couch. An hour later, his alarm sounded. He got up, took the thermometer, and measured her temperature. He was alarmed to see it rising.

Quickly, he wrapped some ice cubes in a thin hand towel, which he then placed on her forehead. At the same time, he also placed towels wrapped with ice on her neck and underarms.

Josie was delirious. She kept mumbling incoherently. Henk bent to hear her. When he took her pulse, she grabbed his hand. "Jeremy, Jeremy," she muttered urgently, "help me. I feel so ill."

Henk patted her arm. He prayed fervently for God's healing on the woman he'd come to love like a sister.

He didn't want her to die. She was the only woman relative of his age range who he could relate to.

He appreciated the moments when he could chat with her comfortably. It was as if he'd grown up with her, since he was a child.

When her temperature rose higher in the next hour, he was alarmed. He decided to sponge her after he fed her with some ice water. Then he took her temperature again. It went down a little.

Relieved, he went to the couch to sit and pray. He must have dozed off, for the next thing he knew, his alarm sounded.

He took her temperature again. It was up one degree. He sponged her again, turning her to the side and on her back. The cold wet towels seemed to absorb the heat from her body. When her temperature went down, he settled on the couch.

A few hours later, Joshua came by. Henk had dozed off. When he tapped Henk's arm gently, he awoke instantly. "Huh? Is it time to take her temperature again?"

"Not yet," Joshua said. "I see you've written her temperature in the notebook every hour."

"Yes, her temperature's like a yo-yo. Up and down. Every hour up," he told Joshua.

"Yes, I can read that," Joshua said. "How did you get it down?"

"I sponged her with cold water. Put some ice on her neck, forehead, and underarms. Um, used those." He pointed to the hand towels.

"After the sponging, her temperature went down. I would have taken her for a shower but wasn't sure if you'd like that."

"Where did you learn to do that?"

"Well, before you left the room, you mentioned about the sponging to me. But at the orphanage, often, when the kids had high temperatures, Matron would wake the older boys in the middle of the night to help her. She taught us well."

Joshua nodded his head in appreciation. "Take your rest now."

"I will." Instead of going back to the annex, Henk went to the couch. Within a few seconds, Joshua saw that he was asleep. Clearly, he could doze off easily and be refreshed within an hour.

The next morning, Ruth came to look after her daughter. When Don came by later and read the readings, he wasn't happy.

"We'll give it another day. Maybe just a bad case of influenza. Does she have a runny nose? Or a sore throat?"

Joshua turned to Henk. "Did she complain of any of these?"

"Uncle Josh, she was so sick and delirious that she didn't say anything coherent. But I didn't notice any runny nose. I spooned a little water into her mouth several times."

"Did you sit her up when you did that?" Don asked.

"No, she was so weak. I supported her neck and shoulders and spooned the water into her mouth."

Joshua sought Don's advice. "What do you think of Josie's condition?"

"Give her another day," Don told him. "We'll see if the fever breaks. It may be lower by this evening. I'll decide then. It's the weekend, and the team taking the test won't come till Monday."

"However, if it's very serious, we might have to take her to the hospital. But let's wait and see. I'll come around later."

After he left, Ruth took the morning shift. Joshua asked Henk, "Are you going into the university today?"

"Nope. Lectures are now online. I'll stay in. Aunt Ruth might need me to take the afternoon shift."

Joshua pressed his nephew's arm gratefully. "Thanks, Henk. Would certainly appreciate that. Why don't you do the afternoon shift then? That way Ruth can rest."

"Will do," Henk said willingly. He left them and went to the annex. Joshua told Ruth of Henk's offer.

She was grateful. Elsa came to help her sponge Josie, while Ruth spooned water into her mouth and took her temperature.

It was still unstable. At two o'clock, Ruth went to her room to rest, while Henk did the afternoon watch with Josie. As the hot afternoon mellowed into a cooler evening, Josie's temperature went down some more.

When Henk came to her bedside, she clasped his arm. "Jeremy, I feel so ill. Where's Uncle Don?"

He merely grunted, "Coming later. Rest. I'll spoon some water into your mouth."

Josie was quite weak. Her eyes were closed all the time. She could hardly sit up. Her neck hung weakly on his arm support.

She muttered, "Love you, Jeremy. Glad you came back to see me."

Not wanting to reveal who he was, Henk murmured, "Love you too. Just rest."

She sighed and rested her head on his arm. Seeing her close her eyes, Henk gently lowered her head on the pillow.

By late evening, her temperature was much lower. When Don came around to check on her, he was relieved. "Think it's just a bad flu attack. She'll recover soon. She's strong."

Joshua and Ruth invited him for a meal. "Want a late dinner with us, Don?"

"Um, just a drink." He left the room with them. In the dining room, he asked Joshua where Henk was.

"Oh, he's in the room with Josie. Didn't want to leave her alone. He's quite concerned about her illness."

"He's quite professional, I see," Don told them.

"What do you mean?"

"His notes describing Josie's fever when it went up or down, they're quite detailed. Also, his sponging her and noting down the temperature changes."

Ruth said, "Er, that's good, isn't it?"

"Very good. It helps me know."

Joshua explained, "He told me he learned it from Matron at the orphanage. She made the older boys take turns nursing the younger ones when they had high fever. Um, even sponging them and giving them a shower when necessary."

He added, "She also taught them to spoon water bit by bit into the mouth."

"That helps considerably," Don commented. "As I said, he's quite professional in his nursing method. He's such a help to you at this time."

Ruth mused, "Hmm, I wonder if he's done a nursing course before."

The next morning when Josie awoke, she saw her mother by her bed, taking her temperature. Ruth smiled at her wan face. "Feeling better?"

She looked at the thermometer. "Why, Josie, your temperature's back to normal. How do feel?"

"Weak."

"Do you want some porridge? I'll get Elsa to make you some diluted porridge. Think you can keep it down?"

"Not sure, Mum, but I'll try." She looked around the room. "Um, where's Jeremy?"

Ruth was puzzled. "Jeremy? He's not here. Still in the States."

"Oh, I thought he was the one taking my temperature and sponging me. Also feeding me some water."

Understanding dawned on Ruth, but for some reason, she didn't reveal it was Henk. "Er, could it be your dad?"

"Perhaps," Josie said. "But he looked so much like Jeremy when he lifted my neck and shoulders to spoon water into my mouth." Ruth was silent.

Josie felt light-headed and lethargic. "Think I'll sleep some more, Mum."

"Let me change you into a new nightgown."

She complied. With Elsa's help, her mother sponged her and washed her face and neck. Then she rubbed her arms and legs with argan oil.

"Um, feels good, Mum." Before long, Josie fell asleep.

When Don came in the evening, he was pleased to see his niece much better. "Think you can move out of bed and sit on the couch? A little movement and sitting up will help you exercise your limbs."

"I'll try." With Don's help, she moved slowly to the couch. As she sat, a little white book on the table caught her eye. It was the one which was usually on her bedside table.

"How did it get there?" she pointed to the book.

"Don't know," Don said. "Your dad or Henk may have read it when they took turns in the night shift."

"Huh? Henk looked after me at night?"

"Uh-huh. He was helpful indeed. Took turns with your dad. Your mum did the morning shift. Henk also helped with the afternoon shift."

Josie was silent. "He didn't attend lectures?"

"Apparently, the university put all lectures online. Your cousin showed great concern for you. It's not easy doing night shifts. Believe me, Josie, I used to sit at nights with you in my arms when you were an infant."

"Yes, Uncle Don, I remember." She smiled weakly. "You came over to look after me at night whenever Dad was away on his business trips. Mum was too tired to do both day and night shifts."

She stretched her arm and patted his. "I'll always remember your kindness. You've been so kind to me, Uncle Don."

He patted her arm in return. "Well, don't forget your cousin's kindness. He looked after you for three nights. Not easy to stay up at such a late time. Don't forget to thank him."

Josie was silent. Did she mistake him for Jeremy? she wondered.

The next few nights, she slept through them. At nights, she was aware someone took her temperature and dropped a spoonful of water down her mouth.

But she was often overcome with fatigue and couldn't open her eyes to see who it was.

Whenever morning came, her father or her mother was always by her bedside. She never saw Henk.

NINETEEN

One morning, when Josie was feeling better and she was sitting with Ruth beside her, Henk came into the room. His eyes lit up when he saw her.

"Ah, Henk, come in," Ruth greeted him. She turned to her daughter. "You need to thank Henk for doing the night shifts when you were quite ill. He's been so helpful."

Josie exuded a wan smile of appreciation. "Thank you indeed, Henk, for your kind help."

He nodded his acceptance. Ruth said, "You're just in time. Josie wants to take a shower. Please stay in case we need your help."

"Sure," he said as he settled in the armchair by the side. Just as they entered the bathroom, his voice called out, "Don't use too much soap." They wondered why he said that.

The hot shower felt good. Josie poured the fragrant shampoo lavishly and scrubbed her head and hair vigorously. Without warning, she had a dizzy spell. She could feel her head spinning crazily.

As she fell, she hit the protruding tap. Pitching downward onto the floor, she felt the water from the shower hitting her body in full force.

Ruth screamed. "Henk, Henk, help!"

Josie heard him rushing in. The next thing she knew, he had snatched her away from the jet of water. Josie heard the water stopping when he closed the shower tap. Pulling a towel from the side railing, he immediately bundled her in it and tucked her under his arm.

Still enfolding her, he started the shower and then proceeded to wash out the ample lather she earlier poured out on her hair. After he closed the tap, he shouted out to Ruth, "Towel!" With it, he toweled her hair dry.

Her mother clucked worriedly as she stood behind Henk, ready to assist him.

"Towel," he barked for another. After Ruth handed him a fresh one, he set Josie on her feet and whisked off the wet one around her body.

With lightning speed, he wrapped the dry one around her. Then he spun her long hair into a twisted plait and encased it within a smaller white towel.

After that, he lifted her up and carried her back to her bed. Before he lowered her entire body on the bed, he placed another small dry towel on her pillow. As he released her, she felt her head touching the pillow.

"Still feel dizzy?"

She shook her head, amazed at his efficiency and speed. What could have been a bad accident turned out well because of his speedy reaction.

Henk emitted a *tch* of concern when he caught sight of her bleeding forehead. The towel was still wrapped around her head. He pushed it up a little to take a closer look on the wound.

Turning to Ruth, who was hovering anxiously behind him, he called out, "Antiseptic."

Ruth dashed to the bathroom to retrieve it from the cupboard. "Cotton wool," he barked. She handed it to him.

He looked at the tube Ruth handed him. "This is cream. Any liquid antiseptic?"

Ruth went back to the bathroom cupboard and returned with a small bottle of iodine. He tipped the liquid onto the cotton wool and gently pressed it on Josie's bleeding wound.

Josie winced a little. He examined the wound closely.

"Quite a deep cut. Let Don see it later." He left the cotton wool sitting on the wound. A while later, he removed it and pressed a fresh cotton wool on it.

"If it bleeds some more, Don may have to put a stitch or two." Josie was impressed with her cousin's skill.

In a crisp tone, he said to Ruth, "Get Josie a warm drink. But see if she's stable enough to keep it down."

Ruth shouted down to Elsa to mix the drink. When she came back, Henk announced to both women, "I'm going to the annex to have a change of clothes."

They looked at his drenched shirt and shorts. The shower had wet his clothes thoroughly.

After he left them, Ruth commented, "Just as well Henk popped in to see you."

Both mother and daughter mulled over what could have been a bad accident.

Henk didn't appear that afternoon. Joshua came instead to relieve Ruth. Naturally, he heard the entire account of Henk's speedy help from Ruth.

Joshua reflected on his ability. "Wonder where he learned to act so speedily? Hmm, it could be the paramedics course he attended. I remember his biodata recorded that he did a part-time course.

"I also recall he attended a nursing course another year," Joshua revealed. "Apparently, the two courses were offered free of charge for those in the orphanage who showed the interest and aptitude for it."

"The principal must have sent Henk for the training," Ruth commented. "That explains his efficiency when our daughter slipped and fell in the shower."

She confessed, "I was helpless when I saw her collapsing. All I could do was scream for him. I knew I couldn't lift Josie by myself. She's too heavy for me."

"When Henk dashed in and took one look at Josie on the floor, he turned off the tap at once. Then he grabbed a big towel and wrapped her up in it."

"With her tucked under his arms, he opened the tap again and washed out the lather on her hair. She had used a lot of shampoo. Now we know why he told her earlier not to put so much on her hair."

"All in one swift movement!" Joshua left out a whistle of admiration. "We're learning more about our nephew each time." Ruth nodded in agreement.

When Elsa brought in the hot drink, Joshua asked his daughter, with eyes of concern, "You need help sitting up?"

"I'm more stable, Dad," she said. "Will sit up and move to the couch. Help me get out of bed." On the couch, he wanted to spoon the drink, but she declined.

"I can hold the cup, Dad. My hands are quite steady." Her parents sat by the side, watching her anxiously.

The doorbell announced Don's presence. When he came to the room, he was told of Josie's fall and cut on the forehead. He examined the wound.

"Looks like a deep cut. See if the bleeding stops by tonight. If not, I'll put two small stitches on it."

"Who applied the iodine on it?"

"Henk did," Ruth told him. "He's amazing. He knows what to apply to stop the bleeding. He's turning out to be such a help to us."

Don prescribed some tablets to help Josie overcome her dizzy spells. "Just take one for the next two days. And don't stay alone. Have someone go with you to the bathroom."

He suggested to Ruth, "Perhaps you should get Elsa to be with her during the day when you or Henk aren't with her."

He checked on Josie's condition and then reassured them. "She's much better today, except for that fall earlier."

Henk came by later that afternoon. "Went to the office. Some of the team members are down with influenza. They're resting at home. The bug is infectious."

"It's not the other virus?" Ruth asked.

"Nope," Henk replied. "The doctor they consulted was certain of that! Their symptoms are mild. Phil and Kye have no fever. Just a bad headache and runny nose. Lea's holding on her own."

Josie took his hand as he sat beside her. "I can't thank you enough for your speedy help."

He bent to take a closer look at her forehead. "The bleeding's stopped." Josie saw a hint of tears in his dark-brown eyes. He lifted her hand and kissed it.

Then he murmured, "My cousin's so precious to me."

A few weeks later, after Josie recovered well, the team resumed their fashion designing. Ruth suggested that they created designs for children's clothing.

"There's a market for them. Currently, all your designs are for adult women," she told her daughter.

"But, Mum, the market's saturated with children's clothing. I see lots of average and lower-quality clothes in the shopping malls."

"I'm thinking of up-market designs. Remember, we're not targeting the average buyer."

Josie recalled Henk mentioning the same thing. His business foresight impressed her.

She knew her mother's clothes were exclusive. Only the wealthy bought them from her boutique. Moreover, to make her boutique exclusive, Ruth opened only one store.

"By the way, Mum, I was thinking of donating some of our clothes to the orphan girls in Mongolia. You know the one which you and Dad visited, where the lame girl, Ariana, had such perfect pitch? What do you think?"

"Josie, not a good idea," her mother advised. "These girls are from poor families. If you donate clothes of such high quality only once, it wouldn't be fair to whet their appetite for such fashions."

"Um, if you want to help them, you can donate average-type dresses from other stores."

"Send them some once every six months. That way, all the girls have a chance to wear them." Josie appreciated her mother's wisdom.

"Mum, when is the international competition in Mongolia?"

"Er, I think it's temporarily stopped. " Ruth informed her.

In the evening, Henk joined them for dinner. He was silent. Toward the end of the meal, he turned to Josie.

"I'd like us to have dinner tomorrow night in a restaurant. I've a Mongolian model coming for dinner. Do you have a friend who can join us?"

Joshua immediately suggested, "How about asking Fred?"

Across the table, Henk asked, "Fred? Have I met him?"

Josie said, "You met him briefly some time back in the office when he came by to fetch me for dinner."

Ruth explained. "He's a childhood friend. Knew Josie even before she met Jeremy." She turned to her daughter. "I think it's a good idea."

Josie mumbled, "Er, not sure if he's free."

"Does he have a girlfriend by now?" Joshua asked.

Josie blurted out, "It didn't work out."

"Why?" Ruth asked bluntly.

"Um, apparently, the computer didn't find him an appropriate match."

Henk looked astounded. "You mean this Fred chap asked a computer marriage maker?" He scratched his head and then burst out laughing.

Josie was annoyed with him for laughing at Fred.

"What's wrong with that?"

Henk stopped laughing. "I'd want to the choose the girl myself."

"Yes, I agree with Henk," Ruth sided him. "No wonder the match didn't turn out right."

"Er, since Fred doesn't have a girl, why don't you invite him to join Henk and you tomorrow night?" Joshua pressed her.

"I'll call him later," she told Henk. "Where would you like to go for dinner? I'll book the place."

"Er, how about the place where you go for *shabu-shabu*?"

"You know about it?" she wondered how he knew.

"Um, I recall catching a glimpse of you there when you went there for dinner."

His words stirred a memory. That was the second time she saw him. The first was at the Asian Golf Tournament.

"Er, was Fred the chap you dined with that night?"

Josie saw Henk had a good memory. She didn't answer him. "I'll book," she answered shortly.

That night, she called Fred. "You free for dinner tomorrow night?"

"What have you in mind?"

"Er, my cousin Henk would like me and you to join him and his Mongolian friend."

"Girlfriend?"

"Don't know. Only know she's a model he met when we all visited Mongolia. Frankly, Fred, I don't know much about Henk's girlfriends."

"Sure," he replied warmly. "I'll go if you want me to."

He asked, "By the way, does she speak English?"

Josie hesitated. Did the woman speak it? She wasn't so sure. Most of the models she met on her last visit could speak a little. "Er, we'll find out tomorrow night. Anyway, you have me to talk to."

"Sure. Want me to fetch you and Henk?"

"Um, he can find his way there. If you can arrive by seven, that'd be fine."

The evening was warm. Fred arrived promptly. When he met Ruth and Joshua, he gave them a broad smile.

"Haven't seen you both for a long time," he said.

"That's true, Fred," Joshua said. "Come over and dine with us whenever you can."

"Would love to, Uncle Josh."

He left soon after with Josie. His eyes ran down the length of her dress. "Hmm, you're looking very good tonight." He added, "Dressed to impress?"

"Stop teasing me. I'm always well-dressed. My mother made sure of that since I was young."

"I'm not complaining. I'm proud to be seen with you. Does Henk know who I am?"

"He seems to. Um, think you met him in passing some time back when you popped into my office."

"Hmm, can't recall."

By that time, they arrived at the restaurant. Henk was seated at the corner table when they entered. Beside him was an exquisitely beautiful woman. When Josie and Fred approached the table, they stood up.

Henk grasped Josie's hand and gave her a kiss on the cheek. Then he shook hands with Fred.

"Fred, I presume?"

He then turned to the model. "This is Aya, my Mongolian friend. She doesn't speak much English. Er, understands more than she speaks."

He indicated the seats opposite them. Josie felt awkward, not knowing how to carry on a conversation with Aya. Her knowledge of the language was limited.

When greeting Aya, Josie remembered to utter the words she learned in her last visit. "*Sain bin uu*?"

Aya gave her a wide smile, exhibiting polished white teeth. Josie could see that Fred was captivated by Aya's beauty. His eyes were fixed on her face all the time.

After they sat, Henk said, "I ordered the *shabu-shabu* Josie. I know you like it. Aya can fall in with the same order." He turned to Fred. "How about you? Something different?"

Fred was accommodating. "I'll take anything you order." With his eyes still on Aya, he mouthed to Henk, "I hear you're Josie's cousin. I now recall we met some time back when I visited her office."

"Yes, I recall we met briefly," Henk responded. "I've been living in her house annex for some months now. Not such a new cousin."

With slow deliberation, Fred asked him, "Have you met Jeremy?"

"No, not yet, but I see photographs of him in Josie's bedroom."

Fred looked startled. "Bedroom?" The word had deeper implications, Josie realized. Fred would want to know what Henk was doing in her bedroom.

Hurriedly, she changed the subject. "Henk, how long will Aya be in Singapore?"

He turned to the model and translated. She answered him with another of her charming smiles. "Two months."

Fred interjected, "Are you doing a course of study, or er, modeling in some way?"

Henk translated for him. She replied in English just one word: "Model."

Henk ordered *shabu-shabu* for himself and Aya. He cooked the *kurobuta* pork slices and vegetables for them, while Josie cooked hers out of longtime habit for herself and Henk.

She couldn't explain it, but she felt uncomfortable. Henk had his eyes focused on Josie most of the time, as if he were assessing her opinion of Aya, while Fred was watching Aya. Whenever Josie addressed him, he answered her with his eyes riveted on Aya.

Midway through the meal, Aya said something quite lengthy to Henk, to which he replied curtly to her. To Josie's shock, she saw Aya's bright-green eyes throwing out flames.

The thought immediately flashed through her mind in dismay. *Oh no, the woman's a shaman!* Josie recalled Boh, who shot out the same fiery look at her in the orphanage in Mongolia.

She panicked. Should she let Henk know? Surely, he should know! Or didn't he? Such conflicting thoughts ran through her mind throughout the meal.

Aya was arguing fiercely with Henk over something he said to her. Suddenly, she banged the table with a fist. From the tone of her voice, Josie knew she was angry. She didn't need to know the Mongolian language to know Aya was angry.

Anger is a universal emotion. It's expressed in the eyes, the tone of the voice, in the tense demeanor.

With eyes flaming a brilliant green, Aya picked up her tiny purse and then got up. She stormed out of the room. Henk chased after her.

Fred was bewildered. So was Josie. "What's that all about? Why's she so angry with Henk?" Fred asked. He sensed it too from Aya's reaction to Henk's words.

The two never came back to their table. Josie and Fred finished their meal in silence. Fred then picked up the bill and went to pay.

They drove back in silence. "You can let me out here, Fred," she told him at the gate. "I'll walk in."

"Let me know what happened between the two of them, will you?" he asked before she shut the car door.

TWENTY

Josie walked by the annex. She saw the bedroom light on. From the window, she caught a glimpse of Henk on the couch reading the book Joshua gave him.

She knocked on his door. When he opened it and saw her standing in the moonlight, he held out his hand and drew her into his room.

"What happened back there, Henk?" she went straight to the point.

He sighed. "It's a long story. I'm sorry our dinner ended like that."

"What happened to make Aya so angry with you?"

He invited her. "Come and sit here. It's a long story."

But Josie just stood over him, glaring at him, still upset over Aya's behavior and their abrupt exit. He looked at his watch. "It's still early. Do you want a coffee?"

Earlier, Joshua had installed a coffee machine in the room. "I don't drink coffee," she snapped at him.

"OK then, why don't you relax? Sit here and hear me out," he said it pleadingly. She consented because she wanted to know the reason.

"It began some years ago. I came to know Aya at a biz convention. There was a fashion show at the end of it to wind up the convention. The wives were present."

"At my table sat three models. Aya was one of them. I was fascinated by her beauty. She had something unusual in her green eyes. I found myself mesmerized by them."

"Couldn't take my eyes off her. There were other delegates who were as fascinated with her as I was. But she seemed to focus her attention on me, possibly because I was unmarried."

"When I went to the washroom, Aya rearranged her seat so she could sit next to me. I realized this when I returned. It flattered me to see she focused on me when there were richer businessmen present."

"We chatted about inconsequential things throughout the dinner. At the end of it, she gave me her calling card and said she'd like to meet me again." Henk stopped and took a sip of his coffee.

"And then what?"

"We dated. Most of the time, she was the one calling me. I was the one paying for the dinner. But I was so keen to get to know her better that I complied willingly."

"When I got to know her better, I realized there was something unusual about her green eyes. They flashed out fires whenever she was angry."

"Oh, so you saw the fires in her eyes. But what did you do or say to make her angry tonight?"

"I don't know. You must believe me. I was always trying to placate her. I was so in love with her."

"But in all those two years, she never once let me touch her intimately. Said it was the Mongolian culture. No touching, no kissing." Josie recalled their custom during her last visit there.

"Hard to believe what you tell me, though, seeing you were so in love with her." Josie wrinkled her nose in disbelief. She paused and then added, "Wait a minute, was she in love with you?"

Henk sighed heavily. "After some months of courting her, I realized she was never in love with me. She was in love with her own beauty and preoccupied with promoting herself for fashion shows."

"She used me to get biz contacts so that whenever there was a convention or even a small meeting, she used me to arrange a fashion show with her as the main model."

"Huh!" Josie snorted. "I don't believe you. She knows you were so smitten by her, yet she never allowed you even to kiss her. Who're you deceiving, Henk? I'm not a child!"

"You have to believe me. I never once touched her. Don't forget, there were many other men. She used her charms to get contracts for modeling from them too."

"That was why I was stunned tonight when she told me, I'd made her pregnant!"

"What!" Josie pulled her hand away from Henk. "How can she expect you to believe that?"

"That's what I told her tonight. You saw her reaction."

"Henk, Henk, we're living in the twenty-first century. There's such a thing as DNA testing."

"I told her that too, but she insisted the baby's ours."

"I don't believe you!" Skepticism was written all over her face.

"You have to believe me, Josie, when I tell you, she's lying. The closest I got to was to kiss her on the cheek. Nothing more. Don't forget, Aya had a lot of other men she associated with. She used them to promote her career.

"There's something else. When I wanted to stop seeing her, she boasted she knew something about my parents and the oil deal!

"Naturally, I was surprised and intrigued. I wondered how she came to know of it. I asked her, but she kept hedging. Just said she heard it from one of the biz men."

"I went along with her, hoping to learn more about what happened to my parents. But eventually, I found she was just using the information to promote her career."

Josie's sharp mind was active. "Wait a minute, who told Aya that your parents were involved in the oil deal? Someone must have told her. Otherwise, how could she come up with such information?"

Henk shrugged helplessly. "Who knows? She said it was one of the biz men. I was so anxious to know more about my parents that I just accepted what she told me without probing deeper."

"I don't believe you!" Josie threw the doubt at him.

Henk tried hard to convince her. "When she told me that she was pregnant with my child, I challenged her. Told her I knew she had other men."

"I reminded her tonight that we never had any intimate moments. She couldn't pin the pregnancy on me. Told her it was probably one of the many married men she dated."

"That's when she stormed out."

Josie sighed. "I just don't know what to believe. But what I do know is that she's a shaman."

"She's a what?" he looked startled.

"A shaman. Don't you know what that is, Henk. I met one in the orphanage you brought me to. His name was Boh. Like him, Aya's a shaman. Didn't you say earlier her eyes threw out fires?"

Henk repeated Boh's name stupidly, as if trying to recall him. "You spoke to him, Henk, in the orphanage. Surely you must remember. Boh's eyes flashed out fires when he thought I was going to donate money. He was angry with me. Don't you recall?"

When he was silent, she pressed in her point.

"Henk remember you told me Boh feared donations. Said he feared that those who donated money would want to change the children's way of thinking."

She continued to pile more information on him, in the hope he would recall the incident. "Henk, Henk," Josie said urgently, "didn't you see the fires in Boh's eyes that day when we visited the orphanage?"

"And tonight, I saw it in Aya's green eyes. You must have seen the fires. She was so angry with you!"

He muttered, "This is overwhelming me. Can't think straight. What I'm worried about is that if Aya told your parents, they won't want to let me stay on with them."

He groaned desperately. "Help me out, Josie."

"I can't, Henk. Don't you see if the DNA test shows the baby is yours, it'll only show Aya's right."

"But I never touched her. She had other men," he protested vehemently. "I asked her to do a DNA test, but she refused. That made me suspect she was telling a lie. Trying to palm off the baby as mine."

"As I said, I'm the only unmarried man. The other men were married. She was using them to get funds for herself."

But Josie refused to be dissuaded. "You'll have to speak to my dad. Come clean. He's compassionate, and wise. He's dealt with cases which are more complicated than yours."

He groaned. "I can't. What if he throws me out? Tells me to leave his house. I know he has a high moral standard."

"He won't, Henk. He's not that sort of person. He'll listen rationally and then weigh the situation."

"I can't bear to leave you, Josie. This is the first time I've found a real blood cousin in my age group. I've come to treasure Joshua and Ruth and you as family."

But Josie was unmoved by his plea. "It's late, Henk. Let's talk about it another day."

"Before meeting you, I've never had a sister or a cousin I can relate to. Now that I found you." He choked and couldn't go on. Tears filled his eyes.

"I have to go now, Henk. It's quite late. Let's talk about this another day."

She left him and returned to the main building, her own mind in a turmoil.

Though the night was late, Josie spent an hour reading about the armor Henk had told her about, more to calm her disturbed frame of mind.

TWENTY-ONE

The knowledge that Aya and Boh were shamans troubled Josie greatly. She needed to know how to defend and protect herself in the event they confronted her.

Where, or when, it would happen, she had no idea. Instinctively, she sensed there would be a confrontation some time near.

She fell into a troubled sleep. Aya's emerald-green eyes kept invading her mind. She tossed and turned. With a pillow, she covered her head, but the green eyes kept piercing her mind, despite the pillow.

After a restless time, Josie got up. She poured herself a glass of water and sat on the couch, sipping the water. To her surprise, a ray of green light suddenly invaded her room.

Someone was flashing the light, as if trying to detect something in her room. She looked around for the intruder but couldn't see any visible figure. It was weird seeing just the green light probing to locate something.

She sank further back in the couch and watched the light. It swept her bed. Then it moved slowly to her bedside table. It shone on the little white book which she was reading before she went to bed.

Fascinated, Josie wondered what the person wanted to do with the book. She saw the light flip the book up toward the ceiling. Josie was amazed that the light had such power to lift a book!

It hit the ceiling and fell with a thud somewhere near her. Then the light went out. Josie heard a shuffling sound. She saw a shadow leaping out of the window.

She ran after it. A luminous green light lit the path to the land beside her house. Josie hurriedly changed into her shirt and shorts and gave chase.

The green light was moving at a fast pace along the margin of land. Her curiosity overcame her fear. She wanted to know if it was Aya who held the light, as well as the real reason she was visiting her room.

At the end of the pathway, the light took a left turn. Josie abruptly stopped and then cautiously trailed it. In the center of what looked like a bald patch of grass was a luminous red light joining the green light.

They were dim when they weren't actively swung around. It was dark, so she couldn't clearly make out the faces in the shadows.

A voice sounded. Its deep bass tones revealed it was a man. Replying to it was a higher tone. It as Aya's voice, Josie recognized. Who was she talking to?

She was astonished when a third figure emerged beside the two torchlights. He said something in a low voice. It was so low that she couldn't identify the speaker.

They weren't speaking in English. Again, by some incredible chance, she understood the conversation.

The tall, broad-shouldered person spoke in a low tenor voice. "Not my child. It's his." In the darkness of the night, Josie saw a hand pointing to the holder of the red light.

The green light screeched, "It's yours, yours!"

The third person insisted, "Tell her, Boh. Tell her it's yours!" Josie gave a start when she heard the name.

The red light growled, "She told me the child is yours!" The rod of light flickered toward the man's face. Josie had a shock when the red glow revealed Henk. She didn't know what to make of it.

She stood there shivering, although it was a warm night.

"Tell him, Aya, tell him!" Henk insisted forcefully. "The child is Boh's, not mine! Take the test, Aya. What're you afraid of? The truth? You know the truth will set me free of your accusation."

Josie heard her sobbing. "I don't want it to be Boh's. I want it to be yours."

"It's not mine," Henk snapped fiercely. "DNA will prove that!"

Boh gave off an evil screech. "Shamans don't have DNA! You can't prove anything, Aya. If the child has no DNA, then it's mine." In anticipation of this, he chuckled with evil delight.

Josie choked on this new information. She hadn't known about this feature of the DNA before this. Was it real? She knew all humans had DNA. What Boh said sounded more like fiction!

Unfortunately, her choke resulted in a cough and a splutter. She heaved a deep breath but couldn't stop her cough. It came out in ragged gasps.

Boh turned his head when he heard the sounds. He flashed his red rod around to locate the sounds. From it, red hot flames hissed out in her direction.

Aya's green light, with its fiery emerald fires, flashed around. Without warning, the red and green fires became entwined into two circles, twirling around the air space above them. The display of lights was strikingly bright, illuminating the dark night.

Josie watched, fascinated. The circles separated. Each spun above and did a midair jig. Then the lights straightened into thick lines. After doing a dance of some sort, they flew toward each other.

The next thing she knew, the lights had created a broader red outer circle and a thinner, smaller green inner circle.

The strong flares of the fires lit up Josie's face in the darkness. The two stopped twirling their lights when they saw and recognized her.

Immediately, they pulled their lights back. The rods incredibly changed into flaming swords.

Grasping their swords, they turned and sprinted in her direction. She heard Henk screaming out, "Josie, run!"

He urged her strongly, "Run, Josie, run! Don't let their fires touch you." She turned and sprinted away. When she no longer heard any more footsteps pounding behind her, she stopped.

In the next instant, to her horror, she saw herself encircled within two circles of hot fires which the green and the red torchlights blazed out. She was trapped within. She tried to break out of the circles but couldn't. They were stronger than a wire mesh. Sparks scattered and burned her hand.

Henk's voice shouted urgently, "Don't touch the fire! Your armor, Josie, where's your armor? Put it on!"

She remembered reading about it when she went to bed. Somehow, earlier, instinctively, she sensed that there'd be a fight of some kind that night. With whom? She didn't know at that time.

She kicked hard at the thick mesh, hoping to break out of it. But the impact only hurt her toes. More sparks flew out at her.

Henk's voice sounded closer. He was shouting out more urgently, "Your shield, Josie! Take out your shield! You can extinguish the fires with it."

Where was her shield? Where had she put it?

In panic, she screamed out, "I can't find my shield!"

"It's within you!" Josie couldn't comprehend what he meant.

Henk's voice burst out urgently, "Use your shield and your sword, Josie!"

Her hand groped her side. Wasn't that where a sword was supposed to hang like a pistol? But all she felt was a belt. And it wasn't the kind of belt which held a sword.

She saw the hot fiery circles shrinking into smaller circles, hemming her in. She screamed, "Henk, how do I get out? Help me, help me get out!"

Henk kept calling out, "Use your shield, Josie, your shield!"

She screamed again. "I can't find my shield!"

"Then say the word. The word which has power."

"What word, Henk?" she cried out desperately.

"It's in the book. You read it earlier after you left me. Use the word. That's the offensive weapon you're given. It's your two-edged sword!"

Josie searched her memory. Several words came to mind. She was cringing by that time to avoid the flames which were enclosing her.

The red and green fires shrank inward a little more, hemming her further in. The fires were singeing her skin. The strong burning odor assailed her nostrils.

She was overpowered by the smoke and acrid smell. Losing consciousness, she heard Henk shouting out from a distance, "Say the word. It has power to destroy evil forces."

Then she remembered what she had read—the Word became flesh! That was the powerful word she needed. It was the sword she needed to demolish the two.

Her voice grew stronger each time she shouted it out. She saw the two shamans staggering back. Its power had rendered the two shamans helpless.

Blazing shafts of fires shot straight at the two shamans. Both collapsed under the power of attacks from Josie on the inside and Henk from the outside!

At the same time, when Josie realized what the shield within her was, she pulled it out from inside her. Henk had earlier urged her to use her shield. With it, she extinguished the flames around. The singed ground around her was emitting a pungent smell.

By the time the fires died completely, Josie was physically and mentally exhausted. All she wanted was to go back to her land. She looked around for Henk, but he was nowhere to be seen.

Where's he gone to? she wondered.

Without warning, she heard a loud hissing sound behind her. She turned. Before she knew it, a long, large funnel sucked her in. Its force was strong. She went tumbling and tumbling along helplessly.

She was hurled swiftly to the other end when the force spat her out on hard ground.

When she landed, her hand touched dry, orangey red soil.

And it was still night.

TWENTY-TWO

Twinkling above, quite close to her head, within touching distance, were billions of stars which filled another vast space above. They were too many for her to put an exact numeral count on them.

There was silence all around. The place was devoid of anyone. Her muscles ached as she walked to the edge of the ground. Exhausted from the earlier fight on the land beside her house, she staggered on.

Not realizing where she was heading, she almost fell over the side. In horror, she pulled herself back in time. She peered down and saw nothing below. There was just a void. No land. Just nothingness and dark, empty space.

Soon, she realized her bare feet were touching cold soil. It had changed color by then. It was more like mud, a dark-gray mud. She decided to head toward what seemed another endless stretch of land. She plodded on and on.

The scenery along the way was unusual. She saw potholes on the ground. Some even resembled tiny craters, like small moon craters. But was she on the moon?

She shook her head in disbelief. *I can't be on the moon! Perhaps I'm on another planet in outer space!*

The stars were so close to her that she could pluck them with her hand if she wanted to.

Her ears suddenly caught the discordant sound of metal clashing in the distance. *If this is the moon, how can there be metal up here?* she wondered.

She was feeling quite weary. She wished Henk were up there with her. But he had disappeared with the shamans they were fighting against earlier.

The metallic clashes rasped louder as she walked closer toward the sound. Just then, she happened to look at the soil beneath her feet.

The thick orangey red soil caught her eye. It had changed color from the earlier dark-gray mud. There were now cracks on the surface.

Not only did she note the change in the color of the soil, but she also soon became aware that her facial skin was parched and cracked.

There's no moisture here, she observed. *Everything is so dry! No trees or plants around too. Like a desert!*

The skin on her hands was dry and shriveled. *How can anything thrive in this climate?* the thought rolled around her head. Her feet soon took her to where the sounds were growing to a crashing crescendo.

She plugged her fingers into each ear. At the same time, her eye beheld an astounding sight—countless humans fighting fiercely with a million or more robots!

Dumbfounded, she tried to make sense of it all. The question *How did these earthlings come to be up here?* ran through her mind.

The light from the stars was bright, several times brighter than when she was on Earth, and it enabled her to identify men and women in unusual outfits. Tunics from the feet up were pulled right up to their cheeks!

Another group was in tunics and shorts, with fish ball motifs dotted all over the material. There was chaos all around. Men were fighting men, and women fought with other women in close combat! There was also another mixed group of men fighting women!

She saw a group dressed in tightly fitted tops with sleeves that ballooned and long bloomers. They, too, were engaged in a fierce battle.

From the expressions on their faces, Josie could see this wasn't a friendly match. They were ugly and distorted, with fury and determination to win!

The mixed group didn't fight with conventional weapons. From time to time, their hands reached upward and plucked a star from above.

The star had six spikes. In front of her eyes, Josie saw each star transformed into a short glass saber. This shortened or lengthened, according to the strength of the fighter. Up close, she perceived that the stars had different colors, some solid reds, yellows, blues, and greens, but others with varied hues.

In a forward lunge, the saber of the combatants grew longer. When they retreated, it retracted and grew shorter. It was a thrust-and-pull action, much like in fencing.

Further on, for it was a large area which Josie chanced upon, she saw big numbers of robots fighting humans! They were of uneven heights, and they seemed to outnumber the humans.

It was a thrust-and-pull action using metallic weapons. Some fell to the ground, but they quickly bounced back, righted themselves, and continued their fight.

That night, Josie was a spectator to a most unusual combat. *Who are they? Why are they fighting?* She was vastly intrigued. Though she was fatigued, her curiosity filled her with new strength to continue watching the unusual spectacle.

She saw a displaced man by her side getting up and hastily approaching her. He urged her, "Where's your weapon? Hurry, give it to me!"

She saw a robot closing in. Fortunately, its attention was diverted when another human came to the rescue of the man and prodded the machine from behind.

"Your weapon," the man rasped out. He held out his hand.

"I don't have any," Josie replied helplessly. "Why are you all fighting?"

"Don't you know we're at war?" he cast her a pathetic look. "Where are you from? Another planet?"

He rightly guessed this. Josie realized he confirmed her earlier conclusion that she was on a different planet! It was mind-boggling!

"Why are you at war?"

The weary-faced man cast her another pathetic look.

"To see who gets to stay on this planet. Don't you know we're overpopulated?"

"Huh? Overpopulated? Is there such a thing on this planet? On Earth, we're looking for unpeopled planets to send our people to occupy!" she exclaimed. "Our scientists are working overtime to discover them."

The frenzied fighting continued behind them as they conversed. Josie then caught sight of a man snatching a shooting star and throwing it at his robot opponent. There was an explosion. The machine disintegrated.

"Where's your team?" the man barked out.

Josie, for some unknown reason, pretended she had one. "They're on the way."

"Huh? How many of them? We could do with some help. The robots look like they're winning. If they throw us off this planet, we'll only be flung into outer space."

"You better hide." He suddenly threw out this piece of advice to her. "If they catch you, they'll inject you with a virus."

Josie gave a start. "Huh, a virus? Why?"

He growled, "We need to win. The robots kidnapped us from Earth and brought us to this planet to do their experiments."

This is getting pretty wild, she thought to herself.

Aloud, she asked, "What kind of experiments?"

"Virus implant," was his reply.

As he was saying this, she spied a robot approaching them from the corner of her eyes.

"Hurry give me your weapon!" He demanded.

"Where're your team members? We need to defeat the robots," he shouted desperately.

But Josie persisted in her questioning. "What good is the virus up on this planet? There's no one here, but the robots and a lot of humans."

"You don't understand. Humans with the virus will be flung back to Earth so that they can spread it to others. Many will die. If they succeed in decimating the human population, robots can populate and rule the Earth!"

Josie had never heard of this ridiculous possibility in all her time on Earth. A cynical look appeared on her face.

"That's not possible," she retorted. "Robots are only machines. They can't procreate. Unless some humans made more of them. Besides, humans have far more intelligence."

She reasoned, "Why should humans want to multiply robots and allow them to decimate humans? Doesn't make sense!"

The man said darkly, "It's just a matter of time, believe me." He snapped brusquely, "Where's your team? We need reinforcements. Many of us are weakened with the virus. Those like me are fighting hard to destroy the robots."

"How do you destroy them?" she asked because she was interested in this aspect.

"Simple. Just disconnect their circuits. Remove the batteries." It all sounded so simple. But Josie knew warring robots would never allow anyone from disabling them.

"Are you sure you have a team?" Josie could tell from his tone that he was beginning to doubt what she told him earlier.

She decided to tell him the truth. "There's just me. One warrior."

He threw her a disgusted look. "You expect us to win with only one of you?"

She looked at him boldly in the eye. "I have weapons inside me which you know not of."

She recalled her armor in her earlier fight with Boh and Aya. Her offensive weapon, the word. Her defensive weapon, the shield.

Comforted with the knowledge of her superior weapon, she was unafraid. She knew she could hold her own against this army of men and robots.

"Let me see them. I can use them too!"

"You can't. They're inside me." He was baffled at her words.

"Are you from this planet?" he eyed her suspiciously.

"No, I'm not," she replied truthfully.

"Ridiculous!" he sneered. "Whoever heard of a weapon inside the body!"

He made a movement toward her. "Let me see it!"

She moved away hastily. Quickly, she revealed, "You can't see my weapons! They're invisible." He looked even more perplexed.

Suddenly, the cacophony stopped. There was a lull, as if there was a truce. The man and Josie looked at the others around them.

He announced, "It's break time."

"Huh, sounds like school!" She was highly amused.

"We don't have schools up here. Everyone's a skilled warrior," he retorted.

Josie looked around. "No children? Why?"

"I told you, we're overpopulated. Everyone's an adult here. There's no space for children."

Josie had no answer to that. She was just too baffled concerning the complicated situation confronting her.

Out of the blue, she heard a high-pitched monotone screaming out, "Josie, Josie, you're here. Have you come for the virus experiment too?"

Astounded, she saw a small machine rolling toward her. It was the little one from the land beside. Since she was in the middle of strange people, she decided to befriend the machine. "Why are you up here?"

"It's my planet," the robot revealed. "My people are here. I came back to look for your creator. I'm hoping he'll be somewhere on this planet. I want a soul."

Clearly, Kin and Henk hadn't deprogrammed that bit of memory in the machine's system. When Kin told Joshua there was a piece he couldn't delete, she didn't know what it was he was referring to. Now she knew. The machine wasn't made in her world. It came from this planet.

"Well," she said kindly to it, "you can't have a soul. Your creator doesn't have the power to give you a soul."

The little machine asked, "Can you ask your creator to give me one? I want to live forever like you."

Sadly, Josie answered, "We're two different creations. When humans die, their bodies disintegrate. Only their spirits live on. I can't help you on this." The machine turned away and rolled back on its wheels to its group.

"What's this about a soul?" the man asked. He was still standing there. "Why does that robot want a soul?"

Josie sighed. "It's a long, long story. And you don't have the time to listen. You're so busy at war up here."

She added, "When you return to Earth, I'll tell you the story. Um, that is if we ever meet again."

Meanwhile, the fighting resumed. Two humans and two robots were fighting viciously. They moved closer to Josie and the man.

Without warning, the taller robot flipped a black rod at Josie. It unbalanced her. She felt herself flying upward and then plunging down the black void below.

* * *

When she opened her eyes, she found herself back on her bed. Just then, she noticed that a plaster on her left arm had come loose a little. When she pulled it off, she noticed a tiny pinprick in her arm.

"Oh no!" She exclaimed in panic. "Did the robot inject the virus in me?" Josie was in a dilemma. Soon, more pink bumps began to form.

She examined it. There was no itch or pain. She saw clusters of tiny oval pink bumps slowly beginning to spread to her arms, legs, and other parts of her body.

What shall I do? she asked herself in dismay.

She couldn't tell her parents. From past experiences, she knew they won't believe her, especially her mother. This time, she knew her account would never be accepted by her parents, for her visit to outer space was even more bizarre!

And Henk? He'd disappeared that night after Boh and Aya disappeared. He didn't travel to outer space with her. Would he believe her?

The dawn was breaking. She saw a stream of light-crimson morning light slowly sweeping across the sky outside.

And it brought panic within Josie, fear, and even despair!

TWENTY-THREE

When she went down for breakfast, there was no one around. She ate her meal slowly, preoccupied with finding a solution.

As she drained the last bit of the *tehsi*, it occurred to her that the person to verify if she had a virus would be Don. She called him.

When he heard her voice, he greeted her warmly, "Josie, how nice to hear your voice. What can I do for you?"

"Um, ah, um, Uncle Don," she faltered. How could she explain her problem over the phone?

"Is everything okay?" he asked, sensing something was wrong from her hesitations. "Did you want to see me?"

In a rush, she answered, "Yes, yes. I need to see you. But not in your clinic."

"My house?"

"Um, is Aunt Jem in?"

"Er, she's away for the day, retreat or something like that."

"Um, anyone else in?"

He chuckled. "Seems you have something mysterious to share with me. 5:00 p.m. OK with you?"

Josie would rather see him immediately, but she knew he had many patients to attend to. His medical skill and experience were great. Over the years, she learned he could identify several ailments which other physicians couldn't diagnose accurately.

"Josie, are you there?" Don asked, his voice sounding more concerned.

"Yes, yes, 5:00 p.m. sounds good."

"Right, I'll see you then."

By four o'clock, the pink bumps had multiplied considerably into bigger clusters. But strangely, there was no itch or pain.

Before making her way to Don's house, Josie wore a long-sleeved blouse and a pair of long trousers. She put on a mask. It wasn't unusual to wear a mask outside the house for, by that time, the virus was sweeping across the nation.

There was no change in the structure of her uncle's house. Memories of her early life spent there flooded her mind as she entered the gate. The large playing field at the other end of the big garden was still there. No one had bought it, for property prices had escalated.

Schoolboys used to fly kites there. Justin and his friends also flew kites there when they were teenagers. But that day, no one seemed to be flying a kite. The computer had superseded the outdoor kite in popularity.

As she stood there, contemplating whether to ring the bell for Elsa, the headlights of a car swept next to her. Don's cheerful face beamed at her. His window screen was wound down.

"C'mon in," he called out as the gate swung open. He drove into his compound. "So nice to see you. You've matured and grown taller too."

"If the matter isn't too pressing, let me change into a fresh shirt and pants. Let Elsa know if you'd like some tea."

Elsa had served the family for many years since Josie was a young teen. Whenever Don and Jem traveled overseas for a long time, Elsa would stay in Josie's house so she could have good meals with the family.

That day, she was overjoyed to see her. "You're prettier, Ms. Josie, now that you're a young adult," she said with a wide grin. "You want some tea? No *tehsi* here, just chamomile or English breakfast."

"I'm OK, Elsa. Just some iced tea."

"It's so warm today," Elsa observed. "Why are you wearing a long-sleeved blouse?"

Josie pretended not to hear her. Instead, she went to the tall antique cupboard against the wall, which Jem filled with souvenirs she bought on her recent trips abroad.

The older souvenirs used to be stored in a glass cupboard in the living room upstairs. But a violent storm several years ago destroyed the glass cupboards in which Jem's earlier treasures were stored, Josie recalled.

Now new souvenirs were stored downstairs in the antique cupboard, safe from the storms outside.

Don hurried down to join her. As if he knew Josie wanted to have a private conversation with him, he dismissed Elsa. "I'm sure you've other work to do, Elsa. Don't disturb us."

After she left them, Josie rolled up her long sleeves. "Take a look. I don't know how I got this. It appeared this morning when I woke up."

Don pulled his seat closer. He took the outstretched arm and examined the skin carefully. "Hmm, looks like allergy bumps. What was the last thing you did before you went to bed?"

Josie looked down, not wanting to meet her uncle's eyes. She was in a quandary. She just didn't know how to explain her adventure to the planet in outer space.

Would her uncle believe her? She heaved a big sigh. In the past, no one believed her.

Don waited patiently. "Does it itch? Any pain?"

She shook her head. He looked at her elbow. "Hmm, this looks like an injection puncture in your skin.

"Did you have an injection? Who gave it to you?" he asked in a kind, concerned voice.

His tone triggered memories of the past when she was bullied by Justin, his son, when she fell and cut herself whenever she retrieved his kites for him. Her uncle had always rescued her and comforted her.

Big blobs of tears rolled down her face. He held out his arms to comfort her as he used to do when she was much younger.

She bawled like a child. When she had no more tears to release her pent-up fears, she wiped her eyes with her hands. "Sorry, Uncle Don, I shouldn't be doing this. I'm too old for this sort of thing."

He said nothing. She was the daughter he and Jem never had, and she was always his special niece. He was ready to comfort her whenever she needed his help.

He recalled he looked after her when she as an infant. He used to cradle her to sleep. Whenever her father traveled, Don would go to her house to do night duty. Her own mother, Ruth, was too exhausted by night to stay up with a crying baby.

It was Don who looked after her when she had a car accident and when she had a fall from the sampan which she and her friend had sat in during a wild storm.

Now that she was older, twenty-one years of age, she needed his help. He watched her troubled face as he poured some water from the decanter into her glass.

"Take your time. Tell me what happened."

She was still sniffing. He reached for the box of tissues and pulled out two, which he handed to her. She was unsure whether to tell him of her weird adventures.

However, there was no cynicism or criticism in his eyes. All she saw was sympathy and deep concern.

She sat back in her chair, took a deep breath, and recounted the night's event. "It happened like this."

He listened gravely to her unusual account. It took her about an hour to complete her account, which was disjointed at first.

Anxiously, she watched him when she ended her account. Still sniffing, she asked, "What do you make of it?"

He leaned forward to take a closer look. "Can't tell at this stage," he intoned slowly. "If it's a virus and you're reacting to it, you may start with a fever." He stretched out his hand and touched her forehead.

"Hmm, doesn't feel hot." He reached for his medical bag and took out a thermometer. After clicking it on her forehead, he read it. "Nope. Normal."

He asked again, "Does it itch? Any pain?"

She shook her head. "No, nothing. Only the bumps seem to be multiplying."

"Stay here for another hour. Then I'll see if more bumps appear. You could be allergic to whatever was injected into you. How about your body?"

"It's all over my body too."

He continued, "And you didn't see anyone putting the needle into your arm?"

She shook her head. "All I saw was a black rod which the robot raised to hit me. The next thing I knew, I was plunging down the abyss.

"I wasn't even aware I landed on my bed. When I opened my eyes, the first thing I saw was the plaster. After I removed the plaster, a tiny pink bump began forming on my arm and spreading rapidly."

"Let's go up to the living room," he told her. "You can rest on the couch there, watch telly if you like."

He led the way. "Meanwhile, I'm going to my library in the annex to read my medical journals. Um, I want to identify what causes the oval-shaped bumps on your skin. Need a drink? Ask Elsa for it."

Josie was too distressed to want a drink. She shook her head. "I'll rest on the couch." She must have fallen asleep, for the next thing she knew, his hand was tapping her shoulder.

"Let's take a look," Don said in an efficient voice.

She screamed when she saw several pink oval bumps all over her hands, feet, neck, and body. She burst out crying, "Am I infected with a virus, Uncle Don?"

He examined the bumps gravely. "I don't know, Josie. What I'm going to do is take you to the Center for Infectious Diseases. They can take a sample of your blood. The doctors there will know. They should be able to identify what you're allergic to."

He pulled her up. "Let's go." Then he helped her into her long-sleeved coat, and called her father on his smart phone.

"Joshua," he said, "Josie's with me. Has an allergy of some kind. Broke out in rash. I'm taking her now to the hospital."

He listened awhile and then confirmed, "Yes, that's the one."

When they arrived, he signed himself in as a doctor. The staff knew him for he often sent patients to the hospital there. They took the elevator to the second floor.

Someone was waiting. "Don," the bulky, balding man greeted him.

Dr. Pao then turned to Josie. "So you're the one with the problem." He had a kind face. When he asked, "Can you let me have a blood sample?" she nodded her head and submitted.

"Hmm, no fever? Only rash which is increasing all over you, you say." After taking the blood samples, he gave the tubes to a technician standing close by.

Dr. Pao continued talking. "From the looks of it, it could be allergy to food or even soil." He peered at the rashes. "However, it looks more like soil allergy. Food allergy may produce rash, but not with this pattern of clusters."

The word triggered a memory. She recalled walking barefoot on the orangey red soil on the outer planet. She also walked on black, gray mud. Which one was she allergic to?

She waited with Don. It wasn't long before Dr. Pao got the analysis. "Hm, looks like allergy to soil. The clusters are similar in pattern to those who are allergic to desert soil."

He muttered, just loud enough for her to hear, "It's indeed very unusual. You haven't visited any deserts lately?" he chuckled at the thought.

It seemed strange to Josie and Don that he thought of desert soil as it wasn't a common source of allergy in her country.

Josie then asked, "Do you have an antidote for it? Am I going to die if you don't have an antidote?"

Don was silent all that while. He was privy earlier to the truth, for Josie had shared her adventure with him.

Eventually, he suggested, "Pao, perhaps Josie can take an antihistamine."

He chewed the top of the ball pen before answering. "Don, it might. Most unknown allergies have been known to work itself out over time."

Josie heaved a sigh of relief. She thought to herself, *This means I don't need to share with him what happened in outer space.*

A thought struck her. "Um, Dr. Pao, how long before my body develops a resistance?"

"Um, depends on how frequently you visit the place which causes your allergy. Or, if you avoid the place altogether!"

"Take chocolates, for instance," he explained. "The therapy today is to feed the patient a little at a time until she's able to tolerate bigger amounts."

He peered at her through the glasses perched on his nose. "Er, where did you say you visited?"

Josie shook her head. "Um, I didn't."

He sensed her reluctance to share with him. "Well, you're free to go. You're lucky your body doesn't itch or cause you any pain."

Josie thanked him. Don clapped him on the shoulder. "Thanks, Pao, appreciate your help."

In the car, Don said, "I'll send you home and give you some antihistamine. Hope it helps. Just keep your hands covered when you go out until the bumps disappear."

When Josie got back after Don dropped her off at the gate, she walked by the annex. Henk's bedside light was on. Through the window, she saw him reading the new book which her father had bought for him

He's diligent, she thought. *Should I stop by?*

Her urge to find out what happened to him the night on the fight with the shamans impelled her to tap on his door. He opened it and stared in surprise at her.

"What're you doing here? It's quite late."

She smiled a little. "I know. Just popped by to find out where you went to after the fight with Boh and Aya that night."

His face was a blank. "Fight? What fight?"

It was strange that he didn't remember, for she knew he had a good memory.

She stammered. "Er, there was a vicious fight in the land beside. You were there. Don't you remember you helped me douse out of their rings of fires?"

He echoed her. "Fires?" he scratched the nape of his neck, as if trying to recall. "Come and sit awhile. Refresh my memory. Which night was that?"

She was quite bewildered. Surely, he must remember! She sat on the couch, uncertain as to what to say to him.

He lifted her hand, patted it, and asked, "Now what were you saying just now?"

Just then, her long sleeves folded back. His eyes caught sight of the multiple pink oval bumps. Without delay, he pushed her sleeves farther up her arms. His eyes asked a question.

Somehow, Henk's continued ignorance of what happened that night irked her. She knew not why.

Well, if he's going to play a game of pretense, I can play it too. She knew he was waiting for an explanation. She, on the other hand, was waiting for his.

She had an idea. Picking up the book he was reading, she flipped to the page on the armor. He was watching her. Then she presented him the open page.

She saw him reading it. But still, no glimmer of understanding lit his eyes.

He really doesn't remember, she thought, quite puzzled. *Was it only a dream for me? Was there really a fight with the shamans? Did Henk really help me?*

Her mind was in a turmoil. *How can that be? I heard his voice. I saw him spew out the words, even heard him. How could he have forgotten so soon?*

"*Agape* love, Henk. Do you know what that word means?" she said in a last attempt to refresh his memory.

A bleak look shrouded his eyes. His eyes had that faraway look, as if he were recalling someone in the past.

She knew he hadn't fully recovered from the loss of his mother. The little boy in him still missed her.

She got up, smoothed down her long sleeves, and then uttered, "*Agape* love, Henk, that's what real cousins have. Didn't you tell me *agape* love overcomes evil? Isn't that what you told me that night? Remember?"

A tear fell from his eyes. "Yes, *agape* love that's what you have for me. That's what my mother had for me."

Since she knew it was pointless to press him for an answer when he was in that mood, she left him and returned to the main building.

TWENTY-FOUR

Henk was late for dinner. The three of them were already finishing the dessert of bird's nest boiled in rock sugar when he rushed in to join them.

After gulping down his plateful of rice and chicken curry, he pulled out two pieces of paper and showed them to Joshua.

"We've two invitations for a fashion show." His breathless voice showed his excitement.

"One is from Zhang in Shanghai. Apparently, Wu, the man Josie and I met in Mongolia, told him about our company. He invited Josie and me to do a show with his company in Shanghai."

He looked at the others before continuing. "The other is from someone in Dubai in the oil business. Ross's wife, Mina, heads the international community of women there."

"How strange," Ruth commented. "Wonder why he wants to do a fashion show in Dubai."

"Aunt Ruth," Henk said, "there are many international businesses in Dubai."

"Well, Josie, do you feel like holding a fashion show there?" her father interrupted them.

"If Wu's friend is inviting us," she said, "what's his purpose?"

"Huh? What do you mean?" Ruth asked. "Do you suspect an ulterior motive, Josie?"

"Mum, the last time Henk met Wu in Mongolia, it's because he wanted to get information from him about his parents." The three fell silent at her information.

"Hmm, Henk, you're the best person to know if Wu has an ulterior motive," Joshua said.

He scratched his temple. "Um, can't say for sure. Wu did mention that Zhang owns an upmarket boutique in Shanghai. It may be just a straightforward invitation to link with you, Josie."

Joshua said, "Well, speculation at this stage won't do us much good. Why not treat it like an open invitation?"

"You think we should go then?" Josie asked him.

"If it's to your gain, yes."

"How about Ross's invitation?" Josie asked. "As far as I know, most Arab women don't wear sleeveless or short dresses. But I must say, I don't really know much about their dressing in Dubai."

"Er, I think the fashion show is meant for Western women," Henk surmised. "As I said, there's a thriving international community there. You can ask Phil to do some research on it."

"I agree with Henk," Ruth said. "Um, suspect the fashion show is more for the benefit of the Western women there."

"Henk, why don't you write to the secretary who sent you the invitation and ask who the target audience is? That way, Josie will know what dresses to design and take there," Joshua suggested.

"How many days are they holding the exhibition?" he went on to ask.

"Both invitations say the show will be for only an afternoon," Henk answered. He turned to Josie. "If you decide to accept both, who in the team are you asking to join us?"

"Probably Phil, Lea, and Anh," Josie said. "Anh is a superb seamstress. She can resew dresses, make alterations on the spot whenever there is a need to. Lea's color sense is good."

The next day, Phil came up with the needed information. Henk told them, "As Ruth guessed, the Dubai show will be for the international community."

"That means summer or autumn dresses, depending on when we're having it," Josie concluded. "Do you know where we're staying during that time?"

"I think Ross mentioned a stay of three days in a five-star hotel." Henk continued, "Um, in Shanghai, we might be staying in a hotel too."

The following week, the team flew to Shanghai as the invitation was for an earlier date.

They found that, instead of a hotel, they were invited to stay in Zhang's large mansion. When they arrived, a limousine transported them there. Josie was impressed by the size of the grounds.

Zhang was there to meet them at the entrance.

"Mr. Henk?" as he said this, he stretched out his hand to shake Henk's. "And this must be your sister."

"Josie, my cousin." He nodded toward her.

Zhang was a tall, slick, debonair man in his early sixties. His thick graying hair was smoothly gelled back. He wore a double-breasted white suit. The cloth was of superior quality.

He was suave in manners and spoke English with an American accent. "I feel your team will be more comfortable in my mansion, Henk." His smile was charming, and he revealed a perfect set of teeth. He added, "There's too much health check in hotels nowadays."

He was clearly impressed by Josie. He couldn't take his eyes off her, although he spoke to Henk. Josie was used to men looking at her, but this man made her uncomfortable with his scrutiny, as if she were an object for purchase.

Before they left for Shanghai, Henk had cued Josie and her team on the quality of clothes to wear. Only top quality, he stressed to them. He told Josie he would introduce himself as her cousin, for he didn't think Wu would be there.

Two maids came forward to take their luggage as they emerged from the limo. The taller maid, Mei, led Josie first to her room. When she opened the door, the sheer size of it stunned Josie.

There was a closed closet opposite the enormous bed. When the maid opened the door, Josie saw within it a walk-in closet.

The bed was covered with the finest embroidered linen coverlet. On it was laid a sparkling white bathrobe. Laid out on a narrow ledge inside the spacious bathroom were bath gels with a variety of perfume, body oils, and shampoos.

On a side table were a variety of white towels and more bathrobes of different sizes.

In Mandarin, Mei told Lea and Anh, "We'll go now to your room." Josie went with them. Mei opened the door, and Josie saw a smaller room within. However, the room layout and fittings were as luxurious as Josie's.

The maid then pulled open the closed closet door. Within it was another closet, which was a large walk-in.

"For your exhibition dresses," she announced.

On a small table close to the entrance was a table with two narrow, upright mahogany chairs.

The maid indicated an earthenware tea set with two small cups on the table. She then led them to the bathroom, where there was a washbasin with a tap which dispensed hot water. "If you want hot water, just press this knob."

Before she left them, Mei announced, "Dinner is at seven."

"I'm impressed," Lea told Josie. "I'm glad Zhang invited us to stay with him."

Josie went back to her room, did a fresh makeup, and changed into a bright-yellow cheongsam with a spray of orchids down the length, her mother's latest creation.

Lea and Anh changed into floral cheongsams. Since her last visit to Mongolia, Lea had done much more exercise and dieted. Her figure had slimmed down considerably. However, despite a thick layer of makeup, she was unable to conceal the pockmarks on her face.

The three walked down the large staircase. When they reached the last step, they saw a butler carrying a silver tray with a large bowl, heading toward an ornate door.

"Let's follow him," Josie said softly.

He led them into a large dining room. The first person they caught sight of was Henk. He was immaculately dressed in a black dinner suit and bow tie and looked handsome in a rugged way. He was seated on the other side of Zhang.

"Ah, the ladies are here," Zhang announced and got up. He went forward to show them their seats. He lifted Josie's hand and kissed it theatrically. His eyes gleamed with high appreciation as they ran down her entire cheongsam length.

As Josie sat, she saw seven tall, elegantly dressed young women seated at the other end of the long table. Zhang waved a hand in the direction of the women.

"My wives!" He announced.

She wasn't sure she heard him correctly, so she fell silent. As if not satisfied with the seating arrangement, Zhang went up to her and whispered, "Why don't you sit next to me? Lea can sit next to Henk."

She complied, although she preferred to sit next to her cousin. Henk hadn't said a word since she entered the room. Anh sat beside Phil.

Zhang clapped his hand. Immediately, the main door opened. Two more butlers entered, carrying two ornate soup tureens which they placed on each end of the table.

Zhang dominated the conversation. "Tomorrow afternoon, we'll hold the fashion show. My friends attending are among the elite in our society," he boasted.

Before Josie could ask who the models for her dresses would be, Zhang supplied the answer, "My wives will be your models."

He turned to Josie. "I hope you're be able to alter your outfits to fit their figures." His eyes ran boldly down her own figure. "It shouldn't be difficult, for they are about your size, perhaps a little thinner or just a little bigger."

"Er, Mr. Zhang," Josie stammered.

"Oh, call me Zhang," he said generously. "Don't need to stand on ceremony." He seemed to punctuate every sentence with a charming smile, which displayed a gleaming row of perfect front teeth. "Now what was it you wanted to ask me?"

"Er, just wondering when I can meet the girls. Can they come to Lea's room?"

"Certainly," Zhang said. "Let's say eleven o'clock, right after breakfast?"

The rest of the meal was eaten in silence. After that, the team silently trooped behind Josie and left the dining room.

Before Josie entered her room, Lea asked her to go to her room. She then pulled her toward the bedside, where there was a bronze carved table lamp. She indicated a small piece ostensibly attached to the top of the handset of a telephone. It looked like a small microphone.

With her hand, Lea pointed to the piece, mouthing a silent "What do you make of this?"

Josie shrugged a "don't know." Lea pointed to the bathroom. When Josie entered it, Lea shut the door. Then she ran the tap fully to muffle her voice.

She whispered to her, "Why put a microphone in my room?"

"I've no idea," Josie replied. "I'll have to ask Henk. By the way, which room is he in?" she asked Lea.

"The one next to yours."

"OK. I'll go there now."

Lea closed the tap. Quietly, Josie slipped out. She knocked twice. It slid open a little way, and she entered.

To her embarrassment, she saw Henk and one of the young wives in an embrace. From the corner of his eyes, Henk saw her. He released the girl's hand wound around his neck.

"Sorry," Josie muttered and quickly backed out his room. It wasn't long before she heard a rap on her bedroom door.

Henk walked in. He didn't apologize as he approached her. "What is it?" he asked calmly, as if he was picking up a thread of their earlier conversation.

Confused by what she saw between Henk and the woman, she didn't answer him. The memory of the microphone in Lea's room also heightened her confusion.

Henk sat beside her and repeated, "What was it you wanted?"

She burst out, "I don't know what this whole setup is about, Henk, but I just want to go home immediately after the show."

"As you wish," he replied. After he said, "Have a good night's rest," he vacated her room.

Josie slept badly. She awoke the next morning with a king-size headache. A rap on her door sounded. She opened it and saw Lea.

"Do you know there's no breakfast in the dining room?" she told Josie.

Josie sat up, nursing her head. "I'm not sure what you mean. I'm still confused over last night's happenings."

Lea commented, "Me too. Why put a microphone in my room? How about your room? Is there one too?" She immediately began a search for one in Josie's room. "There's none here," she announced after a fruitless search.

Josie held her head in her hands. "I just want to get over the fashion show and go home."

"What do we do now?" Lea asked. "There's no breakfast. Do we go down for it?"

Just then, a knock on the door was followed by the entry of two maids in black-and-white uniforms. One was carrying a tray of toast bread, croissants, strawberry jam, and two pots of coffee.

On the other maid's tray were Chinese buns with black sesame filling and a pot of Chinese tea. Without a word, they laid the trays on the center table. As silently as they came in, they left the room.

Lea said, "I'll call Anh to join us."

When Anh came in, Josie left them to take a shower. She felt a little better after the shower, but the throbbing in her head was still there.

She ate sparingly. Although she wasn't a coffee drinker, she poured herself a cup. The caffeine helped her somewhat. She tried to make sense of yesterday's happening. No logical answer filled her mind.

Henk hadn't helped her to understand either. When he saw how upset she was, he had said nothing to explain his embrace of the young wife.

However, when she thought it over, she knew she had no right to ask him for any explanation. He was only her cousin. On this trip, she was learning a bit more of her cousin's nature!

Josie, too, couldn't reconcile that Zhang had seven young wives all at the same time. Did the law of the country permit that?

Promptly at eleven o'clock, the seven young women rapped on her door. When she opened it, she saw their radiant faces and lovely, bright smiles. They were all in their early twenties, she estimated, no older than herself.

"Er, let's go over to Lea's room," she suggested to them. "The dresses are hung there." They crossed the thick carpeted floor and went to her room.

Anh and Lea took out the dresses to see which fitted the girls. They did a superb job of matching the height and weight of each girl. By the time the dresses were donned, they looked as if they were stitched and designed for each girl individually.

One of the girls spoke good English. When she questioned her directly, "Are you going to be Zhang's number 8 wife?" Josie was stunned. She stopped looping the thread into the girl's hemline.

"Huh? What did you say? Number 8 wife?"

"Zhang told us before you all arrived that he wanted our opinion whether we felt you were suitable to be his wife."

Josie recovered from her shock. She snapped, "What are you talking about! Whoever heard of a man having so many wives? They'll only wear him out!"

The girls tittered and then whispered loudly in English among themselves so that she, Lea, and Anh could deliberately hear them, Josie felt, "What do you think Zhang will call her?"

The tall girl turned to Josie. "Do you know he named us after each day of the week?"

The girl pointed to herself. "I'm Monday. The one standing at the end is Tuesday. Now do you get the drift of what I'm saying?"

Josie, Lea, and Anh gave her a blank look. Then Josie uttered sharply, "Don't be so crude! Does your law permit him to keep so many wives?"

The girls tittered again. They ignored her question. Instead, the last one named Saturday said, with a peal of laughter, "When Zhang asked us what name he should give you, we unanimously suggested, 'Holiday.'"

After declaring that, she and the others burst out in hysterical laughter.

Josie was thoroughly upset. Lea and Anh could see that, for her face was flushed with anger.

Lea spoke sharply to them. "Josie has no intention of being Zhang's eighth mistress! She is engaged to Jeremy and will be married to him when he returns next year!"

Josie was grateful to Lea for her intervention. She turned the conversation hurriedly back to the fashion show. "Stop gossiping! It's close to one o'clock. The fashion show will start soon!" She succeeded in distracting them.

"I'll just change into my outfit. Then we can all walk down together. If you know where the room is, show us."

She returned to her room. After a quick shower, she slipped on Ruth's latest maroon cheongsam, which enhanced her fair skin admirably.

Remembering what Henk had told them about the importance of dressing well, she attached Ruth's set of long diamond earrings into her earlobes.

When she returned to Lea's room, the girls sent up a loud gasp. They sniggered audibly. "Zhang has good taste! She is incredibly beautiful!"

Deep within her, Josie was very disturbed when she heard their remarks. Before they could utter anything else, she said firmly, "Let's go!" She followed them out down the stairs, into a room at the end of the corridor.

When they entered the lavishly decorated room, a roar and a clap from the audience present welcomed them.

Josie saw about twenty fashionably dressed women and distinguished-looking men in their late forties and fifties. They were seated at a comfortable distance from one another in silk-covered, cushioned upright chairs.

Henk took charge. Lifting Josie's left hand up, he introduced her to the group. "This is Josie, the owner, organizer, and designer of all these outfits the girls are wearing." She was glad Henk introduced her by her real name. Then he introduced each girl by name.

"Ladies and gentlemen, the models will now walk down the catwalk. The first is Monday, followed by Tuesday."

Henk's announcement confirmed that the days of the week were really the girls' designated names, given to them by Zhang.

A thunderous clap showed the appreciation of the audience. When the parade ended, Zhang came forward and took Josie's hand. He kissed it, embraced her warmly, and pulled her close to him, much to her discomfort.

Then he announced, "Josie is the exquisite jewel of this show. You can now place your orders with Henk, her business manager."

The guests got up and mingled around. One of them said to Zhang within earshot, "You're the best. Always arranging the best for us. Is she your new wife?"

Another man pumped his hand vigorously. "Zhang, you're the greatest. Your taste is exquisite. And your latest collection surpasses all women."

When he said the last bit, he nodded toward Josie. Then he moved off and mingled with the rest of the guests.

Tea was served. Although Josie was disturbed by what the guests said, she deliberately put aside what she heard, for she was ravenous. So were Lea and Anh.

Since they hadn't had lunch, when they saw the exotic dishes and the array of delicacies on the buffet lunch, they headed for it. They mingled with the other guests and were congratulated on their presentation.

The gathering began to trickle out by eight o'clock. The models were no longer visible. Soon, only Josie, Phil, Lea, and Anh were left in the room.

Before long, Henk came up to them, his face flushed with success. "Well done! Your show's a big hit. All the dresses are bought at an exorbitant price! Some have placed new orders too. Josie, your parents will be delighted with the sale."

He looked at the team. "Shall we have dinner with Zhang and his wives?"

Josie shook her head. She didn't feel like meeting them again. Zhang's hugging was too theatrical for her liking.

"I'm too tired. I'd just like to get back to my room. Let's leave on the first flight home."

Henk noted her drained face and sagging shoulders. He spoke to the rest of the team. "You go ahead and have dinner. I'll take Josie back to her room."

But Lea and Anh refused too. "We had a full high tea. We'll go back to our room."

When Josie reached her room, Henk opened the door. He was just about to enter it when Josie shook her head. "I'd like to be alone, Henk."

Her voice trembled. She was on the verge of tears. When she recalled what one of the young wives told her about Zhang's intention, she was thoroughly upset.

Henk looked at her weary face. "Sure," he conceded. "See you at six tomorrow. We fly off at seven."

Josie hastily locked her door. She threw off her high heels and took a quick shower. The shower refreshed her. As she shampooed her thick hair, she thought of the next day's trip home.

She knew her parents would be pleased to know that the show was a tremendous success from the business point of view.

Leisurely, she wrapped herself in the fluffy white robe and left the belt hanging by the side. She intended to change later into her nightgown. With another towel, she swaddled her long tresses in it, intending to dry her hair in her room.

When she opened the bathroom door, she stopped short. Her front door was opened a little way.

Sitting on the large armchair was Zhang with two fluted champagne glasses. His eyes were gleaming with bright appreciation at the sight of her emerging.

"What're you doing here?" she gasped in shock.

"Waiting for you." A sly smile curved his cheeks. He stood up. In two strides, he came close to her. "Let's drink a toast to your success!"

She felt like a trapped animal and desperately looked around the room for a way of escape.

With one hand holding the glasses, with the other, he pushed the robe a little way down her shoulder.

Just then, a rap sounded on the open door. Henk entered the room. When he saw what was happening, he shouted, "Zhang, what're you doing to my cousin! Why are you here? Your guests are waiting!"

Distracted, Zhang half-turned his head. This was the chance Josie needed. Taking courage by the distraction, she quickly shoved Zhang's hand off her shoulder. Then she dashed into the bathroom, slammed the door, and locked it.

There was a loud rap on her door. Zhang's voice pleaded, "Josie, let me in. You haven't drunk your toast with me yet!"

Trembling all over in fear, dismay, and distaste, Josie donned her nightgown. For extra protection, she put on the bathrobe and wrapped the belt tightly around her waist. Then she sank to the ground and began sobbing.

She could hear raised voices outside, arguing, then a shout, and following that, the front door slamming shut.

Soon, Henk's voice sounded. "Josie, Josie, let me in. Zhang's gone."

Frozen with fear and uncertainty, she just sat there, sobbing.

Henk's voice came through the slit again. "Josie, it's me, Henk. You can come out now. Zhang's gone. It's safe now."

She continued sitting on the floor, not answering him. Then she heard the front door slamming.

TWENTY- FIVE

After a short while, she heard the front door opening. Then she heard two voices. Soon, Lea's voice sounded outside the bathroom door.

"Josie, it's me, Lea. You're safe now. You can come out." It took her quite a while to persuade Josie.

When she finally emerged, Josie flung herself on Lea and cried hysterically.

"Henk, what did you do to make her so frightened?" Lea demanded to know.

"I didn't do anything!" he protested strongly. "When I entered the room, I found Zhang in the room inviting Josie to drink a toast with him."

But Lea refused to believe him. "Something must have happened to make her so frightened. See, she's trembling all over!"

Henk was defensive. "If you must really know, when I entered the room, I saw Josie struggling to push Zhang's hand off her shoulder. She was in her bathrobe.

"What!" Lea exclaimed in disgust. "Atrocious! What sort of man is he to do such a thing to his guest!"

She tried to release Josie's hand, but she clung to it desperately. "Don't leave me, Lea!" She implored her, as hysteria swept over her. Fear snuffed out her logic.

"I'll have to stay with her tonight," Lea said. "I can't leave her in this state." She turned to Henk. "How did he get into her room?"

Josie moaned to her, "I locked the door, Lea. I did. I did!" Lea patted her shoulders. "I believe you, Josie."

Henk drew their attention to the large key on the table. "That's Zhang's key. He must have used it to enter the room."

Josie kept pleading, "Don't leave me, Lea."

"I won't. I'll stay here with you, Josie."

Henk offered, "Do you want me to stay in the room with you too, Josie?"

Josie cried out hysterically to Lea, "No, no, I don't want Henk!"

Lea looked helplessly at Henk. "I can't leave her in this state. But I must return to my room and change into my nightgown. Can you call Anh over?"

When Anh came in, she was shocked at Josie's state. While Henk explained to her, Lea went to her room. He offered Josie a cup of warm water, but she refused to touch it.

"Here"—he pushed the cup to Anh—"she needs to drink some of this. Helps to calm her."

Josie clung to Anh, fearful of letting her go. When she heard Henk's offer, "I'll stay the night with you, Josie," she screamed out in fear, "No, no! I don't want you!"

He shrugged his shoulders. "Look after her until Lea returns," he said. Then he left them.

Anh was bewildered by the turmoil but cooperated willingly when she saw Josie's distressed state. It took Lea and Anh a long time to calm Josie down. Even when she fell into an exhausted sleep, her hand was clutching Lea's.

The next morning, although Josie had calmed down considerably, her puffy eyes and tearstained face still reflected the trauma of the last night.

Zhang wasn't there to see them off. Throughout the flight home, Josie sat with Lea. She wouldn't even look at Henk when he asked her if she was better.

When Phil was informed of Zhang's behavior, he was most sympathetic to Josie. Henk advised the team not to make a big thing of Josie's bad experience. "Don't want to upset her parents." They agreed.

By the time the plane touched down on Singapore soil, Josie was much calmer. She thanked Lea for her support when the limo sent her home.

"Anytime, Josie," Lea said. "Have a good rest."

The team of course was elated when Henk told them the figure of the sales and the fresh orders for the outfits.

Ruth and Joshua, too, were pleased. "Well done, Josie." Joshua beamed a congratulatory, loving smile at his daughter.

But she remained unsmiling.

Two nights later, when the three of them were having dinner, Henk was absent. Joshua was sensitive to his daughter's mood. "You've been quiet since your return. Are you not well? Did something happen over there?"

Since he offered her an opening, Josie decided to mention her experience. She finished her melon soup. Then she sat back and recounted what happened.

Ruth and Joshua listened. At the end of her account, Ruth asked, "You didn't think it a compliment when Zhang revealed to his seven young wives about the possibility of your being his eighth?"

Josie wrinkled her nose in distaste. "Mum, how can you even think of it as a compliment! It's an insult to my moral standard. And to think he asked other women for their opinions even before he proposed to me!"

"I think our daughter has a point. Like us, she has a different moral standard from Zhang," Joshua sided Josie. "He was assuming she'd jump at the chance of being his wife or, should I say, his mistress."

He went on to remark, "Zhang clearly has a different set of principles from Fred's dad, Zhou KeLiang. Zhou was upright and behaved in a dignified way. Didn't even remarry after his first wife died."

He was just as distressed when he saw his daughter's distaste. "Zhang's just the rotten apple. I know several Shanghainese businessmen who are dignified, but very shrewd. Um, sharp in their biz dealings. And they have only one wife."

When Ruth turned to her daughter and asked, "What did Henk have to say about it?" she exploded.

"Don't talk to me about Henk, Mum! He's no better than Zhang!" The disgust in her tone was clearly there. Her declaration took her parents by surprise.

"Oh, in what way, please tell." Ruth was curious.

Josie recounted what she saw in Henk's room. Both parents seemed shocked at first.

After a short pause, Joshua rationalized, "Henk isn't married. I'm not surprised if one of the young wives threw herself at him. I feel his response to her overtures is typical of a young unmarried man. Most would react in a similar way."

He offered an excuse for Henk's action. "It's possible that he may be taken by surprise by the woman's entry into his room."

"What do you mean, Dad? I just think his behavior makes him as bad as Zhang," Josie declared firmly.

Joshua replied, "I'm not defending Henk. Just wondered if the woman took him by surprise when she entered his room and embraced him."

Ruth nodded. "That's possible. We'll have to ask Henk what happened."

Both parents saw that their daughter was indeed upset. Her face turned pale, and she was clutching her hand to stop it from trembling when she told them about Henk.

When Joshua saw this, he decided to probe gently. "Did something terrible happen apart from what you told us?"

Josie burst out crying. Her father got up and wrapped an arm around her shoulder. "Tell us, Josie. It's good to let us know."

In between sobs, she recounted Zhang's intrusion into her room and the incident of the bathrobe.

Ruth snorted, "Disgusting!"

Joshua looked very troubled. "Have you got over it yet?"

"Er, not so sure," she stammered. "Lea was helpful. She stayed the night in my room when she saw how upset I was."

"What did Henk do after the show?" Ruth asked.

"Everything's so hazy. I recall Henk returning with me to my room after the show."

"And then?" Joshua prompted her.

"I told him I wanted to be alone. He left. I locked the room door. Then I took a shower."

"The next thing I remember when I came out of the bathroom was seeing Zhang sitting in the armchair. He got up and came to me, with one hand holding the champagne glasses. With the other, he tried to push the robe off my shoulder."

Its memory caused her to choke and sob. Her parents waited patiently. Joshua handed her some tissues.

When she was calmer, she continued, "When Henk entered the room, that distracted Zhang. I took the opportunity to push his hand off, dash back to the bathroom, and lock the door."

Ruth asked, "And then what happened?"

"After a while, I heard a shout and then the front door slamming. Then Henk's voice called out to me. He told me Zhang had gone and I could come out."

"And did you?" Joshua asked.

"I was so frightened and confused that I didn't know whether to believe him. I just sat there sobbing and trembling. I couldn't even get up from the floor." She choked when she said this bit.

Ruth asked, "And then?"

"Henk then must have gone to call Lea, because the next thing I knew, Lea's voice sounded. She called me to come out. Only then did I open the door."

"Are you feeling calmer now?" Joshua's troubled eyes were full of concern for his daughter.

"That's not all that happened," Josie burst out disjointedly. "Do you know what Zhang named his wives?" Her parents looked very puzzled.

"On the morning of the show, when we were trying on the dresses for the girls, they told me that they were named after each day of the week."

Ruth was amused. "Well, go on. What happened after that?"

"At the show, the audience accepted their names as normal when the girls were introduced."

She choked again, before spitting out the word in distaste. "Normal! And that's not all. He had the audacity to ask the girls to choose a name for me."

"Name?" Ruth was intrigued. "Doesn't Zhang know you as Josie?"

"He does, Mum. But the girls told me they decided to name me 'Holiday'!"

Her parents were taken aback. Then, simultaneously, both burst out laughing.

She glared at them. "What's so funny?"

Ruth tried to stifle her laughter as she said, "Sorry, Josie, but it seems so unimaginative!"

Joshua, too, tried to suppress his laughter. "You say the girls were named after each day of the week? Well, I'm not surprised they came up with 'Holiday' for want of a better word."

He went on to offer a reason for their amusement. "As your mother said, it shows how unimaginative they are." Both were consumed with laughter again.

Josie grumbled, "Don't know what you two find so funny!"

When Joshua was finally able to suppress his laughter, he said, "Josie, your circumstances are quite different from some of the other girls."

She asked, "What do you mean?"

"Well," her father said, "You were born into wealth and have morally upright parents. But what do so many of those other girls have? Um, my guess is that Zhang took them from poor families. A woman from a wealthy family would never consent to be his mistress."

Josie snorted. "And he thinks a woman from a well-to-do family in Singapore will? Well, he should think again!"

"Zhang probably doesn't know much about the people here. My guess is that he hasn't even visited our country," Joshua concluded.

His words consoled her. "You might be right, Dad."

Joshua cast her a sympathetic smile. "And don't forget, Henk is a normal young man looking for love. What do you think he'll do when an attractive young woman enters his room and throws herself at him?"

Josie looked at her father doubtfully. "Is that what you think the woman did?"

"I'm just surmising. Just didn't think Henk's the sort to be trifling with someone's else's wife or mistress."

He thought for a while and then asked, "Do you recall if he was in the girl's room, or was it the other way around?"

Josie replied, "I think he was in his own room because I remember telling Lea, I'll go to his room to ask him about the microphone in her room. It was placed on top of her bedside telephone."

"Hmm, then most likely, she entered his room," Joshua concluded. "Um, and probably came to him on her own accord."

"Microphone, did you say?" Ruth picked up this point. "This is sounding stranger and stranger."

Joshua leaned forward. "Odd that a microphone should be in a guest bedroom."

"Yes, it was in Lea's room, fixed to the telephone handset." Then Josie promptly added, "Perhaps Zhang didn't know Lea was given that room by the maids."

Ruth looked at Joshua. "What do you make of it? It wasn't hidden, just ostensibly displayed." She turned to Josie. "On top of the telephone handset, did you say?"

Joshua hazarded a guess, "Maybe he forgot to remove it after an earlier guest used the room."

"Who knows, Dad," Josie said, disgustedly. "He's one sick man, for sure!"

To take his daughter's focus off her distress, Joshua asked, "Did Henk gain any more information about his parents from Zhang?"

"Um, none that I know of. But I was so busy with the fittings and the show that I never thought of asking Henk. Besides, I hardly saw him, except for that night in his room and at the show."

"I'll ask him when we next meet," Joshua said. His love and understanding of his only daughter moved him to comfort her. "You're growing up, Josie. You're learning that the world out there is vastly different from your sheltered life here."

Ruth added, "There's much more you haven't seen or known, child. Be kind to yourself and to your cousin."

"Your mother's right," her father said. "Henk's experience is just the opposite of yours. He's been looking for love and security all the earlier years of his life."

"Well," Ruth said, thoughtfully, "let's hope he doesn't mistake true love for the cheap, sordid love that so many young adults out there are pursuing."

"If it's any consolation, Ruth," her husband said, "we're here to guide him, that is, if he wants to accept our guidance."

* * *

The incident in Zhang's mansion had deeper repercussions on Josie than she knew. Unconsciously, she transferred her fear of him to Henk.

He noticed her nervousness in the office. Whenever he came to stand close to her to hand her a document, she immediately got up from her chair and moved to the other side of her large desk. She made an excuse to say she was busy.

"Um, I'm not free now. Why don't you leave it with me? I'll go over it this evening. If there's any change to be made, I'll write a note by the side to inform you."

Henk offered, "I can always take it home with me and go over it this evening with you. You can always come to the annex."

But Josie was abrupt with him on his offer. "Um, it's not urgent, Henk." But outwardly, she was cordial and polite. She wasn't the warmhearted, trusting cousin he knew.

One morning, in the office, Henk bluntly asked her, "What's wrong, Josie? Have I done something to offend you?"

"Whatever made you think this, Henk? It's just that I've other things on my mind."

Often, he'd catch her sitting at her desk, a moody shadow clouding her face. Her face displayed fear and nervousness whenever he came closer to her.

After two weeks passed, Henk approached Joshua. "I think something's troubling, Josie."

"In what way?" he asked the younger man.

Henk struggled with the right words to describe her, for he didn't want to offend Joshua by saying something out of line. "Um, ever since we returned from Shanghai, I notice Josie's been quite jumpy whenever I stand close to her to discuss our business."

He coughed, cleared his throat, and burst out, "I think she's developed a fear of me."

Joshua put his coffee cup down. "Fear? What's there about you to make her fear you?" Inwardly, however, he was troubled by Henk's observation.

"Why don't you tell me exactly what happened that night when Zhang went to Josie's bedroom?"

Henk scratched his temple. "Um, I recall after the show when I accompanied her back to her room, she told me she was exhausted. She made it clear that she didn't want to join us for dinner."

Joshua asked, "Did she have anything to eat after the show?"

Henk nodded. "She and the two women did. I sensed she was upset about something. After I accompanied her to her room, I heard her locking her door."

"Um, I assumed she'd be taking a shower and then going to bed." He scratched his head and coughed a bit more.

Then he said, "When I went down to join the others for dinner, I noticed that Zhang was missing. I asked one of the girls. She giggled and said he poured champagne into two glasses to take up to Josie's room."

Joshua interrupted him, "Did you see him going to her room?"

"No, I didn't. I knew she was tired and wasn't in the mood to chat with him. So, I went up to her room to check if she was all right."

Ruth asked, "And then, what happened?"

"To my surprise, I saw the door opened a little, heard raised voices from inside. I went in to see what was happening. To my shock, I saw that Zhang had one hand on her shoulder. With the other, he held the glasses."

"What did you do?" Joshua asked.

"I shouted at Zhang and asked him what he was doing to Josie. He turned to look at me. Josie at once pushed his hand off her shoulder before zipping into the bathroom."

"Hmm, just as well you went to investigate," Ruth said.

Henk said, "I heard her locking it from the inside. The next thing I knew, Zhang was knocking on the bathroom door, demanding to be let in. I could hear her sobbing loudly."

"Did you do anything to help her?" Joshua asked.

"Yes," Henk said. "I told him to leave her alone. Then I practically threw him out of the room. After that, I knocked on the door and asked her to let me in. But she wouldn't."

"And then?" Ruth leaned forward to hear his answer.

"I heard her crying hysterically. Since there was nothing I could do, I went to Lea's room to ask for help."

He went on, "It was only after Josie heard Lea's voice that she opened the door. She threw herself into Lea's arms and screamed to her not to let him touch her!"

"Oh dear, the poor child!" Ruth said, quite upset.

Henk nodded in agreement. "Now, this is where it gets complicated. Lea didn't know that Zhang was present earlier. She assumed it was me who Josie was afraid of."

He paused, took a drink of water, and looked at Joshua with an oppressive frown across his forehead.

"Then what happened?" Joshua asked.

"Er, I tried to explain to Lea that it was Zhang who had upset Josie, but she ordered me out of the room."

Joshua interrupted Henk. "So Lea was never present when Zhang came earlier."

"You have to believe me, Uncle Josh." He said this earnestly. "I never touched Josie. All I did was try and protect her from Zhang. You can ask her when she's calmer."

"Right now, Henk, she's so confused over what happened there that she's not too coherent in her account."

Henk sighed loudly. "I'm not sure if she's confusing me with Zhang about that night's happening."

He coughed a lot more before saying, "She could be transferring her fear of him to a fear of me."

After a short pause, he added, "She's been so jumpy whenever I approach her in the office about anything."

"Perhaps the best thing is for me to arrange for her to talk this over with Jem," Joshua suggested. "She is a professional counselor and can handle such matters better."

Henk suggested, "If it's any help to Josie, I'll try to get a room outside. I notice she doesn't even join us for breakfast or dinner."

"Yes, I notice it too." Joshua reflected over what Henk had told him. "I'll try to arrange another accommodation for you. Perhaps, you can lodge with Jem and Don until Josie's calmer."

Henk's frown grew heavier and deeper. "I'm sorry this has happened to Josie. Um, didn't know Zhang's character was like that until we stayed with him."

"Well, don't blame yourself, Henk," Joshua said kindly.

"Um, there's something else," he shared. "Just before Josie came by my room to ask me something, one of Zhang's wives entered my room."

Ruth nodded her head. "Yes, I think Josie mentioned something happened between you and the woman."

"Um, Aunt Ruth, my room door wasn't locked because I don't usually lock it. The girl just came in uninvited. She told me she was lonely because Zhang neglected her. She had a quarrel with him earlier. That day, she asked me to sort out her problem."

"Ah!" Ruth exclaimed. "So that's what happened."

"But I told her that since we were leaving the next day, I didn't like to interfere in her relationship with him. Then before I knew it, she wrapped her arms around my neck and began crying."

"Oh, and so it was at that moment that Josie entered your room," Joshua concluded.

"That's right, Uncle Josh. Um, I could see she was startled to see the woman embracing me. She quickly left my room. I went to her room to ask her what she wanted, but she wouldn't tell me what it was."

Joshua looked at him with penetrating eyes. "You sure that's what happened with the woman. Nothing more? You didn't invite her in?"

"Uncle Josh, why should I lie about it? I knew Josie and the girls were in the rooms next to mine. They could enter any time since I didn't lock my door."

He added strongly, "Besides, I don't trifle with another man's wife!"

Joshua felt his sincerity. "Don't blame yourself, Henk," he said kindly to his nephew. "No one can tell another's character in such a brief time. Just as well, you found out about him."

Ruth spoke to her husband, "Josh, I think it would be good to help our daughter by asking Jem to speaking to her and help her sort out her misunderstanding."

Joshua sighed loudly. "This is getting to be so-o complicated. I'm sorry it's turned out badly, Henk, I mean in your relationship with Josie. Right now, she's upset and fearful."

Ruth added, "We must help her overcome this. It's not good for her mental and emotional well-being."

"I know," Henk replied. "In my case, that night in my room, it was circumstantial evidence which caused Josie to misunderstand me. And then, of course, the incident with Zhang compounded her fears."

"Well, that's one client we'll write off." Joshua's face was grim.

TWENTY-SIX

Two days later, Joshua invited Jem and Don. "Come over for dinner. Josie's troubled over an incident which happened in Shanghai. I'd like you to assess it. Let me know how serious it is."

Don said, "From the tone of your voice, it sounds serious."

When Joshua mentioned to Josie that he arranged for Jem and Don to dine with them, she didn't respond positively. Nevertheless, out of respect for them, she joined them.

"How nice to see you again, Josie," Jem greeted her warmly. But Josie simply acknowledged her aunt's greeting perfunctorily.

When they were midway through, Don said with his characteristic forthrightness, "Have you not been well?"

"Why do you ask that, Uncle Don?"

"Well, you usually take two plates of rice with your favorite fish head curry dish."

"Huh? I didn't?" she replied, looking quite surprised. "Um, didn't realize that. Maybe just not hungry."

Jem suggested, "Why don't you come to my house tomorrow afternoon at four? We can discuss your problem."

Josie exuded a wan smile. "It's that bad, eh? Didn't realize it. Did Dad mention it to you?"

"Josie, my child, we've been looking after you since you were born. We know you as well as your parents know you. Come over. We'll see how we can help you."

She bit her trembling lips and tried to smile back. When dinner ended, she went straight to her room and locked the door.

Jem spoke to Joshua. "You said Henk went with her on the trip? I'd like to speak to him first. Can he come tomorrow at lunchtime?"

The next day, Henk had a two-hour session with Jem. When he left, he was very relieved that the matter was in her hands.

At four that day, when Josie arrived, Elsa showed her straight to Jem's counseling room. It hadn't changed much in structure. Only the furniture was upgraded.

As she waited, Josie recalled Bella, a wayward late teen who Jem had counseled and helped in many ways. She had pressed Josie to help Bella by including her in activities with the youth group in her church. She was reluctant at first, but after much persuasion from Don and Jem, she extended her help to Bella. After some years, she turned away from her former lifestyle.

Her aunt was on the telephone when she entered. Josie looked around the room. It was here that Jem met many patients and helped them through their traumatic times.

Without further ado, once she ended the conversation, Jem turned to her. "Now, tell me what happened."

In between sobs, Josie unloaded her fears and anger. At the end of it, Jem asked a simple question. "Did he touch you at all?"

"Except for that moment when he tried to push the robe off my shoulder. But I was able to push his hand off."

"How did that happen?" Jem asked.

Josie massaged her forehead, as if she was having a headache. "Um . . . um . . . there was an interruption."

Jem pursued the earlier point with Josie. "Who was it who tried to push your robe down?"

Josie hesitated. After a while, she blurted out, "Zhang."

"You're sure it was Zhang?"

"Yes."

"Was there another man in the room too?"

After a pause, she said, "Henk. He came in just as Zhang tried to do that."

"What did you do then?"

"Henk's entry distracted Zhang. It gave me the chance to escape. I dashed into the bathroom and locked the door."

"And then what?"

"I heard Henk shouting at Zhang."

"So, in your estimation, was Henk the one who helped you out of that tight situation?"

Josie paused and then said slowly, "I guess so."

"You're guessing only, or are you sure it was Henk?"

There was another long pause before Josie said, "It was Henk."

"How can you be so sure?"

"I recognize his voice, Aunt Jem."

"It wasn't a female voice?"

"What do you mean? A female voice?"

"Could it be Lea's voice?"

Josie shook her head. "No, I'm sure of it. When I didn't want to come out, Henk must have gone to Lea's room to call her over to help me."

"You're sure of it? Could you be confused over who helped you? Earlier, you said that it was Henk who helped you."

"Yes. That was earlier. I heard him shouting at Zhang. I also heard the front door slamming. Then I heard Henk calling me to come out."

"And did you come out?"

"Um, no. I was too frightened to come out."

"Why?"

"Um, I wasn't sure if Zhang had left the room."

"Then how can you be sure he had left?"

Another long pause issued. "Um, I was sure only when I heard Lea's voice. I knew I'd be safe with Lea there."

Jem probed further. "Didn't you feel safe with Henk there?"

Josie hesitated a long time. "I'm not sure."

"Why not, Josie? Wasn't he the one who caused Zhang to leave the room? Didn't he call Lea?"

"Yes, yes, he did," she replied agitatedly.

"Then how can you say now that you're not sure?"

Josie thought awhile. She muttered, "Because of what happened the night before."

"What happened?"

"I saw him embracing one of Zhang's wives." Josie dabbed her tearful eye. There was a long silence.

Jem asked bluntly, "Did you think Henk was capable of taking your robe off? Why? Didn't he rescue you? Didn't he call Lea for help?"

"Yes, I guess he did."

"Well then, why should he turn on you after he extended such protection over you?"

"I don't know. I was so confused and fearful."

"You don't trust your cousin?"

"No, don't say that, Aunt Jem. Of course, I trust him."

"Has he at any time in the past given you cause to think that he might try to do what Zhang tried to do?"

"No, of course not."

"Did you in the past ever visit him in his room at night?"

Josie gave a start. How had her aunt known? Hesitantly, she answered, "Ye-s."

"How often? Once, more than once? And what was he like when you were alone with him?"

"What do you mean?"

"Did he make overtures to you?"

"Of course not. He was always courteous when I was there."

"And did he look after you alone when you were very ill? Did you fear him on those nights?"

"I don't know, Aunt Jem. I was too ill then. I guess the thought never occurred to me. Besides, as I said, I was too ill to even entertain those thoughts."

"But you thought of that possibility after Zhang made overtures to you."

"Yes."

"Is it possible that you transferred your fear of Zhang to Henk?"

"I guess you may be right, Aunt Jem. My fear of Zhang probably snuffed out any thought that Henk was there to protect me."

"How about now, Josie? Do you think Henk came in at a timely moment?"

There was another silence. "Now that you mention it, Aunt Jem, I realize if Henk hadn't come just at that moment, I might have been . . . might . . ." She burst out crying.

"But he did, didn't he?" Jem persisted. She sat back in her chair and took a sip of water, with her eyes on the girl all the time.

"Now that you're in a rational frame of mind, do you think you owe it to Henk to thank him for his rescue of you that night?"

Josie was silent. In her calmer state, she realized she had unconsciously transferred her fear of Zhang to her cousin. It had caused her to mistrust him.

Her mind rolled back to the earlier times when Henk had helped her. In Mongolia, when he'd taken a jeep for her instead of forcing her to ride a camel.

She recalled the time when she had a supernatural fight with the two shamans. Henk had used his two-edged sword and his shield to help her."

And she realized she'd been unjust in her accusation of him. She whispered, "I'm sorry, Aunt Jem, so sorry to think unkindly of Henk."

From across the table, Jem stretched out her arm and patted Josie's hand. At the same time, she released a compassionate smile to her niece.

"Well, I suggest that you thank Henk the first chance you have for having intervened to protect you from Zhang."

"Yes, yes, I will."

"There are many men like Zhang, Josie. It's just that you've not encountered them before. But let me assure you, they do exist, and they prey on unsuspecting women."

Josie shuddered at the information.

"Let's pray before you leave. Release your fears to God."

"Yes, I'd like that."

That evening, on the way back to the main house, she passed by the annex. She knocked on his door. When he opened it, she saw his eyes wary and his brow knitted in worried lines. He said nothing when he saw her standing in the moonlight. He didn't invite her in.

"Um, I came by to say thank you for rescuing me that night in Zhang's mansion."

In a relieved voice, he replied, "Anytime, cousin, anytime."

TWENTY-SEVEN

The months moved on till it was high summer. Ross Barlow, the general manager of an oil company in Dubai, contacted Henk about the possibility of holding a fashion show. His secretary sent a formal invitation to Josie.

When Henk spoke to the family about the invitation over breakfast, Joshua asked Josie, "What do you think? Feel like going?"

"Um, what's he like? This chap Ross, I mean?"

"Um, only know him in passing. There's an international community in Dubai. Mina, Ross's wife, is one of the main organizers of a fashion show. It's usually held twice a year. But now, I think it's cut down to one." Henk explained.

Ruth encouraged her daughter, "Josie, why don't you hold a show there? Mina is English speaking. You can communicate comfortably with her."

Joshua interrupted them. "Henk, any new information relating to your parents?"

The expression on his face affirmed it. "I learned from Zhang that my parents had invested money in an oil deal in the company where Ross is working.

"Actually, it was Wu who told me to contact Zhang for news concerning my parents."

"This is getting to be more complicated," Joshua said warily.

"Uncle Josh, I learned from Zhang that the money given to my parents wasn't ready cash. They were shares."

"Which means you can't get any cash out of it, and you can't sell their share of it, for they're no longer alive."

"Er, that's the reason I'm hoping to meet Ross and discuss it with him," Henk said slowly. "Um, to see if his company can buy the shares."

"Have you found out if your father made a will where he bequeathed his property to you?"

Henk's creased brow revealed his dilemma. "That's the problem. As far as I know from the people I met, there's no will."

Joshua revealed, "You might have to go further back in time."

"What do you mean?" Ruth asked worriedly.

"Henk has to go back to the time before the plane crash. Someone, a close friend or a business friend, might know if his father made a will. After all, he had a legitimate import-export business."

"Don't forget, Uncle Josh, things were in a confused state after they died. At that time, no one knew who my parents were. Because of this, I was moved to different orphanages over the years."

Ruth interrupted them. "Wait a minute, who were you staying with when your parents traveled? They must have put you with someone."

"Aunt Ruth, my memory is hazy. I was only two. I recall there was a relative I was put with but am not sure about his name."

He scratched his temple. "Um, I think I was put in an orphanage, but er, don't have a clear recollection of that. I was told the government didn't know who my relatives were. Um, during that time, no one even knew I had any living relative."

"Hmm, that's true," Joshua concurred. He paused and took a sip of his coffee. "I had to do a search on your background before I offered you the scholarship."

He went on to elaborate. "It isn't as simple or straightforward as we think. To apply for any inheritance, you must prove you're the real son. Are there papers to show that you're the real son?"

Henk was silent for a long time, thinking through what his uncle had said. "Right now, Uncle Josh, I've no idea what to do. Um, was hoping you'd offer some wisdom to help me out. Er, how did you find out I was a relative?"

"It was a long and complicated search, Henk. I can't even recall all the details."

Everyone fell into a contemplative silence.

"In the meantime, I suggest you make the connection with Ross through Josie's fashion show," he said.

After another long pause, Joshua revealed, "This means you'll have to reveal you're the real son. Ross isn't likely to make deals with someone who isn't the real son."

Josie heaved a sigh of relief. "That means I can go rightfully in as Henk's cousin!"

Ruth smiled. "Whatever do you mean? Have you been saying otherwise?"

Her question put Josie in a spot, for she didn't want to reveal the time when she and Henk went to Mongolia to meet Wu. She was introduced then as Henk's wife's twin sister.

Sensing her predicament, Henk quickly intervened.

"Aunt Ruth, I'll simply introduce myself as Josie's business manager. Um, want to keep our relationship on an official footing."

Joshua said, "That sounds reasonable."

From that day on, Josie and her team were kept busy preparing for the visit to Dubai. Phil did the necessary research on the type of clothing women wore in the summer months in Dubai.

Two days before they were due to fly to Dubai, Henk came into Josie's office. Ever since her talk with Jem, she had been more relaxed with Henk.

He asked her, "Er, I'm booking a five-star hotel for us on Joshua's instruction. How many of us are going?"

"I'm thinking of asking Phil and Lea only. So that'll be four of us. How about the rooms?" Josie replied.

He cleared his throat nervously. "There's one with two single beds on the same floor. On a higher floor, there's one with a large single bed for one person." He paused as he leaned against the doorframe and waited.

"Um, how about you?" she asked.

"I'll make do with a standard room with two single beds. Will share it with Phil."

"Hmm, how about Lea?"

"Well, that's up to you to decide."

"Um, will our rooms be close to one another?"

"Er, it depends. If you take one on a higher floor, then we won't be."

"I'll take the one with two single beds. I can share the room with Lea." Without another word, Henk left her office.

Josie soon realized Henk avoided her as much as possible. Whenever she entered a room, he vacated it. Although she had thanked him that night and shown her appreciation, Henk remained distant when they met in the office.

At dinnertime, he sat next to Joshua and conversed mainly with him. He answered only when Josie addressed him.

Josie suspected that she must have hurt his feelings by her earlier mistrust of him. When Lea learned that Josie had arranged for them to share a room, she didn't say anything about it.

The team packed summer clothing in two large suitcases. Phil asked, "Who will be our models?"

"I guess they'll be the women in the international community," Josie surmised.

Henk asked Lea, "Can you do the alterations?"

"Um, shouldn't be difficult. I know Josie can. Besides, Anh and I made some with large sizes and another lot with larger sizes. There are only three medium-sized ones. Um, we don't expect expat women to be small built."

Phil informed Josie, "We also designed some short-sleeved patterned shirts for the men."

"You're expecting the men to buy them?" Josie asked.

His eyes flickered in Henk's direction. "Henk thinks that some of the men might want such shirts. In fact, Anh designed some in good-quality batik material."

Josie saw Henk watching her with narrowed eyes. She appreciated that he had the sense to include them.

"Thank you, Henk. That's a good idea, indeed." She gave him a wide smile of appreciation. She didn't know how much he valued her appreciation until she saw his deep frown clearing.

Just before they dispersed, Phil asked, "By the way, which hotel are we booked in? How are the rooms arranged?"

Josie looked to Henk for an explanation. "Joshua told me to book a five-star," he said. "The one I selected is ultramodern. There's also a six-star hotel, but it's some distance away from Ross's place."

"Henk, what's the venue like?" Phil wanted to know.

"The one I chose is a venue that's ideal for business and leisure. Um, spacious rooms and posh interiors. There's excellent cuisine. Um, five dining venues and an excellent Italian restaurant. Um, for guests, there's an all-day international dining restaurant offering a culinary feast."

Lea asked, "Is there a Japanese restaurant there? I know Josie likes Japanese cuisine."

Henk shifted his stand and avoided Josie's eyes. "Not that I know of. But we can always ask when we arrive. Ross has arranged a dinner for us on the night we arrive."

He looked at Josie before saying, "Er, you'll like to know the hotel is constructed on the edge of Dubai Creek. There's a golf course close by, a yacht club, a park."

"Henk, we won't have much time for sightseeing if we plan to return the next day after the show," Josie said.

"Um, are you in a hurry to return after the show?" he asked.

All eyes were on Josie. "Why? What have you in mind?" she asked.

"Well, Ross suggested a private desert safari."

Lea clapped her hands in delight. "Ooh, that sounds great. I'm game, Henk," she said.

"Me too," chipped in Phil. They both looked at Josie.

"What does it involve?" Josie asked cautiously.

"Um, the tour is for people who want to book an entire vehicle for their own group only. Each one can accommodate up to six persons. It'll be great for our group," Henk said. "Um, the guide will go at our pace."

"What does it involve?" Josie asked again.

"There's a morning, evening, and overnight adventure safari. I suggest we start with the evening safari, stay overnight. The next day, our group can continue with the adventure safari." Henk emphasized the last point.

"We'll have morning coffee and buns before we start the journey. You'll like it, Josie," Henk said persuasively. "It's just our group." He strengthened his case by adding, "Ross is certain you'll like it. He has arranged such safaris for a lot of his biz friends."

Lea was enthusiastic. "Sounds like fun."

Henk smiled when he saw how excited she was. He turned to Josie and said, "Imagine looking up at the stars in the desert night. Just us, our group. It will be quite an experience."

Josie looked at her cousin in a new light. She hadn't known before this that he had an awareness of the scenery whenever he traveled.

Lea was excited. "Say yes, Josie, it's just our group and the safari guide."

Phil, too, caught the excitement. "Sounds great. I'd like to go on the safari."

With everyone looking at her expectantly, Josie cooperated. "Henk, have you made the arrangements?"

"Ross told me he can make them for us. He knows the safari tour people. Um, by the way, there's a show in the evening with another group."

Josie asked. "A show?"

"Uh-huh. We join them for the predinner snacks and live dance shows. There's also roasted lamb, grilled prawns, couscous, fresh salads, chicken, and stews provided."

"Do the other guests leave after dinner then?" Lea asked.

"Uh-huh. We stay overnight," Henk confirmed. "The next morning, we leave immediately for the safari. There'll be tents and mattresses provided. Um, and breakfast too!"

The enthusiasm on their faces filled Josie with keen anticipation. "That means we leave our luggage in the hotel," she said.

"Yes, and take only the essentials," Henk advised. "The overnight safari is an extension of the evening desert safari."

He went on, "After the others leave the campsite, we stay. The safari begins for us the next morning."

A glow filled his face as he elaborated, "We can relax in the overnight tent, um, even sleep outdoors to enjoy the starry desert."

Henk sounded almost poetic as he said, "The stars, I'm told, stand out dramatically in the dark desert night. Er, and the sounds of the desert at night, apparently, are quite unique."

"It sounds quite romantic, Henk," Lea exclaimed. She turned to Josie. "Pity Jeremy isn't here to join you."

A bleak look filled her face. She knew Jeremy would love to have such an adventure.

"There's always a next time for you with Jeremy after he returns." Henk cast her a kind smile. "Er, in case you're interested, there's a washroom and shower facility at the desert camp."

His kindness for her comfort touched Josie. "In the morning, we can have tea, coffee, and buns before we head out to the desert."

Lea bounced excitedly at this information. "Imagine sleeping under the stars! Never done that before.

"Aren't you excited, Josie?" her eyes sparkled as she asked her.

"By the way," Henk said to the team, "the guide will provide a cloak of some kind for us to don over our head and body when we start out tomorrow. It's to protect our skin from the intense sun." He added softly, "And in case of a sandstorm."

"Sandstorm? What do you mean?" her sharp ears caught his lowered tone.

"Nothing to worry about," Henk assured her. "The summer season whips up a hot, dusty northwesterly wind called the shamal."

As the others listened intently, he explained, "It's known as the desert sandstorm when an area of low pressure develops over the area."

When Henk saw her eyes round with alarm, he wished he hadn't mentioned it to the group. However, later, in retrospect, when he thought it over, he felt he needed to warn the team.

"It rarely happens," he comforted her. "May not happen on our trip as we're taking a short safari only."

He noticed that after he told the group that they had nothing to fear, Josie instinctively moved closer to him for protection.

"Well, let's not get worried over something that may not happen," he consoled her. "Have a good night's sleep. We leave for Dubai tomorrow morning."

The flight took about six hours. By the time they checked out of the airport, Ross was already waiting for them. Mina was there too. She was a tall person on the plump side.

Her auburn hair was cut stylishly. She was dressed in a pair of jeans and a cream short-sleeved blouse. Ross was a head taller than his wife and was wearing a plain cream short-sleeved shirt. He looked more like a Scandinavian with his blond hair, big size, and height.

They greeted the team warmly. Once they got into the car, Ross drove them to the hotel. A row of palm trees like sentinels lined both sides of the road leading to the front of the hotel. He checked them in, while a bellhop wheeled a trolley to take their suitcases.

Clearly, Ross was known here. The manager, smartly dressed in his white safari-styled outfit, came forward to greet them.

In deference to Josie, Henk allowed Ross to introduce her to the suave Arab manager. The bulky man towered over her in height and size.

"Welcome to our hotel." He beamed a wide smile. "I'm Abdul-Alim, the general manager. You can call me Abdul if you like." He shook hands with each one.

"For your information, I've upgraded all of you. You'll be occupying rooms on the 16th floor. They're next to one another. For your comfort, I've given each of you a suite with an extra-large bed."

Josie was dismayed. She didn't like the idea of a suite after her bad experience in Shanghai but didn't know how to refuse the manager's offer without seeming ungracious. So she kept silent.

Lea sensed her dismay. So did Henk. Neatly, he made a request. "Er, is there an adjoining room in case the two women wish to discuss the fashion show after dinner?"

The general manager, looking most surprised, didn't assure Henk that he'd arrange it.

Instead, he said, "I'm sure they'll want to rest after the flight. Mr. Ross has arranged an early dinner. Are you all leaving tomorrow for the evening safari after the fashion show?"

An hour later, just before they were given the card keys to their rooms, Abdul-Alim said courteously, "I've arranged for Ms. Josie to have adjoining rooms with you, if that's all right, Mr. Henk."

Henk looked uncomfortable, but Josie, without rejecting his offer, graciously replied, "That's indeed kind of you, Mr. Abdul. I'll take the room. Which number is it?"

Henk was quite transparent in his surprise at her consent. Lea's and Phil's faces revealed their surprise at Josie's acceptance. None of them said anything as they took the keys to their respective rooms.

Adbul-Alim showed Josie the room. Then he walked to the adjoining door, opened it with another key, and asked the staff to put her suitcase in it.

"Um, how about the extra suitcases with the models' clothes?" Josie asked Abdul-Alim.

"Oh, yes, I forgot. You wish to discuss the fashions with Ms. Lea. Well, in that case, why don't I let Ms. Lea take the adjoining room. Mr. Henk, you won't mind taking the other room farther down? This floor has only suites. Yours are all on this floor."

To cover up her relief, she flashed the general manager her most charming smile. He, of course, was enchanted by her beauty. He lingered in her room, supervising the suitcases as they were brought in.

"Shall I have the staff serve you tea?" he asked.

"Er, don't bother," Josie told him. "We'll all have a quick change and join Mr. Ross for dinner."

Henk vacated her room after giving her a brief smile. Lea entered the next room. She walked through the adjoining door. "Whew! That was close."

She sank into the oversized armchair. So did Josie. They looked around the room. "It's huge. Everything's big here," Lea commented.

"Yah, because they're all suites," Josie replied with a smile. "But it was nice of him to give me an adjoining room."

"I could see that Henk was put in a spot too when Abdul-Alim upgraded us all and gave you and him an adjoining room," Lea commented.

She looked squarely at Josie. "Are you still afraid of Henk?"

"Huh? Whatever do you mean?"

Lea hesitated. "Don't wish to probe, but I sense you've been nervous of him since our last visit to Shanghai. You er . . . avoid him whenever he stands close to you."

"I did? Guess it must be the bad memory of Zhang's strong overtures to me that made me nervous of Henk."

"But Henk was the one who rescued you if I remember correctly. Didn't he come in at just the right time?"

"I'd rather not talk about it." She turned away and began unpacking her suitcase.

Time is a healer. With time, the bad memory receded into the background. And, in a different venue, the bad memory receded even faster.

Following her dad's advice, "Let it go. Don't dwell on the past. It's unhealthy," she set her mind on other things.

"Let's get changed," she said briskly. "Henk will be coming soon to call us for dinner."

They met the five couples who volunteered to be models just as they sat for dinner. All of them were middle-aged and friendly. Clearly, they were impressed by the young team's skill and ability to design dresses which suited different ages and sizes.

After dinner, when they were invited to the lounge for coffee, Josie declined. Instead, she requested, "Um, I wonder if the women can come to my suite after this, um, to do the fitting for the show."

Henk interrupted. "Er, I think there're also two men who'll be doing the modeling. Right, Ross?"

"Um, yes. Barry there"—he pointed to a slim younger man at the end of the table—"and er, Jude, the one next to Barry."

Ross asked, "Will your room be large enough to fit us?"

Henk told him, "Abdul upgraded us and gave us all suites. Josie will take the women. The men will go with Phil. Coffee will be served in the two suites."

Josie had selected the finest cotton and linen material for the dresses. It wasn't difficult to alter the dresses to fit the women. Anh had stitched some large and some even larger ones.

Lea's color sense enabled her to choose colors to suit the women's skin and hair color. They worked right into midnight. By that time, they were able to produce a good variety of fashions for the show.

When Ross and Henk came in later to meet the women, they were impressed. Ross said, with great admiration to Josie, "You're certainly skillful in the choice of clothes."

The women admired themselves as they preened in front of the mirrors. Their hands smoothed down the dresses as they walked around the large suite. They turned back and forth in front of the mirror to admire the dresses.

Ross said with a twinkle in his eyes, "I see the husbands will have to bring their checkbooks and credit cards."

He turned to Henk. "Er, by the way, can we buy the clothes immediately after the show?"

"Certainly," Henk, smiling broadly, said readily. "The women look so good in them that they won't even want to change out of them after the show."

In the background, the women laughed delightedly when they heard his comment.

Henk then came up with a surprise for all the models.

"Wait here a minute. I've something to enhance your dresses." He disappeared from the room. When he came back, he had a large pouch in his hand. He laid it on the bed, opened it, and spread the items out.

The lights of the chandelier bounced on the gleaming stones below. The women squealed in delight when they crowded around the bed.

Henk beckoned to Josie and Lea. "Choose the ones to match their necklines," he instructed them.

Josie was impressed with his ingenuity. He had brought along some necklaces. Immediately, she and Lea set about matching them with the necklines of the dresses. It took quite a while.

Before long, they were parading up and down the length of the suite. Josie and Lea then stored the selected necklaces with the dresses for the next day's show.

It was agreed that they meet in one of the meeting rooms on the second floor at ten the next morning after they came to Josie's suite to dress.

"Ah, before we depart for the night," Ross said, "we have to wind up with the traditional dates and Arabian coffee."

Mina turned to Josie. "You have to try them. They're quite unique." She picked up a bowl and offered her. "UAE produces the finest quality of dates. They're exported all over the world."

Josie picked up one and nibbled it. Its sweetness was palatable. Mina handed her the coffee cup. "This is a special type of Arabic coffee called the *gahwa*. It's a famous traditional beverage prepared with a different ingredient and recipe."

"Smell it," she urged Josie.

"What is it?" Josie inhaled the aroma. "Smells of cinnamon and saffron."

Mina clapped her hands. "Ross," she called out, "Josie guessed correctly."

"That's great, Josie." Ross smiled widely at her. "The two spices give the coffee an unusual taste. Do you like it?"

Josie nodded. "Uh, huh, unusual all right." She sipped a little more of the coffee. Her taste was changing. In Dubai, she came to appreciate the different coffee flavors, especially the *gahwa*.

Ross urged Henk, "Take some back for Josie's parents, will you?"

Then he asked, "Are you all leaving for the desert safari tomorrow? Um, are you doing the sand dune ride? Can be fun, but it takes a lot of guts."

Mina agreed. "It certainly takes a lot of guts. When Ross and I took it with a group, the ride had a 90-degree drop over a high dune. Just as well I was sitting with Ross."

She turned to Josie. "You sit with Henk. He'll be a good support for you. Cling on to his arm, just in case."

Josie looked at him. "Are we doing the sand dune ride?" Before he could reply, Lea quickly intervened.

"Oh, say yes, Henk. I'd love to try it out." Then she offered, "If Josie isn't joining us, I'll sit with you."

When Josie asked "How long is the ride?" he replied, "About an hour."

"That's not long," Lea chipped in.

Henk ignored her remark and asked Josie, "Do you want to ride over a sand dune? If not, we'll scrap that part of the tour."

However, Josie gave in to peer pressure when she saw Phil and Lea looking keen. "So long as I can sit with you, Henk." He looked pleased at her request. He could see her trust in him returning.

"Um, should be safe enough. You'll be strapped in the jeep," he assured her.

As he was leaving her room, Josie asked him, "How're the men doing with the shirts?"

"I nipped into Phil's room and saw them quite happy with their shirts," he told her. "They fit well. No major alteration needed."

"That's good to know," Josie said.

TWENTY-EIGHT

Josie was sleeping soundly when she suddenly found herself on an expanse of land which looked like a stretch of desert. She was alone. Everything was still.

Josie stood there, surveying the surrounding area.

A vast expanse of undulating reddish-yellow sand stretched endlessly all around her. The color seemed to change further on into an orangey red.

She was right in the middle of it. She didn't know which direction to turn to, for there was nothing to indicate where she was exactly.

Just then, a slow wind began whipping up. It picked up sand dust, which began swirling around her. Soon, the wind grew stronger and wilder, causing sand to swirl more strongly and lodge in her long hair.

The fine particles irritated her eyes. They activated her tear ducts. She couldn't find any rock to hide behind because there just wasn't any around.

Panic attacks seized her as the wind grew more violent. More sand enveloped her. She began to cough. In desperation, she sat on the ground and bent her head over her knees. Then she used her hands to cover her head. She didn't even have a shawl or any covering for her head and face.

She recalled going through a heavy snowstorm in Whistler and surviving it. She reasoned that if she stayed still in that position, she could endure this one.

The fine dust choked her, despite her attempt to cover her face with her hands. She couldn't call anyone for help, for she knew there was no one around. After what seemed a long while, the howling wind simmered.

When she tried to stand, she was held down by a heavy shroud of sand covering her entire head down to her body. It was bearing down on her.

She began pushing it off her but found it too heavy. She tugged at it vigorously to get it off her.

She awoke just as she was kicking away at the heavy quilt blanket. When she looked around, she found herself on the bed. It was then that she realized she was trying hard to kick off the coverlet. Exhausted, she fell back on her pillow.

The next morning, when she went to wash her face, she saw fine reddish yellow sand embedded in her hair.

* * *

As expected, the fashion show was a big hit with the group. The room was packed with two hundred and fifty men and women. As Ross predicted, the designs were well liked. The necklaces enhanced the dresses. As a result, they were quickly bought up. More orders for fresh clothes were submitted.

Henk was beaming as he counted the orders. He took Josie aside and whispered, "Your parents will be pleased to know this. Well done, Josie."

She was more than pleased. Her rating in the community abroad was growing. And she knew it was a matter of time before she was invited to hold more shows abroad.

"You've been a great help, Henk. Thank you," she said, and she sincerely meant it.

"Won't be long before our company gets more invitation to do shows overseas." His face was flushed with the success of the fashion show.

They had a late tea and then packed the necessary clothes for the evening desert safari. Their guide was a swarthy Arab, tall and big sized. A thick, bushy black beard filled his chin.

"Call me Ahmed," he said, revealing a set of large, yellow teeth when he grinned. He drove a private vehicle, a newer version of the Land Rover, on the request of Henk. It could accommodate six people.

When they arrived, Josie saw the desert camp safari ahead. Ahmed told them, "We provide a tent, along with mattresses, pillows, and thick blankets."

Lea was round-eyed. "You mean it gets cold at night in the desert?"

"Oh, yes," Ahmed said, smiling at her ignorance. "The temperature drops quite a lot at night. Sometimes, it gets down to even zero degrees."

"In the daytime, it gets scorching hot. You need to cover your skin. The hot sun will burn it. In our bags, we have the covers for you. They will protect you from the sun and also any possible sandstorm!"

With the help of Henk and Phil, he pulled out three large bags from the back of the vehicle. He showed them how to set up the overnight tent.

Josie and Lea laid out the mattresses, pillows, and blankets inside the tents. Each tent was large enough to accommodate two people.

After they set up the tent, Ahmed invited them to join another group for the predinner snacks. Some distance ahead of them was a Bedouin-styled camp, with seats lining a large stage. Performing on it were belly dancers in flimsy, thin clothing.

Ahmed indicated the front-row seats for them. Once seated, they were given an assortment of grilled prawns, roasted lamb, couscous, and fresh salads.

Ahmed explained the origin of the Bedouin tent while they were munching on the food. "The black tent is known as a house of hair. They were traditionally woven from reared sheep and goats' hair. Woven much like strips of coarse cloth, they were then sewn together. This is known as *fala'if*.

"The remarkable thing about this is that when it rains, the weave contracts. This stops the water from coming into the tent. The design originated in Mesopotamia."

"Hmm, sounds intricate and unique," Josie said. Their facial expressions indicated they were impressed.

"Not only that," Ahmed explained, "when it's high summer, inside the tent, it is remarkably cool. The outside may feel hot when you touch it."

"How unique!" Lea exclaimed, with her eyes glued on the belly dancers, who were gyrating vigorously on the stage. When the tambourines stopped, the slimmer girl came down and held out her hand to Henk.

Everyone clapped. But, to Josie's surprise, he kissed her hand and graciously declined. Next, the dancer turned to Phil, who, in turn, pulled Lea up to join them. They both went on stage. It was a fun time for everyone.

"Why didn't you go with that girl?" Josie was curious.

He leaned toward her and whispered, "Didn't want you to be left alone."

"But Phil and Lea were with me."

He grinned. "I knew she'd ask Phil too."

Then he asked, "Would you like to dance too?" She shook her head after she saw the men on the stage taking off their shirts, encouraged by the belly dancers.

Before long, Henk and Josie were given a plate filled with *biryani* rice, noodles, dal, mixed vegetable curry, chickpeas, and sautéed veggies.

Some grills were then added to each plate, such as lamb kebab and grilled chicken. Cold appetizers, hummus, and macaroni salad decorated the large plates in the center of the table.

"That's a lot to eat," Josie commented. "The *biryani* rice, grilled chicken, and salads are my favorite."

"Glad you like them," Henk told her. "Ahmed asked me to make the selection before we set out." He added softly, "I promised your dad I'll look after you and keep you safe."

Josie was touched by his concern, but she wasn't sure she liked the part where he said he'd look after her because he'd promised her father.

It'd be nicer to hear him say he wanted to do it because he treasured her. Jeremy had said a similar thing as Henk years ago at Sentosa beach. She was mad at him then for telling her that and accused him of childminding to please her dad.

Now that she was much older, she was still hearing the same thing but from another cousin. She sighed. Henk looked at her inquiringly, but she didn't offer him any explanation.

Just as they were eating the mixed fresh fruits, the others returned, panting after the exercise on the stage.

Lee said happily, "That was good, but it's exhausting. Didn't know belly dancing is such an energetic dance."

She used her hand to fan herself. Phil laughed. "I'm all sweaty. The dancer asked me to take off my shirt, but I wasn't sure if I should."

Josie grinned and teased him, "Do you have the muscles to show off?" Phil flexed his muscles in answer.

Above the din of the chatter, Henk shouted across to him, "Hey, Ahmed, what time do we leave tomorrow morning?"

"At sunrise. You'll be given a light breakfast with tea, coffee, and buns. Then we set off for the sand dunes."

He added, "We're riding the new vehicle. Our tour company just ordered it. It's a new design, quite similar to the Humvee, tough, um, like a small army tank. Um, but stable and large enough to take all of us."

Phil added knowledgeably, "The Humvee is a military vehicle and still exists. But I understand the Hummer which was designed for civilian use is being faded away from production because of poor sales."

Ahmed interrupted him. "By the way, I've just been told there's a possibility of a sandstorm if the wind kicks up. In high summer, this is rare, but possible. But most storms are quite light."

"I'm sitting beside Josie," Henk informed him. "Phil and Lea can take the last-row seats. Ahmed, how long is the ride?"

"There'll be an hour of sand boarding. It gives you the extra thrills. You young folks will enjoy it. At one point, there'll be a drop of a 90-degree angle, depending on whether we hit an extra high hump. Just hope it isn't a high rock."

When he saw Josie's apprehensive look, he said, "Happens sometimes, although it's rare. Hard to tell as I can't see exactly which ones are the very high sand dunes. Since the rocks are all covered in sand, it's deceiving to the eye because of the glare of the sun."

He consoled her. "Don't worry, Ms. Josie, you're safe. There're five of us. You're not likely to get thrown off because the vehicle is stable. But just in case we're unfortunate and get thrown off, you won't get lost."

He then addressed the group. "May I suggest that all of you don on the robe provided for your head and body as a protection over you from the heat and sandstorm?"

His words didn't comfort her when she recalled her dream. "You're sure the sandstorm won't choke us?"

Ahmed chuckled. "You'll all be safe. Generally, it's mild. So far, we haven't had any reports of any violent storms."

However, Josie knew that with storms, nothing was predictable. In the past, she'd been through many. Earthquakes, volcanic eruptions, and snowstorms. Although they occurred only in her dreams, she knew the devastating power of the upheavals.

But not wanting to appear a wet blanket, she kept silent. Henk patted her arm to assure her. "I'm sitting beside you. You'll be safe."

TWENTY-NINE

That night, Ahmed persuaded them to sleep outside the tent. "It's an experience of a lifetime, especially when you see the stars above and hear the desert sounds."

He added, "You have your blankets which you can use when it gets very cold in the later part of the night!"

The team cooperated and agreed to have the sleeping mats placed outside the tents side by side. They placed the blankets at their feet for night use.

Josie chose the side next to Lea, but Ahmed called her to take the mat next to Henk. He didn't offer her any reason for this. On her other side was Phil. Lea took the one next to Henk on the farther side.

It was, as Ahmed said, an incredible experience. The myriad twinkling stars, which seemed so far away, contrasted markedly with the dark of the desert night.

Josie stared at them until her eyes grew tired and her eyelids drooped. It was a still night with no breeze. The sounds of the desert were more pronounced as the night advanced.

Her eyelids grew heavier. Before she drifted off to sleep, she heard various sounds. There was chirping like the crickets in her garden, but she knew there were no crickets in the desert. She heard what sounded like the croaking of frogs after a rainy night, but Ahmed didn't mention their presence in the desert.

A hissing sound made her wonder if there were snakes in the desert. She hoped not. A pecking sound, like a woodpecker pecking the bark of a tree, reminded her of the one outside her room window. However, she saw no tree around them earlier.

She also heard a *tch, tch* noise and another one with a *cluck, cluck* sound. She wondered which creatures were producing those noises.

Across her, on the other side of Henk, she heard Lea chatting nonstop to Henk. She heard him emitting the occasional grunt in reply. Lea's voice went on and on until Josie drifted off into deep sleep.

The sudden chill of the desert air made her grope for the blanket at her feet.

In her sleepy state, she couldn't quite manage. She was struggling to pull up the thick blanket when she became aware of hands lifting it and gently placing it over her and pulling it right up to her chin. Then they tucked the blanket around her sides.

She struggled to open her eyes to see who it was, but her eyelids wouldn't lift. Soon, she drifted back into deep slumber as she snuggled under the warmth of the thick blanket.

In the early morning, when it was still dark, Ahmed woke them all. The chill of the night was quickly dispersed as the desert heat overtook it and swept across the land.

Josie and Lea arose and went to change into light T-shirts and jeans. Phil and Henk did likewise.

After a light breakfast, they set off just as the sun was beginning to peep over the horizon. Before they set off, Ahmed insisted they don on the robe to protect them from the heat and any possible sandstorm.

As they drove over the desert sand, Josie viewed the incredibly picturesque sight of the panorama before them.

She recalled her much earlier impressions of Mount Batur in Indonesia when the sun was rising. Her memory also took her back to the time of her Mount Kinabalu trek with Jeremy. It flashed back to her visit to Whistler Mountains. Her mind then went back to the time of her visit to the majestic Great Wall of China and the panorama surrounding it. It had unfolded before her eyes as she climbed the Wall, which curved and twisted for a long distance.

As they drove on in the desert, she stored in her memory bank the current, stark, arresting landscape of the desert. She had quite a collection of incredible intangible scenes of the countries she had visited, which she could only pull out from her memory and put onto canvas to make them tangible one day to the viewers!

Soon, they were moving deeper into the belly of the desert. On and on, they drove. At some point, from a far distance, Josie and the others saw a caravan of camels and their Arab owners regally astride them in their long white flowing garments.

Eventually, Ahmed stopped the vehicle. He pointed to vast stretches of undulating curves ahead.

"See those humps?" Ahmed pointed out. "They're the dunes farther up. I'll take you gently up the slopes. But I can't guarantee if the dip down won't be 90 degrees when we descend. The mass of sand camouflages the real height and the rocks beneath.

"We can't see how high the elevation is until we hit it. Sometimes, I know from experience that because of the height, in our descent, the vehicle can skid or even slide down precariously without warning."

"Just hang tight to your seats. Buckle your seat belts. You should be safe enough. I suggest you now pull the hood over your heads for your protection."

Before they set out, Josie had plaited her hair neatly. Following Ahmed's call, she pulled the hood over her head and hair. But it was too large and loose and kept slipping off as the wind began whipping up around them. There was no strap to keep it secure, so she simply held the hood tightly over her chin.

Although Ahmed had predicted a possible mild sandstorm, he didn't reckon for the unpredictable appearance of a heavy sandstorm just as the vehicle ascended a very high sand dune.

The wind unexpectedly whipped up violently as they ascended. Fearsome thick black clouds of sand appeared like a horrible monster from above, waiting to devour the unsuspecting lone vehicle.

Without warning, pushed by the force of the howling wind, the vehicle flew over the elevation. At the same moment, the sandstorm increased in intensity and swirled wildly all around them.

When the storm swooped down on them, Josie heard Lea screaming for help. Her voice was drowned out as the storm swallowed them all, including the vehicle.

The strong impact jerked Josie out of her seat. She didn't know how. She was strapped in when they started off. As the vehicle flew violently over the unpredictably high sand dune, somehow, her belt snapped off.

The heavy force of the wind hammered the vehicle on all sides. Stable as it was said to be, it was buffeted by the ominous force of the storm.

Just as she was flung out, from the corner of her eyes, she caught a glimpse of the others catapulting out of their seats. How far she was hurled, she had no idea.

The tremendous roar of the sandstorm deafened her. It filled her with a sense of dread. She went tumbling and tumbling down the mountain of sand.

When she finally stopped, she didn't know where she landed. Visibility was nil. The cloud of dust which continued swirling thickly around her blinded her. She fell on the ground.

She began choking on the fine sand, which rapidly filled her mouth, nose, and ears. The hood pulled earlier over her head was blown off. She could feel sand punching her head.

When she couldn't see anything around her, she began to feel disoriented. She groped around for something to anchor her but could feel nothing, not even a rock.

She tried to stand but stumbled because of the onslaught of forces too powerful for her to resist. She continued choking and coughing violently as she lay on her side.

She was about to faint when she felt a hand grasping her arm. Whose it was, she didn't know. Then she felt a strong arm sliding her sideways.

Something was then wrapped around her head, and a voice rasped, "Stay on your side. The towel will cover your head and face and keep the sand out."

Hands enfolded her securely as she lay on her side to prevent her from rolling on her back. A hoarse voice croaked into her ears. "Keep very still!"

She lay in that position while the wind buffeted intimidatingly around her. The sand swirled viciously around them. Big gusts of sand slammed into their bodies.

After a long while, she and the others heard the wind lessening in power. The sand dust simmered and settled on the ground.

Then all was still and silent.

Hands then gently released her and turned her on her back. She pulled off the towel covering her head, dislodging masses of sand. She felt hands gradually wiping it off her face, her head, her hair, her nose, her mouth.

Her rescuer was unrecognizable, for his entire body was covered in a shroud of sand. Until he used his large hand to swipe off the sand covering his head, face, and mouth.

Then she recognized him. Her cousin had again come to her rescue!

His large hands wiped the residue of the sand gently off her face. She must have looked like a shroud, with the sand covering much of her. He signaled to her not to speak, for there was still much sand over her nose and mouth. He was wiping it off when they saw some movement in the distance.

She couldn't recognize any of the others as they came staggering toward her and Henk. Everyone was covered completely in the reddish-yellow sand.

It took them quite a while to wipe the mass of sand off. Farther down the slope, they saw Ahmed crawling toward the vehicle which had overturned. It was flung to the bottom of the high dune.

He bent inside it and fished out a huge bottle of water. He then dragged it up the dune to Josie, stumbling a few times. Henk met him midway and pulled it uphill the rest of the way to Josie.

Then, together with her, he began washing the sand off her head, hair, face, mouth, ears, and robe. After that, he poured the residue over himself.

No one spoke. Everyone was busy washing the sand off themselves. Ahmed was the first to speak. "Didn't realize the sandstorm would be so bad this time!"

The men set about digging out the overturned vehicle. It took the three quite a while. Inside the vehicle, there was much sand all over the seats and floor.

The windscreen was caked with sand. Ahmed had to pour water over it and scrub it off with his hands and shirt.

Instead of continuing with the journey, they headed back to the camp. After a much-needed shower and a change of clothes, they decided to return to the hotel.

It was evening by then.

Ross was most apologetic. "There haven't been reports of any all this while. I'll arrange an early dinner for you."

Josie turned to Henk. "I'd like to fly home tomorrow if you can arrange it."

"I'll ask Ross to make the arrangements," he told her immediately.

After a light dinner, he asked Josie, "Think you can make it back with Phil and Lea? Ross wants to discuss something with me concerning the oil deal."

Josie saw his flushed, hope-filled face.

"Sure," she said. "I hope something good comes out of your discussion."

Much later that night, just as she changed into her nightgown, to her dismay, Josie saw some pink oval rash spots appearing on her arms.

Oh no, she thought in dismay, *it must be the sand I'm allergic to.*

She recalled her earlier visit to the outer planet, where the soil there probably caused her allergic rash. The desert sand in Dubai was a similar color to the soil on the planet.

In her room, the rashes multiplied fast. By 3:00 a.m., she felt compelled to call Henk. Her eyes were very puffy. They were almost like slits. She recalled the sand had covered her completely earlier. Clearly, she was now reacting to it.

He came rushing in, his thick hair tousled, his eyes still full of sleep. "What happened?"

He took one look at her eyes and was alarmed at her bad allergic reaction.

Josie lifted her arm to show him. "I think I'm reacting to the sand."

"Hmm, didn't you have this kind of attack before? I recall seeing similar bumps the night you stopped by my room."

She could see his memory was good. "Yes, it was when . . ." She stopped short, not knowing how to explain to him about the last incident, her visit to the outer planet, and her reaction to the soil on the planet.

"Where were you that time which brought on the rashes and bad reaction?"

His eyes clearly indicated he expected an answer. But she couldn't give it without embarking on a lengthy description of her unusual trip. So she just bit her lips and fell silent.

"You're not wanting to tell me the reason?" He sounded hurt at her lack of trust in him.

"Um, it's not that. It's just that it's too complicated and long." Fortunately, he didn't insist on an answer.

Sympathy for her discomfort reflected in his eyes as he looked at the pink bumps and her puffy slit eyes.

To prevent further questions, she asked, "Can Ross get me some antihistamine to tide me over for the flight home? I'll see Uncle Don when I get back."

Henk immediately called Ross. It was 4:30 in the early morning by then. He soon came by with the tablets.

"Mina gets a bad rash because she's allergic to sand dust. Any itch? Um, she used to have a dreadful itch, which caused much pain when she scratched it."

When Josie heard this, she was relieved that she didn't suffer any itch or pain. Henk's frown cleared when he saw her shaking her head in reply to Ross's question on pain.

When Phil and Lea heard about the rash, they were most sympathetic.

Lea clucked, "Oh dear, how unfortunate."

Phil added, "Hope it settles by the time we board the flight. No fever, no itch?" Josie shook her head.

Before they left, Josie wore a long-sleeved coat and jeans. Fortunately, by then, there were only a few spots on her neck, which could be mistaken for pimples. The puffiness in her eyes had reduced by the time the team left Dubai on the afternoon flight.

THIRTY

Don was waiting at the airport to fetch them. "How bad is it?"

"How did you know?"

"Henk texted me. I told your parents I'll fetch you and pass you some medication."

In the car, he asked her, "How bad is it?"

She lifted her sleeve to show him. "It was really bad late last night. I had to call Henk to get some medication from Ross."

"Do you know the cause?"

"Ross told me Mina, his wife, suffers from allergy to the desert sand. Said hers was a bad case. She had pain and itch."

"Oh dear," Don uttered. "Um, I recall you mentioned the sand in the outer planet."

"I recall that time too," she confirmed. "It's desert sand I'm allergic to."

"Well, come back with me to the house. Jem's at home."

"Um, think I'd like to go home first, Uncle Don. Perhaps, Dad can go over later to get the tablets for me. I took a tablet before I left for the airport."

"I've some in my medical bag. Will pass them to you. They'll tide you over for tonight." He rummaged in his bag and pulled out a small packet of red tablets and a tube of cream.

"Here, take this. Apply the cream on your arms. Let me know if the rashes subside. No itch?"

"Thankfully, no," she replied. He dropped her off at her house and then went home.

Ruth was concerned. So was Joshua. "Hmm, didn't know desert sand dust can cause a reaction."

"Looks like it," Josie said. "Mina, too, is allergic to desert sand, and Ross told me hers was a really bad case."

"On the whole, everything else turned out all right?" Joshua wanted to know.

"The sales were good, Dad. Henk was pleased."

Ruth intervened. "How about you? Were you pleased too?"

"Yes, yes, Mum. The women loved the dresses. Henk was clever, did you know? He brought over some necklaces, which were cubic zirconia, simulant diamonds mixed with some semiprecious stones. He had asked Philip to design them."

Joshua let out a whistle. "That's clever, indeed!"

Josie said excitedly, "The women looked so good in them that they decided to buy the dresses and the necklaces!"

Ruth asked, "How did they pay for them?"

Josie laughed. "Their husbands clearly expected them to buy the clothes and the necklaces. They had their checkbooks and credit cards."

"Did the women know how good they looked in them before the show?"

"Well, when we had a fitting the night before the show, Henk produced the necklaces. Lea and I decided which necklaces would best adorn the necklines of the women wearing the dresses."

"That's clever of you." Ruth hugged her daughter.

"Why did Henk stay over?" Joshua wanted to know.

"He told me Ross found out something about the oil deal."

"Well, I found out something interesting too," Joshua revealed.

"You did? What is it, Dad?"

"Don't you want to rest first?"

"No, you've got me so excited. I want to know it now."

Her parents laughed. "You remind us of your younger years, always wanting to know. Curious, just can't wait!"

"Tell me, tell me." She couldn't contain her excitement.

"Let's go up to the living room," Joshua said. "It's a long and complicated account about family relationships."

After coffee was served, Joshua began his account. "I learned that Luke knew Henk's parents, Yanna and Talia, although his memory of them is dim."

Josie leaned forward to hear him. "To simplify, let me go back to the beginning. There were four brothers. The eldest, Joseph, married Sue. The second, Daniel, married Faith. We'll focus on these two as they concern us."

Ruth intervened. "You've investigated a lot."

He nodded. "I learned Joseph had ten children. His youngest son, Ferrel, had several children after he married Rachel. Luke and Zech were their oldest sons. They were later adopted out to Yanna and Talia, who had no children in their earlier years of marriage. Henk came only much later."

When he paused for a sip of his coffee, Josie asked, "What else, Dad"

"I learned Luke and Zech were actually Yanna's much younger cousins. Since Ferrel wasn't rich then, he gladly allowed Yanna to adopt them and send them to Singapore for education at his expense."

Ruth said, "If I remember correctly, in Indonesia then, it was a common practice to adopt children from relatives if they themselves didn't have any."

Again, Joshua nodded his head. "Yanna adopted Luke and Zech when they were only three years old. Um, after Yanna and Talia had their first and only son, Henk, they left for Holland soon after he was born because of business opportunities there. Luke and Zech were left to continue their education in Singapore."

Ruth added, "They must be adults by then."

"That's correct, Ruth. When they were adults, Luke went to Sabah to work and settled there. Zech returned to Indonesia. After Yanna and Talia left for Holland, they lost touch with them. They never knew about their whereabouts.

We know now they died in the air crash. Luke and Zech never knew about this."

He went on, "The other relationships are too complicated to trace. I called Luke the other day. He recalled Yanna vaguely but never knew he had a son."

Ruth intervened, "He and Zech must be grateful to Yanna for having adopted them and paid for their education in Singapore."

Joshua went on. "Luke recalled that his own parents were quite poor. So when Yanna offered to adopt them both, his father willingly released them to him."

Ruth said excitedly, "We know Jeremy was born to Luke and Su Jen, while Zech married Elsie and had sons of their own."

Joshua concluded, "So now Henk has cousins who are his relatives. He'll be pleased to learn of this. I think he's about Jeremy's age range."

Josie, too, was pleased to learn this. "That means Henk has more relatives than he knows of. Um, what happened to the other uncles and families?"

Joshua yawned. "As I said earlier, the relationships are too complex to trace. Right now, I'm too tired to put out any more search. I'm just happy to help Henk connect with one."

Ruth hugged her husband. "You've done well, Josh. Helping Henk to find at least one more relative."

Josie said excitedly, "Then Uncle Luke will know where Henk's birth certificate is."

Joshua let out a loud laugh. "He'll be fortunate if he can find his original one. In those days, it wasn't a requirement by law. The child may be known only in his village or among close relatives without there being a legal document."

Josie asked, "Why's that, Dad?"

"Children were known by the names village folks and relatives call them, not the full passport names."

Ruth consoled her family. "Just as well, Joshua, you were able to trace so much regarding Henk."

Her husband yawned widely. "Feeling tired, so right now, I'm turning in for the night."

Josie went to bed that night feeling more encouraged. After knowing about Henk's distressing days in the orphanages, she hoped fervently that something good would turn up for his sake.

* * *

The morning sun warmed her room as the rays swept over her bed. Drowsily, Josie stirred, stretching her arms upward as she luxuriated in her comfortable bed.

When she saw it was nine o'clock, she jumped out of bed and refreshed herself with a long shower. The pink oval dots had subsided, and only a few dots were visible on her thighs.

When she went down for breakfast, she saw that Teng had bought her *tehsi* and a plate of *chai tow kuay*.

The telephone rang as she was finishing the last bit. It was Don. "How're you this morning?" His warm voice came over the phone.

"Uncle Don, the rashes are down!" She exclaimed in delight.

"That's good to know. I hear Jeremy completed his thesis and handed it in. I guess he'll be heading home soon. And we'll be hearing wedding bells before long!"

"How did you know? I didn't even know it!" She was quite astonished that Don knew it before she did.

"Your dad told me."

"He did? He must have forgotten to tell me. As you know, I just got back from Dubai. Most excited to know Jeremy's coming back soon. Um, miss him so much."

"Well, won't be long now. Take care." He rang off.

Just then, Joshua came to join her at the table. In a rush, Josie burst out, "Uncle Don said Jeremy told you he'll be heading home by next week."

"Oh, yes! Guess, with all that excitement about Henk, I completely forgot to mention it to you. Sorry about it."

At that moment, Ruth joined them. "Yes, we'll have to get down to designing your gown. It'll be the most fashionable one this year."

Joshua chipped in, "I've no doubt about that, Ruth."

He turned to his daughter. "Will you be staying with us after your marriage, or do you want a place of your own? We can buy the land beside. Um, and you can design your house, according to your taste."

"Hmm, haven't given it much thought really, Dad. But I like the idea of buying the land beside. It'll be close to you and Mum."

"Well, discuss it with Jeremy," he said. "Have to leave for a meeting." He gulped down his coffee, kissed her on the cheek, tapped Ruth lovingly on the shoulder, and left.

"When's Henk returning?" Ruth asked.

"Don't really know, Mum. Guess when he has some information."

A few days later, Henk returned. His first question to Josie was "How's the rash?"

"Um, almost gone. Tell us, tell us, what did you learn?"

Henk beamed. "Quite a bit. Let me finish this. Since the account's quite lengthy, I'll tell you all later."

After dinner, when they were comfortably seated in the living room, he explained to the family, "It's really quite complicated! Apparently, I've another living relative."

Joshua whistled. "Fancy that."

"Ross told me that Johan had an import-export business. When my dad, Yanna, was in Amsterdam, he connected with Johan who was running an import-export business there. He left Indonesia at an early age to seek his fortune in Amsterdam, much earlier than my dad. His family's been there for a long time."

When he paused, Josie prompted him, "Well, go on."

"He had two sons, Markus and Jonos. Markus is the older son. He's nearly thirty-five years. He inherited his dad's business."

"Had? You mean Johan has died?" Joshua asked at once.

"Yes. His wife died just before he did. He died soon before the plane crash which killed my parents. His biz was taken over by his two sons. But Jonos, the younger boy, went into the gemology business. The older son, Markus, was left to run the import-export biz."

Ruth said, "This is interesting, indeed."

Henk explained, "Um, you may perhaps know, Aunt Ruth, gemology is the science dealing with natural and artificial gemstone materials. It's considered a geoscience and a branch of minerology."

Ruth nodded knowledgeably.

"Well, to go on, Jonos is a trained gemologist and qualified to identify and evaluate gems." He paused and poured himself a fresh cup of fragrant *gahwa*, Arabic coffee, which he brought back from Dubai for them.

"What did Ross tell you about Markus?" Joshua asked.

"Uncle Josh, here's an interesting thing. Ross said Markus's surname is Lie. Strangely, the government didn't see his connection to me and so wasn't aware he was related to me."

But Joshua's sharp mind saw the connection with Henk. "Is Markus's dad related to your dad then?"

Henk scratched his head and then nodded. "Yes. Markus told me his dad, Johan, was the son of Paulus, who is the third brother of Joseph and Daniel. He is a Lie too!"

Joshua whistled. "Small world!"

Ruth agreed but added, "Sounds complicated if we trace the genealogy of Henk's family."

"I'm not going to try to, Ruth," Joshua warned his wife. "I'm contented to know Henk found another relative!"

He turned to Henk. "Well, what else did you learn?"

"At the time my parents died in the plane crash, Markus was away on business. Jonos was in South Africa on business. The government placed ads in the local paper requesting for my relatives to connect with them."

Josie asked, "And then what happened?"

"Since no one came to claim me, they sent me to an adoption center."

Josie clucked sympathetically. "How dreadful for you."

"When Markus and Jonos came back to Amsterdam a year and a half later, they still didn't know my parents had died in the plane crash. That explains why they didn't contact me."

Ruth asked, "How long before anyone can to claim you as their relative?"

"Quite a long time, Aunt Ruth. I was moved to different orphanages. Now, here's the interesting part. Ross is a friend of Markus through business dealings."

"Henk, what business was he involved in?" Joshua wanted to know.

"Oil exports was one of them. Markus told him that he had a biz, which he wanted to sell, for the owner had died and he was left with the biz."

Joshua replied, "I see."

"However, Markus eventually did sell my dad's share of the business, but not to Ross. With the money he got, he bought diamonds from Jonos."

"What about the oil deal your dad was supposed to have made?" Joshua asked.

"There wasn't any. The person cheated my dad of the money after he passed the message to the other party about the deal."

"How dreadful!" Ruth exclaimed.

"But the good part is that Markus and my dad were partners in an import-export business. The agreement between them was that if anything happened to one partner, the business would automatically fall to the other partner or his children."

Ruth asked eagerly, "What was the agreement?"

"The understanding was that the money would be given to them if the business was sold to another person."

Henk paused again before explaining, "Markus put out a search for me. He told Ross he knew Yanna had a son. But after some years, he gave up the search when he couldn't locate me."

Josie said "How dreadful for you, Henk! Go on."

"In the meantime, Markus used the money accruing from the sale of Yanna's part of the business to buy diamonds from Jonos, his brother."

"Where are the diamonds now?" Ruth asked excitedly.

Henk beamed. "Ross told me he learned that it's in a bank in Amsterdam in Markus's name just waiting for me to claim them."

"But how can you claim it when you don't know Markus and he doesn't know if you're the real son?" Josie chipped in.

"Ah, this is where God comes in." He grinned happily.

"God?" the three chorused in puzzlement.

"Yes, it wasn't a coincidence that I know Ross and he knows Markus. He knows, too, that Markus's surname is Lie. He knows my surname is Lie."

Henk paused again and looked at three anxious pairs of eyes. "Markus told Ross he was trying to find a Henk Lie whose father was in the import-export business. He also told Ross he knew Yanna and Talia were my parents. He said that he met them a few times before the plane crash."

Ruth added, "That's fortunate for you."

"That's true, Aunt Ruth. Apparently, Markus met me when I was only two. My dad used to take me along when he lunched with Markus. He would fetch me from play school and take me to an Indonesian restaurant where Markus joined us for lunch."

"This is truly wonderful news, Henk!" Ruth exclaimed, rubbing her hands in delight. "I'm so glad for you."

She turned to her daughter. "Josie, aren't you glad too?"

"Does that mean that all you have to do is meet up with Markus and identify yourself?" Ruth asked Henk.

"Er, something like that."

Josie suddenly remembered something. "But, Henk, you're much older now. Markus met you when you were only two. Can he recognize you as the same person?"

Another gloom settled on the family.

THIRTY-ONE

Joshua broke the silence. "When can Ross arrange a meeting with Markus? I suggest we fly out to Dubai. Hopefully, we can sort out any problem there which may arise."

Henk looked relieved. He knew that he could trust his uncle. He was so wise and knowledgeable in many ways.

"Can I go with you, Dad? I'd like to meet Markus too," Josie asked eagerly.

Joshua looked at his daughter. Her face was aglow with expectancy and hope.

Ruth urged him, "Take Josie with you. I won't be going."

* * *

They arrived Dubai two days later. Josie took an adjoining room in the suite with her father in the hotel. Joshua booked another suite for Henk.

Ross kindly arranged the meeting in his large house. Mina was there when they arrived for tea at four in the afternoon that day.

When they were all seated in the spacious living room, Ross came in accompanied by a tall, tanned, big-sized man, who towered over all of them.

Josie's first impression was that he must be a descendent of Goliath. He was indeed a giant of a man. He had a mop of dark-brown hair cut short at the nape of his neck. It wasn't gelled or smoothed down.

He wore short sleeves. His long arms had a lot of hair on it. He had the stance of a wrestler as he lumbered into the room.

They all stood up to greet him. Ross maneuvered Markus toward Joshua. "Markus, meet Joshua. Er, I think he's related to you by marriage." The giant pumped Joshua's outstretched hand vigorously.

Ross next introduced Josie. "She's Joshua's daughter." Markus's dark eyes shone with admiration at her beauty.

Then, before anyone could utter another word, Markus turned to Henk. "*Aduh!* My cousin, my long-lost cousin!" he exclaimed with a strong Indonesian accent.

He hugged him tightly, tears in his eyes. "How many years since I saw you? You were only two then."

Henk was overwhelmed with emotion. Tears just flowed down his face. He cried unashamedly. The reunion was touching.

Finally, he held Henk apart. "Let me look at you. How many years since we last met? You were so small then, just turned two."

Henk, in between sobs said, "Can't remember any of that."

"Your *bapak*, your father, had to carry you up when he introduced you to me and Jonos." He looked at Henk closely. "You remember Jonos?" Henk shook his head again. So many years had blurred the memory of the other cousin.

Joshua asked Markus, "How did you remember Henk after all these years?"

"*Aduh!*" he exclaimed. "Can't forget his face. Same shape, no change, only larger. And his hair, plenty, like mine. Dark brown too." He ruffled Henk's mop of hair.

"Um, only difference is that you're taller now." He tipped Henk's chin upward. "Hmm, I see your mole is still there." He pointed to a mole under the lower lip. "And you still have the star?"

"What star?" Joshua asked immediately.

"All the firstborn in our families have a star on the left thigh. That's like our family DNA. Some have it when they are a year. Others a little later, maybe when they are about four or five years old, much like a mole appearing." He roared with laughter, as if he found it amusing.

"We can identify our family members easily by the star! Don't need a DNA test to prove he belongs to the Lie clan!"

"Really?" Joshua and the others were intrigued. This was the first time they heard of it. "That means Luke and Jeremy must have the star too."

"Luke and Jeremy? Who are they?" Markus turned to him.

"Your other relatives. You must come to Singapore to meet them. Luke's in Sabah now. Jeremy returns next week from the States."

"*Aduh!*" He chuckled. "Suddenly, so many relatives!"

"Hey, *adik*, why don't show me your star? That way, we'll all know you are a genuine Lie!"

Henk flushed at his request. He looked embarrassed. Markus emitted a deep-throated laugh. "Shy? Don't want your beautiful cousin here to see it? Go on. Change into your shorts. Then we can all see it."

"Um, don't have it here," Henk muttered. "My clothes are in the hotel."

"Let's go back to the hotel then," Markus suggested readily. "Um, by the way, Ross, where are we having dinner?"

"We can have it at the hotel," Ross replied.

"Good, good." Markus rubbed his hands gleefully.

"Let's go now to the hotel. OK with you, Ross?" He tilted his head toward him as he asked.

"Sure," Ross replied readily. "Let's go now."

Before long, they arrived at the hotel. Immediately, Markus prompted Henk, "Go and change into your shorts."

Joshua suggested, "Why don't you come to my suite? We can have a drink there before dinner. And Ross"—he turned to the man—"let me invite you and Mina for dinner."

Ross cleared his throat. "Very kind of you, Joshua. Sure, we'd love to join you and the family."

They went up to Joshua's room. Markus kept urging Henk, "Go, go, and get changed. We want to see the pink star."

Henk flushed at his demand. When he was hesitant, Markus said, "Why? You shy? Don't want your cousin here to see it?" Marcus steered him to the door in his keenness for others to see it.

Before long, Henk knocked on the door and entered. He was wearing shorts. His thigh was muscular and fair, in contrast to his tanned arms. Josie had never seen him in shorts before.

Markus bent to look at the star. "*Aduh*, just look at that!" He lifted the shorts a little way up on Henk's left thigh and pointed. About a finger space away from the patella was a tiny, faded pink star.

To Henk's embarrassment, everyone crowded around him to see it. Markus chuckled. "Don't be abashed. You have firm muscles." He turned to Josie. "Your cousin is handsome, yah?" Henk flushed at his word.

Josie complimented Henk. "Yes, my cousin is very handsome." She could see a pleased look on his face.

"See, see." Markus had the same way of speaking as Elsie, Zech's wife, Josie recognized. He tended to repeat the same word twice to emphasize his point.

"Now, to talk business," Markus boomed out when the group returned to their seats. "I've the diamonds in the bank. I can pass them to you, Henk, when you fly out to Amsterdam."

Joshua interrupted. "Er, if it's not too rude, can I ask you, Markus, how much it's worth?"

"Huh? You want to know? Must be worth millions and millions of euro dollars by now. We can get Jonos to evaluate them when we meet him. Bought them over the years with the money from the sale of Yanna's share of his business. Have kept them since."

He turned to Josie. "If you're marrying my cousin, you can choose the biggest diamond in that group."

"Er, no, no," Josie quickly said. "I'm marrying Jeremy."

"Huh? I thought from the way Henk looked at you, that he'll propose to you now that he's so rich!"

Then he shot out in his rough, blunt way, "Who's Jeremy?"

Joshua cleared his throat. "Er, Jeremy is also your cousin, Markus. He's Luke's first son. He and Josie are getting married when he returns from the States."

"Ah." Understanding dawned on his face. "Did you say first son? Then he, too, will have a star on his left lap if he's a genuine son. Only true first sons have the star."

"Really?" Joshua was most intrigued by this. "Never knew about it. In fact, Luke never mentioned it."

"*Aduh!*" Markus chuckled. "Suddenly, I am learning of more relatives. He scratched his head in theatrical bewilderment.

Everyone burst out laughing.

"How about having early dinner?" Ross suggested.

He turned to Markus. "Where are you staying tonight? Why don't you share a room with Henk? Can catch up on past news."

"Yah, yah, sounds a good idea," he replied. He turned to Henk. "I know your uncle booked you a suite."

He settled the matter by declaring, "Certainly, I'll share your room tonight. Wah, suddenly your fortunes have turned for the better!" Henk confirmed it with a nod.

Dinner conversation was mainly among four of them, while Josie and Henk sat silently. On his other side was Markus, who seemed to take on a big brother's role comfortably.

Joshua had ordered a set dinner. As the dishes came out, Markus turned to Henk. "Tell me, what have you been doing all these years?"

He was silent, overwhelmed by the presence of Markus and the discovery that he finally found a relative who knew his father.

Joshua, seeing his nephew's discomfort, kindly helped him out by asking Markus, "Why don't you tell us instead what made you decide to convert Yanna's share of the business into diamonds after you sold it?"

Markus sat back, relaxed, took a sip from his glass of beer, and then launched into an explanation. "Yanna and my dad had a loose partnership based on the understanding that if anything happened to one of them, the other person would take over his share of the business.

"When I took over the business, the same agreement stood. Um, no legal contract, nothing. Just based on trust between two relatives. Um, in those days, people were more honest."

"How did the business come to be in your hands? Was it started by your father?" Joshua probed.

"Yah, yah. My *bapa*, Johan, started the import-export and later invited Yanna to join his business. My *bapa* came out to Amsterdam much earlier than Yanna. Um, traded in a lot of things."

Joshua interrupted him, "What happened after that?"

"When he was ill, he passed the business to me. Yanna agreed to accept me as a partner. I was years younger than he was. But he was patient and taught me the ropes of the business. It was a loose partnership, no contract, just an understanding based on trust."

Joshua again passed a comment. "Yes, in the past, there was more trust among family members."

"After my father died, I continued the business with Yanna. Then after he died, I ran the business. As you know, I wasn't aware that Yanna and Talia had died in an air crash until much, much later."

"Markus, what happened initially?" Joshua asked.

"Well, at first, Jonos started out with me. But later in the year, he showed more interest in gemology. When the business grew, Jonos suggested using the money from the sale of the share of the business to buy diamonds."

Joshua asked, "Was that a good move?"

"Although my younger brother is two years younger, he has much wisdom. He said the cost of rare diamonds would, in time, appreciate."

"And then what happened?" Joshua wanted to know.

"I took his advice. When I later learned that Yanna had died, I sold his share eventually. I used the money to buy diamonds. Whatever diamonds I bought with Yanna's money was put in the bank to await the time when I could find Henk."

"Markus, that was nice of you," Joshua said.

"I knew the boy was alive somewhere. After Yanna and Talia died, I made a thorough search for him. Um, learned Henk was transferred to different orphanages. But I couldn't locate him for some reason."

"How did you meet Ross?" Joshua asked.

"Later, by chance, when I did business with Ross, he told me that someone by the name of Henk Lie was trying to find about his father's oil deal."

"Ah, so you made the connection?" Joshua concluded.

"I knew instinctively it must be Yanna's son. The surname Lie isn't common. I also recognized the name Henk."

"Isn't that fortunate for you, Henk?" Joshua said. Henk nodded vigorously.

"Well, to go on. I knew there was no oil deal. Whoever had told Yanna about the deal had lied. Yanna was a businessman. His weakness was that he always wanted to make a quick buck whenever he could."

Joshua intervened, "So there's nothing to the rumor that Yanna had taken money to pass information to a third party about an oil deal."

"Naw, nothing whatever. Joshua, the Russian who told Yanna that, actually swindled him of a few thousand euros."

Joshua asked, "Well, What happened after that?"

"After he was paid to pass the information to another party, the Russian took the money. Later, he sent someone from Shanghai to tell him the oil deal was off. Yanna was hoping as a middleman to make a quick buck from the deal."

"Hmm, so nothing came out of the deal." Joshua mused over the information.

"Actually, Yanna did tell my dad about it. I learned this later. But the good thing is Yanna's business was intact because my father had control over it."

Markus turned to Henk. "Win some, lose some, that's business. The good thing is you now have millions of euros worth of diamonds."

He slapped his cousin on the back. "With all that money, look for a wife. How old are you now? I know you're much younger than me. I'm thirty-five now."

Josie could see that Markus was quite open about his business and his age.

Ross laughed. "Markus, how about you? Isn't it time you were married too?"

The giant roared with laughter. "Haven't found a woman as beautiful as my cousin here. Maybe one day."

They flew home the next day and narrated to Ruth all that happened. Henk stayed on a few more days to catch up on news with Markus.

He indicated he might fly to Amsterdam with Markus before returning to Singapore.

THIRTY-TWO

The night they returned to Singapore Josie called Jeremy. His warm, tender voice brought tears of joy to her eyes.

"Hey, hey, why are you crying?" he asked in concern when he saw her face on the video screen.

"Um, just so happy to know you're returning next week."

"Are you truly glad to have me back? Or have you made new friends? How about Fred and that new cousin of yours?"

Josie laughed. "Jealous? I detect a tinge of it in your voice. Didn't we agree before you left that there'd be total trust in our relationship?"

"We did. But loneliness and handsome, winsome young men can entice you."

"How do you know Henk is handsome? I never showed you a photo of him."

"Ah, but you told me he looks a bit like me, so he must be handsome."

Josie burst out laughing. "Hahaha, such vanity! But if you must know, he can't compare with you. Does that satisfy you to know that?"

She continued, "Anyway, I'm astonished that you can suggest such things of me. Don't you trust me? My affections have always been yours. How about you? Have you been mine totally in love and affection?"

There was a long pause. "Are you still there?"

Jeremy's voice came softly through. "I've never deviated in my love for you, not since you were a baby."

"Mm, that's good to know," she cooed with a smile in her voice. "Know what I'm going to do when you return?"

"What?"

"I'm going to spend the day just hugging and kissing you."

Jeremy roared with laughter. "What, and not let me eat the local food? I've missed it for over a year."

"Don't you want to hug and kiss me too?" she asked in a pretended hurt voice.

"Of course, I do. Let's compromise. In between our kisses, you can spoon some local food into my mouth."

That night, there was much joy as they ribbed each other in the video call.

Josie then said, "I've something nice to share."

"Do tell." His voice sounded eager.

"Dad asked if we wanted to buy the land beside his house. Um, build a house there before we get married later in the year. How does that sound to you?"

"Sounds great. What do we do for money?"

"You're going to work with my dad, aren't you?"

"That's the idea. I've some new technology plans to propose to him. And my dad has invited me to be a consultant for his construction company."

"Sounds good," Josie said. "Well, you should be able to earn some money. And with my fashion business, we should be able to pay for the house with our joint income. I reckon my parents will fund the down payment first."

"You're indeed blessed to have parents who love you."

"Uh-huh. Truly, truly blessed," Josie agreed wholeheartedly.

From outside her window, Josie saw the dawn creeping over the sky. "I'll call off now. See you soon." She threw kisses to him.

* * *

It was late morning when Josie woke up. When she went to the office, she found the team busy designing, cutting, and stitching the clothes for the new orders.

Lea said happily over the lunch break, "We're having more orders coming in. Henk just sent the orders to Phil. By the way, where's Henk?"

"He hasn't come home yet." Josie then filled her in on Markus.

"I'm glad for Henk," Lea said. "He didn't have a happy childhood. Maybe, someday, he'll find a woman he can love."

"You like him a lot, don't you?"

"Uh-huh, but he hasn't looked my way. Each time I see him, his eyes are only on you."

"Well, Jeremy's returning next week. My eyes will be on him alone, you can be sure."

"When are you planning the wedding?" Lea asked.

"Not so sure. Perhaps after we build the house. We're thinking of buying the land beside my dad's land."

"Um, actually, strictly speaking, it isn't beside. It's a little farther up. There's a small stretch of land between it and my dad's land. I never met the owner."

"It's quite easy," Lea replied. "Your dad can easily check with the authorities who the owner is."

"Uh-huh. He did. Learned it's owned by a person named C. Gardner. A property agent told him the owner travels quite a bit. Apparently, he left it in the hands of the property agent."

"Have you explored that land beside yours?" Lea asked curiously.

"A few times," Josie said but didn't narrate to her the adventures with the robots and shamans.

"What's it like?"

"Nice, large, and stretches a long way. I can have a house and a garden comfortably. The good thing is that I can be close to my parents."

When Fred heard about Jeremy's impending return, he was glad for Josie. He knew she missed him a lot.

"Perhaps I can hold a welcome home party for him and invite Henk too. That way, he can meet more girls."

Josie was grateful. "Thanks, Fred. You're so thoughtful. Um, just sorry at this stage, you haven't found a steady girl yet."

"Not in a hurry, Josie," he replied with a smile. "I've plenty of girls to date."

It was a clear, dry morning when Jeremy's plane touched down on Singapore soil. Joshua had secured permission for a private room for him and Josie to welcome him at the airport.

When Jeremy walked in, she rushed forward to meet him. As promised, she hugged him tightly.

"Let me look at you." He held her away a short distance while his eyes took in every detail of her. "More beautiful, more desirable!"

Joshua was very glad for his daughter that Jeremy had returned, for he knew that she loved him a lot and missed him during the time he was away.

He coughed to get their attention. "Er, hate to interrupt you both, but it's time we left for home," he said, smiling.

When Jeremy picked up his overnight bag, Josie asked, "Is that all you have?"

"Uh-huh. Some clothes I gave away to the needy students. Some books I donated to my colleagues. Don't have many though."

Josie asked, "Nothing more? How about your thesis? I'm sure you must have done a lot of reading."

"My research was mainly from journals, interviews, and online resources. The info is in my computer and up here." He tapped his head as he said that.

When Jeremy arrived, Ruth was there to welcome him. He beamed widely. "Truly a great homecoming for me, Aunt Ruth."

At dinner, Jeremy asked, "Where's Henk? I thought he was staying in the annex."

"He's in Dubai," Joshua said. "Met up with Markus, another cousin of yours and Josie's."

Josie excitedly burst in, "Do you know he's wealthy now. Markus invested Henk's late father's money from the half share of the business in top-quality diamonds."

Jeremy let out a long whistle. "Diamonds eh?"

"Yes, and not only that, Jeremy, Henk said I could choose the best diamond for our engagement ring."

"Hang on a minute. I'm the one supposed to buy you the diamond," he protested.

Josie's face fell. Joshua intervened when he saw it.

"Let's see what Henk offers for the diamond. It may be within your price range."

Jeremy scoffed. "Not likely. Top-grade diamonds cost a lot of money."

"Well, let's see what Henk offers you," Joshua repeated.

Josie recalled something. "Oh, by the way, do you have a small pink star on your left lap, just a finger space away from the patella?"

"Why? What's with the question?"

"Do you?" Josie smiled at him beguilingly. "Tell me, then I'll let you know the reason I asked."

All three looked at him expectantly. Jeremy looked at them. "Aw, when the three of you look at me like that, what am I to say?"

"Just say you have the star," Josie begged him.

But Jeremy was in a mischievous mood. He held them in suspense by sipping the hot soup slowly. Then, before answering them, he leaned over and kissed Josie on the cheek.

"Yes. This means you have it." Josie gave a whoop of excitement. "Show us, show us."

"Hah! Sorry to disappoint you but I don't have my shorts here."

"Jeremy, it's in your room!" Josie squealed. "Your clothes are all there. Nothing's been moved since you left. The room's been cleaned regularly."

"Do I get another big hug and kiss from you when I show it?"

Josie jumped up from her chair and gave him that.

"There! I've given you the kiss! Now, show us."

She practically pulled him out of his chair. Amused, he left them to get changed.

They moved to the living room. As he sat on the couch, Joshua told his wife, "If what Markus said is true of the Lie clan, then Jeremy will have it."

A thought suddenly struck him. A strange look passed his face. When Ruth saw it, she asked him, "What is it?"

"I just thought of something," Joshua said slowly. "In Dubai, Markus revealed he was the first son of Johan."

"So what of it?" Ruth asked, puzzled.

"Well, Markus said all first sons in their families have the pale pink star. If so, he, too, must have it."

He laughed. "Never thought of asking him, for we were all so engrossed with the knowledge that Henk had the birthmark!"

Josie agreed. "It's true, Mum, we never thought of asking Markus."

Just then, Jeremy appeared in his shorts. He exhibited very muscular thighs. They crowded around him. Then they saw it.

The tiny pale pink star.

Josie threw her arms around him enthusiastically, hugged, and gave him a long kiss to the amusement of her parents.

"Now, do you want to tell me what this is all about?" Jeremy asked, clearly intrigued by her exuberance.

After the explanation, Jeremy declared, "Then my dad must have it too. He's the eldest son."

"Indeed," Joshua said. "It's good to know." His smartphone *pinged*. "Hmm, I just got a text from Henk. He's coming back soon with Markus."

"Can Markus stay in the annex?" he asked Ruth.

"Shouldn't be a problem," she said. "I'll have a second bed moved in. The annex's large enough. Wonderful, a family reunion!"

That night, long after the parents retired, Josie and Jeremy stayed up, chatting into the early-morning hours. They fell into a blissful sleep on the living room couch, with their arms entwined.

* * *

Two days later, Henk flew in with Markus. When they entered the house, the family was having breakfast.

Joshua introduced them to Jeremy. He looked critically at Henk, even as he clapped him on the shoulder in greeting.

Markus, with his boisterous laugh, proclaimed, "So this is another Lie." He turned to Joshua. "Have you seen his star?"

"We have. He's a genuine Lie!" Joshua confirmed.

Markus wrapped his arms around Jeremy. "Welcome to the Lie clan." He turned to the others and added, "Do you know we tend to have mainly boys in our family? Can't remember there being any girls."

At that point, Joshua said to Markus, "By the way, since you're the eldest son of Johan, you, too, must have the star."

He roared with laughter. "Of course, I have, but with the two ladies here, I won't show it to you people." After that remark, he promptly settled down to his meal.

When they finished breakfast, Markus declared to all, "I've something to show you."

After Elsa cleared the table, from his pocket, he drew out two pouches. He laid them in the center of the table. After he opened them, he used his hand to spread out the diamonds in each pouch.

The overhead lights caught their brilliance. Everyone gasped when the diamonds below sparkled brightly.

Josie exclaimed, "Wow! These stones are so different from the ones you brought to Dubai, Henk, to adorn the necklaces of the women for the fashion show."

Henk explained, "Those were actually cubic zirconia, not real diamonds. The ones for the show were mixed with other stones. Philip helped me design them."

He added, "They're just simulant stones, nothing compared to the real diamonds you see here."

"Yes, I can see the difference," Josie replied. She peered closely at the bright, sparkling diamonds which Markus laid out for them to view.

"Can I touch them?" she asked eagerly.

"Pick what attracts you," Markus said generously.

"Henk has told me he'll let you choose your engagement ring from these diamonds of top quality."

Wide-eyed, Josie exclaimed, "He will?"

Jeremy, from the side, chipped in. "Um, not so fast. Since I'm the one buying it, let me know the cost first."

He looked at Henk, who shrugged his shoulders helplessly. "Um, don't know much about pricing." He scratched his head and, in turn, looked at Markus.

The latter suggested, "Er, why don't you let Josie choose the diamonds first? Then we'll let you know the price."

There were ten large sizes. Their brilliance and sparkle fascinated her. Josie went for the big gleaming stones.

She picked one up, turned it to the left and to the right, back and front, and then put it down. Next, she picked up another one and did the same thing. She placed the stone on her left finger to see if the size fitted it.

While she was examining the stones, the others topped up their aromatic Arabic coffee and sat, sipping it. After a long while, Josie selected two diamonds. One had many white diamonds all around the edges of the stone. The other had blue and white diamonds all over. Both had a center ring around and more tiny clusters of white diamonds within the stone.

She handed them to Markus. He flashed out from his pocket a monocular handheld loupe to magnify the diamond he wanted to inspect, one which gem dealers use to examine diamonds.

He then opened a packet, took out a slip of paper, and read it out. "Those two are 1 carat each in size."

He held up a piece to the light above. "This one, the round one, has a clarity of SI1. Its color is H."

"The cut is rated as excellent. Priced at US$7,900 by a top jeweler." He mentioned the name and then put it down before picking up the other one. He opened another packet and read out the information on the slip of paper.

"This one is 1 carat too. Round. The color is H. The clarity is SI1. The cut is also rated excellent. Also priced at US$7,900/-." He turned to Josie. "You have excellent taste." He passed the two diamonds to Ruth to examine.

She took the loupe from him. After a time, she pronounced them flawless. "Josie, indeed, you have great taste."

Ruth turned to him. "Well, Henk what are you offering? Market price?"

He replied, "I'd like to discuss it with Markus first. Is that all right with you and Uncle Josh?"

Joshua was amused. "You folks take all the time you want to discuss. All that diamond gazing has made my eyes tired!"

Everyone laughed at his remark. They retired for the afternoon.

Meanwhile, Jeremy had taken back his old room, next to Josie's. Before he went to his room, he stopped by Josie's room. "Do you really want the stone?"

She was surprised at his question. "It's most attractive. The jewelers in the city will probably offer about the same price and some even a higher price. Some others may be flawed."

When Jeremy was silent, she went on, "The ones I selected are unset. My mother confirmed they are flawless. Er, what have you in mind for my engagement ring?"

"Um," he hesitated. "Um, er . . . my mother has a few good ones. Thought you might like to have a look at them before deciding."

Josie cast her eyes down. "The ones your mother has are all set. I'd like to have an unset one. Fresh. Not worn by anyone before."

After he heard her, Jeremy didn't offer any further comment.

THIRTY-THREE

After dinner, they went to the living room. Josie was waiting expectantly for Henk's decision. After a while, Markus took the initiative. "Henk has made a decision."

Henk looked at Josie and then at Jeremy. "Since Jeremy insists on paying for the stone, I've decided to offer it at the cost of SGD$1/-."

After a while, Jeremy said, "I can't take charity, Henk. I know the market value is much higher."

Henk spoke boldly. "Don't misunderstand me, Jeremy. I'm not doing any charity. If there's any charity that's done, it's more from Markus, Joshua, and Ruth. And let me add Josie too."

Jeremy sat listening quietly, while Henk continued. "First, I myself don't deserve to get any of the diamonds. Secondly, I don't even deserve to stay with Joshua and Ruth in the annex for free. I'm also grateful Josie allowed me to be the biz manager of her fashion company."

He looked at the others as he said, "And by the grace of God, I've a family to come home to every night. I don't deserve any of these. I'm getting all these free of charge because of this family's love and kindness."

When he paused a while, Joshua encouraged him by saying, "Well, go on Henk, what else do you want to share with us?"

"I learn that freely I'm given, freely I must give. In fact, I want to give it free of charge to her. But I know, Jeremy, you will insist on putting a price to it, so I've decided on the price of SGD$1/-."

Ruth gasped. "Are you sure, Henk?"

In return he said, "I've been blessed beyond measure since I came to live with this family. Now, it's my turn to bless Josie."

Josie leaned forward, keen to hear what else he had to say.

"She's been not only like a sister to me, but she's also shown herself as a true friend. I'm aware she's not perfect, but her imperfections make me realize I'm not perfect either."

There was a pronounced silence as Henk went on. "When I was lonely, Josie offered a listening ear. Sometimes, she tried to comfort me. But during the times when she had no words for me, she sat silently and empathized with me in my sorrow. At other times, she remonstrated me for dwelling in the past."

As he said this, his eyes were on Jeremy. "I know her level of loneliness isn't like mine. I know, she missed Jeremy a lot. It showed in her eyes. During those times, I, too, learned to be a friend to her."

Henk's eyes then swiveled to Joshua and Ruth. "She has loving parents, but somehow, she's been able to sympathize with me on the loss of my parents, especially my mother. Don't ask me how she did it, but her compassionate nature just surfaced each time I was in a morose mood."

He concluded slowly, "That, to me, is a rare quality of a friend."

His eyes swept the others who were listening intently. "Bit by bit, I learned to let go of my past. Over the months, Josie made me aware that there are relatives who cared for me. She made me realize that life isn't only about coping with losses, but about how much I have gained by coming to know her and her family."

Then Henk looked directly at Joshua. "And Uncle Josh has solidly shown me his wisdom. He guided me in areas I was lacking in. He's shown true paternal love to me."

Gratitude shone from his eyes, when he shared, "He offered me a job as a part-time biz manager in the fashion biz. Initially, I could see that Josie didn't like the idea. I'm thankful she didn't reject me."

Next, his eyes settled on Ruth. "I'm grateful to Aunt Ruth, too, for her kindness and understanding. She's always supportive of my plans to move the fashion business forward."

Ruth's eyes teared a little when she heard his words. He continued, "Josie's love and laughter, as well as her parents' graciousness, showed me that there is a God who cares about my welfare, for he put me here with them."

He looked lovingly at his cousin. "In the time I've been with this family, I've come to know what true family relationship is."

He wiped a tear from his eye. "Um, that, to me, is an undeserved blessing. Now, let me bless my cousin with the diamond of her choice."

He turned to Jeremy and looked him squarely in the eyes. "I'm sure you, too, must be grateful to Joshua for something he did for you in the past."

His words struck a chord in Jeremy. He recalled Joshua's kindness and forgiveness. He was rough in his initial treatment of his daughter through his past association with Adil and Carl and their loose and liberal lifestyle.

Yet Joshua had forgiven him. He, Jem, and Don had counseled him and given him a chance to start anew. He allowed him to stay in the annex and even did it up nicely for him. Jeremy had to acknowledge he had a lot to be grateful to Joshua and Ruth that night as they gathered as an extended family.

And Josie, whom he treated roughly, had forgiven him and taken him back. He knew she had many rich suitors. Jeremy recalled Fred, who had an eye on her and who knew her much longer than he did.

He was aware that Fred had remained faithful to her all the years. Yet Josie hadn't chosen him. Instead, she forgave Jeremy and chose him as her life partner.

He sank his head between his face. "Forgive me, Henk. Thanks for reminding me that I've much to be grateful to Uncle Josh, Aunt Ruth, and to Josie."

He confessed, "Uncle Josh took me in when apartments outside were too costly for me to afford. He and Aunt Ruth fed me and gave me a large, comfortable room and other amenities free of charge."

He turned to Joshua and Ruth. "Forgive me for not having shown you my gratitude."

To Josie, he said, "I'll abide by your choice. If you want a fresh stone, why not. And, Henk, if it's in your heart to offer me the stone at SGD$1/-, I'll take it. Thank you for your kindness."

They were all humbled by Henk's and Jeremy's declaration of gratitude.

Henk stood up. Taking the two diamonds Josie chose, he said humbly, "These are yours and Jeremy's, with my love."

Josie stood up to receive them. With tears in her eyes, she said, "You've been such a help to me, Henk, in so many ways. But I'll take only one stone. The one with several white sparkling diamonds around the edges."

Henk turned to Jeremy. "Guard our cousin. She's precious to us all. And now, she's all yours to keep."

Jeremy stood up and hugged him. "Thank you, Henk, for your generosity and your reminder on gratitude."

When Joshua and Ruth looked at Jeremy and Henk, they were touched to know that both men had gratitude in their hearts and appreciation of their family.

They themselves were also glad that their daughter had weathered some storms with Jeremy.

Now that both were stable in their relationship and planning their wedding, they rested in the knowledge that it was something that they, as parents, could look forward to with much joy!

THE END

CPSIA information can be obtained
at www.ICGtesting.com
Printed in the USA
BVHW030948250121
598677BV00003B/45

9 781543 762730